F

"This is a love story and a war story, woven through a beautifully wrought, heart-stopping, spirit-lifting novel of how we survive and grow through crises, and find our way. What Rusty Allen mined was a narrative gold mine, largely undiscovered, of German POWs who toiled during World War II on farms and in factories whose workers were fighting overseas. What a human brew! Young men, grateful to be alive, providing much-needed, war-time labor and getting a taste of America, in all of its complexity—many ended up staying—while Americans met the enemy, up close, teaching them, working with them, relying on them. To this, Allen brings a seamless marriage of research and imagination, mixing worlds together while keeping his eye, ever, on the aching human heart, seeking what it wants. The characters in this book—their travails, their desires, their discoveries—will stay with you. Through them, all is revealed."
RON SUSKIND, PULITZER PRIZE-WINNING AUTHOR OF *A HOPE IN THE UNSEEN*

"Rusty Allen's *Ella's War* takes us back to a well-known time, World War II, but not a well-known place for the events of that time, the East Coast of the United States, where a conflict an ocean away pairs the strangest of bedfellows, women farmers, with German POWs assigned to help keep the farms from failing. A dramatic, beautiful time and place the likes and sentiment of which this country may never see again, in full display by Mr. Allen's excellent literary prose and revealing storytelling. An extraordinary, rewarding read."
CHRIS BAUER, AUTHOR OF *SCARS ON THE FACE OF GOD*

"Gritty and sensitive—a story that is thought-provoking and will satisfy."
STACY CREAMER, EDITOR, PUBLISHING VETERAN

"Rusty Allen's unique perspective in *Ella's War* sets it apart from other World War II novels. The story unfolds on the home front, not the battlefield, and a German soldier is a helpmeet, not a feared enemy. In Allen's sensitive narrative, passion wrestles with patriotism while love confronts loyalty. Like the best historical fiction, harsh facts are softened with tender moments. The tale alternates among four memorable characters. Ella, mother of a young son, struggles to manage the Delaware farm she inherited following her parents' sudden death. Lee, her common-law husband and the boy's father, chafes at being tied down but steps up to tend the farm. Reese, their resourceful child, vows to prove his manhood when his father impetuously overrides his Army deferment to enlist. And Dieter, the industrious first mate of a captured U-boat, strives to make amends for his countrymen's inhumanity. With evocative metaphor, cinematic detail, and absorbing drama, Allen builds toward the book's moral dilemma. Dieter, a prisoner of war, is assigned to work on the farm. Ella, initially wary, falls in love with him. Then Lee, changed by the wounds of war, comes home, ready to 'do right' by Ella, their son, and the farm. Ella is wrenched by the choice she must make. Readers will be torn too. In a conflict without good guys and bad guys, *Ella's War* is ultimately a battle of the heart."
ANN S. EPSTEIN, AUTHOR, *ONE PERSON'S LOSS*

"With meticulous research and literary skill, Rusty Allen's novel takes us back to the American home front during World War II with this exciting and romantic novel. Few Americans realize the impact of that war's Atlantic battles on the eastern seaboard, nor could they imagine that a German U-Boat actually surrendered to a small-town population in Delaware. Yet Allen's *Ella's War* brings it all vividly to life again with deeply sympathetic characters, emotional challenges, and high-risk mortal consequences that still impact those sleepy seaside towns to this day. As the dramas of World War II are beginning to fade from memory, Allen returns us to yesteryear with this superb and compelling tale."
STEVEN HARTOV, NYT BESTSELLING AUTHOR OF *THE LAST OF THE SEVEN*

About the Author

Russ Allen is a career freelance writer who owns The Writers Studio, an editorial and marketing practice located just outside of Philadelphia. He has led advanced novel writing groups and his work has appeared in literary journals, including *Neshaminy*. He is a long-time member of the Rebel Writers of Bucks County, a highly select novelist critique group that was highlighted in *Writer's Digest* in the article "Plotting a Novel Group." Russ studied creative writing at the University of Virginia, has a master's in communications, and has served as a communications director at universities. He is a son of Delmarva and an acolyte of realism in fiction.

rustyallenauthor.com

RUSTY ALLEN

ELLA'S WAR

To Joan,
Thanks for coming to
my release. Enjoy.
Rusty

ʋ
www.vineleavespress.com

To Linda, Beau, and Bailey

Chains tie us down by land and sea;
And wishes, vain as mine, may be
All that is left to comfort thee.

William Wordsworth

Reese Tingle's skiff creaked as it rocked on the bay. In the warm sun, his eyes got heavy. Down by his bare feet, lay a black sea bass and a mess of croaker. Maybe enough for dinner. He'd show her. If she came looking. That he could provide too, if it was to be just the two of them now ...

Reese drifted in the little boat, a fishing line down on each side. Ten years old wasn't too young to go fishing on his own, darn it. His pop had taught him.

A puffy breeze off the cape had taken him back inside the great cove. The Harbor of Refuge. Not a bad float if there might be any flounder to be had. And the drift gave him a good view of the naval pier over at Fort Miles.

Reese eyed the fishery plant, all up and down the beach as he got closer. He'd guessed right that one of the men there, who knew his pop, would let him borrow this rowboat. But the road along the front of the plant was getting too close. So he took the slack out of his fishing lines one more time.

He glanced again in the direction of waterfront. Maybe better to get back out along the sea wall in case she came looking for him.

Reese slid his oars down into the oar locks and let them float, waited another minute, and then began to reel in on one of his rods. Top and bottom rigs on both, with chicken scraps. Maybe rebait them both now so—

Reese stopped suddenly, when he heard or felt a great groan. His eyes rose to look across the surface of the water. Bubbles? All around? He straightened. What the—? The turbulence rising to the top now frothed the water near him in a big swath, where it welled up. Huh? He started to stand. Never seen—

All at once, pockets of air exploded up from below just next to where he bobbed, smelling greasy and metallic. Reese dropped his pole and sat back down hard, his hands scrambling for his oars as the ocean top seemed to erupt and huge creaking sounds came up from below, vibrating his little wooden vessel. A whale, an earthquake? A volcano?

The seas just near him appeared to begin to rise and then part at the surface in tremendous eddies. Reese tried, with a couple desperate swipes of his oars, to move away, but caught only air, almost falling backwards in his skiff. He bent forward again to get purchase with his paddle blades as some kind of underwater upsurge rolled under and past, and then a giant sea creature with a straight-up dorsal fin wider than his boat began to surface right out in front of him. Reese cried out.

His heart slammed and he could not hear his own whine as—but not a creature—a *vessel*—groaning and with water sloshing loudly off its sides and its ... *tower,* which rose before him. Great and gray with a body as big as a train and coming to the top and —

A *sub! A submarine* surfacing! Right here next to him. In the cove?

"Hey! Help!"

No one heard his yells.

Reese tried to put some distance between him and the huge ship, but his arms would not work together. He dropped his oars and grabbed the gunnels of his boat to try to steady himself as the wake from the surfacing sub rocked and pitched him.

But now he could see it! Almost all of it, huge and round, as it came to the surface and then started to loom up above him, but—it didn't look like the pictures he had seen of American subs, and on the high part, were strange markings. And on the bow, it said ... U-858 ... U?! *It was German.* A U-boat ... They were under attack!

Reese hollered and began to row. He glanced toward land to see if he saw her, *please.* Anyone. "Mom!" But he had to face backwards to pull in the right direction, ready to jump overboard if they shot at him or tried to run him over. The black deck gun sat amidships in front of the sub's conning tower, dripping with seawater.

"Attack!" he yelled in no direction and then called again toward the navy pier that was hundreds of yards away, as he saw someone running down it.

Out of breath, he slowed, slack faced, as German sailors scrambled out atop the conning tower of the now-stilling sub. They raised a pole with a big white sheet on it and waved it. A white flag of surrender!

The few minutes after the sub's surfacing became no more than a blur to Reese, as he tried to keep track of all that happened before him. Noises and hollering and sirens from the direction of the base, and patrol boats soon roaring to life. They shot out from the naval pier and surrounded the sub, with the German sailors waving and pointing to their surrender flag. Thank God the Americans saw it and there was no crossfire, as he had feared.

Then, as he bobbed open mouthed, the US Navies unmoored the big mine-laying ship and brought it out to tow the U-boat in. Only with that did Reese feel his chest settle some.

His mom had not come yet, and he would not want her to come now, as he turned his skiff, a few stone-throws from the sub but even with it, in the stilled air and incoming tide.

Wait till he told the other boys! Never anything like this, *ever*.

One by one, the German sailors climbed down the tower ladder and out onto the front deck of the sub, as Reese watched. The wobble still in his knees made it hard to rise up in his boat and see better. It looked like two officers—one short, one tall—lined the enemy sailors single file on the bow of the sub, all of them holding onto the loose back-end of the tow rope that was cleated now to the sub's nose. As the Americans began moving the sub toward the navy pier, he saw, all at once, for sure, back toward the beach ... his mother, driving along the front road of the fishery, in their old red Ford pickup.

He'd gone past his time out here. And that mother had come right down to put him and his bike and fishing poles in the back of the truck.

Reese made certain not to turn his head. He was still far enough out to pretend he didn't notice.

He tried to follow along even with the military flotilla, looking over his right shoulder as he pulled, and now heard planes circling overhead. He studied the devils on the sub's deck. But they weren't golden, like Viking kinds, as in the Nazi posters he'd seen pictures of, but just usual-looking men and scruffy and dirty.

He spun his eyes all the way to the left, without turning his head much, and saw her get out and try to wave to him. He wanted to jump up and yell, "Ella! Look what I found! All by myself."

The Americans had tossed the submariners a US flag, which the Germans had put up on the sub's tower, as the Navy ship drew the vessel along. Reese kept just barely enough apart that the Navies hadn't shooed him off yet.

As he approached the fishery piers and fixed to paddle right under them to stay parallel with the sub parade and the other small boats that had started to collect to ogle it all, he could just barely hear his mother yelling to him. His heart skipped a beat for her and then pounded steady as he passed the pilings and under the great fishery dock with its Ferris-wheel-like net-drying racks and out of sight of his mom, even as he knew she was honking her horn and flashing her lights, standing next to the door of the truck back there in her everyday old farm dress, as she tried to motion him in.

But he kept his heading, bearing toward the Navy pier, until the sailors and army men waved for him and another fishing boat, and a couple pleasure craft that had rushed in to stare, to hold up. But he was the smallest and let himself continue to drift even with the shoreline until he got closer to where they were tying up the sub. As he waited, they began to load the Germans off and line them up on the pier.

And in those moments, as he got as near as he was allowed, here they came—the enemy! Not at all like he'd thought. Not all big and strong. Instead, more like scraggly pirates, all grim and stiff and mangey. Not like the pictures the Nazis put out, but with long hair and beards, and in their baggy sailor shirts, leather pants, and heavy boots. Anyone could tell that they had been out to sea for a very long time, and Reese guessed the something had gone wrong with their sub. Some looked just like the older boys at the high school ... only dirty and tired.

Deadly killers, though!

All the attention was on the giving-up enemy just in these moments, so he cheated his skiff closer along the pier, following almost up under the pilings, where no one saw or cared about a boy bobbing. Army and Navy men from the base formed out where he could see at the end of the dock, as they treated these prisoners like they were under arrest—real regular and careful. Now he could pick out which was the sub captain, black-haired, short and strong looking, standing off and talking gruff to the officers. Where Reese had kept floating up, he could hear that U-boat captain argue about something. Meanwhile, a tall, blond one who was maybe the first mate made his men line up peaceful and take turns to hold their hands up in the air and get searched. The soldier guards and everyone around them stayed tough-faced, some even angry looking, but sticking to business.

By the time they were all checked over, Reese bumped up against the Navy pier, partly hidden in its shadow. He was close enough—much closer than other boats that had been allowed to gather and gawk—that he could just make out a US soldier announcing in a loud voice, "As prisoners of war under the Geneva Convention, you are to obey the orders of the MPs and to halt when commanded." He was saying this off almost in a shout to the submariners and pausing as another soldier, the first mate it sounded like, called it out in German to them. "If, after the third command to halt, you fail to do so, the guards will be ordered to shoot."

Reese suddenly felt like he'd got close enough to all this, and his stomach hurt. With that, he began to row back toward his mother.

Part I
The Calling

1

Ella

Ella Hall threw on her shawl and went to the barn to find Lee. She used her hands to keep her hair from whipping into an even worse bird's nest in the bitter wind coming from nor'easterly and off the bay today.

She found Lee working on a wagon he'd decided needed back in duty. She slid the barn door closed behind her, quickly, so he wouldn't see that she had to put all her weight into it.

"Reese in school?" the boy's father croaked, barely looking up, after she stood there for a minute. Of course he was, and Lee knew it perfectly well.

"Let me help," Ella said. He'd taken one of the struts off the undercarriage of the wagon.

"What's you gonna do, straighten her out for me?" He laughed and picked up his square-head hammer again, held at the end of a forearm as strong as a steel cable.

"Lee, if you won't treat me like a wife, at least treat me like a partner."

Both of which Ella believed she was!

Married in the eyes of authority anyway. Common law spouses—not official. But bound as they'd been for nine years by that mischievous form of life and example of a boy who would return to them at the end of this live-long day, with that darling bounce to his step.

All of them tied together now in another way too. By this place.

"I didn't ask for them to go like that," Ella said. Her parents. So fast, so early, so close together. Untimely, leaving her with this farm. And with Lee, who had been by her side intermittent over the years and, thank goodness, here since the spring and mostly running this farm this past season.

She only wished her man would meet her eyes now. But he was struggling to hold the strut at an angle to hit it just right. She grabbed the other end to steady it. He locked her gaze for a moment, then hauled off and banged again.

She could do so much more, if he would only let her try. Like walk straight off this place, if she took a mind. She'd gotten experience helping to keep a women's dress shop over in Georgetown in those last two years of high school, before she'd started to show, after this bear of a man had seeded Reese into her tummy. He had finished at Henlopen High two years ahead of her and ought to have known better than to take a chance like that first time when they rolled together in the warm sand dunes behind the beach.

But glad he did. And it had been different and fresh between them then. And could be so again, if only they would try and he would let it.

"Stand off, woman," he said, straightening up and inspecting the strut.

But this was his work—everything it took to run a spread like this. He'd helped her family, off and on, ever since Reese had been born, more *on* lately, thankfully.

But how he could work out here in this cold today, she could not understand. Not knowing what else to do, Ella reached for the push broom to help clean up the shop floor, when—BOOM, everything on the shed side of the barn rattled, and they stopped for a second.

Then relaxed again, knowing this sound by now—the guns at Fort Miles, out near the cape … Not but a mile or two away. Target practice from the artillery batteries. For a year, they'd witnessed the fort going up, as other countries had gone to war in Europe and the Pacific. But still, even though he'd heard it so many times, Lee paused and listened in that direction.

Ella shoved the broom across the floor, thanking goodness for the draft deferments. Farmers were too valuable to the war effort to pull them away.

But as the two worked, the wind outside blew again, and came in through the chinks in the shed. This week's newspapers fluttered around on Lee's work-bench, where of course he'd left them open to the war news again.

Lee

Lee Tingle avoided going into town these days—at least, any more than he had to. But the following week, he drove into Lewes like any local Sussex County farmer here in Delaware might from time to time. Lee supposed that's what he was too, no more and no less than a local yokel farmer. He liked it well enough, he supposed—his own family having been at it for as long as anyone could remember. He knew the work without having to think about it too much.

But in this year of 1942, a hundred acres or more had come under his management. A beautiful place, the Hall farm. The finest this close to town. Those good folk of Ella's had made a sad but expected bequeathment to their daughter in their dying days.

They'd never been anything but patient with him over the years—even with his drifting in and out of their lives and their daughter's and grandson's.

But now Ella, bothering him always and ever about what duties she might take on ...

Wondering what had gotten into that woman, Lee played their truck's sticky clutch, banged the vehicle up into fourth gear, and let her roll forward fast. Today, when he'd started up the Ford it had screamed to him again about its need for a new belt. Keeping this truck running had become a bit like fathering that boy who, likewise almost ten years old and just so, had been handed to him and needed tending right often.

Lee made his foot come off the pedal as he barreled into the outskirts of Lewes. Yes, this town indeed had some lovely *skirts,* and he'd gotten under one of the finest, those years ago, when it was young love between them. She was all woman, that Ella—always had been, but — He stopped musing and braked his truck, not wanting another run-in with that trouble-cat of town cop, Hale Truitt.

At home this morning, their boy Reese had been sitting in front of the radio again. Thinking and cogitating always—today asking only about FDR. A fourth grader with an active mind that went quiet and serious when the news reports came on.

Lee downshifted, glad to take a way into town where he didn't have to pass the high school and then the elementary school. Neither he nor anyone else could protect children from what they had to read and hear these days, for a year and a half now—especially, this month, with the bombing raids finally coming to England. An image flashed into Lee's mind of his son back when the boy was not more than six years old, running around under the war clouds that everyone had already felt by then, making a bomb shelter out of a tarpaulin that he tossed over some sawhorses.

Now, those youngsters had to sleep with knowledge of Pearl Harbor. Lee tried to cool his head at that thought, as he slowed his rig.

The road approached the canal and curved into town, and just then Lee heard booming reports far out to the right, to the east, toward the ocean. It was the 155 mm guns, practicing out at the fort.

Lee rolled down the window and, to no one, called out, "Them bastards must be fun to shoot," the cold air blowing his words away.

Out there in the rolling dunes of the cape, where those guns were hidden, he'd had one of his first dates with Ella, wandering in the Henlopen pines back from the point of the ocean and bay beach on a late-spring day. Him already with a job at the clam factory. Then in a great cup of private sun-warmed sand he, *they,* had conceived Reese without knowing.

The sight of the clanky, cold auto garage that he had been aiming for pulled him from that memory now. Just another place where they all knew him. But only a couple older guys and teens remained to work this service station. Lee knew that the younger ones had seen his picture in their high school's sports hall of fame. He chuckled at the notion but didn't argue with it, because none of them trifled with him.

Lee conducted his business, bought a fan belt and didn't tarry. He believed that the proprietor and his mechanics looked at him. He believed he knew *how* they looked at him, and how some talked of him, a vigorous man in draft age who had chosen not to go off to war. In the weeks since Pearl, many of the fellas he had grown up with had run off to enlist. They had flocked to the recruiting centers or answered the draft call.

At the risk of enduring more of the gazes he believed came to him these days, Lee elected to stop over at Herb's, the town's barber and tackle shop, where a guy could get a haircut and the fishing report all at the same time.

Lee sat for a trim in the stuffy little place that had only two barbering chairs and smelled of Wild Root and shaving cream.

Conversation went on over at the front of the shop. Lee listened, as two other customers also lent an ear to a couple of old-timers.

"They sunk one already, you know," one of these two buzzards was saying. He chewed as if he had something in his mouth as he spoke, referring to the first ship sunk by German submarines in this war. "Up New England-way. They're coming. You watch. You mind. Remember I told ya so. Did before."

Lee was acquainted with Pax Paytner, the seafaring oldster speaking, and he knew the man had suffered in the first war with the Germans.

The other codger, Lester Dickinson, who had been a dredger his whole life, slipped a flask out, drew on it again, and handed it to Pax. Lee wet his lips, just as Lester hollered, "Remember the *Carolina!*"

Lee recognized the name of a ship sunk by U-boats near here in World War I. The first ship of a number that had succumbed to torpedoes or mines set by the German Kriegsmarine more than 30 years ago. The *Carolina,* an ocean liner, had gone down just fifty miles straight out east from the capes.

Lee listened as that half-drunk old sailor, Pax, told it again. The submarine had surfaced and fired warning shots across the bow of the ship to provide just enough time for hundreds of passengers to get into their lifeboats before the Krauts sent the vessel down under the sea. But some victims were lost when the boats capsized. Many of the remaining survivors had been brought fatigued, frightened, and only half-alive onto the pilot-boat pier here in Lewes.

Sometime later, as the barbershop telling wound down, Lee thought he caught the inebriated old merchant marine staring at him. Lee stood from the barber's chair and brushed himself off. Then he turned to the counter, paid up with a stingy tip, and bought some lead weights for the trotline he would put out for sea trout in the canal this coming season.

He thought he felt eyes on him. Even wanted to stop and explain. His status had been set by the local draft board. The fellows on it knew his situation well enough that they had fudged him into a III-B deferment—"Men with dependents, engaged in work essential to national defense." It was a small enough county when it came to the people, and the board had given him this disposition knowing he was the main man on a farm, where there was a child of his too—out of wedlock though it might be. They granted him that status, even though he and Ella were not husband and wife by name—not legally anyhow.

So instead, Lee gave a small nod to the other townsmen and left, stepping out into the brittle cold, only wishing these dark months would hurry up.

2

Ella

Ella cleaned up at the counter of her kitchen in the farmhouse, where she had made breakfast for herself and Lee. Her man liked to work a couple hours early before taking his first sustenance, and so often missed their son in the morning by the time the bus had picked the boy up at the end of their lane.

Before Lee, as he sat at the table finishing, were the papers that he couldn't read enough of, today with a headline about some kind of false anti-aircraft barrage out along the California coast, where everyone was jumpy now because of Pearl.

"Farmers are important, Lee. Farming is important," she told him again, as she added a couple farm journals to his reading pile.

Not but a few months earlier, though, she believed she had nearly convinced him on another kind of life. Inland, with real jobs for both of them. All they needed to do was find some answer about the farm, temporary or permanent.

Lee reached for the other reading material and groaned at the things to be kept up with in the state ag circulars.

Ella stepped to him and put a hand on his shoulder. "I'm just glad you're here," she said. Stretches over the last ten years he hadn't been. Not much. Nor had she known his whereabouts when he "took a powder," as he put it.

He was a man who pushed back against anything that hemmed him in. She'd always known it, but she said this now anyway.

"Lee, I love you."

"Same here, Ella."

Close as he ever got to saying it. But she did believe it.

Ella thought back to an almost sort-of date they'd had a couple years ago, when he had started circling back into her world once more. They had gone to the beach right out at the cape. Construction of Fort Miles had only just begun. A large crowd of spectators from Lewes and Rehoboth had gathered to watch the practice strafing runs of fighter planes right off the point. Reese had been back here with his grandmother, who had only started showing the first signs of her illness then. Theirs was a sensitive child. Lee, of course, had wanted to bring him along to the airshow, but Ella had prevailed in keeping him from the military sights and sounds that day.

Now, turning back to her counter, she said, "I had my dream."

They had talked of leaving this place.

"You sure it included me?"

She had worked on him about the war-related jobs springing up everywhere.

"I tried other kinds of work," he said. Other than farming, at the fisheries, the canneries over these past years. And it hadn't taken with him.

"Of *course,* it included you," she answered him. "If you'd just —"

"I'm here, ain't I?" Lee called out and raised his arms, gesturing to the sprawling farm all around them. "Holding on to my deferment on account of this place, right?"

"Well, that ain't the only way you might hold onto it ..." But she would not press him now. Only to say, "You'll turn 30 while this war is going on, which'll help too, to keep you out of it."

"All the same, El," he said in a gentler tone, "this place is still the best way to keep that draft card from coming. Aren't I right?"

Reese

The next day, Reese stood at the end of their drive, dressed for school. He could feel his heart beating as he watched down the road for the bus and kept looking into the back yard of their farmhouse. His pop was off seed buying or such and his mother had packed him up and then gone back to the chicken house.

When the bus driver opened the door, Reese said, "My ma said to tell the school she's taking me to the doctor first."

The bus driver studied him for a second, then nodded, closed the door, and drove off. Fast as he could, Reese skittered down the road, looking back quick to make sure his Laddie dog wasn't following him.

Reese ducked into a bunch of bushes. There, he took his dungarees and old Keds out of his book bag. It was cold but he changed right out here and hid all his school stuff except his lunchbox. Lucky, it was bright and calm this day, but a secret agent frogman couldn't worry about things like weather.

He crossed the couple farm fields till he got down by the canal, where the dinghy was tied up that he and his pop kept stashed there. He could hear the clanking sound of the big tractors from across the water.

Reese rowed in that direction, and at the other side of the waterway pushed through the tidal marshes till he could get on firm ground next to the scrub-pine dunes at the back of the cape. No other way to get in here now.

Oh, how his momma had bellyached when they'd closed down this cape last summer!

"That was the best place for a day's recreation in the whole state," she had complained.

"Most popular one," his poppa had agreed, ever since they had laid the hard-surface road through the middle of it in '37, he said. Built of concrete to hold up under heavy vehicles, his father explained.

But the only proof you could see, from here or anywhere around, of the army base up ahead of him, were the fire towers sticking up against the sky. As he picked through the dead briars and then found a deer path and made his way along it, he knew he would have to fake an excuse note for himself the next day at school. One of the girls who had good handwriting would do it for him. For now, he wanted to get the kind of recon of the fort that the boys would all listen to open- or shut-mouthed.

He had his notebook and the telescope he'd bought from the 5 & Dime. It worked a little bit.

Following the sound of the clatter, he crossed a couple of sand-packed roads, then stepped far enough along that soon he came to a small dune over-looking the activity. He laid on his stomach, watching the jeeps and trucks and construction vehicles going this way and that, some painted in Army green, some regular yellow tractors.

When a pause came, he darted across the main road and made his way toward a great rise overlooking the ocean. He knew he was up on the side of one of the hidden gun batteries that guarded the bay. What luck! This was the closest spot from which he could spy. Hunkered down under the sticker bushes, he could see tents and new barracks rising with fences around them to keep the sand from blowing about. The bunkhouse buildings they were putting up looked comfortable, even warm, as his fingers moved slowly in the end-of-winter weather and he tried to sketch the camp. He started to shiver. But he scratched on. Roads, troop houses, gun placements. This map would prove he had slipped in and scouted right in close. Even big fat-head Roscoe Steeves would have to believe him.

He watched the in-and-out traffic of the soldiers. But after an hour, his head and his outstretched legs felt cranky from the coldness, and he snuck back along the way he had come.

As Reese pushed through the brush to return to the canal, he wondered: If he could get this close for this long and not be spotted, why couldn't German commandos, just as easy? If the German subs were out there right now, shooting torpedoes—and they were!—who knows what else they might do.

Anyhow, he declared today a good expedition, as he pushed his skiff back into the water, deciding this place needed some real soldiers in it, like him! Only nine more years before he could go and fight in this war. *Eight* if his parents would sign off on him when he reached seventeen.

Lee

Lee Tingle slipped toward town once again. Only so many days he could spend cooped up with a woman around while he tried to busy himself with late-winter farm work.

As he drove their rickety pickup through the streets of Lewes, he saw several houses that had service flags hung in the window. In the center of the small rectangular banner's white field and red border, was a blue star for each member of the household who was serving in the military.

Now, he passed the one house he'd heard had placed a gold star over the blue one. Their serviceman had died in action already, a son who had been lost at Pearl. Perhaps blown up while gallantly manning an anti-aircraft gun, but probably killed in his sleep, Lee thought.

With a hard skid in the gravel, Lee stopped his truck and stepped out into a light freezing rain near the bayfront, then darted into the dense warmth of the DeBraak Inn, a tavern named for a famous British gun sloop that had gone down in the late 1700s not far from the mouth of the bay. The low-ceilinged saloon was patronized tonight by a circle of men, regulars and occasionals.

Most recognized him when he came in. Some nodded to him. Some quieted briefly when they saw him enter and then resumed their talk.

Lee circled the bar and, in doing so, ran almost smack into Reverend Nelson Waite Rightmyer, who was leaving the room. Rightmyer, squat and roundly built, rectored St. Peter's Episcopal, the church in the center of town that Ella attended.

"Reverend." Lee greeted him, remembering to take off his wet cap.

But Lee had no interest in this man's attentions at the moment, wondering only where the rector's joviality could possibly come from, when he tended the troubles of a flock as large as his at a time like this.

"How is that lovely—" Rightmyer started to ask but then caught himself. Lee could tell he was about to say "wife" and that he stopped again when his tongue went for "Mrs." He simply finished with "—lady of yours?"

"A wonderful bother, Reverend."

Lee managed to approximate a smile. But, just the same, he knew she was a prize too. No one needed to remind him. Ella—willowy, with light brown hair that had a hint of cinnamon in it, and those hazel eyes, and creamy skin under a dress showing off limbs lacquered brown by just enough farm work.

"Ain't that the way," the reverend said, his stout gut moving when he laughed.

Lee knew the reverend liked to have a little nip in here from time to time, and he could smell it on the man's breath. How could you hold it against him, standing the way Rightmyer did as the chair of the Lewes branch of the Red Cross. It fell to their good pastor to organize the town's provisions and facilities for the shipwrecked who came in from the new War in the Atlantic.

Rightmyer packed his pipe before going outside, as Lee could hear chatter going on about the very events that the reverend had to contend with this month. In an instant, Lee ticked those off in his head, as the two stood silently eavesdropping. After the first sinking, of the *Francis Powell*, right out here off their coast last month, others had come in quick succession from prowling U-boats. Three large fuel tankers had gone down in the last few weeks, with crews of about forty each. Only a dozen had made it to the lifeboats or survived the cold waters on two of them. The third had been luckier, and reporters from the *Philadelphia Inquirer, New York Times,* and other papers had rushed to the landing here to cover the arrival of its sailors.

Rightmyer, who had been with the rescued victims throughout, gave Lee a look and a friendly thump on the shoulder, before slipping out into the dank cold. Was it a pat of warning or a tap of permission? Lee didn't know—or care. He went to the back of the bar and ordered a double shot of rye.

Truth be known, he did not want to be in this place, but wasn't sure where else he could escape to on such a drear night. The men had pulled a chair into the middle of the room for Cal Lynch, one of the sailors who had survived the sinking of the *Francis Powell.*

"Yeah, I'll tell it," Lynch said, as they freshened the man's drink with Antigua Rum, and Lee stepped up to the circle.

He had heard the story, but not directly. Lynch was a seaman that Lee had seen a few times about town. The man had spent days in Beebe Hospital here in town, after the Coast Guard cutter had plucked him and his mates out of their rafts.

Lee edged closer to hear.

Lynch described that night, the one right before the coastal communities had conducted their first blackout test—a night so cold and windy that tops of waves whipped off and froze in mid-air, spraying ice against the side of the *Powell.* "We was running without lights on account of the subs, hugging the coast up toward the cape."

"What were y'all carrying?" someone asked.

"Furnace oil. And gasoline. In barrels." Lynch took a deep swig. "Explosion jolted us all awake and we knew right away what it was. Know'd we'd been hit. Water flooding in everywhere. She started settling fast."

"You call out an SOS?" asked Ty Stillwell, one of the merchant marines in the small group.

"Hell no. The radio shack was busted up all to pieces in that first explosion."

The sailor doing the telling, who Lee knew to be about thirty-five years of age—only a half-dozen or so years older than himself—looked drawn and much older this night. "Most of us got in the boats and one of them almost ran into that damn awful U-boat, just sitting on the surface watching," Lynch said. "We were in a terror that the fuel would ignite around us, as we pulled the other poor buggers amongst our crew out of the ocean and then drifted shivering in the black cold, most of us with nothing but our drawers on."

The rest was just about how the men had tried to joke to take their attention away from the deadly cold while they huddled in the lifeboats, until Coast Guard cutters picked them up the next morning.

The men around Lynch at the DeBraak stayed silent, anger permeating the room. Lee knew how hard it went for them when they no longer felt masters of the great waters before them. One tossed a chair with a loud clatter, mumbling, "… get those bastards."

Conversation broke out in different bunches until another of them called out loudly, "We all got to do what we can." Lee saw who it was sounding off—his old pain in the ass, Hale Truitt, longest serving of their town's few cops, shaking his head, as if throwing the question out to each and every man in the room.

Feeling the warmth of the whiskey, Lee stepped in further and suddenly said, "We *are* all doing what we can," drawing gazes to him.

"Some of us 'least tried," another shot back at Lee. All in the room knew that the man was referring to those who had attempted to volunteer for the service and enlist.

"Get turned down that fast," Lee said, snapping his fingers loudly at how it would be for him if he tried. But suddenly wondering if it were really true.

"Yeah, but there's some managed to just straight up avoid it," one old coot hollered out, referring to the draft.

"And some who went along with what they got 'cause they had a reason to," Lee said, referring to different types of deferments that men had received, as he stood in the circle and looked around at the individuals he knew. "There's for-instances all about this room." A pause told him to go on. "Over there spouts up Hale Truitt, deferred because he's a policeman. Bet he didn't argue. And over here Elwood Colbourn, on the sidelines of this man's war because he helps to run the firehouse in this town."

They knew it was true. These men provided essential services. Exempt because the country couldn't do without them. "And just likewise," Lee concluded, "you think they allow a farmer to just walk off his farm?"

Abandon his land to fight a war?

"No more than they would let Judge Schockley here walk away from his bench to put on a uniform," Lee added, gesturing toward Granville Schockley, the local magistrate, who sat leaning on a table on his elbow, his head on his hand, half lit and half asleep.

But Truitt hadn't seemed to like the speech any more than Lee liked making it—none of them needing to feel any shittier than they already did.

Their town constable stood up and stepped toward Lee.

Truitt was out of uniform tonight, as he got close to Lee's face. "We were *refused*," Truitt spat out, referring to those who had made an attempt, over at the enlistment office.

Lee, who had made no such attempt—had not actually tried to override his deferment—said, "And you make a awful big deal out of that, don't you?" suddenly poking a sturdy finger out hard that stopped just short on its trajectory toward Truitt's chest.

That fast, the off-duty officer went for him. Lee smirked and met him unmoving, except for the quick clench of the man's arm with which Lee stopped Truitt's thrust, all to a chorus of shouts and several hands that shot between them and parted them quickly.

Ella

Ella stopped at the base gate to check in. Winter had stayed around long enough yet, that with the late cold snap it pained her hand just to reach out her identification card to the Marine guard—even on what had become a bright afternoon. Her cousin, Everett Hall, had set up a pass for her. Ev was an officer at Fort Miles, the Army/Navy base newly built into her beloved Cape Henlopen.

As directed, she drove deep into what she still thought of as a park, *her* park, everyone's park—but a park no longer. She walked toward the barracks that she had briefly heard Reese chattering about, wondering how he knew so much about them.

Construction was still underway and she could see, as she came across the rise, that many of the servicemen were still living in tents. A bitter wind had blown the sand up in little drifts against the side of the tents. A quickly dropping late-afternoon sun tried to sparkle the places where the remaining snow had mixed with the white sand.

Ella trudged toward the main barrack, past grasses that had brushed fan patterns before them in the dunes. The grains of sand were like tiny ice cubes again by the time they sifted through the air into your socks and shoes. How relieved she felt when she saw Everett waiting, looking for her out the door that he pushed and held open quickly.

Slim and crisp in his uniform, her cousin gave her a greeting that was as warm as the air she stepped into.

"Hmm, I'm not sure about the mustache," Ella joshed, as she tweaked his lip hair, laughed, and hugged her handsome and dapper buddy, who was looking rather Errol Flynn-like these days.

Everett led her into the brightly decorated day room. It was meant to be a comfortable place for the soldiers to relax, off duty. How out-of-place she felt, as she scanned the pin-up girls on the wallboards. One soldier sat reading a magazine, as another finished up at the phone booth.

Ella and Everett sat on sofas on the far side, but she could hear the ensign on the phone stop to repeat himself before ringing off. "Just like I told ya, the ships are all piled up behind the breakwater a-just off here, waitin' for the okay to go out to sea." He said it in a whisper that nevertheless carried. "You know they must be thinking *subs.*" Then, he seemed to notice an officer sitting to a conference with someone, and he lowered his head and added, "Yeah, we'll get a bead on 'em. Don't you worry."

"It's been a busy day, and I'm sure everyone's got something to do!" Everett said to Ella, trying to drown out the enlisted man who, with the other soldier, politely made himself scarce.

In a quieter voice, Everett said, "They're bringing in the sixteen-inch guns for Battery Smith this afternoon." He nodded toward the dune just nearby, built into and then covered over and hidden as an even greater hillock of sand than nature had intended.

"I can take you and show you the armory and—Hey, what's wrong?"

"Nothing," Ella said.

A lean of his head was all he needed in order to ask. Lee again?

"Yes," Ella said. "Rammy, antsy."

"Drinking?"

"Some." Off and on. "Ev, he just doesn't seem to know from one day to the next what he wants. About anything."

But that was nothing new, and her cousin harrumphed his disapproval, but then motioned to everything around him—a nation at war—and said, "It's not easy for anybody, especially now. And you too, cuz."

Yes, the farm felt so newly hers. "I love it, but ..." Ella shook her head. "I'd need to be allowed to help run it. My own pop never really ... I mean, I watched him my whole life but ..."

As for her schemes of independence? Take Reese, and just go someplace? Not many women she knew would volunteer to become single mothers in that way, especially now. And no one wished to see the Hall farm go under.

Suddenly Ella wanted to get back home before Lee knew she was gone.

"Follow your heart," Everett called behind her, after she gave him a peck on the cheek and strode out into the crisp bluster.

Dieter

As German U-boat 858 surfaced, first mate Dieter Schneider waited to be the first up the ladder into the tower. His navigator had said they were scarcely a league off of someplace called Assateague Island, just east of the coast of an American state called Mary-land.

When the okay came, he shot up the climb, cranked open the hatch, and stepped out through a shower of saltwater and up into the fresh night air. Dieter scanned out across an ocean becalmed but for long, low swells that rolled past them almost imperceptibly. A full moon lit the froth of white still around and pouring off their sub. Out before their vessel, bubbling and hissing in its death throes loomed their prey. Its stern had swung toward them, and Dieter ordered his crewsman to spotlight it, where he read:

San Gil
United Fruit Company

The freighter groaned and creaked as it began to settle, having taken their torpedo in its rear starboard, at the engine room.

Dieter and his mates who joined him atop watched the figures and shadows of the surviving crew in their lifeboats as they tried to clear the ship and its dangerous downward eddies. Dieter sent his gunnery crew to the sub's forward deck.

The Kriegsmarines made ready to administer the death blows to the crippled vessel from the deck gun. With a crank on the magazine, Dieter heard the first shell fall into place.

"Nein. Aufhalten!" he called out suddenly.

The lifeboats had not cleared the sinking wreck yet.

The gunners looked up at him questioningly. "Nicht bis jetzt. Moment, noch." Hold, still, he ordered. Until those sailors were away from the ship.

"Auf geht's," he said quietly down toward his feet, calling the order below. He felt a clank through the sub as the U-boat's driveshafts engaged and U-858 began to glide slowly along the surface, approaching the San Gil and its bobbing refugees, as he gave steering directions while the freighter continued to drop gradually below the waterline.

As best he could in the darkness, Dieter studied the frightened merchant marines nearest them. They stilled as his sub with its eerie forward lights, drew toward them, glowing the water yellow before it, bearing down on the seamen like Captain Nemo's dreaded two-eyed *Nautilus* in the Jules Verne novel he had read over and over as an adolescent. The danger was also U-858's though, having surfaced so close to the American coast, with its planes and sub-killing destroyers. He feared for his crew as he urged the action on promptly. The sin be done now.

But as his vessel eased forward, all was still enough that he could hear someone among the helpless sailors bobbing in the darkness in their rafts call out, "Here they come, boys. Stand by! Steady now."

With his careful instructions, the sub turned broadside to the lifeboats. Then, Dieter leaned out over the railing, summoned what English he knew, and hollered, "Have you any food?"

Not but two minutes later, at his order, three containers of biscuits landed in the lifeboats, hurled from the deck of the sub to the startled sailors. The sub then finished circling the wounded freighter.

Dieter imagined someone in the lifeboats mumbling the same question that he did now, "How can it have come to this between our two peoples?"

At Dieter's command, U-858 delivered the final coup to the *San Gil*, hammering its hull with a dozen loud shots from the deck gun, after which both freighter and sub quietly vanished below the black waters.

Ella

After changing all the upstairs linens, Ella hurried downstairs, wanting to get up some afternoon supper for Lee and their farmhand, Levotas, when— She stopped, seeing Lee standing in their living room. It was noon and sunny outside, the light streaming in the windows as the winter weather continued to relent.

Lee stood looking at a piece of paper. He had his boots on, so she knew he had been bound for outback and more chores before he would break. But he stood reading. A letter.

"It's from Chester Hearn."

Ella's heart caught in her throat. Chester was the fellow who knew them best at the local draft board.

"He says he's been transferred to Washington, D.C. A new head of the board covering Sussex County is in and he knows about our ... arrangement." Lee handed the letter to Ella, who pressed her other hand against the top of her chest as she took it.

"Is it good or bad that he knows?" she breathed.

Just a few days ago, she had telephoned Everett at the base and asked him what they could do if this came to pass—if someone who didn't know them got wise at the draft board, discovering that they weren't husband and wife by name nor law. Everett knew the corps he served with and understood the Army, having joined up even before the war.

"There isn't much you can do," he had said. They had few options to preserve Lee's status, other than the obvious—of getting him to the altar—a choice that her cousin Everett would not bring up.

Ella dropped the letter to her side, spun to Lee, and grabbed him roughly by the shirt. Thank god Reese and his radar-like ears and eyes were at school today. "Marry me!" she yelped at Lee. *Again.* "Then the farm will be yours too. Your deferment will be safe." He knew it. They could get through the war with him stateside.

Lee's jaw tightened in a way that took her back to an evening not three months ago, at the beginning of December, just days before the news about Pearl Harbor—but with all the papers predicting a naval war with Japan in the Pacific. They had taken Reese to the holiday parade in town where strings of Christmas lights had crisscrossed the street. Then she and Lee had gone that evening to the grand opening of the Service Inn, a recreation center near the entrance to Fort Miles.

As they had driven in, a sign farther down the road, toward the newly forming headquarters said, "Chief installation of the harbor defenses of the Delaware," but the powers that be had placed this rec center just outside the base and opened it to everyone.

Lee had looked so nice that night, with an Artie Shaw kind of handsomeness to him, his dark hair pomaded to the side. He needed to do no more than pay attention to her for them to have a good evening. But as they sat near the dance floor, she saw his eyes wander to the uniforms of the hundred or so US Army, Navy, and Coast Guard personnel at the event. The jitterbugging—not his kind of thing—had been wild but she managed to get him out there on the floor until he received a couple of accidental elbows. She pulled him back toward their table, but just then he had turned and barked at one of the sailors, most of whom were younger than him. The sailor had stuck his chest out at Lee, with another rushing in to back his mate up.

Unfairly, it was Lee whom the military police had ushered out of the inn, with Ella at their side working to calm everyone and assure them that she was escorting him home. She remembered how frightening the black "MP" armbands on those big fellows had looked.

Now, on this day that had just begun to change, puffing bright to overcast and back again with its passing March-like clouds, she stepped closer to him, even as his gaze went out their windows and across their land.

"You want to go, don't you?" Off to war.

She leaned her head against his chest. Indecision was surely the pain her man felt most now, and could be the worst kind—worse sometimes than even making the wrong decision.

They held each other close.

"You'd have to show me an awful lot more about running this place before you did," she said, but only as a way to delay him—maybe adequate to keep him here and certainly enough to stay in his arms in this moment.

3

Lee

The season was turning and Lee thanked God for it, despite all the work it would mean. He decided the sun was warm enough this morning that he would start his day with a think, leaning back against the south-facing side of the tool-shed. It was bright and still enough that he hoped for peace for a few minutes before getting to it all. He would read the paper and chew.

He had a sack of rusk and jerky that he kept out here in a tin, safe from the mice. Perhaps the only woman in the world who could ever put up with him and his ways was back there in the kitchen—and he loved her for it—but he needed quietude to start the day.

When Reese had been born in 1933, the Depression had still been going on. It was no time for two teens to get married. Then, by the time they got through the next recession, of '37-'38, well, they'd been together sufficient and satisfactory to be considered married in the eyes of common sense, at least as far as Lee was concerned. Ought to be ample and plenty!

Trying to move his mind elsewhere, Lee threw open his copy of the *Delaware Pilot,* which had more now on the chatter he had heard these last few days on the sinking of the US destroyer *Jacob Jones.* After the *San Gil* had gone down, a U-boat had torpedoed this naval vessel just thirty miles off the coast.

The paper, it turned out, gave only simple details but, from the scuttlebutt he had heard in town and from what he knew, he could fill the rest in. He had spent his share of time on the water and some of his relations had been seafarers off and on for generations.

He could feel the black horror that must have come from being out there in those moments. The concussions and fire that had killed many Navy sailors in their bunks at the moment of impact on the *Jones*... He doubted there had been enough time or able men remaining to even properly launch the lifeboats from that ship. The only thing more that the paper gave was about the few who had made it to their rafts amid the oil fires on the surface of the water. Those not burnt had been slowly pounded to death by the explosion of their ship's own depth charges, automatically detonating as the destroyer went beneath the water.

In the damned safe, warm sunshine, Lee stretched his legs out. He knew how kindly Ella's dearly departed parents had tried to treat him, welcoming him always. Like a son—like the son they had always wanted. The one who could take over someday. Nor had they meddled in matters between him and Ella. They offered him their guest room, always. And swallowed their Christian pride, looking the other way if he snuck into Ella's room with her.

"We're man and wife in the eyes of the Lord," he had told her father, to placate that good man.

And now he had the poor girl thinking a woman could try to take over this place. Ha! Good Gawd...

Shaking his head, Lee at last got to the bottom of the story about the *Jones*. Only eleven of 149 sailors had survived. They had been brought them into Cape May, right across the bay from his town.

Lee leapt up, stalked about in a circle, and then kicked an old, galvanized tin bucket so hard that it rocketed across the barn yard, causing two goats to scatter inside their pen, their old nag of a horse to startle over in his paddock, and their collie dog to low-tail it out of there.

4

Reese

Upon a Sunday, Reese worked at the little desk at his bedroom window. He had nearly finished his school exercises when he heard a voice, singing. He went to the top of the steps.

Her voice. His mother following along to a song about being happy sometimes and blue other times. He went down to the living room, and found his ma was before their Victrola, with her same favorite couple of records out. The one she had on was by Sammy Kaye. And now, like no one was listening, she rocked back and forth, looking across the farmyard, and murmured along with the words about loving someone and hating that person at the same time, and hating that person because she loved that person.

Reese felt a stitch in his stomach. She seemed so lonesome in that minute. "I don't like that song, Momma," he called out.

His mother jumped, "Oh!" and then saw Reese and laughed.

"I know, honey. It's a sad one. But you like this one." She lifted the needle up with a scratch, plopped the other record on, and dropped the arm down right in the middle of the song, where she knew was the part he liked.

Reese heard a familiar clarinet playing low, and the steady strum of a guitar.

"C'mon and dance with me," she said and took both his hands, as she started crooning with singer Tommy Ryan, voicing a wish that it be "you and me."

Reese leaned back and forth, trying to go along with her gentle sway, as she sang along, to the silly lyrics about oysters under the sea.

Reese laughed and started to sing too, a rhyming line about wishing for birds to sing in the trees.

But just that quick, he said, "Okay, Momma," and tried gently to free his hands.

She smiled and finished with song words about having someone to bless us whenever we sneeze, as she tweaked his nose playfully—and lastly accompanied the singer with a wish for love, above all.

"All right. Can we be done now, Ma? I want to listen to the radio."

"Sure, sweetheart," she said with a chuckle and stopped the record, out of breath.

Before long, Reese's knees hurt as he knelt in front of the big radio, feeling bad for having shooed his ma away, but moving the dial back again, trying to find anything other than the war news. Everything had been better last year, before Americans had to join the fighting. He would never forget that Sunday in December when his *Lone Ranger* show had been interrupted by news of the sneak attack in Hawaii.

Worse, one of the teachers in school a couple weeks ago had let slip that more than a hundred ships had already been sunk by the U-boats this year up and down the coast of the United States of America and Canada. He cussed it all again now, but under his breath, so as not to get put in the corner.

Reese settled Indian style on the rag rug, thinking maybe he would just leave the radio settled on fuzz noise between stations. Poppa had been talking last month about a hundred-thousand barrels of diesel that had gone burned up in a giant plume after a torpedo hit another tanker out there, and the survivors had rowed for thirteen hours to get into the shore at Fenwick.

BANG, Reese hit the radio with his hand, determined to find something fun. But then he rolled past what sounded like one of the generals talking in an interview show, and something about it stopped him as he slowly turned the dial back.

"—are indeed concerned about a military invasion of the Delaware. You know that the industrial complex that stretches up along the Delaware River from Wilmington to Philadelphia sprawls with ammunition factories, oil refineries, shipyards, and so on. A sudden thrust up the Delaware Bay could destroy a significant portion of America's war-making capacity."

Reese stood up.

"What's more, the Delaware beaches are almost completely undefended until now. An enemy landing on the Delaware coast could
roll inland unopposed from the landward side. Sussex county is
a flat peninsula perfect for landing an invading army. Once in
these waters and with a beachhead, it could easily sweep across
lower Delaware and the Eastern Shore of Maryland bridgehead
opposite Aberdeen, and there offer equal threats to Washington,
Baltimore, and Philadelphia."

"But general, do you really think that—"

The talking man tried to interrupt, but the general kept on, right over top
of him.

"That army would have little difficulty marching inland to attack
the heart of the nation."

With his feet spread wide, Reese snapped the radio off and then sent a kick
into the air. If only he could kill all Jap and Kraut armies in this world and have
everything be regular again! Or at least have his momma and poppa back more
normal and sometimes sweet together. They bickered over what to do, with
his pop ever bossing his ma too much on everything, and with Grandma and
Grandpa not here to make things right and run things anymore. His pa acting
like his ma didn't know anything, and her acting like he didn't care if she did.

5

Ella

"Here you go, Ma," her boy said, as he handed her down a dusty cardboard box full of papers. Ella stood on the creaky stairs up to their third-floor attic. The box didn't look to her like anything more than old farm annuals that her father had kept. And there was another couple of boxes of *Life* and *Woman and Home* magazines that her mother had stashed away.

"Grab another one of those and come," she said to Reese, as she climbed down. It was a hot darn day all of a sudden for a job like this, removing all the old papers from the attic, to stack in the dining room and then drop over to the paper drive. They were dressed as lightly as they could for the work and—

"What in kingdom-come are y'all doing?" Lee said, as he came into the downstairs hall and surveyed them.

"We are clearing any ..." Ella searched for the word that the township had used, which escaped her until she pulled the flyer out of her skirt pocket and read, "... *combustibles* from the attic ..."

Reese ran up and pulled her wrist down so he could read on. "... in case of ..." He had trouble with the next word.

Lee stepped in to help, "'... *incendiary* bombs?'" He scoffed. "Oh, good God and hogwash. Ain't no bombing going to happen here. And anyway, even if there was, we're too far from town for it to git us anyhow."

"Well, that's what they're telling everybody to do," Ella said, giving an encouraging wink to Reese.

"Poppa, you know they already landed sabotage-ers in America," Reese said eagerly, on his toes to his father. Ella knew it was true because it had been in the news this week. German submarines landed two small groups of enemy saboteurs on beaches in Florida and New York.

"They got nabbed right away," Lee said, with a dismissive wave of his hand as he walked off, but then turned suddenly and grabbed Reese playfully up off his feet. "Nabbed like this," he said, hugging and lifting the boy into the air with a bounce. Reese belted out a joyful call of pretend distress as his dad bounced him up high.

Once Reese had escaped, he bolted to Ella, tugged on the simple, thin, cotton dress she had on today, and asked, "Can I go fishing now?"

"Go, then," she said.

When he had skittered off, she peered at Lee, who looked stiff today. "What's the matter?"

"Bone tired, is all."

"Soon as this war is over, we're selling this farm," Ella declared. It troubled her soul to say it, and Lee just shook his head and pursed his mouth. "Yes, we will," she went on. "Just as fast as we don't need that damn deferment anymore."

A deferment though, that seemed to be holding for now. In spite of the news they had gotten from the board, no draft notice had arrived yet. Had they gotten a reprieve? Perhaps just in consideration of the current growing season upon them?

But the cloud that came over Lee's face when she spoke of selling the farm lingered.

"We're moving to Seaford," she continued. "So I get a chance to do what *I* want to do."

She had never spoken to him so. But, yes, inland in Delaware, to a bigger town. Or over Salisbury-way. How many years had she dreamt of accepting her aunt's invitation to partner with her in her prosperous furniture store there!

"Listen, El, all I know is farming."

"That's not true. You've worked other jobs," she said, as she followed him into the living room. "You could do anything you want. You know my Uncle Orington works in the nylon factory. He could get you a job."

Lee scrunched up his face, obviously having as much trouble picturing himself in a factory job as he might imagining himself stuck in a crab pot.

But she kept on. "They have carpools that they use to get everyone to the plant because of the gas rationing and—"

But when Lee shook his head again, Ella quieted at the verdict.

"They worry it's a military target, anyway," he said about the factory.

Ella walked over and rested her hands on the back of the easy chair that faced toward one of their front windows. It was just in time to see Reese disappear down the road on this bike with his fishing pole. Boys and their poles!

"They worry about it being bombed from the air," she said quietly, as if Lee had thrown an agreeing trance on her.

"How is that possible, though?" Lee said, laughing at his own self now. "Those planes would have to fly from Iceland or some darn place," he added, turning to her and plainly trying for a comforting tone, as he came up behind her. "And then they'd have to ditch after they dropped."

He put his arms around her.

It struck her that he always seemed to enjoy hugging her from behind more than from the front for some reason. She felt nearly naked today in her bare feet and little knee-length frock, with nothing beneath. She had felt self-conscious working around Reese that way, but it was too hot to worry.

"Guess the Germans aren't as crazy as the Japs, huh?" she said.

"Dunno, some these Nazis is damn crazy," he said, softly, as he ran his nose and his lips up along her neck.

Her husband, who had dropped his voice in that way he did when he was clearly done talking, did not seem to mind that she was sweaty and dusty, as his hands travelled across her thighs, drawing her dress up, both of them peering still out the bare living room window. There was no one to see and no one to be seen by. It was that way every day here.

All was safe because Levotas, their Black farm hand, was not due until later, and the postman did not get to them until the end of his run ... She knew that neither she nor Lee wanted to admit to how they listened for the mail delivery, dreaded it maybe, awaited it each day.

Now, though, she let her mind go to him, in that way they had learned together from a tender age. She did not mind the touch of his rough hands. The only man she had ever known in this way.

Anyone walking into their yard—though they knew there would be none— might have stood there and watched their lovemaking through unadorned windows, lit by the same sunlight that heated the golden-brown grass of their lawn and streamed into the room, as Lee's hands went to her pleasure and his forearms drew her hips tightly against his.

Now she pushed her backside toward him and leaned on the overstuffed chair, as she heard his dungarees drop down around his knees.

In the past, she might have declined this moment, what with so little building to it just now. But she felt a new kind of choosing in this—a woman accepting overtures at an odd time and place, simply because it felt good to her body.

The front legs of the chair banged on the floor with a clacking sound. The harder he churned into her, the harder she pushed back against him in a kind of way that caught his attention newly and urged him on, till their movements and their moments became one.

Afterwards, they remained clenched into each other until they caught their breath and he eased his now-caressing grip and they separated. At least this part of their lives, Ella told herself, had always worked.

"Alright, tie me up," Clarissa said, tossing on her blue smock and turning her back to Ella.

Sitting at a chair in Clarissa's kitchen, Ella bowed the apron-like ties at the back of the uniform that marked her friend as a volunteer at Beebe Hospital.

"Won't you please consider coming with me?" Clarissa asked, as she pinned her badge on.

"To there? With *them?*"

"Oh, do come."

"No, thank you. I know what gals lord over all that."

The ladies auxiliary, beset these days by certain other young women that she and Clarissa had grown up with.

"You're the only one among them who didn't snub me back then," Ella said, placing both hands on her stomach, as if she could still feel the baby bump with which she'd had to attend high school in her senior year. "And I can't forget it."

Clarissa, who had been just a year behind Ella in school, stopped in front of Ella as the summer light came in her back screen door, on a block in the middle of town from which you could just see the hospital buildings. "But you used to love it when we candy striped there, as girls," said her dear friend, petite in stature but with ample, solid hips and chest, and a blond bob of hair that bounced in her earnestness about all things—physical attributes that attracted men and that Ella knew she herself lacked.

"Your pop always told us we could do anything we put our minds to—don't forget," Clarissa said, giving Ella's hand a pat on the brightly enameled kitchen table.

It was a reminder that Clarissa had been close to Ella's father, as the two girls had grown up, Clarissa having lost her own dad right out there upon the *Carolina* and its sinking, just at the end of the Great War.

"We miss him, don't we?" Ella said of her father, as she gave her friend's hand a squeeze.

"At least you have memories to miss," Clarissa said, her face hardening a bit, as she gazed out the back door in the direction of the medical center, which this year housed its share of war-related patients, including from the new sinkings.

"You do too," Ella said. "Up there." She nodded at the framed and fading photo on the wall of Clarissa's father, a handsome young merchant marine on a sunny ship's deck in his well-worn and oily engineer's garb in 1918.

Both women got quiet. That man and his crewmates had gone down at the end of a sub's torpedo when Clarissa was no more than three years old. She said she had only the faintest mental images of him to recollect.

Ella glanced at the electrical clock churning in the kitchen and knew her friend had to report soon. "Hey, I didn't come empty handed today," she said.

Ella went out to her truck and came back in, carrying a crate of food. Bread, a huge jar of plum jam, the last of their strawberries just harvested, and jerk-dried turkey bacon.

"Those sick and healing folk, need some farm-hearty food," Ella said, taking out a pack of brown sacks and wax paper. "C'mon, let's quick make up some lunch bags for them."

"Oh, you angel," Clarissa said, and they had just enough time to make jam sandwiches and divvy up the sustenance between two dozen or more goody bags.

"You're lucky to have the liberty for this," Ella said, as she thought of the need to get back and see what Lee might let her lend in on today.

"It helps to marry a little-bit older man," Clarissa whispered. Ella smiled at the mention of Rand Ellis, the fine fellow of a husband of Clarissa's who was off working at the local dairy today, where he was the manager.

"If I can keep him," Clarissa said. Ella looked for a laugh from her friend but saw only a tremor on her face.

"What?"

Clarissa jerked her thumb over her shoulder, to the east, toward the war in Europe.

"Oh, nonsense, sweetheart. Rand is in his *thirties,* and he's married." Ella closed the bags and placed them back in the crate for Clarissa to take. "They won't call him."

"Unless he volunteers."

"What? And *why?* War-making is wrong unless it's forced upon you. That's what I say."

"Well, you know darn well he's already been in the Navy and was in the reserves until a few years ago," Clarissa said, her voice getting higher.

Ella saw tears building in her friend's eyes—tears that came from some long-ago place. What's more, she knew too how badly this couple wanted to have a child after losing two pregnancies early.

"You let me talk to him," Ella said with a smile, hefting up the box of lunch bags to put in her truck, so the girl didn't have to walk to her duty again today. "I'll knock some sense into his head."

6

Dieter

U-858 cruised slowly, almost idled, only close enough to the surface for its periscope to clear the water. First-mate Dieter Schneider knew the ship like it was part of his body, the slight vibration through his feet telling him that vessel's twin props were turning only very slowly.

Dieter stared at the back of his captain's head, as Kapitän Lutz Befehl peered into the long vertical tube, scanning the water to the east, revealing no doubt about what they saw on that horizon. A ship steaming north along the American coast. It was all he seemed to need to know.

Begrudgingly, he stepped back for Dieter to have a look.

Dieter greatly valued the English lessons he'd had as a youth, but Befehl had upbraided him for calling out in that language to their last sinking victims.

Now though, procedure required their Kapitän to let the next officer down in rank view and confirm a target. Dieter reluctantly stepped to the viewfinder, as excitement coursed through every crew member at their stations around him.

He leaned in. He did not have to look hard. Still, he straightened, squeezed his eyes shut for a moment to clear them, put his face to the periscope again, and refocused the lens.

If only it could be a mistake, he thought, or a matter of confusion.

The exchange took place quickly, in clipped German.

"Captain, this cannot be our target."

"It is our mark."

"This is a passenger ship." And *only* a passenger liner, nothing more. The profile of an ocean liner was unmistakable this close. Dieter said it again, loud enough so that the other crew, all of them stilled in their places, could hear.

"Step away," Befehl barked.

Dieter felt the despair again and did not move. How quickly guidance had drifted, even disappeared, leaving things up to men like his captain.

"Nein!" Dieter said. "U-858 crew, stand down."

He knew the terrible risk he took in this. But he had been a party to such a reckless kill once before on this mission—and never again.

"Raus!" The captain shoved him away.

"This is not a military target," Dieter shouted, as two other officers pushed him out of the command room. Not roughly, though. He knew he had the support of most of the other crew members, but they were not prepared to commit outright insubordination. Not yet, anyway.

Ella

"We'll take only the choicest birds. I promise," Lee said to Ella through the screen door, standing on the rear stoop of the farmhouse. She could see he was worked up. He explained again that he wanted to sell some of their broiler chickens to the black marketers who ran them covertly through the wartime rationing restrictions and trucked them up toward Wilmington and Philadelphia for a nice profit.

"I don't know, Lee." She didn't want him to have anything to do with men who would bootleg at times like this, even though she often felt as agitated about money as he seemed today.

"I thank you for asking me, though," she said. It was the one part of the farm he let her help with—the chicken house that he and her father had expanded a few years ago.

Now, though, he blabbered on about how poultry prices had doubled and more since the war began. It was true, but Ella was distracted at the moment by another news bulletin she could hear on the radio in the living room behind her.

"Lee, the survivors have been picked up," she said, as she darted back in to hear. The people who were still alive and floating in lifeboats from the ocean liner, the *City of New York,* had been reached and rescued! The Germans had torpedoed and sunk it south of here, and early this morning an Army bomber and then a Navy blimp had located the lifeboats.

The announcer was saying, "The Coast Guard reports that one of its vessels has plucked both the living and the dead from the rafts."

Ella stepped over and snapped off the radio. Reese was about somewhere, and the boy heard enough of this sort every day.

"I'm doing what must be done, woman," she heard Lee call over his shoulder to her about the birds, as he headed back out toward the poultry house.

It was a fight she could pass on today, though, swapping it instead for a little jump in her step and a special mission. Her stomach surged as she strode back into the kitchen to finish loading a box of their own canned goods to take into town to the Red Cross larder.

The bottom shelf was emptier than she remembered, exposing bottles of elderberry wine that she and her pop had made and stored in there, and which she had almost forgotten about. It took her back to two summers ago, the last time she had worked next to her father on this family tradition, taking the berries from the rows of huge elder bushes they had up along the road over toward the corner of their spread. And standing here next to that dear man while they crushed and strained and bottled. It was the only liquor she could ever remember seeing in this house.

"Reese Tingle, come here, and do you know what's become of some of these jars put by?" she called out, scanning empty spots on the shelves where the Mason and Bell jars sat.

"Already here, in case the bombing starts," her boy said, pulling up a long cloth over their living room coffee table to reveal where he had assembled an assortment of preserved food. As Ella stood there with her arms crossed, he showed her a long coil of rope, his flashlight, a jug of water, tools, and other sundries in his pile of emergency supplies.

Ella made herself stop and count a breath, and not laugh. "I'm glad you're prepared, buddy, but you needn't worry. Now hand me two of them big jars of stew tomatoes."

Ella was thankful for a get-away in this growing season that had turned never-ending, even if just for an hour's reprieve. Driving toward town in their pickup, passing first the far side of their property, she glanced over at the couple of shacks they kept for migrant workers. Her father had only finally agreed to using such labor years ago when truck-farming days had got underway.

But till recent, Levotas had long said that the huts were not fit. He ought to know. There were places over in the Black section of Lewes where he lived that weren't fit to live in either. Ella had taken missions over there with her ladies Church circle. So this year, at Levotas' urging, she had also taken some funds from her parents' bank savings that had come to her and had their two migrants cabins spruced up.

Now though, with the shortage of men, they'd been fortunate to get even a couple-few workers this month to help with the picking and cropping. And that bunch had departed this week and moved on north, following the harvest. Lee didn't much like managing them anyway, when they came up from the south each year for the ripening, but there was no choice.

As she eased on to Second Street, the town's main street, Ella saw notices up on the telephone poles that gas masks would be distributed next week. It brought a pinch to her own chest when she remembered how badly her father wheezed when he came back from the Great War, after he'd got stuck down-wind from a battlefield where the Germans were using chlorine gas.

"The gas alert is two long horn blasts followed by two more long honks from the alarm sirens," Reese had blurted out this week—something he'd been taught in school.

"Oh, Jesus. Isn't anything like that going to happen *here,* I tell you," his father had said.

How many times had she asked Lee not to use the Lord's name in vain in front of their son, Ella wondered.

She parked in front of St. Peter's Episcopal Church, with an image in her mind of that man, just now as she had left, grabbing their son up piggy-back style as they had jogged out back, without even a goodbye, to pick which couple of their few ewes they might auction to butchers as soon as the lambs weaned—the two of them oblivious of her as soon as they were in that father-son world of theirs.

Ella walked up the churchyard path amid the rows of weathered tombstones incised with images of ships, anchors, and angels, marking the graves of generations of pilots, sailors, and patriots. The brick church had been rebuilt in the mid-nineteenth century, but she was proud to know that a congregation had worshipped at this location since the 1600s.

Nelson Rightmyer, her lifelong rector, came rolling out to meet her. She gestured to the crate with jars of preserved food, and said they were for his stores for emergency care of those from downed ships.

She knew it odd that she would drop these in the middle of the week, rather than simply bringing them along on the next Sabbath, and her pastor had only to look at her to say, "Come take a stroll with me."

But she would not talk of Lee! Nelson had heard too much on that subject too many times over the years. And Ella disliked the sound of her voice when she lamented about that man. Since he was nineteen years old, Lee'd had to answer to everyone for Ella's impending motherhood. And to this day, you could see that fear in him of having been tied to any one person or place by accident or otherwise before his time.

"The war is still something new to everyone," Nelson said, trying to prompt her as they strolled.

Their rector invariably weighed in to save a marriage, to support a marriage, to argue in favor of one. On the subject of Lee, however ...

"Season's finishing up," Ella blurted out, "and farming is only going to keep Lee's deferment if he *owns* the farm. But you know that already, and I'm sorry to fret to you, Nelson." She fell in behind him along the garden path. "So don't say a word, now," she snapped at him. "You've been a family friend too long to guide me with that too-careful hand that you would anyone else."

Instead, he put his hands on his hips and cocked his head at her. Before either could open their mouths again, though, they were cut short by a holler from the rectory. Liam, the funny lame boy who helped the reverend around the place, nearly squealed out the window, "Station a-calling!"

Nelson ran in and then back out. "C'mon, they're coming in!"

"What?"

"The poor folk from that *New York* liner, Ella! The one in the news today. Bringing them here into Lewes." He rushed past her, gently taking her elbow. "Come with me. Help me."

They jumped in Nelson's old DeSoto, and raced to the Coast Guard station at the bayfront. When they arrived, the rescued passengers were indeed hobbling into the shelter, looking like wet rats that had been caught in a marsh trap or a saltwater sewer for days. Many were off-loaded appearing barely alive. Those that could stagger across the guard dock and into the station on their own power had sunken eyes. Someone shoved a stenographer's pad in Ella's hands and asked her to take down names and next of kin, as much information as she could from each one that filed in.

Nearly a dozen days lost at sea after the Third Reich sent their ocean liner down!

Ella felt her pencil point snap at the thought. But she whittled a new one with her pen knife and coaxed more words from brittle, baked lips. She scurried between the survivors, flipping back and forth on the pad, getting parts of the story here and there, and stopping also to help Nelson bring in fresh, dry clothes for them from his car and make sure they kept drinking water. And soon a hot supper got laid at the tables, as the doctor arrived from Beebe Hospital.

It had taken just long enough for the authorities to realize that their ship had not been heard from—and the *New York* had been just far enough out in the wide ocean—that nearly a fortnight had gone by on the bobbing waves before these living were plucked from the seas. Ella's hands shook as she wrote information from those with the strength to give it, as passengers told her of riding, huddled and shivering, in a crowded lifeboat, next to their dead companions, who one lady said, "stared straight ahead with eyes that didn't see."

A nurse arrived and sat in one corner, holding a girl who wept. "Her mother died in the boat with us," one haggard man with a two-weeks scraggly beard growth whispered to Ella. "We had to promise her that we would not throw her mother's body into the water, like we did with the rest of them."

By evening everything felt drained from Ella. But with the survivors dispatched here and there, some to the hospital, she found there was little more that she could do. So she walked the mile or so back into town, scheming as she went about how she could keep any of this, *all of this,* from the two fellas who waited for her back home, who just couldn't seem to hear enough about this cursed-damn war.

7

Ella

Ella pumped water into her kitchen basin, as she washed out bowls she had just used to make a pie in advance of the day of thanksgiving. On the kitchen table, the papers lay open where Lee had been reading to her this hour as she worked. She had loved it more in the days before the war when he would read to her of other things.

"They're building camps out in the Midwest to house prisoners of war," he said, running his finger down a column. "German POWs, starting to come in already, mostly from the North Africa campaign."

Ella stopped what she was doing, in mid slosh, and turned to him, trying to grasp the notion. "To the USA?"

"Yup. Make them into labor camps probably."

In the quiet of the farmhouse, and still trying to absorb the notion—just another distant strange-oddity of this war—Ella cranked water into her sink harder and faster than she needed to.

8

Reese

Reese couldn't sleep so he slid out of his bed and went to the window. He slipped behind the heavy black canvas of the blackout curtain and looked out into the icy night. Toward the other brave watchers. Way out there somewhere. People all up and down this coast who had a new duty—aircraft spotters!

"I want to be a sky watcher!" he'd told his ma.

His window faced east and north, across to beyond where the lights of the town and Lewes beach ought to have been, but for the blackout, and to where he should have been able to see another twinkling. Broadkill Beach, and up the bay beyond it to Slaughter Beach and the direction of Fort Saulsbury.

His classmates who had relations up in that way said people in Milford were scared when they heard that, after the guns were moved out of the battery there and down here to the cape, the fort was to be turned into a prisoner-of-war camp. He'd heard whisperings, anyway, that it was true, and he tried to imagine that there might be real—

Reese's thoughts froze when a sharp sound cut in from far away. It stopped and then he heard it again. A wail. The warning siren from down Rehoboth way!

Now came another short blast and another. "Three short blasts with ten seconds in between," just like he'd learned at school. *It was the alert that enemy aircraft were approaching.*

Reese ran downstairs. He flew over to the davenport, remembering the instructions. He threw his hands against the back of the big-long couch and lunged forward with all he had. If they could flip it and get beneath it, they would have a good bomb shelter to hide under.

But it was too heavy and he was forced back and had to drop its feet loudly on the wood floor. Then again.

"What the devil?" came a low voice.

Reese turned to see a dark outline standing in the entrance to the living room.

"Air raid, Poppa! Come help me quick and get Momma."

"Hold on now, buster," his pop said.

"There's no time."

"Come over here, buddy."

"We have to hurry, Pop."

"It's only a drill, son. You know that, right?"

That's when Reese stilled some and realized he was shaking.

"If there was an air raid, they would keep the alarm on—and then one long blast if the planes were overhead," his pop said, as he gave Reese's back a rub. "But that's not going to happen here."

With his pop's hands gently on his shoulders, Reese sat beside him on the sofa. Then the horn startled them. Two short ones.

They counted out loud together in a whisper. Fifteen seconds and two more short blasts.

"You see, the all-clear signal."

"Yes ..."

"It was just a test." He let his father pull him close on this cold night, like he hadn't in a long time. "We're all being tested, every day now," his father added, but with some far-off sound in his voice.

Lee

Lee Tingle felt too fidgety and idle to spend a full day on the farm, a-midwinters. The second dormant season was upon them since the world beyond had turned upside down.

He was not in the habit of looking to his woman for errands. But he found himself doing so now.

He and Ella had just finished loading the truck, and Lee stood by the back door of the farmhouse changing out of his farming coat.

"Pick up a paper, too, if you can. One of the Philadelphia ones, if they have any left," Ella said, as she buttoned up his mac in the dismal weather.

"You know that I will. Maybe see what word I can hear on some of our boys, too," he said about the many townsmen who were long since in basic training or even already overseas.

"Just at the newsstand, though, okay?"

"If you'll kiss me when I get back, you'll know the truth," he said, smiling and putting an arm around her. She would get to smell his breath and know he had not visited the tavern.

She touched a finger to his lips. "All right. Go, then."

"Some of them first boys already getting to see what it's like," Lee said, as he turned and walked to the truck again. "On the front lines, I mean if they're in Patton's army and—"

"We're already *on* the front lines, Lee!" Ella called to his back.

He knew what she meant, and now he'd have to mind how long he was away, on account of her and because they were one of the town's few that had both a phone and vehicle—and that got them on the carpool list, organized to ferry the kids inland to safety in case of evacuation or air raid. Ella knew it to be as unlikely as he did, but darned if she didn't use it to keep him on a short leash.

As he drove out their lane, Lee mulled the farfetched theories he had heard, that the Nazis might-could stage a raid on the East Coast from their Scandinavian airfields. As he headed toward town, he glanced over at the watching platform built in one of the corn fields over in the Tubbs farm and connected to new phone lines, where observers day and night were supposed to report any planes overhead, and call them into the center to make sure they were American. He knew he ought to've volunteered, but such standing about and staring into the heavens was not for him.

Lee drove up to St. Peter's, then to his surprise could scarcely find a parking spot on the streets. He'd never had much business with the church, and now he damned the fact that he'd have to wade into some kind of gathering to drop off this pile of blankets and quilts that Ella and a couple of the neighbor ladies had collected and mended for the Red Cross depot for seafarers here.

Nor could he find limpin' Liam to figure out where to put this load. So he stepped inside the chapel.

A full house ... Virginia Cullen, who wrote for the papers, stood just inside the door, her long, stylish gray coat still on and her short-cut untamed hair falling out from under her beret. She had a reporter's pad in her hand.

"Virginia."

"Lee."

"What is it?" he whispered.

"Service for the survivors of the ships that have been torpedoed this last year."

Sure enough, most of the seats were taken, and among the assembled he could see sailors, some he recognized, many in the front row. God durned if some weren't kneeling in this ancient church—most of them merchant marines but also what looked like citizen survivors of sinkings up there too, a few. Reverend Rightmyer was blabbering off as usual, at this moment reading a prayer of thanks.

When Rightmyer finished, the right rector kept on with, "For three centuries, our fair town has been home to pilots who rely on their knowledge of the winds, currents, and the bay channel to guide ships past the treacherous shoals and sandbars of the Delaware."

Those river pilots had always been leaders in this town, and a number of them were seated on the riser behind the reverend.

"And now the good Lord must guide many more upon the sea," Rightmyer was saying, as he appeared to finish up his opening remarks. Then he cleared his throat and announced, "This service is for and about, and in honor of, all survivors anywhere in the Battle of the Atlantic and any ship caught up amidst it."

Lee thought about slipping out again quietly and leaving his drop-off over on the front step of the rectory, but he found he could not—could not make himself move. His feet would not go as the good pastor sermonized to family, friends, and the luckier ones who had been shipboard on unlucky vessels and were here to witness to it.

"And now a hymn for the lost," Rightmyer said.

The choir started singing, mournful-like.

"Eternal Father, strong to save, whose arm hath bound the restless wave"

Lofty voices rolled like swells on the ocean—like the undulations of the sea that Lee had fished and swam in and boated across his whole life.

"Oh, hear us when we cry to Thee, for those in peril on the sea!"

That's when it happened. That was all the more he needed in that stilled moment, stopped just as fast by what he witnessed now as he was bolted forward by it.

Lee spun and strode toward the door.

"It's a Friday, idn't it?" he asked Virginia in an urgent hush as he went by.

"Why, yes," she said, giving him a confused look.

The draft office would still be open at this time of the afternoon.

Lee got in his truck and drove as hard as the old rattle-trap would take him, inland toward Georgetown, Delaware. When he pulled up and jumped out, a "Closed" sign was looped around the door handles of the office. They had gone home early, at 4:30 ... He rattled the door. Locked.

Locked out and left out! Again. Cowardly relief and disappointment mixed in him equal, as he sat down on the front step of the office.

All he could do now was head back home, and worry about how much rationed gas he had just wasted. And how it fretted Ella when he was gone an hour more than he should.

Lee

One lamp burned in the living room when he stepped in. He stopped in front of the woman who had borne his child and stood by his side.

"I'm leaving," was all he said. "I'm going."

"I know."

In the months since her experience with the passenger-ship survivors, he had seen Ella take a different mind, partway.

She stepped to him and put her arms around him. "If you feel it's your calling, Lee ... then, you must go."

He returned her embrace trying not to crush her lithe, lean body—crush it in the way he worried he just had done to her heart. She dropped her head—eyes hot and flooded—onto his chest.

"I'm for you, Lee. I'm behind you," she said.

9

Ella

She had said it almost as if she could imagine what would happen to them next.

And this morning, she spun her head toward the living room and her wild child. "Stop," she said. Reese had an old broomstick and was holding it up to his shoulder and sighting down it like a rifle, pretending to fire from the upright position as he hopped forward across the room, complete with sound effects.

"Enough," Ella said over her shoulder.

"Pop Lee is going to *get* 'em," her son called out, as he finished up with a couple of kneeled sharp shots out their window. "Blast them Huns, or maybe the Nips, back to where they came from!"

"Eat," she said, commanding him back to the breakfast table.

It had seemed scarcely a 48-hour gust that whirled Lee out of here—signed up, gathered up, departed from Lewes, swept out of Sussex County by the winds of war, and to ...? Where? If only they knew.

"Come," she ordered Reese with finality. He needn't risk missing the bus down at the end of the lane again.

But, by time he was shoveling oatmeal into his mouth, his mood had turned again.

"How long will Pop have to go to war?" he asked slowly.

"We don't know."

"Planting season is coming," Reese said, with his mouth full.

Ella stopped and put her hand on her hip, looking at that boy. "Don't I know it." And how he sounded like his father just then.

"Who is going to be our farmer?" Reese asked.

"I don't know, sugar. Nobody," she declared. "We are going to go to Seaford for a spell, and see what comes next, see what we can work out."

"No!" Reese threw his spoon down. "I won't. And neither would Pop."

But she would not discuss it any further, as she hustled him into his pea coat and cap, and out the door to school.

Hours later, in her living room, Ella faced across to Lida Crouch, the mistress matron of the neighboring farm. With them was cousin Everett, in uniform and with a couple of hours of leave from the fort.

Ella did not like admitting her shrew of a neighbor into her home. But she needed the company of whoever knew and lived and understood her plight.

"It ain't that easy," Lida was saying, about closing down a working farm.

"We'll let out the fields to someone," Ella said.

"If you can find anyone," Lida said. "I can hardly git the labor help to work my place now, with one of my sons and my nephew off to war and with the work shortage and all."

Ella looked at the floor.

"There's livestock to be sold and other type arrangements," Lida said.

"Or maybe I'll just leave Reese to run the farm, since he refuses to budge off it," Ella said, trying to put some lightness into the proceedings, but finding no laughter in herself.

She looked up at Everett, but his face stayed knit at mention of the sadness of the boy who he loved and treated like a nephew.

"If you go upland, or inland, please don't work in any of them plants," Lida said. "It idn't proper," she added, raising her head and looking down that hawk nose of hers.

In the processing plants, so many women had taken over the work, with the men overseas. Most had never had jobs outside the house.

"But some of them are getting a new chance," Ella said, straightening up. "It's a duty. And maybe they even come to enjoy it."

Lida only crossed her arms.

"I've worked outside the home before," Ella said.

Then Lida came out with, "Don't you think your Lee deserves to come back to the farm he left?"

This one fact held over their heads and over the room.

Lida had known and favored Lee his whole life.

Ella had no answer.

Sometime later, the old biddy's departure had left Ella so wrapped into herself that she almost forgot that Everett was still next to her. He rose, though, and was now looking out the stark windows of their living room at the fields and out-buildings behind. She and her cousin had played there and in the yards and woods of this place since they could walk.

Ella's eyes were in the other direction now, through the front windows, locked on the big old iron anchor that her father had put at the edge of their yard. Her grandfather, who had bought this farm and had also worked the ferries to Cape May and the marine yards and fishing boats here for extra money, had come by it somehow, and her pop had painted it black and set it out by the mailbox as a kind of yard decoration.

Everett picked up one of Reese's war comic books from the coffee table idly, but then focused on it and cleared his throat. It seemed hard-won what came out of him next. "She's right, you know... It would be a tough row to hoe either way, but... Reese's dad... What about that?"

He said it evenly, tamping down both sympathy and malice.

With her gut hurting, Ella looked fully into her cousin's face, and those eyes so intensely blue that they appeared violet in the light—those eyes of his that had been so kind to her for as long as she could remember.

"I don't know," she barely breathed.

10

Reese

Deep in the night, lying on his side in his bed, Reese curled into a ball with his arm over his face. Hiding as he cried. Almost as if anyone might see him in the darkness of his room.

He would *not* move away! And leave his friends. Why, would they even be able to take Laddie, their collie, with them? Was his momma a crazy person?

After a while, he got his darn eyes to stop, and wiped his face on the sheet. Not a shred of light came past the heavy blackout curtains in his room. Then all at once, he saw a flash around the edge. He jumped up, pushed back the thick fabric, and gazed out at huge beams of light sweeping out towards the ocean and the bay in great white-gray columns and disappearing in the fuzz of the distant cloud cover.

He ran to his mother's bed and shook her. "Ella, come. Come see."

She followed him up the narrow, squeaky steps to their third-floor attic.

"Look!" Reese said, pointing to the lights on the horizon.

"Yes, hon. The giant spotlights from the fort."

Along the top of the tree line out in that direction, they could see some of the giant floodlights pointed straight out across the sea.

"They've begun testing the searchlights at the fort," his momma murmured, sleepy.

Cousin Everett! "Uncle Ev is maybe running them," Reese said. His army company was ready to spot subs or ships and blow up every enemy they saw.

Now he asked his mom, "How many miles across that water are the American GIs?"

"Oh, thousands, baby."

"Fighting and winning in Africa already!" Reese said. "Maybe Pop soon too."

That father had left a few days too early, though. Just when he and Reese were to go see the bond rally over in Georgetown. Everybody at school had said the Boy Scouts got to be in the parade there, marching. Oh, to see that!

"What it must be to wear a Boy Scout uniform and troop in a pageant with some of the soldiers," Reese said halfway to himself again.

"All right, then," his mother said, as if she'd heard enough about that subject.

All this week, his friends talked about nothing but the Japanese spy sub that was captured and on display at the rally. In his anger at missing it, Reese's eyes got warm again now in a way that made him feel like a baby.

"Oh, sweetheart," Mother Ella said. She pulled him in close but made no more talk this night about her stupid plan to escape their farm.

Ella

In the early morning light, Ella woke in a bed that felt cold. By habit she still slept these past weeks on the side that had become hers for nearly two years, once Lee had been able to make her bedroom his too.

If she let him have his way under the covers, then most every night or two was a rollicking riot that was hard to hush in an old farmhouse four poster, with a child sleeping down the hall.

But now ... she slid her hand over once again and felt only the cool, empty place in the sheets next to her.

At first dawn brightness, she sat downstairs at their roll-top writing desk, scratching a letter to her Aunt Verna with their fountain pen.

> As difficult as staying at this place would be, I wonder now if leaving might be harder. Oh, Aunt V! We did not plan it well.

She blew on the paper, as she thought. She wanted no blots to give the impression that she blubbered over this note.

> Your wonderful invitation, that would allow us to slip away to Seaford now, well ... Can I keep it in abeyance just for the balance of this month, until we see what we can manage?

She posted the note, put the red flag up on their mailbox, and then dwelled in silence with her son at their kitchen table.

"You want to stay on in this place bad enough to help work it?"

She knew it wasn't right to throw it back on him, and torment him with a decision that still escaped her. And what could a child do, anyway?

"Yes, I will!"

"Hmmph." This boy had never been a very enthusiastic farm worker.

They had challenged themselves this morning, just to scratch out a list of everything Lee would have been getting ready this time of year around this place.

"Madness," she said an hour later to Levotas, on their back stoop with Reese. Levotas had worked as a part-time hand on the farm for as long as Ella could remember. But even with him, they could not run this place on their own. "There ain't enough strength in these bodies sitting here," she said.

"Now just one minute, Miss-a Hall," Levotas said. "We make it. I find y'all some more help."

But Ella doubted something she'd never imagined. Much less, her instructing a team on *what* to do.

Worse, she stood shaking her head about an hour later that same day, with nosey, noisy Lida Crouch before her once again. Ella had been hanging laundry in the side yard, and the waving white sheets had been like a flag calling in that busybody of a neighbor from down the road.

"It's none of my bidness, but I don't think you should go it alone," Lida was saying, as humid March winds blew their skirts up and the laundry about.

"Well now, Lida, when I tell you I'm thinking of leaving, you say it can't be done. When I tell you I'm thinking of staying, you say the same."

That brought her beak-like nose down a little. "All I'm maintaining is that you'll need more help, like I've had to get from a few itinerants at the moment. Just want you to know how it is, that's all."

Her real point was what a force of nature Mr. Lee Tingle was around a place like this.

They were also a bit of a kind, she and Lee. Some kind of cantankerous kinship of orneriness had always hung between them.

Ella imagined that this minute she appeared to Lida as no more than a sailboat's sail adrift, as she tried to tame and pin a flapping, uncooperative sheet to the line and decide what to do with her life. But she could only risk so much disrespect to this woman who taught Sunday school to her son, and who had waggled that same crooked finger for so long over an entire generation at her church.

At her farm, Lida had long used a complicated system of male relations to work the place and get a share of the income, plus plenty of the transient workers at planting and picking time.

"Help is short. Even the canneries up and down the shore don't find enough," Lida went on, unhelpful. "And with gas and tire shortages, well, the migrants cain't even move around like before."

Ella knew it was all so.

With one of her narrow eyes nervously twitching, Lida took a high sound to her voice now as she clenched Ella's wrist. "If you're going to depend on the camps they set up for the farm laborers you best know, they bringing in Mexican, Black, poor white—every kind," said she, who could never say anything but that she said it emphatically. And talking now as if about some fourth member of the Axis, invading their homeland.

Ella pulled her wrist away but Lida reached in the basket and took hold of the last sheet to help her spread it on the line, leaning and raising one eyebrow as haughty high as she could and for some reason speaking in a hush. "Germans too," she said.

"*Germans?*"

"Prisoners. Why, yes!"

"Prisoners of war?"

"It's coming this season. It's official. You wait. See."

German soldiers on people's farms? In these *parts*? "That's outrageous," Ella snapped. Or at least hard to believe. Maybe out Midwest-way, on those big spreads, but here? On the eastern shoreboard? With what those demons had already wrought in these waters? "A sin that will never do," she said, grabbing up her basket.

"You don't believe?"

"I've heard tell of it in the middle of the country but this ain't the corn belt or the wheat prairie."

"Well, I'm with you on that, but mind, you heard it first from me," Lida said, as Ella excused herself.

But that next-door woman had said her piece just enough to confuse and confound. And now that bat could waltz her snide self back home in those shoes that always looked too tight.

"What times these are ..." Ella said, noticing as she walked back up toward the house that she was talking to herself more these weeks. And now, *damnation,* she saw Levotas coming towards her from out back.

This past year, she had gone to his neighborhood and his ramshackle house, sat in the lean-to that passed for the kitchen at that back of the place, and schooled some of his younger relations. A handful of his grand babies and nieces and nephews. His people were denied the funds they needed to hire a second teacher at the run-down Black primary school, so she sat with the little darlings and checked to see who knew their numbers as she also taught reading, while the children ciphered and recited. She laughed with these sweet kids, who loved having a story read to them. And when Levotas' grown daughter served up the best sausage gravy on biscuits that she'd ever tasted, Ella had determined she would bring Reese next to help her.

But the war had changed everything, and if Levotas thought she could give up her Saturdays like that still, well then—

Instead, he said, "Stalls all mucked out, missus," with that look on his face like his work was complete for the day.

"More to be done, though, right?" she said. "You want the time, don't you? More paying hours?"

"Oh … yes'm."

Lee always said she paid him too much, but that was one duty he had relinquished to her this past year—being the bursar of this place.

"Well, then hie thee-self over to the chicken house, and start cleaning her out, likewise, my friend," Ella suddenly said to her helper.

Always-congenial Levotas paused at that, looked at her with a surprised head tilt, but then headed off to the chore, with a "surely be," and Ella stopped and stood there for a moment realizing what she had just done. She'd given marching orders to a worker on their farm. And it had felt pretty good.

11

Dieter

Twenty miles north of Lewes, along the bayfront, Dieter Schneider and his shipmates from the surrendered U-boat 858 piled out of a military truck and trooped into a facility that the Americans apparently called "Fort Saulsbury." Fearing the worst, Dieter walked at the front of his men into the fenced compound of what was clearly an old, converted gun battery from the Great War. Dieter knew only that, here, something would be done with them or to them.

But days later, they milled about the yard still, smoking and chatting, stunned that they had been brought to this camp just to be kept and quartered. Clad, fed, and housed in barracks newer than they'd seen any Wehrmacht soldiers in.

This day, in a budding spring that smelled sweet to the captured U-boat's junior captain, Dieter stood talking to one of his mates, a lieutenant from their crew. Befehl, their captain, had been sequestered in another part of the compound. If it was because their captors did not trust him, most of his crew believed they were correct in this.

As for the rest of them? "Why do they treat us so?" Dieter mused to his fellow—the conditions so humane and relatively comfortable.

"It's as they told us in the speech," his shipmate said, both men speaking German in the chewy northern accents of their home state of Schleswig-Holstein. "The United States is conforming closely to the Geneva conventions."

Dieter's nostrils flared pleasantly at the thought and at the bayside air he breathed, so full of oxygen and reminding him of their Baltic Sea homeland—the atmosphere here especially sweet after months in the fumy, stuffy, metal cylinder of a death trap that had been their U-boat. So fine and unexpected now just to be alive!

He thought of all the suffering among nations back on his home continent—block-to-block warfare in cities, refugee families streaming in every direction, and starvation. "Still, though, how can they act so responsibly with German prisoners?" he said. After what Germans had been doing to them and their allies—especially right here in the shipping lanes?

They could just see the bay in the distance, through the tree line. And smell the salty air, which reminded Dieter of their U-boat base in Kiel near his home in the little town of Plön.

"It's because they want to make sure that their own prisoners are treated the same in Deutschland," his crewmate quipped.

Certainly, and yet ... Dieter wondered if it was more than that.

"They question you still?" the other sailor asked.

"Yes, they still want to know what happened to our ship. I explained. The fire that destroyed our electrical system," Dieter said, and his shipmate, who was one of his confederates, gave a knowing but tight-lipped nod.

"The captain doesn't understand and wants to question us too," the other said.

"Forget him," Dieter said.

"He has authority on us still."

"Never mind."

"Will they let us write to home to tell our loved ones we are here?"

Dieter did not know the answer, only reminding himself that he must be careful who he claimed as family through such letters.

But now he put his relations and their ship's commander out of his thoughts and instead thanked his own good sense to have told his shipmates to grab up anything that might be used as a souvenir before they left their ship. By today, they had already given nearly everything to their eager guards—flags, medals, hats—as a gesture.

Still, Dieter had one small pennant. The red and black of the German Kriegsmarine. On an inspiration, he went and fetched it, found the officer of the guard and offered it to him.

"Here," he said, "I don't want this anymore. I never want it again." Dieter knew that his pronunciations in English turned Ws into the sound of Vs and other heavily accented sounds and articulations but, still, he made himself understood.

The corporal looked at him with surprise. Dieter understood that it was because he spoke English. And that skill was thanks to his aunt, his Tante Petra, who taught at Universität Kiel and had given him English lessons every Sunday when he grew up.

"Mine self und mine men, we are humans too," Dieter said, wondering if he could be understood, and not caring if he suddenly lost his poise and made a spectacle in front of this American soldier. "We have *morality*." Dieter had studied this word in his English-Deutsch dictionary.

The soldier arched his eyebrow and made a "hmph," but accepted the offering of the pennant.

"We have principles!" Dieter declared, as another guard walked up, listening.

"Well, you'd better use them then, you want any freedoms around here," the second soldier said.

The first guard seemed to agree and, gesturing at the POW installation and the men contained in it, said, "The locals in Milford just a few mile from here have gone from curious about all this to resentful about it, just so you know."

Dieter had seen on a map that this nearest-by, very English-sounding-named town was just a few kilometers inland. And he and his crew had found immediately that they were not the first to arrive in this camp. Others, including a handful of Afrika Korps troops, had been here a few months.

"I seen it too," the second guard said. "Last time, I passed through that town square, one of them men belted out to me, 'Hey, Army, y'all keep them Jerries awful damn comfortable, don't ya?'"

"I got asked why we feed y'all the same kind of food that everyone else in this country is rationed on," the first guard added.

"Meanwhile, you rats out there," said the other, nodding angrily in the direction of the bay and ocean as he took a step closer to Dieter, "with orders to kill our brothers and sons and friends."

Stepping back, Dieter got most of what they said. He dropped his eyes and replied, "Ja, das ist understood," as he bowed slightly to them and walked away.

Ella

Ella could not sleep. Before the night was far along, her bed already felt like a wrestling mat, where she grappled with decisions made so far in her life, plus just as big ones needing made now.

She walked out back in the darkness, then stood in their drive, over at side of the house. Some minutes later, she saw headlights approaching down the road. In moments, she guessed who. A squad car approached. Part of a squad of one, these days.

Officer Hale Truitt, their town policeman often finished his nightly patrol rounds with a drive-by, a-way out here, on his farthest loop out along the perimeter of their village. Normally, she would have ducked inside but, just that quick, the lights were on her, and she would not be seen running away.

He slowed before the road here curved past their place and took him back toward the canal and town. Now he turned partway onto the shoulder and let his headlights linger across their house and farm. He switched on his brights as much because he saw her standing here, as in spite of it.

"That's rude, Hale," she called out into the blinding cone of light, as she put her hand up to shield her eyes and pulled her light robe around her. Under it, she had on only a thin nightgown, in the gathering spring warmth.

Truitt cut the lights and his engine, and got out of the car. How many years had she had to experience this?

Hale walked up to her.

The smell of the barnyard drifted across them, carried on a light land breeze this night. The odor of the animals and the compost and the fields dragged slowly across them.

"You know how I enjoy illuminating this place," he said, his eyes running up and down her. "But I don't normally see such loverly signs of life out here this hour."

Squarely built but in a softening body, and still shadowy to her as she tried to blink her eyes back to the darkness, he said, "So Mr. Lee Tingle done left his livelihood here, huh?"

She said nothing.

"You're better off. Fine woman like you ..."

"I don't see it that way, Hale."

She believed that this man drank sometimes when he was near the end of his duty-shift. She had only been a high school girl when he, as a young officer, had begun his little stop-bys.

"Had enough run-ins with that hell-raiser of yours, that I can tell you better," Hale said, putting his hands on his hips and equipment belt.

When she stayed mum, he stepped closer and added, "Never did quite find the grounds to arrest him."

He tried to make it a joke and laugh.

"Then, maybe it was you who was in the wrong, Hale."

"I don't make no problems," he said, straightening up. "I just take care them. You want my advice? Grab your stake from this place and run. Hightail it out of here, while he's off warring with the Huns."

"That's a mean thing to say, Hale."

"You know, they got some of them bastards up Slaughter Beach way now."

She had heard chatter of a POW installation right here in Sussex County, but even if true it was just another mystery of this war that was of no importance to her.

"He don't deserve a delicate lady like you," Truitt said, in her space again now, "or having come by you and captured you up wrongly."

"Go," she said.

"Best close this place down and move on, you got any good sense."

She flipped her fingers at him to shoo him away.

"Shutter her up and come move on into town with the rest of us ..."

"Goodnight, Hale," she said, without budging, even though he was scowling now. She knew too that over in Levotas's blocks his people hated the man.

"Maybe we all get lucky and that trouble-cat Tingle don't return," he said, his voice madder and lusher both.

"Get out of here, Hale."

"Or what, you'll report me to the ...?" he asked, leaning mockingly at her. "... the *police?*" He threw his head back and belted out a laugh that she worried would wake Reese.

With a dismissive sound, he turned and ambled off, got back in his car, and eased the vehicle forward but strangely with the lights off till he vanished in the darkness around the bend.

Even now, weeks after his encounter with the sub and his witnessing the surrender of that U-boat, Reese still occasionally hurled himself from room to room with excitement and with the telling of it—recounting it again to Ella and everyone. Ella knew that they had indeed witnessed something historic and something that Reese would be telling his own grandkids someday, Lord willing.

Today, though, several of Reese's chums were here to organize and outfit their Guardians of the Beach League, as they called it. But Ella knew only that, in this month of April that would bring the fate of her farm, Levotas remained confused about what he ought to be doing. So today, she brought in the teenage boy they used for odd jobs and tried to help direct them in delayed start-of-season clean-up around yard and field. Those fellas would keep watch on the boy's club here too, so she got in the truck and drove toward town, watching the gas gauge as always.

But as she rumbled along, in the seat mostly occupied by Lee this past year and more, she clenched and unclenched the steering wheel. If it was to be, she and Reese needed to load up and go now, hire someone to do as they might with the farm and animals, or let the fields go fallow, even in this time of need in the nation.

This hour, it all just made her wanted to go somewhere dark to hide. She decided on the movie house.

The lights were still up as she walked into the Lewes Auditorium. The few Blacks in attendance at this matinee were required, as always, to sit up in the balcony. Such wrongness and unfairness added to the knot in her stomach. This time, she made a note to ask Levotas how that felt to him—what with Blacks pulling a lot of the same duties as whites in this wartime and showing the rest of the nation that—

But suddenly, she noticed something missing.

"Where's the old player piano?" she asked the usher.

"Hauled off to be melted down and turned into war material, ma'am," came the answer.

Feeling no escape, Ella plunked and sunk in a chair. Alone in the welcome darkness, she realized of course that before the afternoon feature, *A Lady Takes a Chance,* with Jean Arthur and John Wayne, would come the newsreels and funnies.

As a war short came on, she thought perhaps she would close her eyes for a few minutes. But before her, all at once, vast scenes of American farmland began to play. And narration welled up about the effect of the war on farms. As the reel spoke to her, she gradually sat back up. Here was some kind of film by the government and ag companies, called *Soldiers of the Soil.* And as she released herself to it, came a heart-rending fictional story, imbedded in that message, about one brother who went off to war and came back blind, while the other struggled with his desire to enlist, knowing though that it would leave no man in their family to work the farm.

By the end, Ella sat riveted by the film's argument that the role of farmers in the war was just as important as the role of any other Americans. A propaganda film to keep farmers from leaving their land, yes, but a promise to them, too, about the improvements that the new programs could offer and assurance that they were patriots in full—as it finished with great sweeping vista-like shots of American farms.

The swelling music was enough, but even before the endorsements at the end for new fertilizers and seeds and equipment, Ella leapt up. As the sales messages of sponsors and the products of the DuPont company, located a-just north from here in New Castle County, trailed her, she rose, gathering speed, and rushed out of the theater. Before the credits ran on this little film, she was already moving out toward the light, her cheeks wet again, but her stomach starting to untie itself. Sometimes it took only a small thing to tell you what you already knew.

She stopped out on the sidewalk of her town, as the warm, moist, fecund air of the new dawning season struck her. Of course … Yes, it was a duty. But was it *hers?* If so, there wasn't a day to lose.

"Momma, what are you doing?"

Ella heard Reese's voice behind her as she wrestled a heavy burlap bag across the floor of their supply shed, in the early morning. She straightened up and pushed her hair back out of her eyes. She had not rested well the last two nights, her decision taking her every thought. Early this day, she was already hot and dirty.

"Trying to sort through these seed bags your pop bought this winter and that he put up here."

"Why?"

"'Why?' Why, because we're going to save this farm, that's why."

"We— What? We ain't *moving?*"

"We are *not* moving."

But for this rambunctious, impressionable youngster, she needed to try to preserve a lot more than just this farm. When you'd been with a man for so long, through so much and mothered a child with him who set so much store in the man, and with the man so linked to this place ... well ...

Reese was already spinning circles around her like a puppy dog.

"But that's only if you're my partner," she added, straightening up and putting arms akimbo as she faced him. "We got a lot to do—and only if we do it together."

"Heck yeah. Momma, other children get to stay off school to help with the planting season. Can I stay off school?"

She had to accept some of his will now too, if he was to be part of the effort.

"Here," she said and handed him a ground-digging pitchfork, "you go start turning those rows in our kitchen garden where we put the greens. We're a platoon now and that's your victory garden from here on, Private Tingle."

He snapped up and saluted her and then actually went *running* off to a chore, the pitchfork dragging behind him—probably more thrilled to be playing hooky than anything else.

"I got to go see Cousin Everett for a bit!" she hollered after him.

Levotas was working back there, if the boy needed any guidance, though Reese had studied his pop's every waking day enough that the kid was more likely to manage Levotas than the other way around.

Ella felt a rush inside her as she made her way over to the Service Inn, out in front of the base, where she had set up for coffee with Everett. "I'm determined to take steps," she declared. "There's government support programs, aren't there? And farm workers being brought in, for labor."

In a voice surely meant to slow her down, he said, "Yes, Ella, it's true. And there are loans for equipment and buying land and everything else that could be needed. But that's just part of what you'd be up against."

But she insisted on knowing what he'd heard. He showed her a government update that had come across his desk about how fast farm production was already rising in this country as anticipation of the war had come on.

"We can still salvage this planting season, if I hurry," Ella sung out hopefully.

Everett gave her that sad expression of looking at someone who was about to pass up some important dreams of her own.

But she would meet his eyes for none of that. "And what's this news I've heard," she asked, "about prisoners of war being allocated to work some of the farms down here?"

Part II
Soldiers of the Soil

12

Reese

When Reese's mother told him to go check on the milking cows and move them to the back paddock to graze this early in the day, he knew something was up. They usually only gave these milch bossies a few hours in the afternoon out there. As usual, these dairy cows had already been fed this morning. She was making a chore to get shed of him, he was sure.

So when he disappeared along the fence line, as if heading straight to that job, he simply stopped, stepped sideways, and hunkered down along that weedy row, in all the overgrown grass and shrub there, already greened out by the warm season.

And he watched. A good place for it too.

This was his and his pop's spot. From here, Reese had bagged his first kill when Poppa had set them up, last fall, small-game hunting. The perfect hiding spot in this growth here, because you never knew what might come by and did! Squirrel, rabbit, dove. With Pop Lee helping him aim his .22 rifle, Reese had shot and killed a big old hairy pest of a brown groundhog they'd been after, with his father laughing and clapping him on the back. And darned if old Levotas hadn't butchered up that gnarly wild old "whistle pig," as he called them—so that they'd even made a stew of it that—

Reese spun his head. Sure enough, a car had just pulled up. An Army car! Cousin Everett.

He stayed low in the brush pit as he saw his mom and Everett walk out back, motioning and talking about the fields and the barnyard. They ended at the far back corner of the farmyard acres, where the farm's two biggest fields came together and spread behind into the distance. There, Poppa Lee had built a little platform, so you could see out across the rear of the land. He'd used it as his deer blind the last few autumns and let Reese sit up there with him, teaching and showing him everything, but promising only that Reese could take his first deer when he got to be twelve.

Spy tactics were Reese's best though, and so it was an easy matter to sneak silent down along the hedgerow and crawl right under the lookout where his ma and Uncle Cousin Everett were talking. He held his breath and listened.

"—it for real?"

"Yeah, they're coming down this way too. Already on some of the farms in the county."

"You're kidding me. How are they even here? I mean, so many that they could make any difference? I don't understand where they're coming from."

"The English. Mostly captured by the Brits, who don't have the resources to house them. There'll be thousands of 'em in work camps in Delmarva before it's all over."

The Germans! Reese suddenly realized they were talking about *Germans* ...

"When one of our supply ships comes back empty, they've got German POWs on them from over there," their Lieutenant Everett was saying.

Reese, holding still as a chipmunk, could see them partway up through the cracks of the boards above his head, the bottom of their feet, shifting about. Like him, Momma had no brothers or sisters. How lucky she was to have a cousin like Everett! Who knew everything and acted every way like her brother.

But Reese could guess that his mother had a hard look on her face now. Like she got when, in truth, she was just worried or scared—or confused.

"Well, now, and here's the thing, Ella, and what I came to tell you," Everett said. "We just got word at the fort to help organize them."

"The German POWs? Oh, Ev. You?"

"And so here you go—if I play my cards right ... I think I can get a couple-few of them assigned to you here quick to help out. That's what you want, right? And need? More hands? Quickly?"

The enemy? *Here?* "No!" Reese hollered, and stood up so fast that his head banged on the deck above him.

"What in God's name!" his mother yelped. And, "Ho!" from Cousin Everett.

"That little muskrat." His mother ordered him up on the platform, practically pulling him up by the shirt collar, and scolded him for eavesdropping again.

"Now, now," Everett said with a chuckle and pulled Reese against him in a hug.

But Reese pushed away. "You won't do it!" he hollered at them both. "There's no Germans coming to this farm!"

"Listen, little buddy," Everett said, putting a hand gently on Reese's head, "your Hall farm needs help, from you and others, and needs it now."

He said it like a question to his ma, but she didn't answer direct. She just said, "It's really been the Tingle farm lately."

That quieted Reese and he said, "That's right, Momma." She knew who the man and father of this farm was!

"Well, then, the Tingle Farm. And mind you, these men are supposed to be working at the fort, but I think I can get a few sent over this way. So this is a special dispensation, at some risk for me, don't forget," and he turned and waggled his finger at Reese. "So let's be good soldiers. Loose lips sink ships, buddy. This has got to go well and *quietly*. All right? No one needs to know. This is the first farm down this way gets any allocation like this."

"They're enemy-men," Reese said, turning away from them and throwing a punch into the air.

"Don't worry, pal. They'll have a guard with them, or so I'm told. Y'all'll be fine."

His momma just looked beat and mixed up, casting her eyes about like she could neither vision the amount of work his pop did on this place in the course of a season, or how a bunch of strange, hateful foreigners could be made to do the same.

"I won't let it," Reese yelped at them, feeling his face all swoll as he stomped off.

Ella

Days went by and no Germans appeared at their farm. If they had, Ella could imagine at least a couple different neighbors of hers who might walk across and shoot a German soldier if they spotted one here. But she was at a loss on how she might manage this planting month otherwise.

"Let 'er out easy," Levotas had called to her from behind the tractor, after they'd figured out how to get the machine started and Ella had jumped the clutch a couple times as they tried to get the hitch lined up with the tiller, which could plow five furrows at a time.

But then darned if they hadn't indeed turned most of the main field on their own, Ella bouncing along up high in a way she could never have imagined, riding atop that clattery beast, wearing overalls.

Reese had finally gotten off his fit about the idea of prisoners. At least for now. But it only switched him up to his new mania, which was about the Civil Air Patrol. You could easily see the flights of their small planes up and down the coast every day.

"They're looking for subs, Ma!" Reese said.

This morning at breakfast, it was, "I want to join the Air Patrol school and learn how to be a junior pilot."

"That's wonderful, honey. But you're not old enough yet."

"Well, anyway, Gil and I are going sub hunting today."

His request surprised Ella, who was unsure her son really wanted anything ever again to do with subs after the fright he had taken. But Reese had asked permission and she had given it, for the first time since the sub surrender, to go back down to the bay in front of the fishery with his buddy, and row a skiff around, like he had done that momentous day last month when he had witnessed the surfacing of the U-boat. She knew his chances of spotting anything again were nil. And the papers had been able to give only scant and vague information about the sub that had surrendered to their town—just that mechanical problems aboard the U-858 had nearly caused the sub to have to ditch at sea.

The screen door smacked shut as Reese plunged out and to his bike to head to the canal bridge and on toward the fishery. Good that he would not be here. If today was indeed the day when their new ... *help* was to arrive—against her better judgement.

And not but minutes later, the sound of a truck! As she moved to the back door, she instinctively tugged once on the padlock that Lee had on his gun cabinet, then felt up high atop it to confirm where the key was hidden. Well, the doors on this cabinet were rickety and loose, and all someone had to do was punch the glass out to steal a firearm, but ...

A big green truck, with its double tires, backed in rumbling and crunching to the top of their clam-shell driveway. Feeling her pulse accelerate, Ella stood in the back yard, apart from where an Army private with a rifle slung casually across his shoulder came around and opened the back gate of the truck. Three men, with odd-looking leather boots, gray trousers, and baggy shirts that had a big "P.W." painted on them, got out.

Germans had arrived on her soil.

And only one soldier guarding them!

Was she the traitor now, for having allowed it? All at once, she wanted to cancel this gambit and tried to wave them off. "Go on," she said. But the US Army man closing up the tail of the truck only scrunched his face up incredulous at her, like that was no longer possible.

As the foreign soldiers stood waiting, the one in the middle, a tall blond, looked more at ease than his fellows. Dressed otherwise though, the three men who stood in her yard might have been mistaken for any three young American men walking down the street.

"Don't expect me to ..." she started to say, as the Army private walked to her.

She and Levotas had sat at their kitchen table and worked out a list of jobs needing done. She fished it out of her skirt pocket. Of course she could not save face if she backed out at this moment, and she'd have to answer to Everett if she did.

The Army guard, lanky and all green in his uniform before her, wasn't here to waste time.

But he had carelessly turned his back on his charges! Ella took a step back and waited for them to dash or hijack the truck.

But when nothing happened, she reached the list of work she had to the guard. "Stink like sauerkraut, do they?" she said to the guard, who only shrugged.

"Well," she said, "I know they're trained to follow any orders—brainwashed that way, so go ahead and start them on something easy."

The Army private reached languidly up under his helmet and scratched his head.

"Potatoes are still planted by hand here," Ella said curtly to the absent-looking guard. "The sacks of seed spuds are over there by the toolshed and the acre plot just yonder. Get them to that first today, and come to me if anyone didn't know how. The instructions are all writ right there. Since they cain't read American, you'll have to show them, I guess."

And so began a new thing that felt thrust upon Ella, as she kept to the house and chores there the next hours, watching out the window and with the back-door locked. But it got too quiet with enemy on her property. So, a-midday, she stepped around back. Reality felt as though it skidded sideways, as she watched the three gray-clad figures working down a row out there.

Approaching this work detail, she at last acknowledged fully to herself what she had let transpire here this morning. Her husband had vanished off a farm that had been his livelihood, like the loved ones of so many across the farming towns of America. Soon to be sent overseas to contest the war. Materialized in his place before her eyes, *captured Germans,* taking on the jobs he would have done or overseen himself this very day. She wondered if she was in a dream that threatened to turn bad, as she spotted the Army private napping under a tree with his helmet tilted down over his face.

At best, here she was, Ella Hall, commanding a little squad of the same devils that Lee was training at Fort Benning, down Georgia way, to kill. Here they were, working her fields, treading where Lee had trod not but a couple of month ago. What kind of cruel trick was this?

The guard spotted her, popped back up straight and ambled over to her.

"They went right to it, Miss. No complaints."

There they were, bent over or on their knees, with trowels in their hands and moving, as a threesome, slowly and steadily down along the rows of these couple acres.

Ella shook her head in wonderment. It even looked like they were doing it properly.

"Helps that they're still in shock, ma'am."

"Shock?"

"That they weren't executed or mistreated—that, instead, they're being managed real civil-like," he said, with a yawn.

"Well, they're making headway anyhow," Ella mumbled, watching them, halfway across the plot by now.

"They're good workers, ma'am—you might not know—but I can tell ya it's so."

"Thank you for showing them what to do. How to plant the 'tates correctly," she said, nodding her approval as she looked on.

"Oh, I don't know nothing about farming, missus. Like I said, they just went right at it with the big one in charge."

Ella looked at the guard with alarm, and saw her written instructions still folded in his breast pocket, then back at the POW workers, as she strode up along the side of the field. But, avoiding their glances, she was pleased to see that they were spacing out the potato halves right and placing the cut side of the spud down.

"They knew already," the guard said with a shrug, when Ella returned. "Er, the big one seemed to, anyhow. He showed them."

She could see that the strapping, blond, Nazi-poster-looking one was directing them. She marked how he encouraged them along and spoke to the other two, though she could not hear anything from here. Now, he helped one of them move his sack of potatoes and clapped him on the back, before stepping back to his own row.

But Ella didn't care. All she wanted was to get this done. And if she could have them for the next few weeks and they could be taught the field planting, well ... Then she'd get them the hell off her farm just as fast again.

13

Reese

His momma had lied to him about who was working here during the day—till he got home from school early enough one time to get a look at them.

"They're Germans, Ella Hall," Reese said.

"They're whoever gets the work done," she said, and then wouldn't let him back out of the house till they were picked up.

He had only ever heard his poppa talk in such a way to him—like the boss of this farm—and he had to stare at that mother for a few moments. But then he refused to speak to or answer her for two whole days. Well, one and half anyhow, but he was pretty good at it, just like he was good at stare-down matches at school, where he knew he must not let on to anyone who the men on this farm were.

Then, this week, he got home only to find that she let them run Poppa's tractor, with the planter hooked up and all. He could tell she had done so, by the look of the fields and, when he scurried into the barn, by the smell of the tractor and its engine still clanking as it cooled.

How long would this go on? Cousin Everett was due here again today, and he meant to ask.

"You might as well listen in, since you've got to know everything," his mother said, as they heard the roar of a jeep coming.

She let him stand beside her out in the bright warm sun in the drive as Everett parked on the shoulder of the road and strode to them, with a crisp crease to his green Army pants.

"Ev, that soldier from your base only spent the first day here," said his momma, who seemed tired and worried always now. "It's been weeks since they had any guard on them a'tall."

"I know, El," Everett said, swiping his Army cap off his head, wiping his brow, and sort of kneading his hat in his hands, as he peered back toward where the prisoners were working. He looked spanky, though, with his lieutenant bars on his collars. "Tell the truth, we're not really sure how to do this. No one in the Army here has had much training or experience with prisoners of war."

"Shoot them," Reese said.

"Shhh!" his ma said.

"We don't have enough men to put a guard on every place these guys are assigned. To keep order and manage it all, it's up to their officers and NCOs, like that one." Their cousin nodded far out to the edge of the farmyard, to the pigsty, where they could see the bigger one of the Germans finishing up directing the other two on watering the hogs.

"Ella, now let me ask, as of yesterday your fields are planted up, are they not?"

"In the main. Mostly."

Yes, just in time too.

Reese's mother had told him that the one who was the leader of them had seemed to know a lot of what to do and could read English, with instructions wrote out by her and sent out to them and sometimes delivered by Levotas, who complained bitterly about it and said they didn't seem to want to take orders from him or try to understand him when he spoke.

"And the summer is here and the growing season is underway," Uncle Ev said. "And not everyone can say they got their fields set. So let's count it as a battle won and now I'm afraid you got to give up some of this help."

All of a sudden, his momma didn't look sure about that either.

"Here's what I think I need to tell you. We got to move these men on to someone else's place or back to the fort."

"No, sir," his mother suddenly said.

Reese's neck hurt from craning up at their faces. Was she disobeying a lieutenant of the United States Army?

"It'll all be for naught, if you do that," she said. "There's—"

"I know. There's always more to be done, but—"

"You're going to keep sending at least one of them to us," his ma suddenly commanded, all at once, as if she'd made the decision on the spot.

Everett rubbed his chin.

"One of them at least to keep coming and lending a hand with every other thing around here," his mother said again. It made Reese want to put his hand over her mouth.

"I can only try, El," Everett said, as the prisoner truck that had followed him in backed up their drive. The soldier got out and whistled up the prisoners.

His ma tried to shoo Reese back in the house as the prisoners came right in, but he stood his ground.

"If I can do it ..." Everett was saying, "which one of these would you want?"

That left Mother Ella blinking for a second. But for the first time, Reese was close enough to get a good look as the three Germans stood behind the truck's open tailgate. They were rough and dirty but with their hair well barbered and in place now.

"You care which one?" Everett asked in a hurry, like he had to get on.

"The big one, I suppose," his mother said quietly.

That one because he was stronger to help around here, Reese guessed. According to Levotas' whispers, he was the one who seemed to know what to do, without anybody having to tell him much.

Now, that same German faced squarely around and nodded to them as he and the other prisoners waited for the order to step up into the truck. All of a sudden, something went through Reese ...

He took a couple steps toward the prisoner.

"Hey," his mother said to him, hooking a finger in the back of his collar.

He recognized this German ... That was him! He spun to his ma. "Ella, it's one of the U-boaters." On his toes, he tried to keep his voice below a holler. "One of the U-boat captains! I saw him." Out on the pier where they had surrendered this spring. "An officer from them."

His mother drew a strong breath through her nose, and her nostrils flared, as she looked back and forth to everyone. After a moment to swallow it all, she hissed, "Is it true?" at Cousin Everett.

"As a matter of fact ... I do believe so," he said. "That one I think was some kind of first-mate or something off that U-858 that came in here, yes, sorry. They're sent around random, Ella. We sure don't pick 'em by where they came from or why they're here."

"Get him out of here," Reese's mother snapped.

"Now, El."

"You get him reassigned somewhere else immediately," she hissed.

Reese watched Everett's Adam's apple rise and fall. "Listen, cuz, as an officer he's not even required to work, but this one insisted on making himself available for whatever duty his men are put on. There's got to be something to that at least."

His mother huffed her consternation and ordered Reese back inside, but he heard what was said behind him.

Everett was trying to convince her. "I think you should keep the best one you can, because—"

"With what they've done *out there?*" his mother practically spat at Everett in disbelief, darting her eyes and her pointing finger east, in the direction of the bay and the sea.

"Look, yours is the only farm right near town that's gotten some POW help so far. You best stick with what you got. Think on it and I'll see what I can do."

But Cousin Everett did not make good on that. And so, back came that same prisoner. Reese saw him not but two days later. The torpedoer!

Their great President, Mr. Franklin D. Roosevelt called the U-boats "rattlesnakes of the Atlantic," and that's just what this sneak was.

The German stayed off and quiet, to himself, working, not needing to be instructed much. Not wanting to, his mother said, though she wrote him out chore notes. Reese watched in amazement as his mother somehow figured what needed to be done next and took charge.

"Watched your grandpop and pop my whole life, didn't I?" his ma said. "I ought to be able to ponder out what's next."

Reese heard a new kind of sound in her voice, as she carefully handprinted orders that the prisoner could somehow mostly understand when they were taken out to him, though he would not heed or reply to Levotas hardly.

Reese hated him.

Then, that same week, he found his mother lying on her bed. A woman who was never not on her feet every minute of the day!

This afternoon, she was lying on her tummy, partly crossways on her bed, her head in her arms. Now he heard snuffling and quick pretended not to.

"Ma, how long till Poppa comes home, do you think?"

"Home? Oh, Lord, I don't know. Could be years, *if* he comes home to us."

If? He could tell she hadn't meant to say it that way and her head popped up and she did a quick groan at herself.

He took a step back, his eyes feeling hot, his fists balled up so tight his arms hurt, his ma looking like no more than a sheet tossed on a bed. And her now not going out back times when she needed to because of the stranger.

That was it.

Was he Reese Tingle or not? Was he Lee Tingle's son or what? He was the man of this Tingle farm now!

"You help your ma out here, champ—in any way that needs be," his pop had said before he left.

And now he knew what needed be because there was a criminal on their farm. Time to do just what his Poppa would do when he went to war—that pop who he might never see again because of fiends like this taking over everywhere!

Reese went down to the closet by the back door and got his BB gun out. Squeezing the stock of the thing hard in his anger, he shook it to make sure there were BBs in it. He started for out back but then stopped, knowing he needed to make this real and do it once right or not.

He spun and quiet-footed it back into the hall to his pop's gun cabinet. These doors were loose enough, with only a big old padlock holding them, that ... he could part them some, slipping his hand up in enough to grab the butt of his .22 rifle. He lifted it up easy and quiet, and slid it out the bottom. With his fingers, he pulled the little cardboard box of rim-fire rounds out after it.

Reese hurried out back, carrying both guns. Toward where he knew the prisoner was working on an open rise on the near field. He kept to the tree and shrub line again, to that same hideout, in the grasses and growth, that he and United States Army man Poppa Lee Tingle had used on their game hunt last autumn.

Keeping amidst the center of the brush ... he saw ... *There.* There was the *Hun,* as his teacher at school called them. Bending and toiling in the field not fifty feet out across the dirt from him.

Reese tried to quiet his breathing, as his hand shook and he placed a .22 long-rifle round in the gun and closed the breach softly.

Americans had started invading islands in the Pacific and bombing Italy. Everybody had to do their part. And this one out before him, all dressed in gray and working out in the dust, was a boat sinker. No one would naysay an action like this.

As he put the butt to his shoulder, leveled the gun and aimed it, his stomach crimped on him and he remembered all the rules of shooting that his poppa had taught him. Muzzle control. "Imagine a great fan out in front of you and never raise your barrel if anyone is within that."

Reese realized there were tears streaming down across his face, and his hands were quivering. He put the .22 rifle down with a toss. Sting him first, then run him off with the rifle! That's it! He grabbed up his BB gun. Or turn him first, so you can shoot him right in the chest if he comes straight and attacks. Yes.

He had already pumped the Red Ryder. He raised and pointed it, held for an instant, and then shot. A whack sound and the BB hit the German in the back haunch. The prisoner raised up quick like he'd got stung by a bee and put his hand on his thigh, then somehow turned and spotted Reese immediately, and started for him.

Reese's hands scrambled for the .22. He dropped it and grabbed it again, but it seemed the German was on him in just a few long strides. Stepping through the tall brush, just that quick the enemy stood above him. Reese fell backwards in this little dugout foxhole, staring up at the huge blue-eyed man.

The prisoner's face looked only surprised and stern. He bent down and picked up both the guns, looked at them for a second, then began walking back toward the barnyard, one of the weapons in each hand. Reese leapt up and took a wide sideway back to the yard, hollering and crying at the same time when he got ahead of the German.

"Momma, watch out! He's coming."

Murder at the hands of a Nazi, because of him!

"He's got guns!"

All because Reese had flubbed his shot.

His mother came running out onto their back stoop. When she saw the German with a gun in each hand, just as Reese reached her, his lungs burning for breath, she whipped Reese behind her and barked, "Stop," at him, with nothing else to raise but her hand.

He did not stop, till he got closer to her. But both barrels were pointed toward the ground. He handed the BB gun to his ma, who took a hesitant then quick step to him and reached out and snatched it. Then he pumped the breach open on the .22, turned the gun sideways, and let the bullet drop to the ground. Gray lead nose and shiny brass casing, it landed in the dusty dirt between them. He closed the breach and held the gun out for Momma Ella, whose gaze was fastened on that bullet that had dropped out before them at their feet, until she turned and looked at Reese with more fire in her eyes than he'd ever seen.

14

Ella

Ella feared for her son now. How God-awful close they had come to a catastrophe.

First, he tried to lie. "I only just set up out there in the field to pick off the crows that bother our crops." Until she stared him down. Then he swore he was only guarding the man. At last, he stuck to a story that he'd only planned to shoot the gun in the air to chase the prisoner away.

Two days was a long time to confine him mostly to his room, she knew, especially in the summer heat, but busy and with no man here to take him in hand, she could not chance the boy. Any time freed up, she made sure Reese met with their doctor and with one of the deacons at the church, and even talked to Everett. The men consoled her. No way for even the boy himself to know for sure what he had meant to do. Worry less, trust to the goodness of your child, and try to let it pass, they said.

And meanwhile having to keep an eye on this prisoner herself now. Just the same as before the incident, he kept to himself. Neither speaking nor approaching nor meeting their eyes—but somehow, between following Levotas' lead and interpreting her notes. Seeming to understand his tasks.

She could see that the German sailor never wanted to be under a roof any more than he had to. Sensitive, too, to smoke whether it was coming from the farm's meat curer or exhaust from the tractor engine.

When Everett came by, he wasn't surprised at any of it.

"Conditions were pretty bad for these men, El. Choking down there in those sub cans for months, never getting up for much air or sun, or expecting to get home again. This U-boat flooded from some leak on board and their power went out, or so I hear."

Her cousin went on about what it must have been like to have to hand pump while they decided to abandon or surrender.

"Some of that U-858 crew said there was a near mutiny. But that one right there," Everett said, nodding to the prisoner, whose name she learned was Schneider and who they could see this day at the back of the yard moving wheelbarrows of feed grain, "probably had to keep it all under control, as the second in command, because—"

"What if he tries to bolt?" Ella asked. "What if he gets the idear to slip down to the shoreline and try to signal for a rescue."

"No, hon," her cousin said, "and good luck to him if he does." Everett laughed. He recited it to her again: there were thousands of prisoners working now on the peninsula and nothing like that had happened yet.

"Could just walk off into the woods ..."

"And where would one of them go, then? Wouldn't get too far."

"I suppose. And, well, you-know-who up there," Ella said, pointing to Reese's window where the boy was in his last hours of confinement, "watches his every move anyhow."

But soon came a day when Ella was overseeing the help from her back step and maybe studied the prisoner too much. As she looked on, Schneider was putting away a tiller. When he spotted her, he walked toward her. She stiffened. He had the lunch pail in his hand that she had left for him.

How she found enough sympathy to even feed his kind, she did not know, but the farm was now succeeding or failing by any labor they could find, and so today she had put an extra helping of farm bread and thermistor of peach-flavored ice tea in that box that he handed back to her now, from where he stood a respectful few feet away. She was conscious of her bare legs below her knees, but was not hardly going to rearrange herself for one of these types.

At last, someone needed to speak. "You work hard," she said, wondering if he could understand.

He nodded. Almost bowed.

She had spoken to a German prisoner! And now it got her nerve up. "You're welcome to work double hard like you do, if you want, but I can't pay you nothing extra."

"Natürlich. Of course." His voice for the first time. Clear.

Everett had said this one had been the go-between for them with the crew of his ship.

"I got to pay the US government for your work," she said, not caring how much he followed. "Forty-five cent an hour I got to pay for you when you're here."

That's the way it worked, she had learned. By the rules of war. Then, by the conventions, the government had to pay the prisoners.

The German said nothing until he cleared his throat and pronounced, "They pay us eighty cent for a day, when we go out to work."

Despite his heavy accent, his command of English dizzied Ella for a moment, just as, at the edge of her vision, she spotted a shadow around the corner of their house and knew what little man was listening in on this—no doubt thinking that was a damn lot of money to be paying a captured Kraut.

15

Reese

His ma had finally sprung him loose. Back to regular freedom again. Most of the way, anyhow. And given him a mission too.

She sent him to town, to the grocery and drugstore. Just for a few things, to bring back in the basket of his bike. More probably to get him out of the way for a while.

This summer, though, he still woke up at first light, like he always had. Got his momma up sometimes.

But she forbade him to go into town until later in the morning. "After the morning rush is over," she said. So many vehicles—military and farm—moving through town these days.

So Reese promised to fish by the canal first, under the train trestle on the way in, one of the best places on an incoming tide. He strapped his pole to his bike and his Hopalong Cassidy watch to his wrist.

But he rode slowly, in truth feeling no lust for fishing today. At the last minute, he veered in a different direction, to the far inland side of town—yes, toward the war-salvage yard, which he had visited before with his pop. They'd took a couple of old spring beds, some license plates, a set of wood-stove irons, and a roll of wire and such to leave off there.

As he breezed toward the yard, he could think only of the letter they had from Poppa Lee. At last! Momma said that he had finished boot camp fast and was now one of the infantry men assigned with First Armored Corps. From there, someone had neatly sliced the next couple sentences out of his dad's letter before it went through. Ella didn't say it, but Reese knew she believed he was out to sea somewhere already, which put a surge of fire in Reese's tummy. His mother for her part just clutched at herself when she read it all, and then sat straight down to write him back again.

Reese had held his pop's letter up to the light, squinting through the long square lines that the censors had cut out of it and imagining ocean swells of the Atlantic crashing against the bow of a big, gray transport ship.

First Armored Corp! In its honor, Reese had armored his own vehicle today, with trashcan lids strapped on each side of his bike.

All real weaponry at the farm was now locked in a trunk in the cellar. But his pocketknife was in his pants, and he had lashed to his bike the big shillelagh that he and his pals used to play stick ball. As he went flying along, he made snare-drum sounds through his pursed lips, like a military parade, in his own pictured, armored half-track, until at last he slowed and stopped in front of the metal collection depot, looking out over mountains of junk. In the pile, he could make out toasters, doorknobs, hinges, kids wagons and other toys, a vacuum cleaner, a coal stove, plumbing, batteries and other car parts, as well as some bicycles, lawn mowers, and garden tools. But then he saw something else. Shapes he recognized, in colors of ... the miniature cars he used to ride at the boardwalk in Rehoboth. For the war, someone had scrapped this old ride from Funland. It made him feel even hotter, sitting out on the shoulder of the road on his bike, on this still summer day.

So he let it be and sailed into town, where he wasn't supposed to go this early. No one would notice—what with how many people rode bikes these days on account of the gas shortage. Just in case, he stopped, pulled a big red handkerchief out of his back pocket and tied it around his face, under his eyes—a bandanna just like wild west robbers used.

He went first toward the market, arriving with a good long skid mark in the gravel there—but then, just as fast, spotted a problem. A couple of the older boys from school sitting on the bench in front of the place ...

"Ha, look at Tingle over there," one of them hollered. "Who you think you are, Roy Rogers?"

It was dumb Roscoe Steeves.

Reese remembered the kerchief around his face, and yanked it down around his neck.

"Your mommy send you to get her condensed milk again?" one of Roscoe's sidekicks called out. "Gonna stick up the place with your six-shooter and steal it maybe?" The boys har-harred loudly.

"You don't know anything," Reese said. They had all the milk they needed at the farm, and Roy Rodgers would never play a bad guy, unless he pretended to be one to catch them. Anyway, Reese was more partial to Gene Autry and Tom Mix, but he wasn't going to argue the points as he went right by the older boys and pushed open the door to the grocery, with its clangy bell.

Reese walked across the creaky wood floor, amidst the spicy smells of the food store, and stood at the counter, in front of the bins of crackers, cookies, and other loose items. Off the list, he read the man what his momma wanted, and the grocer retrieved the items from the high shelves with a long squeeze-grip grabber, like the kind that Reese wished he had in class to grab girls' hair from behind.

Reese bided his time with the paying and all, glancing outside to see if those boys might move on, when all of a sudden a military convoy came by—jeeps and trucks with trailers.

It was just the noisy distraction he needed to slip back out, put his goods in his bike basket, and skedaddle, over toward the drugstore.

The main street of town was busy with people, and with men in uniforms everywhere. Cousin Everett said that thousands of Army and Navy men were living at the fort now.

The few old men who always sat up in front of the drugstore were gabbing and, as Reese paid for the paregoric that his mother wanted for her stomach and head pains, he listened in on the old guys talking.

"This town lived through attacks by injuns, pirates, and British and—"

"Mosquitoes, jellyfish, and green-eyed flies like *you.*"

"—and, like I say, I think we can buck up against lily-livered welts like these Germans. Bunch of bullies who—"

"And well, here they be now!"

Reese spun and saw a big Army truck pull up. In moments, German POWs began to climb out of it! He could see that this corner of town was a drop-off point, where some of the prisoners were picked up by others to be sent to farms around this part of the county.

As the prisoners lined up out there, the men in the drugstore got louder.

"You know they got studies at that camp where these dirtballs can earn college credits that count back at the universities in their damn Fatherland. Can you imagine that?"

"Hell, you say. And then, they distribute bottles of beer to them up there, too, and feed them better than army chow."

As Reese opened the door of the drugstore to go out, one of the men hollered out to the Germans. "Must be pretty nice up there at the Fritz Ritz! Why don't you stay there."

Out on the sidewalk, the sound of his taunt brought some jeers and catcalls from a few other townsfolk at the prisoners. Reese could see that a handful of people gathered to watch this, perhaps each day. He even heard some cusses and curse words from the watchers.

The older boys he'd seen at the grocer had caught up and were out in the street, moving along next to the prisoners and pretending to goose step, though Roscoe was such a lug he could hardly do it. Reese felt flushed, and his heart pounded at the scene.

"Yeah, why don't you—" he started to holler at the enemy soldiers, along with the other voices, with his hands cupped around his mouth, but then stopped a-midsentence, when he saw their Schneider step out of the truck.

Near the vehicle, a couple of the other villagers took a different turn. One townie was giving cigarettes to the prisoners and another lady handing them books to read in their imprisonment. A couple of farmers who picked up their hands directly, waved their men down by name and with a howdy-ho. And the Army truck soldiers from Fort Miles, who watched over this disbursement, greeted some of the PWs as they jumped down from their camp truck and looked for where to go for their day's assignment.

Reese turned back to the angry faces. But at the same time, there went Schneider—who would now step into the local Army truck for transport out to their farm. The Hall-Tingle Farm, Reese thought with pride, and then realized, all at once, that none of the hecklers out here had probably ever met one of these Germans.

Just then, friendly Mr. Rickart who ran the fountain at his apothecary stepped out front and said, "All right, now, that'll do," trying to get everyone to settle down and move along from the front of his place. He turned and saw Reese still cupping his mouth, ready to belt out, and gave him a look. Reese slowly dropped his hands back down.

Lee

Lee Tingle drowsed in his bunk, deep in the hold of a transport ship. He was certain that Ella and Reese and all stateside family members of the soldiers of his infantry group had no notion that his corps had been reassigned to the Fifth Army while crossing the Atlantic. The group that held Lee and his fellow GIs was headed toward the straits to form up in the Mediterranean as part of Operation Husky—the Allied invasion of Sicily, but no one who didn't need to know was permitted to know.

Moving in and out of a broken slumber, Lee drifted into a half-dream. In it, he was home during the first hour of a morning on the farm, seeing Ella and Levotas toting water to the chicken house, and imaging his son sleeping in for once, perhaps due to the night's lingering heat—slumbering, with that boy-face of his, deep into a close, peaceful morning.

Dieter

On a hot, humid day at the POW compound at Fort Saulsbury, Delaware—near the bay and the small town of Milford—Kapitänleutnant Dieter Schneider sat at breakfast with his fellow officers among the prisoners. He preferred to eat with the other men, with the rank-and-file soldiers, but this is how it was done.

Across from him, an Afrika Korp officer, Helmut Kanzlitz, tossed a piece of American white bread into the middle of the table and in the truculent Bavarian drawl of his German said, "What is this for an excuse for bread?"

Dieter's Captain Befehl from the U-858 spat his coffee back into his cup, and in his clipped Prussian accent agreed. "And they call this coffee?"

Next to them sat another officer who rarely said anything. He had a scar down one side of his face, and Dieter was sure he was Waffen SS. Every evening, all of the prisoners were forced to attend the lowering of the United States flag out in the yard, and this strange officer led some of them—even some with sensible beliefs—in raising their arms in the Sieg Heil salute during this flag ceremony. Dieter at first had joined them out of pure habit, but now had given up such things.

Later that day, deposited for his work on the Tinkle farm on a blazing mid-summer's afternoon, Dieter fretted over the tensions among the men of different beliefs at the camp, as he dug out a ditch to improve the drainage along the side of Frau Trinkle's property. He found it remarkable how little the mistress of this place knew about running her manor, and yet how quickly she was learning or guessing or recalling correctly, as she rolled up her own sleeves too. She had been sadly protected from a lot of the farm work as a mother and then lady of the house, he supposed. But it was something to witness, as she took the reins.

Dieter stopped his digging for a moment and wiped his brow, then thought he heard something, all at once, a high-pitched sound, like a yelp. But it did not repeat, so we went back to his sweaty toil, with the smell of the rich muck under his feet. Here, near this west side of her land, between the edges of their fruit-tree orchard and their sorghum field, it flooded in heavy rain. The bottom of the swale needed trenching down to where it met the culvert along the road.

He had met Frau Tinkle in this very place, just over there, some days ago, and he thought about it again now. He had seen her inspecting the apples, and so he had taken a bucket and gone to her. He had found her holding and inspecting a branch upon which a bunch of three apples was trying to grow, clustered tightly together. Each already the size of a German meatball. She had neglected to have anyone thin the fruit last month! But the apples could never grow to their fullness, left like this. He lifted the branch from her hand, and snapped off one of the little green apples, showing her. Along each branch, pairs of two were the most that should be allowed, so they would thrive together.

He had dropped the apple in the bucket and handed the bucket to her word-lessly. These hard, sour apples could be saved and used too, if they were cooked in a sweet sauce, not just discarded. She needed to learn more of the things his own farm had taught him growing up.

"Mit Honig und butter cooking," he said. And not just honey. It wanted cinnamon and nutmeg. But he did not know the words.

She had understood, though, and nodded gratefully and begun quietly working around the tree with him, doing the same—reducing all bunches to not more than two in any one place.

This afternoon, as his mind lingered on how pleasant that had been, working alongside her, he thrust his shovel deep again into the sandy soil of this part of the world and his thoughts switched to where he must return at the end of this day. Remarkable, he mused, how, despite all that went on in the POW camp, and how often the guards questioned the prisoners, he never heard one of his fellows admit to actually being a Nazi or even—

Dieter's head popped up when he heard it again. A second time. A cry for sure. A holler. A young voice. He straightened and looked about. "Stop it!" came a yell from down the way, along the road. A boy's voice?

Dieter stepped up and peered just over the berm he had been working below, looking along the road toward the town. *There.* A boy, *the* boy, of this place. Running along the side of the road. Two bigger boys running behind him. Chasing him! Taunting.

As they quickly got closer, Dieter could hear one of them call out, "Keep Krauts on your farm, do ya?" and then laughing, as another slid to a stop quick, picked up a pebble and threw it at the Tinkle youngster's back, and then commenced the chase again.

Dieter put his shovel down as the two bullies chanted the name he'd heard called out on the farm. "Reez" or so was the boy's appellation.

"Reez pees and pees his pants!"

Dieter stepped along behind the berm to where it came close to meeting the road, just in time for the smaller boy to pass by. Reez slowed, gasping, and put his hands on his knees, barely able to run anymore. At the next moment, with the other two closing in, Dieter stepped up on top of the berm, rose all the way, and in his biggest lieutenant-commander's voice shouted, "Was gibt's denn hier?" *What is going on?* "Halt!"

The two bad boys looked up as if they had just seen a specter from the under-world—or as if dropped into a scene from the most feared moments they'd heard of in the war across the sea. They skidded to a stop so fast in the gravel that one slipped and fell backwards.

"Raus, ihr zwei!" Dieter bellowed, big and low, throwing his arms up in the air. *Get out of here, you two.*

Dieter tried not to smile at the wild speed with which the two turned and ran back in the other direction.

As he watched their rears receding, their fear of a German soldier brought pride, but also a pang, to Dieter.

He looked down at the farm boy. Sweat poured off the young master, as he straightened up, trying to catch his breath. He looked up at Dieter.

"Thank you," he said at last, and then went wobbly toward the farmhouse.

16

Ella

On the last day of July, Ella had found a note that Dieter had slipped in the back door. It was scribed in a careful, intricate old-world hand.

> *Frau Trinkle,*
>
> *I say sorry I quiet and hiding like on the farm. Feel better now. Needed away from so long under the Wasser. Try to work hard still. You can be sure, and can help you in your ~~Bauernhof~~ farm. Keep tell me anything what you need. Thank for your kindness and good foods.*
>
> *Dieter Schneider*

Well, she had no choice but to take him at his word and take him up on his offer. Picking time was here and she needed all hands, and after all, he was easy to manage and ... not so terrible to look at.

Ella had gone to the extension office to apply for more worker help. Fortunately, the Farm Security Administration had recruited men from West Virginia. When her truck of pickers arrived on the first day, it also included some Black men from the islands, Bahamians they said. There were even some Boy Scouts from Wilmington and a couple of privates from Fort Miles. She was glad to have the soldiers at the start to keep order so that the rest of them weren't forced to take too many instructions from her or her German prisoner.

And what other way was there? Schneider knew their place from months now and seemed to understand what needed to happen. Besides, she required Reese and Levotas around the farmhouse and yard, including in the kitchen, helping her to make the noon meals for the men. It was hot work, and she let Reese luff now and then, but they got it done.

Out in the field, when the food was brought out, her German would give them the signal to take a break.

"Nehmen Sie Platz!" They didn't understand his words but knew he was waving them back under the trees to find a place to lunch and rest.

"These are no longer your sailors you are speaking to," she whispered to him. But the two GIs from the fort looked entertained, thank God, at the Wehrmacht-sounding commands and the working alliance between her and her POW.

On water breaks, Ella would stand with the German and he would fastidiously go over the count of the pick with her—number of bushel or peck, coming from the plots of tomatoes, string beans, zucchini, and all that they were wagoning back to the top of the lane for when the cannery and table-market trucks came by. He would hand her the counts that he meticulously penciled onto pieces of cardboard.

And in those hours, something about standing next to a strong, conscientious man, out on her land, and conferring with him so, gave her hope that perhaps she might just pull all this off after all.

At the end of a day in the first week of August, when the picker trucks and farm trucks had left, and the couple itinerant families had retired to their farm's two migrant huts, Ella stood with her German helper in the slowly cooling shade of the backyard. The sun had just dropped below the roofline of the barn.

The POW stood close. Clarissa, whose grandparents were from an Italian neighborhood in Philadelphia, had explained to Ella that polite space was different among people from the European continent, but ...

"Thank you for being *der Chef* out there today," Ella said, using the German word for "boss" that she had heard one of the soldiers mildly taunt him with today.

He brightened at this.

"Only way for me is this—this kindt of work," he said, his hands behind his back—one of the few times she had seen those big hands not busy. "Ins Fabrik I cannot go."

The *factories.* "The plants. The canneries?"

"Ja," he said with faint shudder, as if imagining a low metal ceiling over his head again, with machines grinding and smells. "Or don't want spend mine daytimes at the Lager too." *The prison camp.*

They'd stood then in silence, Schneider scuffing the dirt with his boot, as Ella made overly much of folding the apron she had just taken off.

Despite the reason he had come to their shores, she somehow felt badly for the man, wondering if he was here by choice, and it occurred to her that she ought to think about inviting him to table with them—at least to be cordial and show American manners. And to try to get Reese the rest of the way off his snit about it all.

Schneider slumped when they heard the truck coming down the road to take him back up to the old battery-fort. To distract him, Ella came out with a notion, an idea she'd been chewing on.

"I hear tell we could grow a lot more chickens than that," she said, waving to their long, thin chicken house.

Schneider straightened. "The prisoners say others farms already doing that," he said, nodding yes to her, vigorously. He seemed to rise up at hearing a challenge, as she noticed again his solid, chiseled body strain against the thin T-shirt he wore.

Reese

Reese sat quietly in the dining room, poking at his potatoes. At the other end of the table sat the man whose name they had learned was Dieter Schneider. He was concentrating on his food. In between them sat Mother Ella.

With glances between Reese and his ma, they both marked the skillful way in which the man used his knife to move food onto his fork for each bite, some kind of foreign habit, a thing his mother had taught Reese never to do.

Looking across, under his brow, Reese eyeballed the prisoner, as the man's jaw worked. Nobody said much.

When Ella asked Reese to help her clear and bring dessert, Reese caught up to her in the kitchen and whispered, "This just ain't right, Momma."

"Other farms done it with their Germans. I've heard it. We got to be kind to these people. The war has brought suffering to everyone—them too."

"We *been* polite. Now, we got to be respectful too?" Reese asked, distracted though by the smell of the lemon meringue pie she had made.

Last time they had sat at this table, and in this stiff old room that never got used hardly, was with his Poppa Lee, for a Sunday meal. And before, every Sunday with his grandma and grandpa, who he missed bad.

This mother of his needed to mind herself! What with the way talk was already going on about Germans... On the other hand, maybe if this got around and turned into gossip, the jabber would rectify her. Alls he would need to do was mention it to the widow Crouch over next door. Then the spreading about would take care of itself.

Lee

Lee Tingle stood in the bowels of his troop transport ship floating in the Mediterranean. He quickly folded up the letter he had been reading again, as the briefing in the common room was called together. Mail for him and a few of the men had actually caught up with the fleet.

In the note, Ella was talking about nothing and everything. One of her sentences had been blacked out by the censors.

The Army and Navy finally completed construction of ███████████
███████████.

He was sure that the rest of the sentence said something like "the protective gun batteries at Fort Miles." On their Cape Henlopen in Delaware, where they had once frolicked and—

"Soldiers!" Lee turned his attention to the officer. "You men know that the Fifth will not be landing in Sicily," the senior midshipman announced, as he commenced to tell them more of what they already knew through scuttlebutt. No, their army riding on the sea had been pushed further north, by whatever lofty plans or grand events were in play, into the Tyrrhenian Sea, preparing for landing, probably near Salerno the men had guessed. The officer prattled on through an all-hands, all-stations briefing on damage, flood, and fire control if they should take a fish—a torpedo. Mandatory prep on every ship in the fleet.

Listening, Lee felt it start slow but then come upon him fast. As if he couldn't breathe. As if he might suffocate down under here in this stuffy hold, as all that he knew and had seen of the dead, injured, and survivors of U-boat action off of Lewes came washing over him. Fear that this meeting might bring it all up was why he had stood in the back. Now he strode from the room and then ran up gangways of the oily-smelling ship to the deck, to topside.

Outdoors, he felt like he could get air again. And there he found a place to sit, even though a warm rain had begun, a light but steady downfall, as the fleet sat far out at an anchorage for the night.

By the time he sensed more movement around ship, with the briefing concluded, he looked up to see a couple of his fellows coming toward him. He'd gone through basic with these two, who surely weren't used to discovering him looking like his wits were out of whack. He was getting steadily wet, trying to push the worried grimace off his face, where he sat unmoving as the evening advanced quickly.

"You okay, pal?"

"Sure."

His two buddies exchanged glances.

"Talk," said Luke Maloney, a big Irishman from Poughkeepsie.

"What's eatin' ya?" said Bart Olsson, a squat farm boy from Ohio.

"Nothing, just how shitty the planning is on all this," Lee said, raising his hands to indicate the armada, its other ships visible in the form of great gray shadows upon the ocean in the dimming light and gathering fog. "We're sitting ducks."

The Kriegsmarine had sunk so many merchant and naval ships in this theater that Lee suspected the numbers were intentionally kept from the men. He felt the difference between his instincts and those of enlisted men like these two who had not grown up by the sea, some having never been out on the wide water before this voyage.

"Like that one there," he said, motioning to the ship at rest closest to them, a munitions vessel, looming and hulking but riding low in the dull metallic light, the water line on its hull higher than it ought to be. "That one's just a likely to blow of its own accord," Lee called out. "Overloaded and—" Set up for this stoppage too close to them. One of his friends turned and faced him with a calming shrug, while the other put a comforting hand on his shoulder and then convinced him to come back below with them.

But on this particular night, Lee could not rest or toss down there. If the worst came, he refused to die in his sleep in a fiery, flooding, screaming dark box. He'd give it up on land if he had to but not down here in a coffin of black water.

So he gathered a blanket and went back up and found a sheltered place to sleep above decks, like a few men had done on sweltering nights, but which he did now because his gut and the salt in his veins told him that *this* fleet detachment especially, full of thousands of advance-unit soldiers, was being hunted from below the surface every hour by those two-tubed devil fish.

Dieter

"Why'd you save me from them boys, anyhow?" the Tingle child was asking Dieter with a scowl on his face. "Why'd you do that?"

They were standing in the yard behind the farmhouse, and it seemed to Dieter that the heat was getting to the boy. Both were in shorts and undershirts in the still, fetid air.

"Now everyone thinks I have a German guarding me."

Dieter understood.

"Next time, mind your own bidness," the kid said, his lower lip quivering.

"Well then, next time, you guard yourself," he said. "Turn 'round on them. Give them some fighting. Then they think about it next time."

This silenced the boy, who nodded and stuck his chin out.

"You know how?" Dieter said, putting his hands up in a boxing position.

The boy did the same, modelling Dieter's stance, and seeming to suddenly remember to keep his elbows in tight, rather than flailed out to the side. "Sure, my pop showed me," he said.

Dieter took hold of the boy's left fist and gently pistoned it out toward him a couple times. "This one to bother them and keep them away," he said. "To ready. Then this one," he added, pushing the boy's jab back fast and pulling his cocked right fist out quickly. His cross.

He could see that the boy was still angry. Mad at all that was happening in his life right now.

"Tries it," Dieter said, stepping closer to the boy, dropping his arms to his side, and tightening his stomach muscles. "Here, right," he said, smacking his own midsection and inviting the boy to punch it.

"No," the Reese boy said, looking around quick and awkward.

"You know Joe Louis?" Dieter said.

"Everybody does," the boy said. "The heavyweight champion of the world." Then more quietly, the boy said, "He's a Black man."

"You like him?"

"Sure. He can beat ones like you."

"Ja, he beats our man." Louis had needed only a couple minutes to knock the Nazi's Max Schmelling down and out of the fight just before the war started.

"Try," Dieter said.

"Joe Lewis is in the service now ..." the boy said, as he straightened up.

"Come!" Dieter said, banging on his torso again. "Go. Like him."

All at once, the child's eyes got big. Then he rocked off his back foot and launched forward with a hit from each of his hands on Dieter's stomach.

"Ah!" Dieter said. "That's it. More."

Suddenly, Dieter could see the boy's frustration—the absence of his father, strangers in his world, and war fears—as it all rolled into his arms and he began pummeling Dieter's gut, grunting and socking as hard as he could. Dieter absorbed the blows easily and let him go on for some moments.

"Okay, then," Dieter said loudly, groaning and laughing at last. "Okay, okay. Oww. Ist gut!" He caught the boy's hands. "That's it," he said, with an admiring smile. "Just like that and no ones come chasin' you anymore."

17

September 1943

Ella

Ella stood up abruptly at her kitchen table and smacked the newspaper spread out in front of her. "Is 'VI Corps' the same as the Fifth Army?" she said, to no one, though Reese was close by.

She had thought that Lee was in that Corps but there was only news of this larger Army to follow now, and perhaps these divisions had been melded or just renamed into one. The landings in Salerno, Italy were taking place. Was Lee part of it? And what was wrong with this man, that he was such a terrible correspondent? She'd tried to write to him almost weekly, at least with something short, news about the farm or about their son—but where did the letters go?

They'd had no more than a couple notes from him since he left, and these in that labored hand and manner in which he expressed himself. Meanwhile, here she was, figuring out every day what needed to happen on this farm, especially again in this do-or-die month of September, what with—

"Come, Momma." Reese was at her side, taking her hand. "We want to talk to you."

Dieter and Levotas were waiting in the back yard, loitering next to each other, standoffish. Dieter still would not directly address a Black man. Ella wondered if he'd ever met one before, or ever even *seen* one before coming to this farm.

"You wanted us git the wheat fields turned?" Levotas said.

Ella nodded yes. As they had discussed. She believed that was the next urgency here. She'd guessed and asked others. She tried to remember. Summer wheat had been harvested. And as for the corn? Well, they had planted it for feed corn

104

and would let it go to that. No rush yet, as it dried on the stalk. But the winter wheat was needed in the ground.

"No petrol for the tractor," Dieter declared sheepishly, as if it was his fault.

Of course. They were low on gas. "Farms always get their gas rations," Ella said, but suddenly realized she had not done her part. She had gone up town a few days ago to see Reverend Rightmyer, on excuse of helping him organize his supply room for shipwreck victims. Really, though, she just needed someone she could speak to. She knew he counseled other women in his parish left behind by the war. The reverend had reminded her to go pick up her allocation of gas cards, as other farm families did regular. Distracted, she had failed to do so and the extension office would not open again until next week.

"The old way, we'll do it," Dieter offered. Ella was not sure she understood, but she could see the three of them had some kind of plan.

"We'll yoke up old Barney, ma!" Reese said.

Their aging plow horse?

"That old cuss?" Ella said. Reese treated him more like a pet. "You think he will pull?"

"Horse? Yes, he will work," Dieter said. Under his growing mop of straw-colored hair, and behind the ginger stubble on his chiseled face, nothing seemed to bother this man, and it caught on with the rest of them.

"Like grandpa used to do," Reese said. And, how did he even remember that?

"I can see he want to work." Ella was not sure if the prisoner was talking about the horse or Reese.

"Old nag like me can still do it," Levotas said with a laugh.

And damn if that afternoon Dieter didn't show the boy how to hitch Barney up to the old plow and Levotas showed him how to drive it.

The horse couldn't walk a straight line, though, so Reese ended up leading him, while Dieter and Levotas took turns stepping up on the plow and steering it. The more loud voices she heard, the longer Ella watched them from the back acre, as they worked up and down the field in a kind of competition that broke out between the two men to see who could plow fastest and longest, down how many rows before needing a blow, both hipping up Reese and the horse till Reese was jogging and laughing and Barney was sweating with his tongue lolling out.

"Best let me have my turn, now," Levotas would call out, goading as Dieter passed by. "You pooped. No shame in that."

"You should let a stronger man do. You will hurt yourself," Dieter would bellow, while the other took his turn.

Ella tried to remember when she had chuckled so hard that she felt it all the way down to her belly.

And for it, they made good progress and by the end of the weekend, she had thanked them in what little ways she could, after taking them lemonade and cookies in the fields.

Sunday afternoon found her sitting at their beat-up picnic table in the back, a plate of sliced watermelon between her and Dieter that she had put out for the men, as she and the prisoner waited for the pickup from the POW truck. He leaned on his elbow in a tiredness that seemed to feel good to him, and it was never hard to catch his eye now and that cobalt twinkle that was always in it.

"You know a lot about what needs to be done around a place like this?" Ella said, at last feeling ashamed that she had made so little talk with the man.

"I know it from my homeland," he said humbly, but did not seem to want to offer more.

"You have a place and family?"

"No," he said and shrugged, "not anymore."

It could get quiet with him sometimes, but then even mighty quieter around here once he got taken away.

She looked back toward their chicken house. "I hear the price that broilers are bringing these days is out of this world," she said.

"We make that shed for much bigger chicken house," he offered suddenly. "Build it out." With his fingers on the table, he outlined a far larger footprint for the house, and then walked her back and showed her the place for the footers that he had already marked out. "Here und here," he said, in a way that would extend their chicken operation.

As he spoke, Ella's head swirled with the question of how she might put together funds for such a building—her mind spinning too with the momentary feeling that she was under the command of a German officer, or at least in alliance with him.

Dieter

Several days later, Dieter Schneider stood watchfully at the back of the mess hall at the POW camp. Nearly a couple hundred Germans and a lesser number of Italian prisoners now populated the installation. Many were transported daily out and about the county on various types of work details.

With all the contact this created between the populace of southern Delaware and the prisoners, the authorities and community worried about it going too far, and he and the other POW officers had been briefed on it. Mostly about fraternization between the prisoners and women. So this evening, the mess had been cleared, tables and chairs to the side, and a social was to be held between the POWs and local American women, so that all could take place safely, under watchful eyes. Dieter wondered at this idea and the wisdom of this but supposed it would bring more peace and calm.

He fidgeted in the corner where the other officers had gathered, awaiting the arrival of their fair visitors.

As they anticipated the entrance of the American women, one of the few other prisoners who knew English paraphrased and translated what he was reading in one of the American newspapers. "They believe the allied forces will capture Rome by October."

Dieter heard a couple of guffaws from the men. Others shook their heads. Reluctantly, Dieter agreed. The naïve Americans did not understand who and what they were up against. The German mountain troops, artillery corps, and Panzer divisions that the fresh, green Yankees were about to throw themselves at were the finest, most-experienced, and best-equipped fighting troops in the world.

To Dieter's mind though, worse fools abounded here—those who still believed in an ultimate German victory. Such delusions were perpetuated among them by a few. For this and other reasons, Dieter found little friendship among the officer corps in this camp, though he attributed it to the influence of those same few. Those grim ones near him now had been talking disdainfully of the Italian prisoners in the camp and the surrender of that government, putting the brave German defenders of the peninsula on their own and in conflict with the Italians as well.

Dieter wondered if the men around him understood the responsibility that their people held for the events of this world, so he endeavored to change the angle. "This Schloss was built because of us, you know," Dieter commented in German. As he said it, he indicated the low-slung, decommissioned gun battery across the yard that was the main structure of the camp, with its great, thick cement walls.

Befehl, his captain from the U-858, who stood nearby, sniffed at the comment. Months later, he remained still suspicious about the extensive electrical calamity that had caused the rare surrender of a German sub—his sub—at sea, and Dieter had so far elected to give him no satisfaction on the subject. The U-boat captain, who was now allowed to move freely about the camp under his own recognizance, studied out the window at the age of the emplacement that Dieter pointed to and said, "Nein."

"Ja," Dieter said, "it has stood guard here since the Great War."

Dieter was prepared to argue the point, but just then several busses arrived, and handfuls of American ladies began entering from the opposite end of the hall. Straightening, Dieter stood struck at the sight. How fresh and ... *American* they looked! With their skirts up to their knees and low-cut socks, flat leather shoes, and curled hair. They and the prisoners were immediately as shy as he had expected, the young ladies looking *so* young—girls really. No doubt many had come just out of curiosity, but Dieter admired even that.

As he kept to the back of the hall, looking out vigilantly, he could hear more talk, under their breath, from the troublemakers near him. "Mongrels," his captain hissed about the women. The Afrika Korp officer next to him grunted and nodded his agreement. Kanzlitz was an underminer of all things, but not stupid. He was one of the few who secretly had command of English and—

Suddenly, Dieter skipped a breath, his thoughts tumbling, when he saw Frau Ella step in the door with another group of women. What ...?

He almost didn't recognize her. But it was certainly her, and how *different*. Put up so. Her sun-streaked brown hair wrapped up in waves and circles atop her head, accentuating an elegant neck. And wearing a crisp dress with a sheen to it. His only first instinct was to disappear out the back door, before she saw him here.

But she spotted him immediately, when instead, he moved directly across the space to where she was shepherding young ladies in the door.

"Frau Ella, you are here," he said.

"I am here."

"You should *not* be here," he let out, agitated. He spoke without thinking, upset that she should see this place and him in it.

"You should not be here either," she said, a comment to which he could not assemble a reply.

"Refreshments over there along the side, ladies!" she called, directing the young women. Dieter could smell the delicious aroma of the baked goods and other foods that the women had brought with them.

"The rector at our church asked me if I would come along as a chaperone. *Escorté,* you know?" she explained.

Yes, he understood.

And, well, if she wanted to see his world, he could do nothing about it.

But how mature she looked among these young women. Dieter had seen her identity card lying on the kitchen table back at the farmhouse. He knew her to be twenty-eight years old. Just a few years younger than him.

"Well, now that you have these women here ... you must understand that our men are long from home und ... friendship," Dieter said, searching for the English word for companionship and not finding it. For a year or two before coming here, some of his fellows had not seen women, except perhaps from a distance in brief port calls with no leave.

"Then please keep your charges among these men under control and know what behavior we expect," Frau Tingle said, bringing her nose up in the air. Dieter took her meaning and turned away. To antagonize her back, Dieter thought he might click his heels to her—maybe even bop his mouth or salute— but instead he walked stiffly back through the crowd.

For the next couple hours, he and Ella Tingle watched over the proceedings and each other from opposite ends of the mess, as Army soldiers from the camp guard sat in the shadowy corners of the room, while timid, awkward flirting and halting communication went on between the prisoners and the ladies. Dieter and Ella only nodded to one another from time to time.

Noticing Dieter's glances, one of his bunk mates whispered, "Ganz hübsch, diese." *Very pretty, that one.*

Embarrassed, Dieter nonchalantly replied, "Schön aus der Ferne, aber alles andere als schön." *Pretty from afar, but far from pretty.* In fact, he had quite the opposite opinion.

But as the social began to wind down, Dieter lost sight of her, just as he heard a disturbance at the very back of the room.

The Afrika Korp officer, Kanzlitz, was over in the corner interrogating one of the camp's guard corporals. As Dieter stepped close enough to hear, Kanzlitz said, "You say your name is Mandel, oder?"

The young corporal said yes, looking intimidated by this big veteran German. "That is a Jewish name, ja?"

The corporal nodded, taking a step back.

"We will not be guarded by any Jews. This is not permissible. You tell your commandant and—"

A quick glance told Dieter thankfully that Frau Tingle had slipped out with her church group. So, as the exchange before him now threatened to turn into a browbeating, Dieter quickly positioned himself between the two and the others, and simply encouraged the rest of the men to continue to exit out a side door and back to their quarters, now that the social was concluded.

But when the problem went on, Dieter spun, stepped to Kanzlitz, and said, "This is nonsense that you are speaking!"

"It sure is," he heard behind him, as two other guards rushed in and grabbed each of Kanzlitz's arms. "Some time in the cooler will set you right, ya big bastard," one of them said, as they rushed him out.

Time in a dense, dank room in the old gun battery across the yard!

Dieter had never spoken out in quite the way he had just now about the hatred of peoples and against it. But, as they exited the hall, a few of the hard-core Nazis clapped each other on the back after witnessing the confrontation and the speech of Kanzlitz, including their strange, silent Waffen SS man, Kühne—who had achieved Sturmführer rank, according to the gossip, and behaved with the men as though he was still their leader among a troop of secret police.

Dieter had heard whisperings, rumors only maybe, of violence breaking out in other camps between prisoners who felt they should cooperate and those who still believed they should resist fully.

When all had quieted, though, Dieter felt somehow lightened—perhaps by the justice he had witnessed here in this moment and his small part in it—with Kanzlitz consigned now to the dark, moldery armory across the way. In fact, this new sensation, drove a decision that had torn at him for months. He motioned to Corporal Mandel, the still-rattled guard to meet him behind the quarters. Dieter made as if to visit the outhouses but then circled around to the shadows of the building's rear, where he could speak to the corporal.

"These very hard Nazis are bad for me und bad for the men," he said, as the stench in this spot of the latrines at the backside of the camp rippled over them. "The other prisoner are afraid to speak free to you or your soldiers, from them bad ones you see just now. So you know."

The guard was grateful for this information.

"If you make a secret with us—just you and me—I can tell you on them, as I see these things. Who they are und what they do," Dieter added, no longer caring how much personal risk he took in this from his harsher comrades.

Ella

Driving up along the canal, Ella pulled off Pilottown Road and into the parking lot of the dairy out on the north edge of town near the inlet. She had just come from inland at Georgetown, fetching her last bank check for the construction credit that had been approved by the extension office. That was not her most important mission today, though.

Yesterday, she had driven down 2nd Street and seen her girlfriend Clarissa's husband, Rand, talking yet again to a bunch of gobs in their sailor suits. He had been good this past year and minded and tended and kept his peace amidst this war, but not contentedly. She was sure he acted out yearnings like Lee had, in Rand's case keeping with his naval reserve buddies at the Service Inn and volunteering for watch duties. Ella's instincts told her she hadn't a moment's extra time to bring the man to his senses.

At quitting time on a Friday like this, you could get the day-olds for half price—tubs of curds and extra gallons of buttermilk that had to be sold off. She knew that some of it came from milk from her own farm, but this saved some trouble and was good for breakfasts and desserts for her fellows.

She fished her buys out of the ice table and knew she wouldn't have to wait long. Rand Ellis always spotted her.

"Ella Hall. Always put out fine," he said, standing there in his white coverall, smiling as he gave her a friendly look up and down.

Ella laughed, but only for an instant. "What's this I hear you're thinking of some foolishness?"

He knew what she meant.

"Saw you hanging out again with a bunch of tattooed pop-eyes."

He shrugged, shook his head, and looked down.

"You have a responsible job here," she said. He was foreman at this dairy. The draft board wouldn't take him from that.

"I know it sounds corny El, but the sea always calls to me too."

"Oh, where'd you hear that line?"

"Well, there's plenty of families been here for generations that feel that way. Got to protect it."

"You been watching too many movies, Rand. I don't think any torpedoes going to hit your fishing boat."

Rand had a big old scow of a trawler, a cabin cruiser that he kept together from his father before him, and that he took tourists out in for tuna on weekends. Or at least had until the diesel rationing.

"What about your wife, does the sea call to you more than she does? And just when you're ready again to try to get in a family way?"

Rand smoothed the ice out around the bottles and tubs.

"You run off to the Navy and this war, and I'll run her off to the first handsome young man that comes along. Mind, now."

18

Reese

"Yes, you will," Reese's mother said. "If you're not working out back today, you will run these errands. Now, go dump this fat and collect the grease pail."

It was a duty that Reese did not enjoy. They saved all types of fat from cooking any kind of meat. His mother strained it into a big coffee can and his job was to take it to the outside cellar steps under the Bilco door where it stayed cool and ladle it into a big pail that had a screw top. It stunk and made his hands smell like onions and bacon and such.

"Must be a pound or more in there now. You fetch it out and take it to the butcher to collect," she said, where she sat writing another letter to his pop. Reese looked over her shoulder and read:

> We trust you came through the landings okay, and only hope and pray
> that you stay safe in your movement up through Italy. We are so proud
> of you and all the men. Please be careful. We need you. I need you

She stopped as if there was more to that sentence that she didn't want to finish as Reese watched.

"Will he even get it?" he asked, walking toward the door.

"We have to believe he will," she said curtly, then changing her tone to nicer. "Now go on about your assignment."

Reese threw on his jacket in the morning coolness, put the pail into the basket of his bike, and rode into town. When he arrived, uniform colors—army khaki and navy blue—were everywhere in the streets on a Saturday like today.

Reese asked the teenager working the counter at the butcher, "What do you collect this mess for, anyway?" referring to the lard pail he handed him.

113

"To make glycerin for artillery shells, boy, don't you know?"

Reese then took his empty pail, left that young man who wore a bloody apron, and walked his bike over to the grocery store, where he found two friends from his class, like he thought he might. But, sure as eggs too, there was Roscoe also and Tanner, another of the older boys who helped give them such trouble, lording over the corner here. They had backed off Reese a bit after he'd stood his ground with his fists up once in the hallway at school, but still sat on the bench this day and teased him and his friends when they went by.

"Feeling dry out here, Tingle," that fat head Roscoe sung out. "Why oln't you fetch me a drink in the grocery when you come back out, unless you want to be wearing your shirt backwards when you go home."

Inside the store, Reese had the quarter that Ella had given him to buy a pound jar of peanut butter. But now the thought dawned upon him that this was enough money to buy a soda for himself and all four of the boys out front.

"Well, ain't you a regular Joe, now," Tanner said, as Reese handed them all a grape pop.

"Yeah, and maybe now you can lay off some," Reese said.

"All right, then," Roscoe said, with a mean laugh that Reese did not trust. "C'mon squirts, let's ride over and watch the prisoners get trucked in."

Reese did not want to watch that again, out in front of the drugstore, the daily dispersal of POWs, but somehow he got into the pack of boys anyways because everyone had their bikes today. They took the way down around past the canal park, where several old cannons sat, in honor of the town's battle in the War of 1812.

"They won't ever take our cannons to melt them down!" Reese belted out. He heard the older boys laugh like anyone knew that.

On the main street, the trucks were arriving and the prisoners were moving about among the supposed-to-be-watchful soldiers from the fort. He was surprised to see that, in the drugstore window, Mr. Rickart, who never had a disparaging word for anyone or anything, had hung one of the government war-bond posters that said, "Deliver us from evil" with picture of a sad child's face in front of a swastika.

As Reese tried hard to figure how he might skunk on out of here, he spotted Dieter standing across the street with one of the Army lieutenants. Today, their POW was to finish building a new feeder in the big chicken house that he and the other men had added at the back of their yard. Reese was supposed to help again, too, on the final construction, with Dieter showing him how to finish laying the tarpaper roof on. Then they could move all the grown-up baby chicks to where they could eat and water freely with—

"Hey, Jingle Tingle, you a German lover, right? So why don't you go git some candy like the other babies," Roscoe called out behind him. Reese turned and saw that some of the Germans were giving out treats to the younger kids.

Suddenly, his two pals his age didn't care and launched themselves in the direction of the handouts. It was just the distraction Reese needed to slip across to Dieter, pushing his bike in front of him. If he did nothing and was to stay here, the bully boys would boss and heckle and hound him all day.

"Guten Morgen," Dieter said. Reese looked up at him a little forlorn. Reese could tell that, with just a few glances, their German saw what was happening behind him among the big boys. And Reese could not turn back, now that he had gone up to speak with a prisoner.

Dieter snapped his fingers quietly, like he had an idea. He leaned over toward the Army sergeant next to him and said something low down.

"This is a very good boy," he heard Dieter say, as their German slipped his hand into his back pocket. "You give him und his bicycle a trip back to the fort in your truck—is a good thing he will remember."

Then he saw Dieter hand the soldier something. A five-dollar bill!

Reese knew darn well that this mother slipped Dieter extra money once in a while when he was such a big help. Dieter told her he didn't need it because his chit tickets with eighty cents a day printed on them went so far at his barracks store at the camp that he couldn't use them all, but she kept pressing extras into his hand, like the crazy-person kind of mother she was.

Now the soldier shot his eyes left and right, slipped the bill in his pocket, and said, "Schneider, you keep them Jerries of yours in line like you been, and we'll sure do you a good turn now and then."

Before Reese could believe it, the Army man picked up his bike, put it in the back of the big green truck, and told him to jump up in the front seat with him. "Come help me ride, pal. You sit up here and be lookout for me, okay chief?"

Suddenly, Reese was easing out of the square to the roar of a big engine, leaning out the window over the big white star on the side of the door, with a smile on this face, as his two chums ran along next, yelling, "Reese! What? How did you?" and the two blockhead boys just stood on the curb with their dumb mouths open as Reese sailed by and gave them a salute.

Ella

As the sun dropped behind the trees on a fall evening, Ella watched Dieter and Reese working together. Herding their vastly enlarged flock of white broiler chickens from the outside pen toward the enormous coop they newly owned. The German took the time, now and then, to give an instruction to her son. Reese clearly took note, by the way he paused.

Had it been *her* bossing the boy around, she would have gotten an entirely different reaction. In fact, Reese groused at her about having to round up so many birds each day. But Dieter's instructions were delivered in the gentle but firm man's way needed with such a boy.

Now Reese waved his hand dismissively at the straggling hens, wanting to be done with this work.

"No, we must keep all these Hühne in the house," she heard Dieter insist loud and jovial, using his foot to direct the remaining cluckers. "They grow faster this way, just like you because you have a nice warm house to sleep in."

That night, as Ella lit a fire in the hearth in their living room and then dreamed over some fashion magazines, while Reese did his school exercises, spread out on the floor, she realized that she didn't just need a POW to keep this farm going, she needed *this* POW—the one they'd already found.

By the time it had darkened, and she had gone out back and checked on everything in the farmyard, then came to tell Reese it was time for bed, she walked into a smokey smell and found her son snuffing out their hearth flames with the fireplace shovel.

"Because if there are enemy pilots up there," he said, "they can look down our chimney as they fly overhead and see the glow."

They had all indeed been taught such things by the civil patrol, but … She gently relieved him of the shovel and reassured him.

Then, as she tucked him into bed, she said, "Just want to remind you, buddy, we need to keep it quiet about Mr. Dieter around here. It's our good fortune to get him so regular—and him in particular, you know. Can I have your promise?"

He only murmured what she thought was assent.

She finished the night at the kitchen table. With one lamp burning to light the newspaper in front on her, Ella held her head in her hands, her hair hanging down around her face. Every day, to keep their world going, she felt as though she was shot out of a cannon before dawn, going nonstop all day, until this time, not long after dark, when she could no longer put a foot in front of the other and could only fall over sideways in bed.

She had gotten the Philadelphia newspaper at the drugstore yesterday, from cheerful Mr. Rickart, but who had gone sad-eyed when she said she had no word from Lee. She had narrowly avoided running into the town cop, that bothersome Hale Truitt, who might only relish bad news about her man. Truitt, a fellow with a short fuse to begin with, looked noticeably grumpier now that his only brother had been shipped overseas to fight in Europe.

In these minutes—her last moments of wakefulness this day—she decided to take the paper to bed with her. But the lines and columns of words swam before her eyes as she tried to follow reports on the 5th Army, which it sounded like was partly stalled out in front of the German defensive lines in central Italy.

And Lee—maybe having forgotten about them altogether—was not communicating. By letters or any other way. Except silently perhaps ...

19

Ella

Ella moved down the narrow aisle of the grocery market, her basket on her arm, as she checked her war-ration book to see what she would be allowed. A few necessaries, some canned goods, a couple sacks of flour. Lord knew, they grew enough wheat at their own place but damned if they were going to mill it themselves and darned if the local mill could ever get it as fine and white and—

\ All at once, she picked up chatter from the next aisle over. Voices that sounded familiar. Women. Then she heard a name, *her* name. And *Lida Crouch's* voice, from the baking aisle.

"He's there every blessed day," Lida was saying.

"Oh, do tell." From other ladies.

"That's what I've heard too."

"A big handsome one, huh?"

"He the man of the farm now, ay?"

How could Lida even know such things for sure? Ella turned into the aisle and walked up to the clutch.

"He's the hardest worker we've ever had, save my dear husband," Ella said, putting a startled, even shocked, pause to them all. She knew she should stop there. Of all the farms near here, she'd had POW help the longest and steadiest from the same prisoner. So she added, "You would all be glad to have a hand like this one."

There was a titter from a couple of them. Then another who said, "Oh, you and Lee are married now?" even though this biddy knew damn well that they weren't official.

"In the eyes of the Lord," Ella said, as she budged on past them and went about her business.

At the end of that very same day, and keeping the incident to herself, Ella ended up in their chicken house—which was twice the length of their barn now. Dieter was instructing her about the new watering system that they had just completed for the birds. He had built it with the farm contractor they hired for such improvements here and there on the place. Outside, were water barrels set at a certain height.

A couple of Army guards, detailed to check on all assigned POWs, had rolled by in a jeep earlier in the day and questioned Dieter about who was managing him, and he'd had to claim Levotas. Somehow it had passed muster but reminded Ella that she needed to stick close.

Inside, with all the cluck-cluckers around their ankles now, he explained how to adjust the height of the drip hoses to make sure they turned on or off according to how the water level in the trough compared to that in the barrel. Lee had never taught her anything like this.

As they knelt and he demonstrated how to pinch off the hoses, Ella noticed a moment when their arms were against one another—their skin touching from their wrists all the way up to their shoulders. Nor did they pull away for long seconds, until she thought of the gossip in the grocery store and quickly straightened up.

Dieter

Nights were long at the prison camp. Especially when you wondered about family members back in Germany. And in Dieter's case, whom you might allow to *claim* you as family …

But, at least in this camp you knew when it was night and when it was day. Not like the hell-hole that had been the U-858. They had been at sea, off and on, for nearly six months altogether. Few U-boat crews returned alive from missions even half that long.

But now, the cold had come into this new world. It was nothing really to someone from the northern-most parts of Germany, except that this weather forced him inside this day, which meant into the officers' barracks. Last night, they'd had the diversion of feasting on a big round strudel, or "pie" as she called it, that Frau Ella had made from her own apples that he had helped to harvest.

Other men likewise returned sometimes from their workdays with cakes and other küchen. Dieter felt endlessly thankful for such kindness, experienced by many of his boys.

This season coming, though, he would be forced to sit long evenings with the handful of officers that included unsavory characters such as Befehl and Kanzlitz.

"We are all duty-bound to try to escape," his captain felt compelled to remind the others, flecks of Ella Tingle's pie spraying from his mouth as he spoke and as they sat at the common table in the middle of the room.

From talk overheard from the guards, and from stories of a couple of prisoners transferred here, they understood that a few such attempts had already been made. Not from their camp, but from other camps on this great farming peninsula.

"You must remind your men of this," Kanzlitz, the Afrika Korp officer, said. "They are obligated to try to get away."

It appeared other escapes had been short, harmless ones before the handful of escapees had been rounded up and had all their privileges removed back in their camp. Dieter had no intension of encouraging such things among his men.

But it was on his mind the next morning, as he lined up his soldiers for the headcount and march to breakfast. At least one was missing, and the count of the officers seemed short as well.

Possibly a couple had gone ahead or to the latrine? "Lead them to the mess hall," he said to one of his NCOs.

Dieter stepped back into the men's barrack again, but found no one. When he stilled though, he heard a muffled sound from the rear, outside.

He strode through the door and around. The commotion came from a spot he knew, behind here, poorly visible from anywhere else in their camp.

As he turned the corner, he saw Kanzlitz looking on, as Kühne, the Waffen SS trooper, struck one of their fellow German corporals with some kind of club.

"When you tell the guards of our talk, you commit treason and this is the required punishment," Kanzlitz was saying to the soldier who was down on the ground and bleeding from the head.

As the trooper reared back again to strike the corporal with the thick broom stick, Dieter had two-stepped to full speed. Just as he reached Kanzlitz, the man spun to him and Dieter dropped his shoulder and head into the SS officer's midsection. He struck the man with all his weight in the side of his ribs and sent him sprawling with a loud grunt. The Sturmtrooper hit the ground with a groan.

Dieter kept his feet, grabbed the club, and turned toward Kanzlitz, who stepped back and then fled. As the SS man moaned on the ground, fighting to regain the wind that had been knocked out of him, Dieter heard footsteps coming around the barracks, and suddenly his captain, Befehl, stopped abruptly before him, seeing all that had just happened.

"*You,*" he said, spreading his feet and arms wide, ready to fight, and Dieter felt a soreness suddenly in his shoulder from tackling the SS man. "You have always been against us. Against me," Befehl hissed.

"Against *you,* ja," Dieter said in the flattened, lowland German of his north country to this Prussian tyrant of a man. "Did you really think you would keep us trapped under the sea forever, against orders, helping you to fire on ferries and steamliners, full only with innocents, until we finally died?"

"*You* did it."

"You think a shipwide failure of our systems happened that easily on its own?" Dieter asked with a smirk.

"Now I know."

"Perhaps we had a little help from God."

"You sabotaged our ship."

"We simply let a problem go unfixed until it got worse." To bring down a rogue officer and his mission gone mad. "I had help."

"You will hang for this when the war is over."

"No," Dieter said with a bitter laugh, "when this war is over, it won't matter. And maybe you will be the one to hang!"

The men took a step to rush each other, but at that moment several camp guards arrived at a run around each side of the barracks, and grabbed them, pulling Dieter and Befehl's arms behind them, as the German corporal who had been struck sat back up, wiping blood from the cut on his brow, and hurriedly explained to the guards what had happened.

Ella

"Is your arm sore?" Ella asked Dieter, out in the chicken house on a crisp late-fall morning. She saw him favoring his right arm as he moved the large bags of chicken feed. She always got a laugh when he called these the "ein-hundred-pound bags."

He had remained in the camp for several days, and he would not give much of an answer about why.

"No. A little bit. Ist nothing," he said, hefting the load mostly with his right arm. "Just slept on it false last night. That's all."

Ella put her hands on his shoulder and inspected it, to see if she could feel anything amiss there. She worked her hands into it a bit to see if she could take any of the stiffness out.

All at once, they looked at each other—him with that blond stubble on this face and bright white smile. She dropped her hands quickly to her sides.

"Come," he said, with a pleasant look on his face. "Let me show you this Apparat." They went to the end of the poultry house, where he had completed a task that she had ordered this month. Dieter had run an electric line from the farmhouse out and set up a heating unit. Just in time for the early cold snap that was upon them.

He showed her how to turn it on and off, and adjust the heat of the electric coil and moderate its blower so that their ever-expanding number of hens would not be in danger. The broilers were supplying this farm with its first-ever steady flow of cash.

She and Dieter stood close to each other in the warm rush of air, with the smell of the chicken house—earthiness that mixed savory and sour scents with ammonia smell—all around them. As he often did while he worked, Dieter was telling her about other things of which she had no ken, today going on in his sometimes-broken English about the bath and spa towns of Europe and Germany. "To Bad Bevensen near Lüneberg we go, for hot mineral springs, rich in salts," he was saying, and she tried to imagine such places. She wanted to ask him so much more, only wishing the fan had drowned out the Army truck's horn that sounded from their drive, here to fetch Dieter and leave her by herself again in these chill and darkening weeks.

She had asked Everett to be on that truck today, so she could speak to him.

"Why can't Dieter stay for supper?" Reese had asked.

With her shawl over her shoulders and a scarf over her head, she stood in their lane and likewise asked Everett, "Why is he sent elsewhere on some days?"

"Well, El, I can't control it. They need to move the officers around so they can check on the detachments that the other prisoners are working."

"Well, that just won't do, Everett. I can't run a farm that way." Subject to every whim of this Army!

"Remember, officially he's assigned to duty at the fort," Everett said quietly. "I'm doing the best I can on this, hon."

She shrugged, her thoughts turning to tomorrow, when she would see Clarissa and other women at their ladies' church-circle gathering, and then take a drive up north along the highway toward Dover, using her farm gas allocation to help her girlfriend go find fabric and wallpaper she needed for what she hoped would be a child's room in their house someday—but mostly to hear whether Rand was keeping his wits about this war.

That trip would make for some company, anyhow. Still ... When the engine noise and lights of the Army truck disappeared down the road that evening, she knew again her lonesomeness.

20

Ella

Ella stood in the far corner of her living room reading a letter by candle. To see the scant missive in her hand during the blackout hours, she held what her grandmother used to call her flashlight. A candle holder with a wooden handle beneath it and a little mirror at its back, so that it reflected the light forward. The candle flickered as she read again the first correspondence she had received in a long while from Lee, complete with edit strips cut out by the war censor.

> *As you probly know, the 5th is fighting up the west side of the Italian*
> *peninsula. We are moving 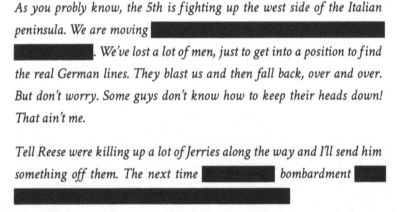*
> *. We've lost a lot of men, just to get into a position to find*
> *the real German lines. They blast us and then fall back, over and over.*
> *But don't worry. Some guys don't know how to keep their heads down!*
> *That ain't me.*
>
> *Tell Reese were killing up a lot of Jerries along the way and I'll send him*
> *something off them. The next time ▮▮▮▮▮▮ bombardment ▮▮▮*
> *▮▮▮▮▮▮▮▮▮▮▮▮▮▮▮*

Ella blinked. She stared through the slice-outs as she tried to know what that last sentence might have said, but found only darkness in those holes. She read it over again and again. Her man in such hell … She would in no way pass that message of his on to Reese!

Lee

What Lee didn't want to tell was truthfully how many thousands of men they were losing just to get into a position to assault an Italian mountain ridge called Cassino. He and his fellows knew that the enemy was using the chance to pound them and then retreat to more defensive lines north, where they would probably set up for the winter.

Lee was glad that he had written that note when he did, his hand shivering as he sat in a tent, holding a pencil with fingerless gloves, because the next day he and his men took it hard. Positioned in a ditch along a roadway that they were trying to secure, they flattened against ground that had started to tremble again with rumbling cannon fire from the hills. Then came the first time his platoon had experienced the whistle-whine of a shell passing directly over their heads. It thudded thankfully to their rear, but they heard the scurry of engines as the supply column behind tried to get off the road and conceal itself.

Lee rose up, sure that their roadhead, several hundred yards in front of that column, was not the target. But the next moment, an incoming got louder than it should and suddenly a percussion rattled their helmets and the ground and their ear drums as dirt and stones from across the road rained down on them. The explosion was so close and jarring that Lee could barely hear the screaming over the ringing of his ears as he raised his head. The hollering came from across the way, where another platoon of his regiment had crept up along the fields on that side.

"Cover!" he hollered to the men he had guided into this gulley. He had somehow become a corporal over the last two months. His order meant for these PFCs to both stay covered and cover him. But there was nothing for them to shoot at.

As Lee moved up and onto the roadbed, he made a quick explanation to Ella and Reese, "because I had to," but not an apology.

As his feet rushed him forward, he thought too of the medics behind them who'd had to cover the red and white crosses on the side of their helmets with mud because they found the insignias of corpsmen made them more of a target, rather than less, to the bastards in front of them, who ignored the rules of warfare.

Lee crossed the wide cinder road at a crouch and turned up its other side. The source of the yelling came out of the smoking hole right in front of him and straight at him. A soldier missing an arm but, in his momentary shock and confusion, having picked up that arm in his other hand, came shrieking past Lee as the man rushed back toward the column they were supposed to be clearing the way for.

Lee ran into the black hole and grabbed the only thing he would see moving there, a solider whose pack remains were still smoldering on this back as he lay on his stomach quivering. Lee pulled the man up onto his shoulders in a fireman's carry and began moving back down the road, as another explosion rippled Lee's clothes and vibrated his insides, and opened up a huge crater between him and the trucks he was making a dash back towards.

Dieter

Dieter felt as though he now presided both reluctantly and thankfully over a long table of prisoners in the POW camp's mess hall. His U-boat commander, as well as the Afrika Korp prisoner and the SS swine had all been removed from the camp. Dieter was not supposed to know, but it had been whispered by the guards that the three had been shipped to a camp in some state called Oklahoma that kept committed Nazis. It left Dieter as one of the ranking officers here.

This evening, though, on this Christmas night, he felt that if he heard the men sing "O, Tannenbaum" or "Stille Nacht" one more time, he too would try to escape from this camp. So instead of that, he jumped into a pause in the warbling. He stood, raised his beer glass, and gave a loud toast to everyone's health—and to a quick and merciful end to this war. His salute was met with a wave of agreement across the room.

They had been given a special meal this night. Pork and potatoes and great big bowls of steaming spinach. But Dieter poked at his.

He wondered what festivities, if any—perhaps none—were taking place at the Tingle farmhouse.

Last week, he had heard Reese Tingle say, "It's coming on Christmas, Momma."

"Yes, it is, child," his mother had replied.

It pained him to think they might have invited the negro, Levotas, to join them, but not him. They were a team and yet he was kept in this country and in this camp as an enemy.

126

Still ... Ella Tingle was an ever-more ingenious woman, and she would find a way to light a light and bring warmth to her home, no matter the circumstances and no matter who could join.

Around him, each man in the camp had been allocated an extra glass of beer this evening—or at least the piss-water that passed for beer here in America. Thinking about the family in Germany that he had long left behind—his parents, the girl who had tried to claim him—he felt guilt. Why must it be so? And did he still even have them to remember?

But beer glasses were banging on tables all around him. He knew he should not be surprised. Most of these men were in their early or mid-twenties, just a few years younger than him, but still, younger ... And so of course the bawdy conversation, a rowdy, ribald din of tongues from every corner of Germany turned to the subject of American women.

"They dress so plain and simple and light, it's easy to see their shape," one was guffawing next him, with his mouth full of food.

"I love this farmer's daughter so much that I will always love her," declared a private at the table, talking about the family on whose place he sometimes worked. But it irked Dieter to hear such blather.

"My American woman friend who works on the line next to me is full of sweetness," another was bragging, referring yet again to a lady with whom he worked in the cannery, and to whom he passed notes. "I will marry her someday, even if I have to run away, or if I have to escape back to America after the war—we will marry, then—"

"Enough!" Dieter shouted, slamming his hand on the table. "You are fools," he hollered at the three men, silencing and clearly shocking many at his end of the table.

They would not marry these women. It could never be.

21

Reese

Something woke Reese. On a cold winter night, after it had taken him a long time to fall asleep, he pushed the extra pillow off his head.

Nothing, though ... Not even a breath of wind against his loose, usually rattling window that surely must be frosted up behind the blackout curtains.

He knew he ought to go bank up the coal stove or the wood stove. But instead he slipped his bare feet onto the icy-feeling floor, put his corduroy robe around him, and went quietly up to his observation post, the dormer on the third floor that looked toward the canal and then the cape and, beyond, the ocean. This window up here needed no cover because the attic was dark.

All he could see were the searchlights out at the fort ... Out east, it was as if two giant carpeted runways of whiteness had been laid out longways across the sea. Straight across the Atlantic. Maybe to where Pop Lee was.

He could see them scanning slowly upon the glittery surface of the water.

One of the engineers from the fort had told their fourth-grade class, "The lights are five feet across and each has 800 million candlepower."

Reese had raised his hand and asked if they were for spotting infiltrators too. The soldier had hemmed and hawed and lied to them when he tried to say no.

Next day, at breakfast on a mean old winter morning, Reese didn't even pause to properly chew his eggs when he asked, "Hey, Moms, why do they burn and shoot those giant searchlights at night, when all of us back here have blackout, huh?"

"I don't know, darling." It was the way she answered when she wasn't listening. Too concerned with putting together the perfect lunch pail for Dieter and whoever else today.

"And then if the town monitor comes by and so much as sees the glow of our radio dial through the window, he'll cite us!" Reese said, but immediately wishing he hadn't.

His ma turned and gave him a look.

"You sneakin' down again to that radio at night?"

Reese kept his head down, scooping on his bowl of cooked millet.

"The rules are just the way they are," his mother said about his question. "Here and everywhere."

It was the kind of thing she'd let out when she didn't know the why's or wherefores. Instead, she gazed out back.

In a softer voice, he asked, "Anything from Pop yet?" and once again regretted what his mouth said sometimes. So many weeks since they'd heard!

"Not just now. You know he can't sit and send post back when the Army's on the move." But he saw one of her hands go to her tummy for a moment and the other to her temple—the places that pained her when she fretted.

Reese went over and leaned against his ma, and she put her arm around him. She'd acted upset yesterday morning too, because the drip spouts had froze up in the poultry house. She got so dang worried about her tremendous flock of hens! Dieter had been out there busting the ice on top of the barrels to bucket the water into them, and Reese sure didn't feel like helping with any of that today on a day off of school, because—

Suddenly a knock came on the door. Reese bolted toward the hallway. A truck had stopped in front of their place. Boys jumping off, with blue or brown uniforms and caps on, and yellow kerchiefs over their winter coats.

All at once he knew. The Cub Scouts and Boys Scouts were going by, collecting for their rubber drive. He and his ma had nearly forgotten about it and now they scurried. His ma found a few old Mason jar rings and a rubber glove to give them. She forbade Reese to donate their garden hose when he tried to get it from the back stoop.

As the scouts loaded up and started to clamber back on, Reese quickly threw on his hat and gloves, and ran behind the old broken-down tool shed that his grandpa had used to use before they built the new one. "Wait!" he hollered to the truck and flipped an old car tire up out of the tangle of dead winter weeds. Grunting, he started rolling it out into the yard.

The scouts scrambled back toward him. "Give the shrimp some help," one of the older brown-shirt boys called out with a laugh.

Afterwards, Reese just stood in the kitchen with his arms folded, glaring at that mother of his. He didn't have to say a word for her to know that he demanded to hear again why he could not join the Boy Scouts.

"I don't know, Reese. You're already missing too much school and homework time for your farm duties," she said. "You're a farm boy and most of them ain't."

Reese walked out back with his flap hat still on, groaned and socked the sky a few times. She was a darn mean momma! And like he'd heard biddy Lida Crouch whisper to the other old ladies when they walked by coming out of church last Sunday, "She takes liberties." She *certainly* took liberties, whatever that meant, and Reese intended to get her back for it.

22

Ella

Ella drove through a cold night. At the entrance gate to the fort, the guard checked her off on his clipboard.

"For Lieutenant Hall," she said.

Everett had left her a pass.

"Yes, ma'am," the guard said, as he looked at her identification. "Have a good evening."

The sentry saluted and lifted the gate for her, and she drove her smoky, loud old pickup onto the base.

Ev had asked her to meet him at one of the big, tall, cement watch towers.

"Well, look at this coming. Mm-*mmm*," one of the guards said, thinking Ella couldn't hear him, as she walked up to the tower.

"Evening, fellows."

"Lieutenant said to look for you, miss. You're welcome to wait in here."

It was only slightly warmer inside the huge cylinder of concrete and steel, with its winding stairs.

The two soldiers on watch politely stood outside but she could hear their chatter.

"Wish we were nice and warm like the dang 198th right now."

"Hell, yeah, camping in Tahiti. Goddamn."

"Like they'll ever see a Nip there."

Ella knew of others from Sussex County who had been assigned to the coastal artillery unit they were referring to, and she'd heard they were building emplacements on an undefended beach in some place called Bora Bora.

Just then Everett came gravel spinning and skidding to a stop in a jeep in front of the tower.

"Sorry, El. I was down watching the festivities at the National Guard camp in Bethany."

"Which are?"

"C'mon, we might be able to see some of it still," he said and led her in the couple-minute climb up the equivalent of several stories on the spiral stairs of the tower.

What a view of their world from the open-air observation deck! Out across the bay and up and down the seashore and back behind, across the dark inland, the entire circle of their world, spread out and vanished in the distance, 360° around them. It would have twinkled with lights if their lives had not been so blacked-out by the war. Only a bit of moonlight permitted her to distinguish the lines between the land and ocean and sky.

"Look," Everett said, pointing south. Far in the distance, she could make out what appeared to be tiny round clouds lit from beneath with spotlights and occasionally with what looked like a single string of red fireworks streaking up towards them.

"They conduct their antiaircraft practices day and night down there. Hundreds of people come to watch. Those are balloons illuminated by the floods below, and that right there, those are streaming red tracer bullets from the machine guns. Why if one of those rounds strikes an aircraft it will—"

"Ev. Look, I can't stay long. This is one of the first times I've left Reese by himself at home."

"Oh, he'll be fine," he said, flashing that bright grin of his. "He'll be all filled up with it."

"You never can tell what that child is going to do. Listen, what's this you wanted to tell me about my farm help?"

"Just that I can't continue to guarantee it."

"You need to."

"It's just unpredictable and getting more so, and you need to know that. It's hard for the Army to manage, because there's more of these POWs coming into the camps all the time. And we got to keep them in bigger groups and keep 'em corralled and we don't want people to get scared, seeing them all over the place, and we got almost no one left who is in uniform and can speak their language that isn't over there," he said, jerking his thumb to the left, in the direction across the ocean, "and that makes it harder."

"My farm idn't 'all over the place,'" Ella said, as she narrowed her eyes at him, wondering what he was making excuses for, as her temples started to throb—whether from the bone-chilling cold or maybe from what he was leading to she was not sure.

But he no more than rambled on. "And your typical Kraut recruit don't parlez much American. But your Schneider there, he's been a real big help in that way and, well, it falls to me to parcel out these prisoners with that in mind."

"Keep parceling just the way you have been."

He looked at her, first questioning and then beseeching a bit. She knew that never in his life had he wanted to see her disappointed about anything, and it was part of the reason she loved him so.

"Do it on the sly if you have to," she said.

"That's just it. I'm going to have to do it part way off the books starting now, if you're going to continue to get ... *his* ... help, especially this time of year. If that's really what you need."

It was the one stretch of weeks in the one season that everyone knew farmers could take some time off.

"What do you mean?" Ella said, pulling her coat more tightly around her.

Then he said it. "I can't assign these men to keep people company."

"Ev! There's still plenty to be done," she said, but hearing the conviction quaver in her voice. "We've got a poultry operation that's running year round and ... I need him on my place."

She would not be chastised for befriending her prisoner!

"I wouldn't never interfere, El. I'm only just sayin'. It might get hard."

The next morning, Ella walked across their front lawn, such that it was, with bright frost on everything that still sparkled in the sun. She had scrawled out a short note to Lee, mostly just asking if he had gotten her last couple-few letters to him. She didn't think that mail was reaching him or the other men in his company, wherever they were. One of her letters had simply been returned, and it gave her a chill.

But as soon as she opened the little door of their tin mailbox, she saw it—a letter from him. The postal truck must have come by much later yesterday! Why the postman didn't toot his horn when he saw the service APO she could not imagine, but she had been distracted.

Since the moment her son had gotten home from school yesterday, she had been busy prompting him along on a report he was supposed to write for history on Caesar Rodney and his ride through the night to make Delaware the first state to sign the Constitution.

Whenever her shaking fingers closed around a letter from her man, Ella snatched it out quick, then found a private place to read it—now leaning up against the west side of their house, under the eaves in the late-winter chill. Had it been almost two months since she had received anything from him? Daily, she had to hide her fear. She flipped open the crinkly paper and Lee greeted her and then said,

> *You may of heard about the fight for Cassino.*

Of course she had, and she had suspected he might be there.

> *Sorry it's taken me so long to tell you about our part. Our division started at it about the middle of last month. We'd hardly had time to get ready* ▮▮▮▮▮▮▮▮▮▮▮▮.

She imagined the sentence finished with something like "with how bad beat-up we were already."

> *Three months of rough stuff it taken us just to get here from more down Naples way, like I had told you about before.*

But she had received no such letter! Another one lost in the mail.

Lee

In writing to his woman, Lee had paused there and elected not to tell her any more about the bombardment they had endured just to get up to the real German lines. He marked the shake in his hand and worked not to pass it on in his handwriting, much less his words.

> *Well, then we made some progress through the valley about a month ago. At last our regiment assaulted across the river. But we didn't have the armament we needed and hell rained down on us from every kind of fire you could imagine. The lousy Krauts have some crack troops all set up that pushed us back and we took a lickin'.*

On an errand to a hut they were using for command, Lee had lingered and loitered to catch any skinny he could, but had come away only with what he had spotted on an intel communique, typed up and lying on their colonel's desk: that they had run up against Generalleutnant Eberhard Rodt's 15th Panzergrenadier Division. Well, whoever the hell it was had pounced back on Lee's company and other units with counter-attacking tanks and self-propelled guns that day.

> *I don't like to say it, Ella, we gave them what we could but we had to retreat back across the river. By chance, I was one of the ones who was okay. Not sure how.*

> *I'll bet you heard from the papers and news reports that the bombers pounded the damnation out of Monte Cassino, way up on the point north of us, but it didn't help us none. The Jerries came back and dug in harder.*

> *The divisions from other countries fighting next to us have been getting pasted pretty good too. And now the I-tal winter has been upon us and the rains and flooding are so bad we can't do anything. The weight of a jeep can't even get through. We're hunkered in huts and tents here and it ain't exactly the Waldorf Astoria.*

Lee hadn't been sure if this would get through the censors, and he had decided not to tell her just exactly how miserable it was, with men getting everything from trenchfoot to pneumonia. He also had no intention of mentioning that, over the past month, a good half of the men in his battalion were either killed, wounded, missing in action, injured, or sick.

Ella

As Ella read on through the longest thing she'd ever known Lee to write, she leaned against the clapboard wall of the house she had grown up in, trying to catch a little breaking sun but staying where she could not be seen from any of the windows. And now she came to the end.

> *I hope y'all are getting by. That's all you need to do for now. I'm sure things are meager, but I thank you for staying the course on the old place.*

> *I hope too it's working, the way I set it up, for you to draw down on my Army pay from the bank, and hire help, but if it gets too tight I say tap*

*in to that little nest-egg your folks left you in the Wilmington Trust that
I know you didn't want to touch, but ...*

Anyhow, we're mustering up again here shortly, so that's all for now.

When his letter ended just like that, though, Ella dropped her hand to her side, put her face in her other hand, and stayed that way for longer than she should in the cold, as much because of what he hadn't said as for what he did.

23

Reese

In the rushes of warmer, humid air, Reese could smell the spring getting ready to bust. He wanted nothing like he did to just be in the out-of-doors, free again.

If only he could do like his pop, outside all the time soldiering. Adventuring every day as they chased enemies back where they belonged.

He knew for a fact that his ma wrote Pop letters that she didn't let him see. On other times, when she gave him some space of his own at the bottom, he didn't know what to write.

> *They say the big rock fish have already started running up into the bay.*
> *And it looks like your persimmon trees have took hold. I see green on*
> *them already.*

He couldn't figure what else, and he felt stupid. He only added,

> *Shoot straight, Pop. And hurry on back.*

Meanwhile, he could tell that this strange mother of his looked at him with both pride and surprise when he came home from school each day and said he was going to go out back to the farm to see if he could help Dieter—or he came out there and found her and him together and he lent in, like today, changing out the straw bedding for the cattle, making sure their few heifers could still stay warm one more month till the weather broke the rest of the way.

In the cattle stalls, Dieter said, "Mr. Reese, every morning ist fine work you do, feeding these Kühe and pushing hay down for them."

He showed Reese how to feel the belly of the one that would calf soon to check if everything was okay.

Finally, Reese sat back and asked him, "Were you a farmer?"

Dieter glanced about and then he said, "Ja. All the time when I was a young like you. Our farm is in the country between Kiel und Lübeck."

"Why'd you quit to do something bad, like drive a submarine?"

Dieter shook his head. He brushed off his hands, tossed the gloves he had taken out of Reese's pop's toolbox, and sat down on a feed crate. He patted the other end of it for Reese to come sit with him, in a way Pop Lee hardly ever did—just to invite Reese to have a talk.

"Was already five years ago now, I could take a chance to learn mechanics in meine Schule, if I sign up. Ist what I liked best and wanted. Then the war came and we got put in it. It was verboten to say no."

Then he went on about war training and rallying and marching.

Just the day before, Dieter had taught Reese about the wires he had run out here—which was the "hot" and which was the "negative" and Reese tried to memorize it, like for a quiz in school. But he thought now of the other kind of Nazis, the murderous ones that his father might even be fighting right this minute. "It's good you are different from those other Germans," he pronounced, sliding his feet around in the sawdust so he didn't have to look at the man.

"Not really different, Reese. Not so much."

Reese stared at him, wondering what he meant.

The next week, Reese went back out to their livestock barn and found Dieter working with a pair of snips and wire cutters near the new calf, come just this hour, who was sleeping in a big hollowed-out cup of straw they had made for him. Dieter switched on the lamp he had just finished hooking up and the orange-red light from the heat bulb gently warmed everything.

"This one came out early and in a mess, so we have to care," the German said, looking at the little one with smelly afterbirth still stuck to him. Reese knelt, pulled a piece of the dried mother's sack off the little cow's backside, then grabbed a cloth and dampened it, and wiped the bloody stains off the baby as Dieter took off his gloves and helped wring out the rag.

"You are braver than they are," Dieter said.

"What?" The prisoner's accent was still heavy and Reese sometimes wasn't sure he understood.

"Those other few boys who trouble you at school. You are stronger than them."

Reese said nothing to him for a long time, then asked, "Are the prisoners sad that they are penned up and can't fight anymore."

"A few," Dieter said as they watched the calf stretch and try to sit up. "Lots of us glad we captured, though, and don't go along with this war anymore, don't like what our country done."

Reese looked at the prisoner. His history teacher had said that the Germans had only lied about everything to the world for a long time.

The big man with the "PW" printed on his shirt looked sad, though, so Reese was glad when their Laddie collie came in and licked Dieter's face. For his part, though, Reese said nothing, only picked up his poppa's gloves and put them back in the tool chest where they belonged.

24

Ella

Ella was glad to leave her shoulder-wrap on its peg this afternoon, as she started out back. Even as this middling season turned mild, though, she was not feeling well—worried that she was coming down with the grippe. She only hoped that this change in the weather would help her more than the news reports were.

The radio these past days had been talking about a break by the Allies through the German lines in Italy, but it was impossible to tell which divisions this meant or even know for sure which units Lee was still fighting with. Imagining the conditions these men must be experiencing, she felt shameful for having complained in a letter to Lee about how cool and wet the spring had started off. Who knew if he even got the note—a strained and lackluster missive in which she could not possibly tell him that one of those Germans he battled with was now an essential part of their farm.

For all her troubles, too, she'd surely caught a late cold that had stayed with her and was in her chest. They'd gotten the spring-greens acre in, and now she was feeling it.

As she headed toward the chicken houses, though, a sunbreak warmed her, as did the chortling she heard back behind the farm sheds. Earlier this month, Dieter had figured out how to hurl a line up over a big, high branch of the huge cottonwood tree there and pull a fat hemp rope up on its own slip knot to make a rope swing for Reese. It was just the thing to entice two of Reese's buddies to come out to the farm this afternoon.

As Ella reached the back yard, she came upon the scene of the boys whooping and belly laughing as they took turns swinging high on the tremendous arc that the rope made. And it was Dieter powering those flights!

140

She saw him run up under one of the boys and lift the little wooden seat of the swing over his head as he ran through underneath and finally leapt up with his hands all the way above his head, giving the youngster a tremendous push, a dozen feet into the air to start a great long swing.

"Zooper!" called out Dieter, who had so much mud on his boots from the fields that he looked like he was wearing mukluks. But the over-the-head push was something Dieter and Reese had invented this past week. Dieter called them "zoopers" and Reese called them "super-highs" or just "supers."

Ella turned on toward the chicken houses, well imagining—and worrying— that between meeting a real German soldier and then playing with him, these boys were going to return home with a story to tell their folks.

She went in a side door to their chicken house, which had been expanded again. She had given Dieter and Levotas permission, in their slow time during the winter season just past, to build an extension onto this long shed for egg layers. She had even helped them, as they had used all the scrap lumber and tarpaper left over from the main chicken house. She had held boards while they nailed and sawed in the cold.

He and Levotas worked in a kind of competition—not just about who was Reese's chum—but about who was the main hand on this farm, neither of them quite willing to take instruction from the other, but both knowing what needed done together. And in it all, Ella experienced moments when she forgot what was men's work and what was just *work* as she leaned in.

Instead of that newness today, though, she felt only hot and cold waves, as she finished loading a crate of egg boxes, which she heaved up and carried into the main chicken house. They must be ready for the grocery truck tomorrow.

Just then, Dieter came inside. She had rigged up a partition to separate the broilers that were big enough for market and those still too young, and for part of the next hour the two of them hand sorted birds that were growing faster or more slowly, passing them across the divider.

Surveying the market side before them, full of almost two hundred white cluckers, Dieter asked, "You want me crate them all or ..." and he made the motion of culling the few dozen smaller birds—big enough, but marginal— back to the other side. The trucker would offer them a price based on his assessment of the birds. Would they make more selling all or by leaving out the slighter ones?

She was unused to a man turning to her so often for such decisions.

"Let's crate and sell them all, please," she said.

Then she turned back to the egg box, as she started coughing again. She and Dieter had set up some shelves on the steps down under their Bilco doors into the farmhouse basement, for an extended kind of root cellar where they could keep eggs at the right temperature for a night or two while they were waiting for the pickup. But Ella began wheezing.

Dieter immediately took off his jacket and put it around her. "You should not be out here," he said, as he picked up the egg box, balanced it on one hip and led her out. "You should be in your bed."

As he walked her back to the house, supporting her across her shoulders with his other hand, she knew she had never experienced a man's arm as big and long as this one. How good it felt, and how distracting and interesting to hear him prattle on about things she knew nothing about, including about some leaf called eucalyptus that he said was imported to his country and put in steam pots to help with chest colds, like he would make for her with whatever lavender or thyme or other dried herbs they had about.

Better the next day—no one ever having really encouraged her in her grown-up life to take a day off and lie down and rest—she was able to meet the poultry trucker out next to their house, at the top of their drive. They counted and haggled a bit. When the pricing was all done and agreed upon, the driver said, "I've got several boxes of hatchlings on the front of the truck. Broilers—and layers, some—come from the farms up at Nassau and Red Mill Pond. They raised up too many and asked me to distribute them—for a price."

They were not cheap and would be a risky investment. How many would live, and how many could they accommodate? She looked over to where Dieter was helping the men load the last of the chicken crates on. But she realized that look-over to a man came from a lifetime of habit.

Having heard the question, Dieter smiled and simply winked at her.

"We'll take a box of the layers and three of the broilers," Ella said, the words seeming to spill out of her.

"Well, all right then, missus," their poultry man said and credited her a chunk of their proceeds today to the purchase of the new chicks.

"And then there's Ella's fellow, fighting it out to win this war for us," Lida Crouch pronounced, as she cleaved off a big piece of an easter-egg-shaped coconut cream cake.

Against her better judgement, Ella found herself sitting in Lida's stiff old-fashioned parlor at a ladies' Good Friday gathering. She would have had to come up with a whale of an excuse not to be here at the neighboring farm today.

"A more handsome, rugged fellow than Lee Tingle you'd be hard-pressed to find anywhere," Lida was proclaiming to the clutch, about Reese's father. Matronly Mrs. Crouch had no compunction about the affection she had always harbored for Lee. In that mischievous alliance, the man could do no wrong in her eyes.

And at these audiences of the ladies' circle that she called from time to time, the woman invariably singled out any lady she considered younger and attractive, to test her a bit. Ella was first in line today.

"What's the latest word—good word, I mean, God willing—from that man of yours, Miss Ella?"

Ella was aware of how still she became. She could not possibly allow as how rarely she heard from him or got any news otherwise. "There's nothing good to be said about the fighting on the Italian peninsula," she replied simply, shaking her head and looking down at her teacup.

"Well, we just hope for the safe return of all our boys," one of the other women cut in.

"Oh, yes, indeed," Lida sung out.

Ella wanted to holler. All our boys? They already knew that hundreds of thousands of them would return only in boxes or wheelchairs or—

Ella bit her tongue. Lida could afford to be smug, with one son safely assigned to a supply depot in England, while the other remained here working a job at the Lewes fishery. The fishery was exploding in growth for the war effort, now that they'd figured how effective it was to put the massive catches of menhaden fish not only into fertilizer but also into meal for livestock feed.

But agreeable chatter covered Ella's reticence.

"Because lord knows it's so hard for a body to run a farm without the men," Lida was going on. "If I had one like your Lee, I could have this place humming along." It gave the appearance before the others of trying to cheer Ella.

"Some are getting by with the POW help," one of the ladies said.

Ella focused down quick on the couple of petit fours on the side of her plate.

"I wouldn't abide it," Lida called out strongly. "Couldn't. I'd rather the place go under and turn to weed than have someone who was a *German*, much less a German soldier on my farm."

The comment brought a mixed murmuring of agreeing and uncomfortable responses, and it seemed to Ella that Lida tried not to look directly at her.

"Certainly, I'd feel the same, about accepting any help from that lot," came the response from one of the ladies who lived in a fine home a way up on Pilottown Road.

"For what those buggers have done right out here!" said another woman who ran an inn up on King's Highway that had benefitted greatly from the war traffic.

All at once, Ella raised her head. "It's easy for you town ladies to be so sure about that, idn't it? Why, if only you knew what's required to keep a farm place going out this way and during this time …"

The room silenced. Lida sent a dagger of a look in Ella's direction, but tried to cover over. "Well, I'm just not sure how some places manage to get that kind of prisoner help and others don't," Lida said directly to Ella.

Lida had likewise known Everett her whole life, and was damn well aware of who Ella might go to for POW labor.

"It ain't easy driving a plow tractor or running a planter if you never have before—or loading a cheeken box on a poultry truck if you don't have the back for it," Lida kept on. "I'd like to mend fences too, but I cain't."

Ella doubted that, but worried more how this woman knew the details of Dieter's presence about their place. She realized they must go to greater lengths to conceal it.

Lida pursed her lips and dragged her eyes off Ella, and suddenly the threat became clear. Help her get similar aid or Ella's arrangement could become much more public. This fight would not stop here.

But Ella could not push Everett an iota more than she already had. And the last person he was going to risk his neck for was the one whom he and Ella had always laughingly referred to as the Wicked Witch of the West.

Ella's heart pounded as she saw Lida turn to another woman next to her at the dessert table and say something in a confidential hush to her. If she spread rumor and it gathered falseness to it and got talked about, it would get back to the servicemen and then back to Everett's superiors.

25

Dieter

At a table outside his bunkhouse, in the warm spring sun, Dieter held a pencil over a single sheet of letter paper. Before him in the yard, prisoners played Fußball, or soccer as they called it here.

His fellows, especially those from the north of Germany, enjoyed the mild climate in this place where spring came early and lingered as a proper spring. In any normal time of life, this would be the season of amour ... Regardless, it had certainly become so for him.

He had never met a woman like Ella. She was lovely and caring. Lithe and healthy. Bright. Hard working. A fast learner. And willing to give and sacrifice of herself.

"Toll!" he shouted, as one of his shipmates scored a goal.

But his posture dropped back again. The things he permitted himself to imagine!

What's more, he needed to return to the task in front of him. The war had been going very badly for Germany. Perhaps that was as much good news as bad, but ...

And so he wrote:

> *Dear family,*
>
> *I have seen another life. I have seen many things and a different world. If I return home, I may not be returning the same or all the way.*

He was not sure there was anyone left to whom to send this, but if so, the postmaster in Plön might know, or perhaps how to forward it to his parents or

145

whoever else remained who he had known—though certainly not to that one who had claimed him ...

Ella

"Lida's question was fair, in a way," Ella said to her cousin Everett, where they'd met up along Savannah Road, on the excuse of monitoring the prisoner trucks that were loading back up again at the end of the day. She felt jittery about finally putting it to him, but she had learned from him that 20,000 or so more prisoners had arrived this month to the US—put in the empty Liberty Ships returning from England. "They keep it kind of secret, don't they?"

"Well, not exactly a secret, but on the down-low, you know? It keeps people from getting alarmed or up in arms about it."

"Seems like the folks up in Milford got used to it," Ella said, about the cross-roads farm town closest to Dieter's camp.

"Mostly," Everett said. His hands were shoved deep in his pockets as she worked on him at last, against her better judgement.

"What do you think, Ev?" she asked, a kind of desperate crack in her voice. "Can you divert some help her way? Lida's?"

"It idn't really my job. I'm only in charge of the handful of POWs assigned to the fort here at the cape. Lida Crouch needs to apply regular, through the extension office."

"Says she already has and they're only sending them to the biggest farms. And she seems to know that my farmhand is not coming by the normal routes," Ella said. "Ev, damn it, she's going to spill on us, if we don't do something."

Dieter

The very next day, Dieter lingered with Ella near her back steps, telling her of the leisure time he and the other prisoners were given, on good behavior, to go into the village of Milford.

"The townspeople trust you, right?" she said.

"They are quite polite. Most of the time."

He could see she was comforted by this. Both knew the great prejudice that Americans had thrown against all things German—German immigrants, German names, German food. All of which were so numerous in this country.

"It's not nearly as bad as the attitude about the Japanese," she said.

As she let him linger closer to her than he ever had before, she told him a story about a man she had read and heard about in Delaware. "This poor fellow, by the name of George Yamamoto, was driven clean off of his farm by the hostility thrown at him."

When Dieter saw her eyes well at the sadness of it all, he declared again that he knew her soul, and he took her hand. She colored and started to pull her hand back but then looked down and stopped resisting.

"I have something for you," he said.

From his pocket, he produced a fancy handkerchief that he had bought her on a day when he'd had a pass into Milford. It was wrapped in tissue and tied with a small ribbon.

She unwrapped it and turned it over in her hands—chortling at the pink stitching around its border and around the cut-out and needlepointed image of a butterfly, her joy seeming muffled though by whether she should accept it. She closed her hands gently around the little gift—made of the most delicate cotton and died powder-pink—and he closed both of his hands gently around hers. She shut her eyes and held still, as Dieter's eyes dropped too and he looked intently at their four hands clasped together.

Ella

Clarissa and Ella had pulled two chairs close together in the living room at the farmhouse, so their knees almost touched, as they attempted to knit socks.

"He bided another six months and more, after you spoke to him," Clarissa said.

Rand had told Clarissa about the talking-to that Ella had given her husband out at the dairy this past fall.

"The day he enlisted back in the Navy, he said, 'You just keep doing for the war and so will I. Then I'll be home in a jiff!'"

Ella could only shut her eyes.

"How do you like that?" Clarissa went on, knitting faster and faster. "If that's how he cares ... How 'bout if I just call the Civilian Defense Volunteer Office and ask to get trained up as a nurse's aide? Do just what he says. See if he likes that."

She dropped her hands and got louder. "I wish I'd-a darn gone to nursing to school like I wanted instead of getting married sometimes. I could join straight up to the Army and Navy Nurse Corps Reserves. That would show him! Oh, yes, that would get old Randy's attention." Clarissa leaned forward, trembling a bit. "Get out there in front of the war before he does!"

Ella let her friend calm first, then said, "You could still decide to join the WAVES, honey." The Women Accepted for Volunteer Emergency Services was a smart alternative to daydreams like being in a forward field hospital. "There's dozens of different kind of jobs they could give you. Why, you could get taken up to any of the bases around here. Aberdeen or some such place."

"Well, maybe I just will," Clarissa said, having stilled her needles. She looked hard at Ella. "And that's all he said to me before he straight old re-upped and headed out to sea."

Rand had taken a great chance, in more ways than one.

Clarissa tossed her cute little head, and looked out the window, in the direction of the coast. "All this, when the doctors had just now told us it was okay to try again—everything looked all right and just keep on trying."

To get pregnant once more, just when she and Rand were ready to put the sadness of the lost pregnancies behind them ... Ella gave up on her own hands and held up the lopsided tube she'd been knitting—a terrible excuse for a sock that got a laugh from both of them.

"Did you get a chance?" Ella asked. "You know ... I mean before he left?"

To try?

Her friend's face opened and colored a little.

"Maybe," Clarissa said. "And maybe once more for the hell of it before he went out the door."

They tried to laugh, but Ella could tell it must have been a happy-sad, maybe loving-crying, bitter and thankful interlude for them before he stepped out and vanished.

And surely it was not just for the fun of it. There was more. Clarissa wanted nothing else like she wanted a baby. Perhaps more than she wanted Rand, it sometimes seemed.

"At least you have this huge place to keep up, for the effort," her friend said and brightly added, "You're part of the Women's Land Army." Ella supposed it was true, the Hall-Tingle Farm now part of the US Crop Corp. But before Ella could reply, Clarissa switched her gaze out the back window, to where they could see Dieter and two other POWs he'd brought today, who were filling the seed-corn boxes on the planter they were getting ready to drive. "A lot to keep your eye on ... And I guess it makes for company for you too. All the help, I mean—and especially them, and the main one I suppose ...?"

"Oh, they're quiet and polite, and diligent enough," Ella said quickly, not sure what Clarissa was fishing for. "I don't have any more to do with them than I need to," she added.

But her friend arched her eyebrow at Ella. "Must be a ... *comfort,* though, to have a man around."

"It's so, and more than that," Ella said, standing up quickly and turning away, but then clamming up, only wishing she could ask Clarissa—who did not press—what some of the moments that had passed between her and the prisoner meant.

Reese

With the weather warming fast now, and school allowing days off for the farming children, Reese found he only wanted to be out on their acres with Dieter. Anything, really, other than being cooped up in a classroom, where he would get caught again daydreaming out the window. Plus, their helper showed him stuff.

In school, teachers bossed you. But around the farm, he was the boss, as long as Ma Ella stayed up at the house. He could choose to lend a hand or loaf as he wanted, and couldn't anybody say anything to him about it, because he was the Tingle-man of this farm now.

And the best laugh out here was to just tag along with Dieter and Levotas and listen to them go at each other. Wouldn't either of them take direction from the other.

Today, Levotas was trying to lift up the tongs of the cultivator so he could bang one of the blades back in shape with a hammer.

"Why ain't you get yo' snow-white German ass over here and he'p me out," he grumbled loud at Dieter. Reese wondered if he had ever talked to a white man like that.

"When you could speak good English, then I could better help you," Dieter came back at him, and Reese threw his head back and hooted at both of them.

Levotas was grumpy, though, because his favorite nephew had just enlisted in a new Black army unit training in South Carolina. The soldiers in it were separated from the white soldiers and treated different and less in every way, their helper said.

But as master of this farm, Reese could tell them to stop chirping and just get back to it.

Dieter would snap to attention as he brought his feet together quickly. He would rock forward on his toes, and then back again, and say, "Jawohl, Herr Meister Reese."

"Oh, yes-sah, masta Reese," Levotas added, putting the deep-south in his voice.

Something about those answers would make Reese hush up and go over and help out with whatever they were doing.

Soon, though, they had to manage the labor brought in to finish the planting. Migrants, volunteers, and some not-volunteers. Some high school and college students from all around, and even a couple men in like jumpsuits that Reese asked his mother if they were jail criminals, but she would not tell him.

His mom had taken more of their land and put it into new and different crops. She had "invested," as she said, in a whole truck load of strawberry plants and committed another few acres to them that needed to be hand dug. And on and on, such that she had gone around the house repeating the word "diversify" like some kind of new gospel for them.

At midday, the men from the labor truck set out long plank tables on sawhorses and everyone got fed. His ma had brought in a couple of girls, and they had been cooking for two days. Reese sat at the end of the table with the men. Two of them said this farm work was their duty because they "objected" to the war. They refused to go? Reese studied on them and they seemed pale churchy types to him, and yet the kindest people he had met all spring, asking him all about his life here.

Dieter served the people he had helped to manage all day, running up and down the table, making sure everyone had all they needed. Levotas made special confabbing with the Blacks among them, who his mother had barked at Dieter would indeed eat and sit just the same at the table with everyone else.

Managing it all, his ma smiled at how Dieter at last made polite, even friendly, with the Mexicans and the few darkies from islands of the Indies among their handful of workers.

Dieter had shown Reese's mother how to take the mint and lemon balm that they now grew and crush and strain it into a tea that his mother sweetened and was now serving all around and calling it their spring tonic.

Standing with his ma and watching how hospitable their German tried to be, Reese said, "More so than Poppa ever would ... who has maybe forgotten all about us here," sticking his jaw forward.

"Oh, lovey. Let me show you something," she said and marched him inside, where she took last week's newspaper down from atop the icebox. She pointed to a story on the front and said, "Your poppa helped with that." It said some place called Monte Cassino had fallen and been captured in Italy. And the allied armies were on their way to Rome!

That was all, though, and she suddenly turned back to Dieter to help carry out more vittles to the workers.

Reese watched again on the next and last day of the hired field help as Kapitänleutnant Dieter Schneider and Miss Ella Hall or Mrs. Ella Tingle, or whoever his mother thought she was, signaled and directed each other with their eyes. At midday, they stood shoulder to shoulder, looking satisfied that another huge lunch proceeding and workday of the planting weeks was in good order.

Reese swung in the nearby hammock that Dieter had rigged up and, through its rope mesh, studied on his ma. A happy look stayed on her face, and dwelled. One of the few times he could remember that lasting so long, even before this blasted long war had started. Meanwhile, Dieter acted nothing but thankful for everything all around him and just to be here.

"Tschüß," Dieter called to Reese when he got back on the truck at the end of the day. It was one of the German words he had taught Reese. A way to say goodbye.

"Tschoose," Reese called back, grateful for their big-strong helper and holding his hand up in a wave till the truck was out of sight.

26

Ella

With the heat upon them this month, morning was the best time to get things done. Ella came from the chicken house, where she'd dumped eggshells, meat tailings, and other food scraps that the cluckers liked to peck at and fight over. Crossing the farmyard to the barn to go make sure Levotas was mixing feed for their heifers, she stopped.

Farther out back, Dieter was replacing fence posts. She watched as he worked with the post-hole digger, raising it up high and plunging it into the ground. It had been a season since she had seen him with his shirt off. His body moved under ivory skin that would soon take on a rich tan. He had muscles about his arms, his chest, shoulders and back, but especially his torso, in places where she didn't even know men had muscles. She became aware of her bare feet touching the warm dirt of the ground and the breeze travelling under her skirt and up her legs.

With that, Ella put down her buckets and turned quickly up toward the house. She cleaned herself up hastily, got in their pickup truck, and drove off, letting the wind come in the window and brace her.

But she was still gripping the wheel and pushing away the surge she had felt by pressing her thighs together, as she approached town and encountered traffic. The roadway slowed and then clogged as she neared King's Highway, which she could see was thronged with military vehicles. Another column or caravan or whatever they called them, this one probably headed toward the fort at the cape.

Her mind drifted randomly to one of the few details that Lee had given them in his letter, some weeks ago.

You wouldn't believe who we are fighting with. Our 5th along with the British Eigth Army look like the damn league of nations. Theres divisions here from every Brit and Frenchie colony you ever heard off—New Zealand, Canada, India, north and south Africa parts. Jews and a-rabs. Even Polish units! And anti-nazi forces that slipped out of the slav countries and Greece. Plus I-talians that have joined up with us against the Axis and the Reich. There's even nigroe American and Jap-American units fighting next to us.

I swear I'll send you a picture. And the next one will be of me in Rome before long. In front of the coliseum, Ella!

Wonder and gratitude and admiration all mixed inside of Ella, and yet ... the few lines he deigned to share with them now and then, or that got through, were as if the world he had left behind here no longer existed.

Inching along, annoyed in the heat of the cab, Ella gave up resisting, parted her knees, and pushed her hips forward. Her hand slipped under her dress.

Was it the balmy heat?

Just then an Army truck with a driver's view down into her window, tried to edge her out. She sat back straight quick, returned a moist hand to the steering wheel, and laid on the horn at service vehicles in front of her.

Into the flow and soon down a street in Lewes.

St. Paul's was one place where it always felt as though peace reigned and where she never wondered whether she was welcome.

Off the seat next to her, she picked up a pile of Lee's clothes, tied up with string, that she had washed and folded to donate to the supplies for ship survivors—though thankfully the pace of sinkings had abated.

She felt lucky to find Reverend Rightmyer alone. He looked unkept, as she had seen him at Sunday services a time or two. His duties on the seafront for the Red Cross might have been enough for most normal individuals, but he also oversaw three other parish churches in nearby towns.

When she came to him now, though, he reached out and took her hands.

"Lee is far away and the absence is hard ..." she said.

"At least you have ample ... er, a good team on your farm?" he said, stumbling a bit, then added, "I mean to keep you *occupied* on your Hall Farm."

That was *not* what he meant. Not exactly. And so here it was again! Ella's chest and neck and face flushed.

Lida Crouch ... Nelson had clearly heard gleanings.

Maybe lewd and scurrilous whisperings and imaginings?

"You continue to buck up strong, partly for Lee," he said, but clearly he meant *with* Lee or because of Lee, like he always had.

"There's a farm to be kept and war to contribute to. And there's a child that's part of it too."

"Of course. And your marriage, if that's what it is, which must be decided on its own merits. Not by a war. God will dictate that it survive and prosper, or whither—all quite separate from anything that this time has imposed upon you, Lord willing. And you must see to that."

Ella wasn't sure about her good pastor's reasoning, but was positive she wasn't the first woman in Nelson's parish to whom he had given some version of this speech. However, she had come here for a just bit of fellowship, not to be preached to.

"His will be done," he said, "only through your help and love and obedience and patience ... and forbearance ..."

Reese

Reese Tingle scanned about from the front window of the town drugstore. He'd been given leave to tarry here this hot, still day. Mr. Rickart's store was a cooler place. It sat on the shade side of the street with trees and awnings out front and all the windows open. Fans whirred and chopped everywhere, overhead and on the counters. In addition to the cold boxes he had behind the fountain, Mr. Rickart had two floor fans at the back of the store and he'd put a big galvanized pale in front of them with a huge block of ice in each. The air that blew across carried at least a little of the coolness to where Reese studied the summertime goings-on of this main street.

He and two of his chums had bought sacks of licorice and sat and chewed, till his two buddies had to scurry off for the bus they took afternoons to a summer beach camp down Dewey way that Reese had been denied, because he lived out of town and had farm duties.

He put it out of his mind, for he knew his momma worked to make it up to him, giving him more radio time when he was tired in the evening and trying to cheer him. He smiled at the thought of her when they had listened to a speech by FDR this month. She loved the man even more than Reese did, and she had put on a pair of his grandpa's old wire-rim spectacles and then let a hay straw hang out of the corner of her mouth like the long-stemmed cigarette holder that their President smoked from, as she side-ways grinned and spoke all snooty like him, till she had Reese laughing.

But Reese lost his smile as he watched a young man in a navy uniform who had come into the drugstore wearing a black eye-patch over one eye. Already a returned veteran of the war!

The sailor watched outside, a-midday, as more vehicles rolled into the main street with another bunch of the POWs to load onto the work trucks. "They're animals," Reese heard the Navy man say suddenly.

"We try to treat 'em civil," the proprietor, Mr. Rickard, called out to him, from behind the counter, in a now-now voice as if he was tired of explaining it to folk. "We try to set an example, you know."

"'Civil?' 'Example'?" The soldier said in a voice loud enough that the one other customer in the store and the two old men sitting in the opposite front corner from Reese turned and looked at him. "Those people out there don't know nothing about that," the Navy man said.

"That's right," one of the oldsters called out in agreement.

"Darn tootin'," said the other, stomping the floor.

The woman who had been browsing, came clunking in her marmish shoes to the front of the store, glaring out at the prisoners. "They don't understand the rules of civilization," she said.

Reese looked at Mr. Rickart, who closed his eyes, knowing this was all that was ever needed to spill people out the door to start a problem.

Sure enough, all of them drifted out to the sidewalk to watch. "You ought to been sunk by your own kind when you shipped over here," one of the oldsters yelled at the POWs.

"Yeah, better that y'all'd gone down than the poor people been rescued back into this town," the other coot hollered, pointing up to St. Paul's.

As Reese stepped out with everyone else, drawn by the excitement, several other passersby gathered with them and joined in the shouts, even as other townsfolks out on the street approached the angry group before the store and asked them to stop.

In a minute, Officer Hale Truitt—who Reese knew from safety talks he gave at school and who had been sitting in his patrol car—approached the ruckus, but slowly, as if he wanted no part of it.

The teenage boy who worked behind the fountain counter had stepped out behind Reese. "Truitt's in no mind to baby these bastard Krauts either," he said in a hush to Reese.

"Officer Truitt's brother is part of the great invasion," Mr. Rickart said to them, as he stood in the open door.

The landing on the European coast! Walsh Truitt would maybe part of it ... Perhaps on the shoreline of Belgium or France. He'd heard Cousin Everett whisper his theories.

"They're free to speak," Officer Truitt announced to the nicer townsfolk about the hecklers.

Just as fast, a couple of the soldiers who had arrived in a truck from Fort Miles, and had rifles on their shoulders, positioned themselves on the sidewalk curb.

Mr. Rickart put his hand gently on Reese's shoulder and said, "Just remember, chief, that most Americans—and most of the people of our Sussex County— even some of these here, don't hate the German soldiers, but instead blame the German government for the war."

That's when Reese spotted Dieter. It struck him that their man here was used to the angry shouts, as he hurried to get the POWs transferred between trucks. Suddenly something flew by and struck the side of the prisoner truck. Then one hit a prisoner on the shoulder. Tomatoes. Other things were tossed at them from down toward the grocery store. With that, Officer Truitt ambled back to his patrol car, pretending not to see!

In a minute, Reese watched Dieter give one quick look around to make sure everyone was out of the transport and up into their assigned pickups, as he mounted up himself. Ducking in before these objects might become stones or bricks!

"It's their leaders done this to them," Mr. Rickart said to Reese about the Germans, as they watched the prisoners driven off. Reese wasn't so sure, though. Dieter had kind of taken over around their place too, like his kind seemed to want to do everywhere.

"Go on with your business, please," Mr. Rickart called to the people in front of his establishment. "Git on about your day," he said, waving people along.

Dieter

On a warm day, Dieter stood with Levotas at the top of the Hall farm's drive, as they received a sudden set of orders from Ella.

"Hook up the tire wagon to the back of the truck and give me twenty bale of hay loaded up and in," she said. "Get goin'."

She left no room for questions, and as they turned toward the barn to comply, Levotas whispered, "Wha's got in her crawl, las' couple days?"

Dieter did not understand the man's words, but he took the general meaning. He had wondered the same, though it was not very charitable of the Black man, considering how long and passionately Ella had lectured Dieter last year on treating Levotas respectfully and in every way as an equal.

"Lida Crouch is short on hay for her few milking cows," Ella barked at them when they set the wagon tongue down onto the pickup's ball hitch. Dieter looked at her questioningly. "She's got only one field with summer grass in it and it's not enough," she snapped. "Now get a move on."

It didn't seem to make sense, but with the load in, Ella called out, "I only need one along," and then pointed to Dieter. "You." As she started the truck, Dieter reached for the passenger door.

"Nope. In the back," Ella said, and whistled him to go around and get in the bed of the truck.

Dieter complied, puzzlement on this face.

At the neighboring farm, Dieter recognized the matron.

"Howdy, Lida. Howdy, Baxter," Ella said to them.

It was the next-over farm lady and her son.

"Well, lookee here what kind of dirty demon just rode in with this load," her son, Baxter, said, glaring at Dieter and his "PW" shirt, as his mother gave a knowing nod.

Ella snapped her fingers at Dieter, telling him to help this man unload, as she spoke to Crouch without even a look back.

But the Lida woman surely meant for Dieter to overhear her every word, each time he walked back to the truck.

"They all smell sour, these Krauts, like vinegar," she commented loudly to Ella.

Dieter paused for a glance at his employer, but she seemed to have decided, in advance and for all the world, to endeavor not to disagree with anything that was said.

And the next time, "They're completely godless and hold satanic beliefs, did you know?" the old Frau was saying. "Have you seen the films?"

After a couple more comments, he could at last hear Ella attempting to change the conversation, but the woman bellowed, "They're all hypnotized and programmed by their Führer and operate like robots." She clapped her hands down low at him as if to a bad cur she was trying to drive off. "They've had all the feeling trained out of them and only know how to follow orders, without a thought. You see how this grim lout of yours works."

Dieter did not understand everything she said, but got it in the main.

How easy it would be to correct this person! But this was not his privilege or his boss' mission today.

Dieter paused to wipe his brow at the back of the truck, hoping that Ella Tingle had heard enough.

"Oh, and you know about this plague of the kamikaze too? On the other side," Baxter croaked out.

"Slant-eyed, pie-faced monkeys, who—" and with that the Lida woman almost lost her breath, and Dieter thought she might lose her dentures with it. He missed some of what was said next as he stowed a pitchfork, but straightened to hear the neighbor woman spit out, "They're dirty, sneaky beasts that ain't even developed into full humans."

"Oh, they're worse than that," his Ella said, as if delivering a line that she had rehearsed for a purpose. But who was she speaking of now? "They're like a plague of rats," she said.

His people? Dieter lost his grip on the last bale he was heaving and had to heft it up again.

"Is that brave G.I. of yours giving them what they deserve?" the neighbor asked Ella, as her Baxter son stood about, slacking off. This man was coarse in that way Dieter had seen among some in this locale, including certain of the men who worked at the fishery and the canneries. This one had a kind of nerve-twitchy affliction about him too and bad teeth, and Dieter suspected he hated lifting a finger around here.

"I don't know, to tell you the truth," Ella answered. "I got a notice from the Army that his battalion was supposed to be relieved from the combat front and fighting theater soon, but I don't know if it's true or when it would be or how he and his men are faring."

"Well, they're our heroic boys, pushing that nation of brutes back," Lida practically hollered in Dieter's direction, her neck shooting out like a turtle's, vessels protruding.

"How 'bouts I go give this one a good kick in the seat of the pants to thank him for his help?" Baxter Crouch suggested, with a big yuck-yuck, eyeing Dieter up.

"I don't think so, today," Ella said, as if another day would serve just as well.

"Stand down, Baxt," Lida said in a wise estimation, as Dieter mused on just how easy it would be to bend this gangly provincial in half—but mostly just wanting to get out of here and be done with whatever nightmare was taking place before his ears and eyes.

"We'll let this one slide," Ella said, "this time." She narrowed her eyes at Dieter, who only felt that something otherworldly had just happened. Perhaps he had made a terrible mistake. In his heart. In his dreams.

He'd gotten it wrong. He had let his trust and feelings and friendship run far ahead of sense.

By the time they arrived back at the Hall Farm, with him bouncing around in the empty bed of the pickup, Dieter had firmly concluded that he was still the idiot he'd always been, especially when it came to women.

Ella

In her rearview mirror, Ella saw Dieter climb out of the truck without a look at her when they got back from Lida's, or even an offer to unhitch tire wagon and back it into the barn. Instead, he went to the shed, retrieved his knapsack, and walked out to the road to await his end-of-day Army transport back to the prison.

Ella knew suddenly that she should have explained to him beforehand. She called to Dieter as he walked away, but he would not turn to her.

She opened her mouth again, but perhaps it was as well for now, she thought, to draw this out a bit. Make life easier. On them both. Leave it that way.

Ella felt she would weep, but simply closed her eyes till it passed. Everything had been out of character for her for so long that it no longer mattered who she thought she was.

From their sitting room window, she watched the Army truck disappear down the road and she felt a thud inside her. And another. But real ones, it turned out.

The big guns at the base were roaring out in practice.

Soon, all the guns were going at once, rattling the glass in her windows. Before her, a small, framed picture of her and Lee was vibrating slightly, threatening to move precariously to the edge of the polished roll-top desk on which it sat. She picked it up and laid it flat. Then she picked it up again and laid it face-down flat.

27

Ella

Reese and his chums were wonderful about entertaining themselves during this warm season. They had farms and fields and waterworlds to traverse. They had their bikes and their boats, and the bay. The canal, the marshlands, and the dunes. Far more than most boys, but they couldn't be expected to bide themselves every day, all summer.

So, on this sunny hot morning, Ella loaded the truck to take them to the ocean beach at Rehoboth. Umbrellas, rafts, picnic baskets. She believed she and the three boys then could all fit in the front seat of the pickup, and that the fellas would get a kick out of riding hillbilly style like that.

Nor could Ella be expected to toil every live-long day of her young womanhood on the same hundred and more acres she had lived her whole life on. While others had their adventures ... Clarissa certainly was. She had done it! Her do-gooder friend had signed up for the WAVES and had been accepted for training at the naval shipyard in Philadelphia.

Ella could only imagine ... And yet she was thankful for the boys' company and the purposeful feeling they gave her.

Dieter still had scarcely a word for her these past weeks. And more days, he allowed himself to be assigned elsewhere, it seemed. He might have reasons—every reason—Ella knew.

When all was ready for their trip, and the boys were running circles around, Ella took one minute to go fetch their mail from yesterday. In the last moments she would have to herself, with these rambunctious boys to cheer her up the rest of the day, she walked out to the road to their box to retrieve the post.

In those few steps, she recalled another trip to Rehoboth that she had made in her earliest days with Lee. She had been a couple months out of high school and Lee would have been a couple years out—if he had finished. They had met up that day with other young people their age. At the end of hours of bathing, in which Ella had worn what she called her pink-and-white peppermint suit, they had pulled clothes back over top and gone up to the new Avenue Theatre to see a movie show. Like the Auditorium in Lewes, it had separate seating for the Blacks. Ella had thought of Esther, their cook and cleaning lady that she had grown up with till she was fifteen or so and who was part of their family.

"That makes me sad, when I see it," Ella had said, looking back at the Black section.

"Why?" she remembered Lee replying.

As soon as the show was over, it was time for the young men to don their beer jackets. With prohibition just over that year, it had become all the rage among older teens and young adult men to gallivant about in these get-ups. It was one of the few college-boy-like things she could ever remember Lee doing.

The beer jackets were white like a doctor's coat, and made of heavy material on which the young guys collected signatures of friends, doodled drawings, and wrote quirky messages. Lee had let her write the names of all their favorite songs from those years of 1933 and 34 on the back of his jacket.

"Love In Bloom"

"Blame It On My Youth"

"With My Eyes Wide Open, I'm Dreamin"

"P.S. I Love You"

All the tunes she waited to hear on the radio back then. She remembered how dark and tan and handsome he had looked that day. On the big hip pocket of his coat, she had written the name of another of their favorite songs of the day.

"You Oughta Be in Pictures"

By that July, though, Ella was already several months pregnant with Reese and not feeling well. As darkness had fallen around all the honky-tonk lights and sights, and yells and smells—vinegar French fries and candied kettle corn—they had made it not very far along their promenade of the boardwalk when another wave of nausea overcame Ella, and she'd had to scurry to a trash can and lean over it retching.

What stuck with her was how it was another young gentleman in their group who had come to her aid, placing a hand kindly on her back and offering her napkins. Meanwhile, Lee had stood aloof, smoking a cigarette and watching. To be fair, he'd seen his share of her morning sickness already by then, but—

Ella snapped out of the recollection as she snapped open their big, galvanized metal mailbox and spotted Lee's handwriting on an envelope.

"Momma, c'mon!" Reese hollered, as the boys were clambering over and in the truck.

Without sorting through the other post, and keeping her hands in the box, so her keen-eyed son would not see, Ella tore open the letter and scanned it. That took not but a few seconds, as there was scarcely a handful of lines.

Nothing much new except for this cryptic last bit.

> *Damned General Clark has let the Jerries slip back up and reset their lines. The only thing we can do now is* ███████████████████████ ███████████████ *dugouts.*

That part of the last sentence was blacked out by the Army censors, but Ella assumed it was something about making sorties into those hills to assault their enemies where they were dug in.

Ella reminded herself to breath as she hurriedly folded the letter and shoved it in the pocket of her cover-up. Knowing Lee as well as she did, she worried about all he left unsaid and how deep the war might be pulling him in. In the last missive she had sent, hoping it would reach him, she had said,

> *Please don't put yourself needlessly in danger. You don't have to win this war yourself. You have a family and place waiting for you. You'll do what you have to but please keep your head down. We have so far to go.*

She felt clumsy in the writing of this but he was not a man to ever do things halfway. And when it was over, if he could not step away from this war in body and soul, if he was not Lee or better-than-Lee when he came back, what then?

28

Dieter

In the American heat, Dieter felt as though he worked listlessly at best around the Hall farm this month—as though the war had, at last, inflicted its greatest and most grievous wounds upon them all.

But if he didn't want to work on this Bauernhof and land here, it would then be his choice, as an officer, to sit in the sweltering POW camp, overrun by mosquitoes, no-see-'em biting gnats, and bloodthirsty horse flies from the marshes. Or he could oversee prisoner gangs clearing fields, or digging ditches, or running production lines in brick buildings or under tin roofs.

Ella Hall had begun asking him again to take lunch with her out back. But he did so cautiously.

"As you may know, I'm experimenting with sending Levotas to the Lida Crouch farm some days to help," she said, as they shared open-faced sandwiches with meat and mustard, in the way that Dieter had showed her they did back in his home. "I believe it might assuage the widow and get her to back off of snooping and insisting I can somehow get her prisoner labor for her place too."

Then, in simple, halting conversation, Fraulein Ella Hall began talking of Herr Lee Tingle for the first time—her man and beau, the father of the boy, who had mastered this farm before going off to this war—and in whose very footprints and handprints Dieter worked on everything about this place.

"He's something," she said. "There's nothing around here that he can't do."

Dieter buttoned his lip. He saw some things that long needed attention.

But upon a third day—as they sat at that table and bench under the shade of the orchard trees, eating peaches as sweet as anything he had ever tasted and sweat ran down their legs in the humidity of the afternoon—she began sharing bits of Tingle's letters home to her. Dieter wondered if either he or Ella understood what was happening, as she did this.

He tried to help. "I can't say much for sure about that front, Ella," Dieter said, of her man's campaign up the Italian boot.

This past year, Dieter had read and listened to and spoken as much English every day as he could. Now he tried to explain in words she would understand. "These American farmers fighting up against very strong German troops."

She tossed down the letters, put her head in her hands, and said, "If you only knew how many nights he spent carousing down in Dewey, on Whiskey Beach, when I was living here with my mother and father and a new infant."

He tried to understand. When she straightened and it seemed she would cry, he put his hands gently on her wrists and rubbed her arms.

After it passed, she picked up one of Tingle's fingerprint-besmudged notes again.

"The Italian line in the mountains," she said, as if talking to herself and trying to imagine something she could not.

"That is not an Italian line, that is a German line," Dieter said, and tried to explain that those American soldiers would probably encounter deeply dug-in German mountain divisions and very experienced paratroop units. She must know the truth.

But when he saw her shutter, he said no more. He was sure he would have felt a shake go through her now if he were to reach out again to comfort her more, but when he placed his hands on her shoulders to brace her against her worries, he felt a different kind of tremble go through her.

Ella

Ella dangled her bare foot as she sat on their back steps, talking to Dieter, on another balmy, still afternoon. He stood before her, his body cut and outlined in the thin, tattered rag of a T-shirt he wore.

Nearing the end of this third, long wartime summer, it seemed to Ella that everyone and everything had changed. But this hour, she and Dieter spoke only of small things and nothing—haltingly—and of the arrival of the pickers again soon, which would mean only bustle for several days.

"I'm sorry," she said, "about how I acted in front of Lida Crouch those weeks ago, when—"

"I know," he said, as his eyes clearly lingered on the view he enjoyed of her in her thin work dress and her bare limbs.

"I was trying—"

But he shook his head for her to hush.

She had on a shoulderless frock, just spaghetti strapped at the top, her shoulders otherwise bare and nothing from her knees down.

"I only wanted her to think that—"

"I *know*," he said.

Smiling, he stepped to her, placed his hand under her ankle and lifted and admired her leg, as her heart pounded hard. Then he slid his hand up past her knee and onto her thigh.

He leaned forward and kissed her. It was soft on her lips. Her hands were on his chest, awaiting the will-power to push him away. But then they looked at one another, and he kissed her harder—a kiss that she gave back equally.

Lord forgive her, then, she pulled him in fully.

Just as quickly, she straightened him back up, looking in every direction. Their faithful Black man, Levotas—good God—was mucking out the chicken house. She rose and felt Dieter's old shirt tear a little, as she pulled him along and into the big tool shed to one side of the barnyard. If she was to sin, it shouldn't be stupidly.

He lifted and partly carried her as they passed into the dark shelter.

But Reese was due back … she wasn't sure when, from a crabbing float trip in the canal with his pals. Dieter already had her dress up around her waist and she had unbuttoned the top of her flounce where he was burying his face between her breasts.

His Army truck pick-up was due soon, she knew, as she tore at his belt buckle. For some reason, it came back to her now what they had told Dieter last year—that if ever a prisoner was not waiting at the appointed time and place for pick-up, they would assume he was escaping and would draw their weapons and come after him.

Dieter set her down on the edge of the low heavy worktable. She leaned back, opened her legs, and wrapped them around his hips. How could a man be so hulking yet without an inch of fat on his body! Had she worked him that hard? But she had little to compare to. Lee, the only other man she had ever been with in this way, had a kind of strength that was more compact and coiled, hidden.

He drove into her without pause and effortlessly, with a hand under her waist and rear, and she was fully ready and received him. Her timing was safe this week, she was sure.

Now she would cross into another place, willingly as another person.

How badly she had wanted and needed this for so long!

She pulled his hand from where he was caressing the side of her face so that she could hear any noises from outside. But she was sure they had minutes now in safety, and the heat helped to propel her pelvis open and up into his.

She put her head back, knowing she had never felt entered like this before. So deeply and fully. With looks of wonderment and joyful play, each placed fingers gently over the mouth of the other so that a minute later neither roared out when their moments came together.

29

Dieter

"Deutschland will still prevail and rise victorious," one of the prisoners was saying, sitting at a table with a group of others in the commons area.

Nearby, Dieter was rustling through paperwork that had become his responsibility to check over in the record-keeping for new prisoners. But all tasks came effortlessly for him these past couple weeks, and he worked now with that same glowing ease that had been with him all the time since—while still keeping one ear today to the gab that came in all the different sounds of German that every region of their homeland produced.

"We will have to pull back the lines of the Reich and redraw them, but it will survive," said another.

They were two of the few true Nazi-leaning POWs still in the camp, and they had been here for some time, their main reference to the conflict from years ago, long before the war had begun to crumble so badly for their country. They were speaking to a group of the newer prisoners, a large number of whom had come into the camp over the last few weeks. Dieter did not complain when, as the tenured officer in the camp, he was tasked with helping to process them. In fact, he noticed he complained about nothing these last few wonderful weeks.

"How can you still believe that our country will win?" asked one from the newest group of prisoners, almost all of whom had been coming in from capture in the north of France, the Wehrmacht having trouble reeling back fast enough from the battle at Normandy. These new ones knew of the slaughter on both sides there and the persistence of the invaders, and their overwhelming numbers and equipment.

"There is no way. They will keep coming with three men for every one of ours. Five tanks for every one of ours. Ten planes for every one of ours."

"Is that the attitude that you bunch back there take now?" one of the two long-time harder cases kept on. "Giving up? Surrendering? Deserting? That makes you traitors."

"Make us—? Do you know how we bled and died near that coast and across Brittany?" one of the newcomers said, standing up abruptly.

"Did you say 'traitor?'" another of the newly captured ones barked as he lunged across the table. He grabbed the Nazi speaker by the collar and the back of this head and slammed his face down onto the table with a mocking, "Heil Hitler, then!"

Dieter was between them in one movement and helping the crowd to pull everyone apart. When he could get them all settled enough to quiet the room, he commanded, "Let everyone have their say here," addressing the newcomers in particular. "We will not let fear of speaking freely come into this camp. That is gone now. Forever, I hope."

In truth, Dieter was glad that one of the Nazi believers now held a towel against his bleeding mouth and nose. It also eased his frustration at having been kept here at such tasks as this when the loving of Ella Hall was his only want these days.

When the dispensation of the prisoners concluded that afternoon and all were situated, Dieter took a small portion of the considerable money he had saved and bribed one of the younger guards whom he trusted most. Dieter stated that it was merely to borrow one of the camp's bicycles to ride into the nearby town of Milford for a bit. This was no great thing.

But as soon as Dieter was out of sight of the camp, he went off the side of the road, pulled out of his knapsack the civilian clothes that he had purchased at a second-hand store in the town and changed into them. Instead of going to the little farming town of Milford, he turned down the main coastal road as he walked his bike, then thumbed a ride to Lewes. A gentle, older man in a motorcar big enough for his bike to ride in the trunk gave him a lift. Dieter feigned that he was deaf, so that he only had to speak a little to the man, in American but in a thick-tongued way.

Dropped off at the five-point crossroads, he rode the final mile into Lewes, to a service station where he knew he could put a nickel in the phone.

Ella

Ella Hall had not been expecting any calls, so when she heard the phone ringing, she scurried in from where she had been beating a rug in the back yard. She guessed it was someone from church advising them on volunteer assistance, or it was Lida Crouch insisting on knowing already what labor Ella could offer her in the coming week.

When she heard Dieter's voice, her heart jumped.

"I am here, in the town."

"Why? How?"

He explained quickly, "I slipped away."

"No, go back. Before you are discovered." It was too dangerous. For them both.

But he refused and told her to come meet him. "When it gets dark, down on the front street, by the Wasser."

He said he knew where he could stash himself till evening fell. Perhaps in some back lot or park brush?

How quickly this and her conscience had spun out of control. Ella would never have agreed to such risk taking, and had already told him this must stop, but he was here in Lewes now, so she scampered. She gave herself a quick stand-up bath at the pump out back, since no one was about. She tied her hair back and put on a summer dress because the weather had remained so warm.

When Reese and his pal Trevor Horn arrived back from the fort they were building in the woods at the back of the farm, Ella told them that she had to run in at the last minute to help Reverend Rightmyer.

"Has another ship gone down, Mom?" Reese said.

"*No*," Ella snapped, wishing again that this boy would not ask so many questions. But she quick changed her tone before their company. Trevor was to stay the night with them. "You two can be on your own for a bit, as long as you stay here in the house. Set up in the living room and listen to your radio shows. There's popcorn to be made. You know how."

It was the best she could do. To steal a little bit of the evening and try to manage this situation that she had let loose. She had spent the last eleven years of her life taking care of others and of a child mostly on her own, and she would do what she pleased in this moment.

"If I'm a fallen woman, I must manage what I've wrought," she said to herself, trying to talk herself through the fear, as she got in her truck. Yet, that feeling again of being engulfed by a man was still so fresh ...

Just yesterday, she'd had a call from Clarissa, who had regaled Ella with stories of living in a big bunk with other volunteer women in the naval yard in Philadelphia. "It's pretty simple, but we all throw in and make the best of it." Austere but fun, she said. "So far it's still clerical work with ship assignments," she had said, "but they're about to teach us how to train sailors on the .50 caliber deck guns!"

Everyone was having their adventure, but she forced herself to take a slow, unobtrusive route into town at this darkening hour. She put her truck on a side street and walked toward the canal.

She stood near the corner of Bank and Front Streets, in a quiet end-of-summer nighttime that had just barely fallen. She felt like a stupid, lustful, sneaky teenager, just as likely to lose her nerve and skulk back home. The town darkened as she waited, but the moonlight was good, sparkling on the tide running out the waterway here and past the fishing piers that—

"Excuse me?" A gruff voice came from behind her and she jumped. "Is that your truck a block back there, miss? Ah, well, it's Miss Hall."

The town warden! Mr. Gleeson was a funny little old guy, with ears that stuck out, but not someone to be quibbled with. She knew him as head of the Masonic lodge here in town too.

"My duty to intrude, I'm sorry to say, but why are you in here at a time when you'll need to use your headlights to git home? Might I ask?"

Ella was back on her heels, in a violation of a black-out rule. "Meeting a friend in need. I'll try to keep 'em off as much as I can on the way back." She was just glad it was not the town policeman. Hal Truitt had it in for anyone like Ella who had anything to do with the folk over in the Black section of town or, of course, anything to do with Lee Tingle.

"If we're seen, we could get shelled, you know," he said motioning out toward the bay and the coastline.

Anyone would deem that pretty unlikely by this point in the war, but Ella humored him. Standing, as they were, just near the historic Cannonball House here, which still held one of the cannonballs from the British bombardment of the town in the War of 1812—displayed where it ended lodged in the bricks of the house's outside wall next to the historic marker—she didn't feel she could argue.

Gleeson seemed to give her the benefit of the doubt and ambled on about his rounds. But Ella thought she would flee now—worried that Dieter might have been apprehended.

Dieter

But Dieter had been watching her with some amusement these past minutes from the shadowy side street next over, and now he let out a soft whistle.

When he stepped out just enough to be seen, his new lover darted to him. She began wagging her finger at him and scolding in a hushed and frightened tone. But she resisted only weakly when he pulled her into an embrace and in a moment their faces were buried in the nape of each other's necks.

She felt and smelled so good that Dieter made a grateful sound. For the past couple weeks, she had been "in his nose" as the saying went—intoxicating him again every time he breathed in the scent of her skin.

Reese

Back at the Hall farm, Reese was making popcorn. He had banked up the kitchen stove with wood and gotten out the big pan with the tin top.

He and Trevor were in a rush to get the popcorn made before their favorite show, *Lights Out,* came on. They were indeed going to turn out the lights and see how much fright they could take.

Dieter

In that moment, Dieter had drawn Ella into the alleyway within the block, a sort of back drive between the homes and buildings, and they could not stop kissing. Then she guided him into a sheltered, partly enclosed garden gazebo at the back of someone's lawn, as they yanked at each other's clothes in the darkness.

Reese

Reese had just poured the cooking oil in the hot, spattering pan when his friend reached across to help and knocked the bottle of oil. It spilled across the cook top of the oven's counter and splashed on the wall. Some of it poured down toward the oven's leaky old fire box and caught flame. The fire leapt up and across the oven and climbed up the wallpaper in an orange burst. Both boys screamed.

Dieter

Bright moonlight came crisscross through the lattice work of the little pergola hutch with its bench. The glow lit Ella's milky skin in diffused bluish diamond shapes as they joined into each other. And hard now, locked and rollicking, trying, in this place where they hid, not to make the old settee creak—Dieter held her with his arm that was farmer-tanned from the biceps down, and she wrapped her arms around his neck. Hard torsos undulating into each other, as they roiled together, her leaning partway back, knees in the air, until came the muffled flesh-and-blood version of a cannon's report and its equal softer receipt.

Reese

Reese remembered immediately where the big red fire blanket was stored under the table. He grabbed it and flung it open. "Help me," he shrieked at his friend. Together, jumping and thrusting, the boys covered the flames with the fire-retardant blanket and snuffed them out.

Ella

When they had caught their breath, Ella wiped sweat from Dieter's temple and laughed quietly, as he tenderly brushed hair back away from her face and kissed her cheek.

Reese

They had their hands on each other's shoulders, leaning on each other. "We did it," the two boys were saying—Reese wondering how much trouble they would catch. But they had put out the fire and saved the day.

Ella

"How will you get back?" Ella whispered to her lover.

But Dieter only murmured, wanting to stay in their warm clench, until at last they knew again the risk of lingering in this backyard and they detached and then put themselves back together, and stood and rocked gently against one another kissing more, still in the shelter of this arbor for which they were so thankful now, and he finally said, "Come, I will show you."

Back out in the alley, one side of which ran behind some of the stores on the main street, Dieter drew his bicycle out from behind a row of trash drums.

"All the way back to your camp? That's a good twenty mile, isn't it?"

He kissed her to hush her. "That is nothing."

"Well, I'm supposed to drive home without any lights on too, so there you have it," she said, hoping the brilliant moonlight would be enough, as they both chortled trying not to make any noise. Ella knew, though, that he dreaded having to go back to the camp.

"I've an idea," she said quietly. "Everett mentioned that a couple of the other prisoners assigned to work here at the cape have been overnighting at the fort. Right here. I'll ask him to see if he can fix it up for you too."

Dieter stilled. "This could work!" he said as loudly as a whisper would allow.

A dog started barking from somewhere down at the end of the block. Ella thought about Hale Truitt and how badly that policeman would deal with an AWOL German prisoner and what once-in-a-lifetime ammo it would give him to find Lee Tingle's woman with one.

"Mostly don't let them assign me any elsewhere each day," Dieter said. He explained that a newer sergeant of the guards there at the camp, who was angry and hateful to his Deutsch and Italian charges, had said he would put together another detachment to go spend their days raking the oil off the beaches— fuel residue that came from freighters and other ships that had been sunk by U-boats off the coast.

Ella felt her grasp on him loosen at this mention.

Dieter

Dieter did not tell her that he had openly refused the suggestion of the sergeant, who then replied that Dieter was perhaps the most appropriate person in the camp to be on his hands and knees scrubbing the beaches of the Delaware coast and if that was distasteful to him perhaps there were lots of excuses they could make to place him in solitary confinement there in the three-foot-thick cement bowels of the old battery that centered the POW camp.

The nightmare of solitary in that place, though, did not horrify Dieter as much as did the thought of combing through, and staring at, the flotsam on the beaches down along the Delaware ocean front.

Ella

But then it worked. Ella's proposition to Everett had born out, and she exhaled over the days that followed. Everett agreed to give it a try and got Dieter assigned for a few days, continuous, at Fort Miles.

And yet, Ella felt equal relief that they could find almost no time to steal away on the farm. All at once, the season was too busy, with help here for harvest and slaughtering and so much else, and Reese having days off for the cropping time. Too risky. And then the Army would arrive at the end of the day to at least spare Dieter the camp up at Milford and take him back to the cape.

On top of it all, Reese's radar was up. And his back. Her German had been divvying out too many To Do's around here, including to the boy.

Ella came upon the two of them in the farmyard, where Dieter was trying to hand Reese a scythe to get after the weeds around the out-buildings. Reese was standing with his arms crossed and feet spread, refusing. But Ella was in no mind for this and she gave the scythe to her boy, who dragged it after him sullenly as he stalked away.

And so the following days passed until another night when Ella lay turning in her sheets, thoughts of her trysts with Dieter making her want to go out back and pump cold water on herself, when—

She thought she heard a sound below the window. Then again. "*Pssst.*"

She rose to see a figure below. Someone out there! She leaned into the screen. "Guten Abend," came the whisper. *Dieter down in the yard ...*

Escaped again! He waved to her and blew her a kiss.

She knew that a smart woman would shoo him away, but instead she moved like a breath of air through the hallway, where she paused to hear Reese breathing deeply in his sleep. She closed his bedroom door silently, and then tiptoed down the stairs and out.

With no wait for permission, her big muscular lover engulfed her in his arms. She could do nothing but let herself fold into his wide chest. "How?" she breathed, but he covered her mouth playfully with his hand as they sought a place—until the only thing they could think to do was to slip quietly into the cab of her truck.

The base at the cape was easy to sneak out of, he explained, since it ran openly into the scrubby pine woods and tidal wetlands. He had walked out of their bunk as if to the latrine, and then across some roads and through the dunes, until he could pick up the rail line, which he had followed the bed of cautiously, crossing into town at the rail bridge over the canal, which by luck was not drawn, and then light-footing it the rest of the way here down the road. His shirt clung to him, and she could feel and smell his sweat, after his dash across the distance from town.

Ella had not felt anything like this since the first weeks in which she and Lee had found one another and consummated their love over and over on the sly. But she was not, in the eyes of the law or the Lord, a married woman, she told herself again this night. Which was fortunate because she felt none of the will that would come with that. And for the next hour, in the front seat of the truck, she and Dieter did all of the things that lovers can do for one another when they can't quite lie together. Nothing failed in that way—even as she kept an eye towards the house for any signs that Reese stirred—and afterwards, they sat closely in the dark, each curled into the other, muted for *another* hour or so that crossed so far beyond their carnal needs that all at once she said, "You must go." He had to reverse his arduous trip and make sure he was back in his bunk well before first light.

For the few hours of that remained after Dieter's midnight visit, Ella expected to sleep deeply, but dreams plagued her. First, her walking after Reverend Rightmyer down the beach but unable to catch up as she called to him. Then Lee and Lida dancing arm in arm. Finally, she woke from a nightmare of some stupid young trigger-happy MP, who had been left frustrated and stateside by all the war's action, marching toward her farm with townsmen carrying shot-guns and hunting rifles. Torches!

Ella staggered downstairs, glanced at the newspaper from yesterday, and was reminded again that sentiment was still strong to deal differently with the German POWs. The war in Europe was at its costly worst these weeks and months. The fighting in Italy and France and Belgium was terrible. The allies were losing thousands daily as the Wehrmacht threw everything forward then backstepped desperately over and over.

But inland, near Georgetown, Delaware, the Army had opened a camp for another five hundred German soldiers. And right here on the outskirts of Lewes, they had just turned the old Civilian Conservation Corp camp into a new POW facility. She saw captive Germans working in road gangs and many places, now.

Why, she'd even heard the resentment from Levotas. "You know what I seen? I seen it in dis very town. Heard about it from up Milford way too," her hired hand said about the Germans. "How come those bunch 'llowed in restaurants and such where my kind ain't? Prisoners can come through the front do'. Don't have to sit in the back, neither. Now you know that ain't right!"

No, it wasn't but nothing was right during this wartime.

Dieter had been standing next to her last week when Levotas said it and he had as much trouble as she did coming up with an answer. He could only look down at his feet.

"Well, that ain't any different than it was before the war, now is it?" Ella had said impatiently to her long-time helper.

This morning, though, she waited till a respectable time and was fortunate to catch Everett on the phone when he could speak freely.

"Can't you make it so that he can just stay here? At least sometimes," she asked, squeezing the receiver so hard that it shook, not caring anymore if she shocked him.

"Special treatment is out of the question," Everett said. She knew the chance she was pushing him toward.

"It would make everyone's life easier, Ev." To try letting him overnight here.

"Everyone's but mine, El. It just idn't done."

When Ella's phone rang a few days later, Everett started out with, "Look my cousin, since we were kids, I haven't seen you as happy as I have these last few months."

She supposed he meant "in love," or suspected it, but didn't want to admit to having any knowledge or even hunches on that. "Here's what I done," he said and explained that as of today the powers that be at the Milford camp understood Dieter still to be assigned and reporting back daily to Fort Miles, while the powers that be at the base here understood that Dieter had been re-assigned and reporting back daily to the new CCC camp at the edge of town.

"Let's try it and see if we can get away with it, at least for the harvest season," Everett whispered over noise and voices that Ella could hear in the officers' quarters.

"I love you, Everett," she said, as they hung up.

And so began Dieter's stay on the farm—his round-the-clock-residence with them. Ella set up a cot for him in the big shed out back. She told Reese that they'd gotten permission for him to stay with them for the rest of the farm season. It was a special favor, and so he was to tell *no one*.

At last, the danger was less for them to find one another, and on nights she could give in to a kind of lust that she had never felt before. She could go to him easily, as the rest of the world slept. What no one else knew didn't hurt anyone, she told herself, even being able to imagine, in those inky nocturns, that the rest of the world didn't exist—or care.

Yes, this arrangement gave them the chance to give into their pleasure fully, even too much, but ...

Soon, she had to confide with someone. When Clarissa finally called her by phone, on leave up in Philly for the day, it tumbled out. She swore her friend to blood-oath secrecy, even knowing that with this woman she didn't need to.

Clarissa was struck speechless and yet not as scandalized or aghast as Ella might have expected or that she could detect in the silences over the phone line. Her friend understood! She and the other volunteer women were surrounded by robust young men at the shipyard.

"In this life," Clarissa said, "sometimes you have to seize something for yourself and just *have* it."

Something had changed in her friend, and Ella wondered what.

"Just don't get caught," Clarissa said.

Sundays, Ella mostly stayed away from church services. She knew that her absence might draw attention, but she was not feeling much in a church way these days.

Still, she had gone up upon a Friday to volunteer in the kitchen and the pantry. Some of the other ladies who helped and who lived along Savannah Road said that they could hear the prisoners at the CCC camp singing at night. Going by that way, heading home at dusk that evening, Ella had slowed, with her windows down, and sure-as-heck heard it too, coming from the barracks. She pulled over to the side of the road, just across from the fence, and turned off her engine.

The singing came to her plain as could be, through open windows not a hundred feet away. It was sad and beautiful both—rough but catchy too, even rollicking at moments. All in German of course, and she could not understand the words, but the chorus carried the name Lili Marlene.

Then they sang that part again in English, about wanting to be with a girl named Lili Marlene.

That very night, the sound of the men's voices still in her mind prompted her back out into the warm mid-September darkness behind her house. Against her faltered will power, as always.

When she padded under the stars to the shed, Dieter took her hands, where he sat on the edge of his cot, jokingly complaining about missing his beer allocation up at Camp Saulsbury. Her smile before her German, though, did not linger, as she thought of the brief note she had received earlier that day ... from Lee ... She knew from all the news that his 5th Army was stalled out in fierce fighting along what they were calling the German "Gothic Line" in central Italy.

She had not heard from him in so long ... The only words that told her anything about his situation were these:

> The Germans have set new lines to the north and the fighting is some-
> thing fierce. We're trying to get up into the mountains with the Brits.
> We're ████████████████████████████ ...

His last couple of sentences were blacked out, but she had read that the American and British divisions were attempting to move up into the mountains, and she guessed that's what he had written here.

She was a bad person who needed to end her lark with one last full indulgence in it she declared *again.* And so, feeling drunk without have taken a drink, Ella surprised her Herr Dieter with a bottle of their own elderberry wine that she had found in the basement and brought along.

They indeed drank, and then tumbled together till at last their parts wouldn't work anymore. Yes, Ella took her own good time to sin this night, and then fell back with such a swirl in her head as she wondered if she had ever felt.

"Just because a war is going on should not determine who should love who," she murmured in a lush dream-driven hush, convincing herself that she was paraphrasing her rector at the church and that she was making any sense.

"We should run away," Dieter said, rousing her with the thought as he gathered her again in his arms.

"Do you have no one you would be leaving behind?" she asked, realizing how little she had asked him about his life back in his country.

She felt him stiffen. "No one left that matters in this way," he said.

"Yes, then, we should get in the pickup and just drive," she said, with her eyes half open and a sense of falling softly, floating, like a body settling slowly to the bottom of the cool bay. "Leave all of this behind."

"Ja, take all of the tankards of petrol we had for September put them in back of the truck and motor west."

"You could dress like an American and become one," she heard herself say.

"I am very good at pretending American," he said, suddenly removing all hint of his accent so thoroughly and convincingly that it surprised Ella.

"Take Reese and just vanish … Become new people," she said, her head spinning.

"When?"

"Soon maybe," she said, but trying to quiet him so their voices would not carry across the farmyard.

Before they slumbered in each other's arms, she whispered to him about the German song she had heard.

"Lili Marlene, ja, of course," Dieter said and then explained that it was the most popular song with the men, and among many on both sides of the war.

All at once, he began to sing it quietly in her ear.

He was *singing.* In German in her ear. She could not understand the words but it lilted and she drifted, transported. Oh, how fully she had surrendered in this moment, flowing along to a song about a girl named Lili Marlene.

"What does it mean?" she asked in a voice almost too soft to hear, her body folded against his. He sang it again, as he translated, halting but steady, about a soldier standing near a barracks and a gate, under a lantern, where he dreamed about meeting a girl named Lili Marlene once again and forever.

Reese

The next morning, Reese stood on their back stoop, and hollered out, "Mom?" Then he cupped his hands to his mouth and, looking out back again, yelled, *"Mom!"*

He was going to miss the bus. Where was she?

Suddenly, she emerged in a hurry from the big tool shed, wrapping her robe around her quick, and fast walking up to the house in her bare feet. She looked a mess, her hair sticking out crazy, her eyes all baggy.

"I'm sorry, honey. I— I had to speak to Dieter quick first, and get things organized for the morning." She was mumbling.

And in that moment, he at last knew what a terrible liar she was.

The hurricane of 1944 was about to hit. It whipped up the Delmarva coast with 150 mph winds, and the warning had been sent ahead.

Out of school, Reese spoke little to his mother, only doing as she said, running around shuttering, and helping to lock up, and put away, and tie down.

As the full blow finally arrived, his mother hollered to him to get down in the basement with her, where she had set up for them to wait it out. But Reese stood in the back hall, looking toward the big shed out back, with his hand on the phone.

What if he just went ahead called the police station to say that a POW had used this storm to run off—and that he was loose here, and that Reese could see him darting about and hiding among the farm buildings?

The wind began to sound like one of those trains you could stand next to as they passed through town here and out toward the cape with military cargo. The windows rattled and he could feel the house bend and groan.

"Git down here!" his ma shouted.

He knew the number for the town switchboard. Even in this blow, they'd come out here and cuff up or shoot an escapee.

Out back, he saw a bushel basket fly across the farmyard. That main tool shed, where Dieter was almost surely hunkered down, seemed to sway, its corrugated metal roof rippling.

But at last, Reese let his hand slip back away from the phone, just before his mother's head popped up from the basement steps and ordered him down.

And over the night, it passed.

Out back was clear and bright the next morning. Only a couple trees uprooted, but it left Reese home for days on account of the power outage.

And just that fast came their prisoner of war Herr Meister lieutenant-commander Dieter Schneider ordering Reese about, making him do pick-up, and help haul things to here and there, all about the farm for clean-up from the storm. And now that German, who had tried to be a friend of his but was also a stranger and an enemy soldier, and who thought he could do anything he wanted here, including on a cot at night, was about to ask him to wrassle and wheelbarrow sacks of feed so they could be torn into and scooped out of at a poultry shed that no one had asked him to build out so big in the first place, and—

Well that was it! By the third day of it all, Reese stormed back to the house, and stuffed his rucksack with a blanket, overshirt, crackers, can of peanuts, jug of water, a pocket knife, a cap, matches, and other supplies. He was barely able to balance on his bike as he escaped down the road with his fishing pole and tackle bag lashed on.

The power had just come back, so he would miss the comedy of Amos & Andy tonight on the radio, but those were the kind of things a ranger and a guard and a watchman and an Indian brave had to give up sometimes.

He got along the road littered with branches, and at the turn kept on down a sandy gravel lane that he knew so well—to a foot path, where he got off and walked his bike in a hurry past shrubs and marsh grasses. Would it still be there after the storm surge? On that little hidden landing was where he and Poppa Lee always kept it ... Reese hadn't used their rowboat since this summer when he took his pals crabbing.

But there it be, partway down the bank! Upside down, as he had left it, but now with its prow down in the water. Saved only because he lashed lines to the gunnels and staked them. Pop would be proud.

Yet, he was but one person, he suddenly realized, as he tried to flip the water-logged vessel over. "Sheiße!" he hollered at this heavy old wooden scow. The curse word he had learned from Dieter. *Shit!*

He tried again, and was able to get it almost far enough up to roll over but then had to drop it again. If he could not get across this way to Cape Henlopen and the fort and base there, then he would go with his back-up plan. He would hitchhike, like everyone did these days, down to Rehoboth Beach and live under the boardwalk at the beach, if it was still there.

But with one more great shout and his arms and legs driving upward and extending all the way, he managed to turn the boat over. He pushed it into the water and oared his way across to the other side of the inland waterway where he once again pulled the boat up as far as he could and hid it under the scrub pines. Then he hiked toward the sea. His new life as an independent patroller living by himself, hidden here by the oceanside until the end of the war, would begin today.

He navigated southeast, with the help of his compass. When he came to the main base road—set up, he knew from his spy mission here two years ago, to cover the mile or less between the two main batteries—he approached it on all fours, his backpack clanking and sloshing around. When he was sure all was clear, he darted across and then, within earshot of the surf on the beach, found a perfect cupped alcove in the dunes, hung over by the loblolly pines, protected and hidden. There, he set his camp.

The first order of survival in the wilderness was food, so he took his fishing gear and sack of dried chicken skins for bait and went straight to the beach. Walking north, he could see, up near the top of the cape, the Great Dune, or the Walking Dune, as his science teacher called it because the constant sea breezes whipped the sand from the tall dune landward and caused it to migrate several feet a year. He had seen pictures of the grand old lighthouse from colonial times that had finally been undermined by the moving sands here this century and had fallen into the sea.

But catching nothing, Reese moved south along the beach to find a better place to cast. All at once he noticed something sticking to his shoes. Along this section of the beach ... Balls of tar. From the American fuel ships that had been sunk!

Damn these German skunks, like the one back there, all of them trying to ruin his bayside world. Now he knew why he had come here ... From a farm invaded and a mother acting like someone else. Setting up as a sentry and frontiersman here was all a boy could do. It mattered not what that Ella woman thought.

After a night trying to sleep, rolled up in his blanket, it was time to recommence his job of fisherman and lookout, walking the dunes to find German agents sneaking onto the beach. Venturing down along the strand again—but not too far so that he would be spotted by the Herring Point battery—Reese scavenged for finds along the waterline. In the days after a big storm, who knew what might have washed up! His grandpa had sworn that when he was a kid, people used to find gold coins from the wreck of the DeBraak along this stretch.

Reese was more hoping that the mullet might have started to run. He had a small hand-throw net that he could use to at least get a few of them and—

Suddenly, he slowed when he spotted two figures approaching him. He thought to dash and hide back up in the dunes, but then they did not look like soldiers. Smaller. Other boys?

He would not run, as they came toward him. Sure enough, he was now approached by two of the older boys from school! Some of the ones who had given him such a hard time in the past. Part of Roscoe Steeves' posse.

Well, at least it told him that school was probably out again today.

"What are you doing here, Tingle?" Tanner said.

"Watching out for enemy."

"Yeah? You? Thought you were a German lover."

"Plenty of Krauts for you to watch over back at your own place, right?" Vic said.

Reese's face reddened so, it felt like it would explode. But he explained that he had snuck out to the shoreline to rough it out here and keep a look-out all up and down the beach for infiltrators.

"Why, that's what we're doing too," Tanner said.

Reese kept talking at them about all he and they had seen, including the Army encampments here and then about the gulls and the terns diving just off the beach on the schools of baitfish in the becalmed ocean, which meant that beneath were almost surely bluefish and perhaps stripers or even sea trout.

But the other boys had seen the tar balls in the surf too, and the three stood and debated whether the oil was from sub sinkings—because those had slacked off—or the wreck of the big tanker that had beached itself on Rehoboth a few months earlier.

Finally, Vic said, "All right, Private Tingle, we will accept you back as a patriot for now." Then they made him recite off a special sea-watch pledge they had made up. Reese followed them as their unit beachcombed further up for a while, until all three came to a standstill at the same instant. Before them, washing about in the surf, was a child's shoe. They looked down at it in silence, not sure whether to touch it or—

Suddenly, something huge came toward them from the side of their vision. Rushing at them from the dunes and then slowing to a trot came a man on a horse, with a uniform on. One of the Coast Guard Mounted Patrol!

"I think our jig is up," Reese said to his comrades as the officer approached. Sitting way up high above them, he barely gave them time to explain what they were doing, as if he already knew.

"I need to take you boys up on out of here," he said, nice enough but stern, about their having snuck out to a shoreline that was part of an off-limits Army-Navy base. "You cain't be here."

They pointed to the shoe, and he dismounted and plucked it out of the foam quick, grim, silent—gave it a look and put it in his saddle bag. "I can only take you," he said, pointing to Reese, the smallest one in the bunch, and told the other two boys that he'd send a jeep for them. None of them knew whether to be scared or excited.

Next thing, the mounted patrolman lifted Reese up in the saddle behind him. Reese saluted his two fellows sea-watchers as the mountie turned the horse. The patrolman took Reese to his little camp and allowed him to collect his things, and then Reese had to explain where his rowboat was. The coast guard rider was kind enough to go back through the woods and set him home, but Reese's face turned gray as he rowed across the canal. To go back under the command of the submariner who had come ashore and annexed their farm and his mother? He would not!

30

Ella

Only when Reese had not come home after that night of his vanishing last month did Ella realize why he did as he did. But with a child missing, the whyfors hadn't mattered.

She had tried to keep calm, knowing how resourceful the boy was. She had gone to the Lewes police station at dawn the next morning, where they had sagely asked her where the kid liked to get away to on his own. Hearing the bay and the canal and inlet and seashore, they had put out the notice to Fort Miles, which had relayed it to the mounted patrol, which in just a few hours had located him with some other boys and retrieved them. How long he might have tried to stretch this runaway she did not know.

Ella endeavored not to make much of it with him. He had retreated behind the closed door of his bedroom, and she dared not punish him at this point.

She let him be, and then, as always, shut and darkened her home at nightfall. She had not felt right having Dieter up to the house for anything other than the occasional meal. And on the second night that her son had refused dinner, she'd had trouble sleeping once more. And she had been excited by Clarissa's call.

"They've relieved me of my position up here," her girlfriend said over the phone.

"What?"

Fired? Let go from the WAVES at the shipyard?

"I couldn't hide it anymore," Clarissa said.

"Hide what?"

"My baby bump."

"Girlfriend!"

She must indeed have had a nice last-minute send-off and lie-down with her husband, Ella concluded. Four months or so ago? But her Rand was now out to sea, already aboard the destroyer *Davis*...

Still, why hadn't she at least tried to get word to him?

"I wanted to make sure this one was for real first," was the excuse Clarissa gave, hurriedly.

"God is great!" Ella had belted out. "Forget about all that up there, girl. They'll get along. Just get you home here, where we'll take care of you."

It had felt good to tell someone to just forget about this damn war! Especially the next evening, as a chilly October night descended and she sat at the light of a small, sheltered candle, trying again to pen a letter to Lee, wondering what she could say sincere that her conscience would permit her.

The newspaper reported that Lee's 5th Army had captured Monte Battaglia on the Gothic Line in Italy. Her pencil hung in the air. She wasn't clear on whether some of her earlier notes had gotten through to him. If they had, then ... all she could do again was to tell him that she was in awe of his army's doings. But even talking about how well the farm had done this season seemed—

Bang, bang, BANG! Ella jumped. Someone was pounding on their front door. She had waited for the day that her confidences were betrayed and Officer Hale Truitt came and arrested her for harboring a fugitive or just went out back and shot Dieter. She moved quickly through the front hallway. Truitt's young brother had been lost paratrooping into Holland on something called the Market Garden Operation. All the town had grieved with the Truitts, and she had paid her respects to the man at the service at St. Peter's, but she believed that Hale was not altogether right-minded from it at the moment.

As she threw the latch, she told herself that whatever came through that door she deserved.

A lone figure. Official looking in the half-light, with his cap and epaulets on his shoulders, but then she recognized the neighborhood warden. Mr. Gleeson again—that same irksome little spy of a fellow who had upbraided her last month for driving into town after dark.

"There's a light from your window," he barked.

A black-out violation. She relaxed a little.

She could see the man's car running with no lights out by road.

"I'm sorry. I had a candle burning in the kitchen. I'll be sure—"

"No, up there," he snapped, pointing to their second-story window that marked Reese's room.

"I don't know why..." she said, as she turned and stepped back in. She looked up the stairwell and could just make Reese out, peering from the darkness of his room.

As she rudely kept the warden standing on her front step on a night that had gotten chill and gusty, she called up to her son. "Were you burning a light?"

"My flashlight."

All at once, she feared he had been signaling the warden.

"I'm sorry," she said quickly to the man and put her hand on the door to show she would like to close it. "I'll see to it."

"Mind the rules, please," he croaked, but a bit softer, as he turned and left.

Ella shut the door and breathed out, all but hearing how Dieter would probably be snoring out back now.

As she went up the steps, Reese tried to close himself in his room again. But she put her foot on the door just in time.

"Why?" she asked gently. "Why did you have your flashlight on? I'm not angry. I just want to know, since our farmhouse can be seen from far away."

"Reading my book, for school," he said. Then he mumbled, "Thought I was all the way under the covers."

"Very well. Please go to sleep now."

"Why do you always want me to make sure I'm asleep so early?" he said.

"...Just read your book in the morning. And we will keep this open," she said, leaving his door ajar.

But after that, Ella didn't want to toss in bed again, thinking about the way that their neighbor lady, Lida Crouch, eyeballed their spread all the time. She feared the bitter old wasp was honing in on it all.

Downstairs, Ella watched the searchlights on the horizon, then finally crept back up and into Reese's room. She got a surge in her stomach when suddenly she could not see him in his bed. She tiptoed quickly around pulled back some of the covers and found him sleeping with the flashlight turned on again under a tent of pillows, comforter, and sheet.

She clicked the flashlight back off—darn the rascal—and gently slid his book from his hand. *All Quiet on the Western Front.* She knew of this book but had not read it herself.

Sick of all that comes with war, she wanted to hurl the little tome out the window, but instead placed it on his desk. As she did, she spotted the report he had been so anxious about writing on this reading assignment. She slid the black curtains back from the window before the desk, so that the moonlight came in.

Yes, here was his little essay, started at least. Partly written. Stopped where his pencil lay.

> *I think this book shows that soldiers on both sides of the fight are kind of the same. The Germans and their enemies were all humans beings. They are stuck in a bad situation and trying to save themselves or get by the best they can.*

> *Sometimes they do right, but sometimes they*

He had stopped there and Ella tried not to imagine how he might complete that sentence. She closed the curtain quickly. He must let her check this assignment before he took it back to school. And she only hoped that the understanding she saw in it would help him keep his lip buttoned to the world.

Reese

On a Sunday, Reese looked up through the window-well of their basement. Before him, a note to his father and an envelope for it. Yes, he had easily copied the way he needed to address it from his mother's letters—and he knew how to get a stamp up town and drop this in the post there. Writing it this hour, he had said every dumb thing he could think of, about how their pumpkin patch had put forth this fall, about the tautog fishing doing so well around the sea wall this month, and how a boat parade was to be put on here for Halloween. He and his chums might dress as pirates and row their skiff into it, pretending to be Captain Kidd, who had come to Lewes way back when and maybe buried a chest in the dunes.

As he wrote that last part—and worked to keep his promise to himself to stop there—he looked up and out toward where he could see their front step and the neighbor ladies starting to come to their front door. His mother's church circle was gathering at their house today, and it was part of the reason he'd been sent down here to occupy himself.

Among them, he saw Mrs. Crouch, toting a canvas bag, which meant the ladies were bringing baked goods to share, which meant he would at least get some fine pickin's when it was done.

Yes, his mother had directed him this hour to the basement, first to start up and stoke their old furnace, which they used only sometimes and then only if they had coal in the coldest part of the winter. Reese didn't understand why they needed it when the wood stove was running fine and hot upstairs in the living room where the ladies gathered on this chilly late October day.

But his mom had made darn sure that both he and Dieter were scarce.

Earlier today, back in the barn, he'd stuck his head out of the loft and heard the way his mother and the German tried to boss each other, like an old ma and pa. His mother had told the German to spend these hours today at the back of their property. She wanted him to make an inventory of which trees in their wooded acres at the back were large enough that they could cull them and send them to the lumber mill for money. She asked him to mark them, but then he had countermanded her and said the day back there must first be spent clearing two trees that had fallen into the field during the hurricane storm last month. They'd had to drive the harvester around them, because there had been no time to remove them these past weeks.

Forgetting who was boss of this place, Dieter had also ordered his ma earlier to place a notice at the high school for more help. Now, on weekends, they had one of the oldest boys from the football team come for an hourly wage to lend a hand. So, today, that sub-lieutenant of a sub had taken the older boy and the tractor and the wagon and the two-man saw and axes and chains and the lunch pails that his ma had prepared and disappeared over the rise.

But Reese had been pointed down to the darn basement. Here, his mother had stashed his entire collection of comic books when he had lost privileges for them, on account of having run away last month. She had tossed them sloppily into a couple milk crates, and now sent him down to those boxes, telling him to straighten them up and stay out of the way.

Reese spread all the comics out on a worktable and put them in piles by date and series. Captain America fighting Hitler and the Nazis here. Nighthawk, the team that flew their skyrocket planes to fight dictators, on this stack. And, of course, Superman, who was strong enough to win the war all by himself and fly down and punch out a whole army of Germans in one swoop if he wanted to. Reese thought of the years of saving to buy each one of these, and all at once wondered if he cared to collect them anymore.

As he worked, Reese could hear the ladies talking upstairs. Their voices came down through the living room floor's open heating grate that was in this cellar's ceiling just above him. Reese went over and looked up through the opening. Spying was one of his best skills, so he climbed up on a big old wooden ordnance box underneath the grate and could see the side of one of the living room chairs and a bit of the lady's dress who was sitting in it and her handbag next to it.

"The older girl who used to live across the street from us was a passenger on the *Carolina* when she was sunk out here in '18 by one of them bastards," someone was saying. Reese was surprised to hear a curse word. "When she set foot back on the cape here, she was tired and hungry and scared and barely alive!"

Above his head, he could hear Mrs. Heinz, a church lady from in town, piping up too. "The way I hear it, they always come up and shoot warning shots over the bow to make sure the lifeboats get filled before they torpedo her."

"Damn if they do!"

Another cuss!

"Now, ladies," he heard his mother say.

"Well, at least they do after the first torpedo, before they blast her the rest of the way and send her to the bottom," Mrs. Heinz corrected herself.

"Mostly."

Reese wasn't at all sure which ladies were talking, or how they had got on this subject, or why he even cared to listen to blabber like this that would just make him madder.

"Yes, I always remember hearing that at the *Carolina's* sinking, the U-boat crew came out and waved a cheerful auf wiedersehen from the deck of the sub before they put 'er down and then submerged again."

"My pappa was on the oil tanker *Pratt* when she hit the mines that the Huns left out there at the mouth of the bay in that war."

Then everyone was talking at once.

"We all heard the patrol boats firing after them that day when we was kids."

Reese had a hard time following all that was said and told himself that this old-time stuff didn't matter.

"Well, that's in the past," he heard his mother call out, trying to bring some order to the room. "I say we have to concentrate on the here-and-now, and make the best of what's right before us, in this time."

"I'd say you certainly have," he heard, in Mrs. Crouch's voice, which seemed to make an awkward quiet up there.

Then another round of talking from the ladies who had farms, all saying they'd assigned the running of theirs to someone, a nephew or brother or even a neighboring farmer—with Crouch claiming her one son still remaining here took care of it, though Reese knew dang well he had quit his job at the fishery and worked most of his time now at the clam plant. She was getting by with Levotas assigned there almost every day, for some blasted reason, making Reese's own chores the more.

"Why," his mother suddenly asked, calling out above them all, "do any of us need to title a man with charge of our farm? Even when it's us doing most of the bidding and sweating—and us holding down the place?"

As his mother went on, bragging upstairs about the part that women were playing in the war effort and on farms, Reese stepped down and finished his letter to his pop, feeling at last like he actually said something.

> *I decided, Pop, I aim to defend our place here. Just like you're defending the world. I'll figure out a way to protect it, till you get back here to do it yourself.*

He knew it was bad trouble-making to say anything more than that, so he folded the letter, but feeling hot under his collar. Above him, he could tell that his mother had probably gotten the room's full attention again, as he heard her spout out with, "As far as I'm concerned, I am head of my farm and will remain so until further notice."

That drew claps from a couple and, from what he could tell, sniffs or surprised silence from others.

Reese suddenly stepped back up. "That's a lie!" he yelled through the grate.

There was an "Oh!" and some other startled sounds from the ladies.

"There's someone else running this farm," Reese called up through the floor. A German! And he—"

"Well, there's that youngster of mine," his mother said quick and loud, over his voice so all his words got drowned out, "playing tricks on people again." And that fast, he heard ma Ella clip-clomp over to the grate. "I suppose he thinks he's the man of the farm and that's what he means," she said, putting on a fake laugh. "Let's just let him play where he loves to downstairs while we talk."

Reese opened his mouth to correct that, but a throw-rug suddenly landed on the grate, blocking and blacking out his view above.

Reese got down slowly off the box again and smacked one of his piles of comics, sending them flying onto the cellar floor.

She was a terrible fibber!

Lying about things was not her talent!

When he'd cooled off, Reese snuck upstairs. He stuck his head around the corner and, when he was sure the ladies weren't looking, grabbed a brownie off the table and then climbed the steps up to his room, trying not to let them creak. Last thing he wanted was for his mother to grab him and put him on display before all these crows!

And in fact, his mother had told him to dress in school clothes this afternoon so that he could make just such an appearance. But he had not! Instead, he went to his desk, still in his old khaki pants and torn-up sweater, and pulled out another sheet of lined writing paper. With his pencil, he wrote:

Dear Mrs. Crouch,

It's not true what my mother said. Our farm is under the command of a boat-shooting German officer. <u>And he's here all the time.</u>

Yours truly,

Reese Tingle

He snuck back down the steps to the foyer by the front door and slipped the note into Mrs. Crouch's canvas cake-carrying bag.

31

Ella

At her kitchen table, Ella slid a cup of hot chocolate across to Dieter. It was one of his favorites, made up with whole milk from their mooing Elsie's and Daisy's and other kine out back, but also in the way that Dieter had showed her with a dash of cinnamon and nutmeg. She had been able to swap some ration coupons and actually get a box of cocoa powder. Outside, a cool fall rain fell, but Dieter had split wood these past weeks and built them a larger box for it in here. He rose and banked up their stove before returning to her.

They were poring over a catalogue of fancy new tractors that the extension office had provided her. Another loan had come through to them from the government program that had been expanded for the war

"This one will go best in the wet soil," he said, pointing to a spanky new Ford with big fat tires. They both liked it and excitedly voted it the one, with a squeeze of each other's hand.

With Reese safely in school, they could spend time like this. As Ella began filling out the paperwork for new equipment, Dieter, a man usually always in motion, sat contentedly instead today and gushed over some of the other farm implements on the pages.

She had gotten cross with him only once this week. On the shelves in the basement, she had been stacking jars of canned food that he had helped her put by. He had gone up to the kitchen to bring more crates down when she heard a knock at the front door.

Darn if that German had not gone straight to the front hall and answered the door. God bless, it had only been the deliveryman from the notary, dropping off bank papers for her to go over.

With the other part of the loan and with the profitable poultry production they had now, Ella had bought more land. A forty-acre parcel adjoining their farm just south. Her father had talked about that piece of property off and on for as long as she could remember. He and Lee had hemmed and hawed on it, worried it might get too wet sometimes, flooding after storms, but it hadn't, and Dieter told Ella he could do some grading and deepen the swale that ran across the middle of it, and so the thing was done—on no one else's idea, decision, or say-so but hers.

At the door with the notary, Dieter had merely taken the packet from the man and, in the most straight-up flat-out Sussex Country drawl, said, "I thank you kindly, sir."

"Don't ever do that again," she said to Dieter.

Nothing seemed to come of his mistake, though, thank goodness—the clerk having taken him for a local.

The God-fearing Mrs. Lida Crouch, though, had become a different story. All Ella's instincts told her that Lida's understanding of Dieter's movements, or lack of them, had become clearer.

And so when the day came, Ella just stood and took it. She had been before her house with the high-school boy, instructing him on raking and cleaning up the front and out along the road when she saw Lida marching toward them purposeful.

Upon her face something had changed.

Without a hello, and dressed in her gray stiff-collared old-fashioned dress, she said, "I know about your ... *arrangement* here."

Ella remained motionless, wondering how much Lida did know.

"You have the German as much in residency here as anything else."

Ella looked back poker faced.

"I will somehow manage to keep my effrontery to myself, since you continue to send help my way," Lida said.

With great effort and hoping she didn't flush, Ella remained expressionless.

"If you will not prevail upon your cousin at the fort to see clear to provide me the same amount of ... farm help that you have, then I think it only fair that you continue to send Levotas Clark my way—each and every day now."

In not so many words, she demanded help from Levotas nearly full time, or as full time as Levotas ever got, at Ella's expense—or else.

Ella had an impulse to tell the woman to go pack sand, but reminded herself of Lida's life-long affection for Lee and how close to the bone this skillful busybody was coming now.

"Very well," Ella replied, but wondering how long it would satisfy. "If it's something I can do to continue to help you, then, as you say. I'll do it. And for *that reason.*" To cover the horror and danger she felt, though, she gave the woman her back and went inside.

For the expense of this set-up with Levotas, she continued to use the part of Lee's pay that he was able to send home. It would have been more if he had just damn married her official and could declare her and Reese as dependents! But, yes, that's how it lay. Lord help and forgive her—that's what she used Lee's war pay for, to bribe a neighbor not to gossip about her set-up here as she colluded and co-mingled with the enemy—with Ella trying not to tremble and sicken each and every time she put the cash in the good and gnarled Black hands of her innocent, unknowing, and confused helper.

The following week, as she sat with Dieter in unseasonably warm November sun out in back of their farm at the new picnic table he had made for them, came a moment when she stopped wondering if she could ever reclaim herself—or if she cared to. All were better off for what she and fate had created here.

Lida stuck to her agreement, stopped her snoopiness for the moment, and remained in quietude. Meanwhile they prospered, on a farm worked hard and proper, with her always as the final decision-maker.

And now, in this last Indian summer warmth, she and Dieter rubbed their feet together under the table and smiled at each other. She had put the end-of-season apples in the press and made a cider. Dieter had requisitioned a bottle of spirits. From where, he would not say. Ella was not sure if it was gin or brandy, but he put a generous glug in each of their cider glasses and pronounced, "Apfelschnaps!"

Thanks to salvation from above, Reese had joined the after-school sports club. So her sprite of a boy was occupied and, thankfully, tired at the end of the day. It all made it easier that very night, for her to slip back out to Dieter at a reasonable hour. The shed had no heat and she was not sure what they would do about that by the end of the month, but they had found a better bed for him—a frame and single mattress. Ella slipped under the mound of old quilts and covers, as Dieter finished his work outside.

A grand harvest moon had come up like a giant peach above the ocean this eve and later had climbed up to become a silver dollar in the sky. The brightness of the fall night came through the door as Ella could hear Dieter moving bags of fertilizer up against the outside of the shed. With the cash flow they had and all the advising from the state ag people, they were buying and using more NPK, and Ella had already seen the results in some of their totals this season.

As Dieter worked, Ella could hear him whistling. She listened and recognized his tune—"By the Light of the Silvery Moon," a wonderful song played on the piano and sung by Fats Waller that they heard on a radio station that played some of the Black music. Dieter had gotten up a fascination for American music and couldn't get enough these days.

"I'm coming," he called softly to her, his voice finishing the universe she had in this moment.

Ella laid back, reminding herself that other families got several letters a week from their man in the war. Ella and Reese were lucky to get one a month, with a few lines that were only about war. She realized, that with Lee vanished to his own circumstances—not communicating and not once in the better part of two years saying that he missed them—she had faded away into her own life just the same.

"I tell my man Coco let you slide on in, but you know that you gots sit in the balcony—now, mind," Levotas said to Ella and Dieter.

He had invited them to slip into a Black musical show to listen, and Dieter had jumped at it. It was the kind of gesture that was long in coming from their POW's sometimes nemesis. Ella's lover acted humble in his acceptance.

The "git down" as Levotas referred to it was to take place at the Happy Day Club, a small band house over in the Black section of town. Yes, the little neighborhood was a part of Lewes, but its own place—just a few blocks really, on the northwest side of town that Ella had not got back to much since the war had started, just a few times to pick up her helper there. Not many white people frequented that part.

"Performing is Cab Calloway, I do believe," Levotas said. "You know him?"

Ella's mouth dropped open. Of course she knew him. She had heard of him since she was a child. And loved his music from the radio. She wondered if this was true. Here in their little town?

"He coming down from the Cotton Club," Levotas said, with some obvious pride. "In Harlem," he added bringing his chin up in the air. "Touring down 'long the coast only in a few Black joints, to get away from it all."

Ella had heard of a couple performers who, just the same and just as unlikely, had stopped through the Happy Day Club here over recent years, including Lena Horne, she believed.

"Goln be some wild jazz, now ..." Levotas warned.

Ella hurriedly assured Levotas that they could handle it. And by the good complicity of the Almighty above, the show at the Happy Day was to take place upon a Saturday night when Reese had set up a sleep-over at a chum's house.

That night, she and Dieter found their contact, a very dark colored man, at the side door of the club. He gave them an up-and-down. But, aside from their whiteness, Dieter looked like any other white man from the county when dressed in casual civilian clothes.

They paid their entrance fee, adding in a nice tip as Levotas had advised. "Upstairs with y'all, though," Coco said with a *fsst* from his lips and whip of his head.

But stepping in brought a moment of hesitation. And Dieter stiffened as they entered the poorly lit joint, a small concert hall, yes, but with a ceiling barely high enough to have a balcony at the back. It was crowded and close. She pushed her lover along in front of her, not wanting to be seen, and they climbed the short flight to a narrow upper level of seating, where were also mostly Blacks and a smattering of whites.

If anyone here at an event like this noticed her, or maybe even thought they recognized her face, she doubted they would know her. Or even if they did, they would have no idea who Dieter was, looking like any other local as he was tonight.

The Black crowd below was loud, and it roiled as soon as a piano man came onto the stage. A ragtime band with a small brass section had apparently warmed up the assembled before Ella and Dieter had arrived, and now that combo returned, with jackets on, and seated themselves. The air was dense from the press of bodies below and from the smoke.

Long minutes of waiting ensued, in which Ella wondered if it had just been a rumor, but she pinched herself when all at once they indeed introduced Mr. Cab Calloway and he stepped out in his shiny zoot suit with long tails and his white bucks on. He was a handsome Black man and light skinned, with a thin mustache. It seemed he was going to pull this off somehow without his usual big-band section behind him—announcing he had wanted away from the bright lights of New York for his own special "Back-Door Tour."

"Don't tell nobody," he said to the audience, with a big, wide, bright smile and finger to his lips, bringing laughter.

The crowd shoved the tables and chairs out of the way and pushed forward toward the stage, as the floor filled, shoulder to shoulder.

"Y'all know how to scat, ain't ya?" With that, he and the small line-up of players burst forth with a sound like Ella had never heard in person, and words about what to do when your sweetheart tells you that everything will be all right, with a lot of be-bops and skeetle-de-days added in.

How the man could sing, with a great voice that he could push out across a room with no help at all! This crowd all knew it and rejoindered with their own bop-bop's and doo-doo's in rhythm and synchronization with the singer.

The dense mass below them was swaying and jittering. Ella took her eyes off the scene for just a moment to see Dieter sitting back with bigger whites to his eyes than anyone in the place.

When the first number ended, Calloway wiped his brow and announced, "All right, all you big daddies and cool kitties, I think you're ready for some jumpin' jive!"

On he plunged with a lot of hep-hep's, and the crowd hollered the sounds back and pressed forward and twisted till she thought this little band hall would come apart at its joints. A man was next to them, putting glasses with whiskey and ice in front of them. Ella looked over to see Dieter stop nodding his head and rocking to the beat long enough to hand the man some crumpled bills.

And so the hour went, sweatier and more raucous with each number, till Calloway went into the finale with his slowly building "Minnie the Moocher."

How the man could dance! By then, Ella and Dieter were long since on their feet too, clapping and swaying, as Calloway sang about a woman who he called both a red-hot hoochie-coocher and the toughest frail.

Ella and Dieter were leaning into each other and bumping their hips like teenagers, as they sang the chorus back, with a lot of hi-dee hi-dee hi-dee hi's answered by everyone with a lot of hi-dee hi-dee hi-dee ho's.

When it was all over and Calloway had wished them a goodnight and vanished as quickly as he had appeared, they spilled out the side door with the rest of the noisy crowd. Ella and Dieter stood against the band hall and caught their breath, thankful for the cool air. Dieter took Ella in his arms. She could see the faint mist of warm air pouring out of the door of the place they had just exited, along with the other patrons, in the brisk November night.

His arm went around her waist, but she pulled him into an alcove, so they wouldn't be seen. They kissed deeply, whiskey tasting, and pressed against each other. In this bunch around them, with the catting and cavorting going on, Ella was sure no one would notice. She could have been standing here naked and kissing a Black man and she doubted anyone would have cared. She tried to imagine even in her next lifetime spending an evening like this with Lee. If she and Dieter could enjoy life like this, then—

"Let's go tonight," Dieter said, with his mouth next to her ear. "We put the boy in the truck and go."

Simple. Just vanish.

But Ella was glad for the chilly air blowing on her face, returning oxygen to her lungs, and bracing her back into the real world—or trying to.

And just then, over Dieter's shoulder, far across the block, under a street-light, on the distant corner that marked the cross-over back into the white neighborhood, she spotted Officer Hale Truitt leaning against his squad car gently smacking his baton stick in his hand, keeping a careful watch on the direction that any of the Black revelers might spill.

She felt horribly for that man and the terrible loss of his brother, but it ought to have taken the meanness out of a person, not put more of it in him.

Ella tugged Dieter away from the direction of the cop's glance and thanked herself for having thought to park her pickup a way over on Pilottown Road. She pulled Dieter into the dark night along a back path.

Lee

In the Apennine Mountains in central Italy, Lee and the men in his platoon occupied a dusty, boulder-strewn dugout along a ridgeline. Nothing to be seen in any direction but more rocky peaks and crags, distant valleys and summits. They had spent the summer and fall in fierce fighting to break through the German lines, only to get stuck here along this front when the Wehrmacht fell back again and re-established its emplacements in a high, rocky, east-west barrier just to the north of the position that Lee's men held.

Lee and his fellows could sometimes see the enemy—their posts, their units moving about, well-hidden but not so far away, in gray and camo uniforms among these granite hills, or manning their mortar pits, machine gun nests, sharp-shooting hideouts, or small artillery positions. Occasionally, a member of one of the two opposing forces would hail the other in a more human way, but more often it was a loud gesture of malevolence. The foulest insults echoed down the chasms here in both directions in the hopes their foes could hear.

This afternoon, Lee and his men sat back, smoking and trying to enjoy the warm sun, which was crossing farther and farther south, to their backs this season. Here in the dry alpine, with no tree cover, the temperatures rose quickly in the day and plummeted at night. It was enough that they had baked in the foothills through the summer, but now that the Italian winter was coming they would get the reverse treatment in their high redoubts.

Two of the fresher PFCs were among them, this day, talking about home, and then about when they might get to return there.

"Ain't no such thing as a 'stint,' son, or a tour," one of Lee's men said with a laugh. "You might as well know."

"Partner, you're here for 'the duration of hostilities,' as they say," agreed another.

"'Duration of the war plus six months,'" Lee recited.

And for that reason especially, no one spoke of the many thousands in the 5th who up to now had been killed, or the tens of thousands wounded.

For his part, Lee could not stand hiding in these outposts like a varmint. Sitting in a hole all the time.

The only relief? Go out on patrol, where you could get a nice walk or get popped off by a sniper. Not really a patrol these weeks, but a link-up. They were under instructions that once every day or two, a couple of them were to move to the next west-most dugout along this line to relay an all-clear and get a report.

Lee was preparing to send his next pair of men on this loop within the hour. It was their turn, and—

Just then, he heard voices. His head popped up brightly. Chatter coming up the trail that led to the next-over watch-out about a mile or less to the east. This would be a welcome reprieve! A team of English soldiers garrisoned that position. British XII Corps had been a God-given addition to the force of the US 5th Army. The arrival of some Brits up here to their spot to check in every day or so brought camaraderie because they were good blokes, tough, trusty, and loyal damn fighters, and they carried their manners and good sense of humor to every confab—not to mention usually a box of biscuits, or can of tea, or whatever treats had been airlifted and trucked to their basecamp.

Lee rose to greet them. Looking down that steep path that led to out of their trenched position. Just a few feet past the big boulders over to their right, he saw—

A rounded gray helmet climbing towards them and then the top of another, at the same instant that he heard the harsh, clipped throatiness of the Teutonic language—

"*Enemy,*" Lee hissed, trying not to give his men away in the same second. But just that fast a German mountain grenadier, then another one, walked and stumbled into their hidden encampment—before realizing what they had done. They stopped, stunned, right in front of Lee's trench.

All in an instant, Lee's men scrambled and fumbled for their weapons, without even time to drop the cigarettes dangling from their mouths, as Lee crossed their ditch in a single rush, stepping on legs, and made it to the first German, colliding with him, as the hollering exploded. He grabbed the Kraut around the collar before the man had a chance to raise his weapon and threw him to the ground hard, keeping his own feet. A second German came immediately behind, with what looked like three others suddenly scrambling for cover on the trail just below when they saw what was happening. This second German had stepped through the cleft in the rise, between the boulders and right into their midst, with equal shock and terror on his face, but with enough time to level his automatic assault rifle down at his waist and begin firing into their trench, hitting some of the men before Lee could fall into him, grab the gun, and push the muzzle down to the ground.

Lee managed to spin and pull the man down with him, but the German landed on top of him. Lee's shoulder crunched into the ground and his bare head struck hard on the rocky shelf behind him. Things went black for just a moment but not so black that he couldn't keep ahold of the enemy, clenching him close. Lee shook off the purple stars as more firing started, just in time to roll back on top of the camo-jacketed Gebirgsjäger and push the soldier's weapon up under his chin, where Lee put all his weight and force into it. The vessels of the German's head and neck bulged as did his eyes, above his clenched jaw as he gasped, while shots were fired in both directions through the cleft in the rock.

That's when Lee suddenly felt a hot, burning thrust go deep in the small of his back.

The first German had evaded the clasping hands of Lee's comrades as they scrambled out of their trench, several with their weapons out of reach. The grenadier had pulled his knife and stabbed it into Lee's back. No pain had ever been like it and Lee felt the strength go out of his lower body.

The three other Germans in the patrol had dropped to the ground just below the ledge-like rise, as a nearly face-to-face firefight between their machine guns and the M1s of Lee's riflemen ensued. The first German, behind Lee, crashed back to the ground when two of Tingle's men pulled him away and fell upon him. Lee heard the click and boom of a .44 and saw that first German's head explode next to him as the second German's throes began to subside and life slipped from his body under the thrust of Lee against his gunstock and neck. Then Lee saw an M1 barrel thrust into the eye of the German beneath him and the back of the man's skull part from the rest of him in a messy explosion.

Lee tried to straighten and pull his pistol, but the quick deadly exchange of fire concluded just that quickly, with his platoon leaning down over their post's stony summit here pulling the triggers on their rifles as fast as they could into the remaining Germans who had little cover below. Lee dropped down again, feeling the warmth of his own blood flowing quickly over his hip and haunch, as he heard the wounded among his men—thank God, only one or two perhaps—in the ditch behind him calling for help. But by then, he realized he could not sense or move his right leg as he felt fainter with each second.

32

Ella

As light dimmed out of the western-facing windows of their farmhouse in still-shortening days, Ella rustled through a basket of scarves to find one to go with her old mauve coat.

"I don't want to stay here," Reese was complaining.

Ella was hurrying up to the town hall, where a meeting was soon to begin.

"Mrs. Bunting from down the road will be here any moment. She is going to help me get ahead on some baking while she minds you and—"

"I don't need minding."

"She'll be here all the same."

"But—"

BANG. Ella and her boy both jumped at a loud noise, a single thumping rap at their window.

"What was it?" Reese asked quick.

"A bird." Ella had seen it out of the corner of her eye. "It flew into the glass." And bounced off, to a loud thwack, and then dropped.

Reese pointed to the window. "What did Grandma used to say about that? When that happened?"

"She said that..." Ella's mother had used to say that it was a bad omen. In fact, that it meant someone you knew was going to die. "Oh, just that it was bad luck, but that was a silly old wives' tale. Now open your books."

Ella saw Mrs. Bunting's beat-up Studebaker pull into their drive. "You get your practices done before I get home," she said, waving to Reese's arithmetic primer and tousling his hair. That's when she spotted a comic book hidden under his textbook and snatched it out. Another of these confounded endless stream of war comics that they put out for boys! He had spent another ten cents on *Flying Aces: Wings of the Hell Diver, Death Flies Tonight.*

She put it up on top of the cabinet. "You can have this back when I get home and see your drills done."

In no time, she was walking into a crowded hall up in Lewes. Poor Everett had the job of running a meeting tonight for the citizens of the town. There was unrest about the numbers of Germans all about the county now, especially around here and particularly from the people who lived in town, here and in Milford, and points from which they were distributed for each day's work.

Ella stayed as far to the back of the room as she could. But Everett came and found her, as people were still filing in and milling about.

"Why do you have to do this?" she asked.

"Everywhere, the government is getting bucketfuls of letters bitching about how well the prisoners are being treated," Everett whispered and raised his eyebrow to her. "But really, people just want to bellyache, and so we're here to answer their questions—so they don't worry."

He'd had to do this a year or so ago, and Ella had only heard about it second hand. "This is the last time," he declared and then he walked to the front of the room, where several town officials sat. Among them was police officer Hale Truitt.

Everett called the gathering to order and gave a brief, perfunctory speech about how well and productive the management and working of the German POWs was going, and how peaceful those proceedings had been. "And this meeting is to hear more about that," he announced. Then, in a voice that seemed tired, he added, "Or, any feelings to the contrary." He opened the floor with, "I know there may be concerns."

One man stood up right away and said, "Wouldn't be hard for a mess of them to just slip off, from what I've heard."

"Hadn't happened yet," Everett said.

"What if they come down this way for sabotage on the rail line or the fort?" a lady called out.

"Or on our drinking water..."

"Hasn't happened anywhere else," Everett said, "and there are hundreds of camps like this all over the country. South, West ... Any problem-makers would be caught up quick."

"All the same, you treat 'em pretty royal, don't ya?!" someone called out.

"Not at all," Everett corrected. "We're firm but fair with them. That's the way. And their lives remain that of a soldier. Living conditions just the same. 'Three hots and a cot,' as we say—nothing more."

Officer Truitt's face looked purplish, like it might explode, as if he had been told he was not to say anything during this meeting.

A portly man rose now. Ella recognized him from his overalls, then from his profile, as a fellow farmer from nearby. Harmon Grace had a hell of a peach orchard up Milton way. He had the day's newspaper in his hand open to the page where they listed American casualties every week. Horrible and growing daily at this point in the war.

"You see this?" he barked. "You know what this is?"

"I know it as well as anyone," Everett said.

"We should kill every one of these rats. Bring 'em out of that camp and execute them for what they done to our boys." This brought approbation from a good half of the room.

"And, sir," Everett said, as he rose and clearly tried to keep a measured tone, "what if we set that example, and consequently they did the same to all our prisoners? How'd that be?" He seemed to force himself to pause. "My friends, let's try to remember the worldwide conventions on this as well as our own Christian ways, and work to find some of the spirit of the coming holiday season in our thoughts toward everyone caught up in this awful conflagration."

Another man stood, but faced the complainer, not Everett, and said, "Don't you know? POWs got to share same bed and board as the soldiers guarding them." Ella recognized Roland Derrickson, a veteran of the Great War. "Same everything. That's what the law says, and what we always done."

"And they got to be paid like soldiers, too?" someone barked back at him.

And on it went for a good half-hour, with some lending in with fair comments about the prisoners but then getting drowned out again. Ella had stayed to the rear, leaning against the back wall, pushing against it and thinking it might be time to slip back out.

All of a sudden, as Ella was sure the meeting must be winding down, a woman stood up. Lida Crouch! Ella felt her neck tighten. Levotas all but refused to work for the old crow anymore, and Everett had tangled with her, too, having to tell her again that she needed to consult up at the CCC camp if she wanted POW labor.

"There's some of these Huns aren't kept proper track of," she started out, searching around the room and then spotting Ella, as Ella's stomach did a flop. "I know for a fact there's some aren't accounted for properly all the time."

She had turned all the way back toward Ella and stared at her as she went on. "There's some maybe think they're above the rules and some these sneaky prisoners who think they've become part of our families or worse."

Ella only wished she could blend in and become part of the wall and so vanish from the room, as confused heads turned to try to see who Crouch was speaking to.

Meanwhile, all the color had drained from Everett's alarmed face. "That's enough," he said, waving for her to sit back down.

But people were still looking to see who Lida was glaring at all the way across the room. Some surely knew that Ella had POW help.

"We won't have it!" Lida said, down in her seat again, but going on nevertheless. "Take matters into our own hands, if we need to."

A few cheered that.

"Nonsense," Everett said. "You have no idea how many times a day there's rollcall and headcount with these prisoners, so it's malarkey for us to go at each other about such things."

Ella only wished her feet weren't stuck to the floor now. But to flee would call attention.

"Very well," Everett cut back in quickly as Lida started to open her mouth again, "I think everyone has had a chance speak their piece, this hour." He checked his wristwatch in an exaggerated manner. "I'm calling this meeting to a close," he said, shuffling his papers and standing quickly. "We are adjourned," he called out summarily, to a murmur of only partial satisfaction about the room and his glance at Ella to get lost.

Ella drove home with sweaty hands and her mouth still dry. She was convinced that Lida knew or at least suspected most everything—though not sure how—and that she was going to spill it, next chance she got or when she felt the time was to her advantage or when she could prove it.

She had warned Dieter. Told him to be more careful to conceal himself nights and mornings. But his nature was incautious, not worrisome. Evenings, he remained in his own world of Dieter bliss, despite the chances they took continuing to carry on with each other.

"If you don't escape with me, I'm coming back here after der war," he had said just the previous night, engulfing her as she curled more into herself than into him under a mound of blankets in the shed.

"How can that be?" Ella had barely breathed.

"Other men are talking the same. They have been well treated. Und have fallen in love with this land here." As he spoke, he had gently rubbed the place between her shoulders that got so tight sometimes. "But I have something else to love, even more than this country," he said, drawing her in and, as was his wont, humming a tune to her.

At his urging, she had found a radio station that broadcast the live concerts of the Philadelphia Orchestra. Their recent past conductor, Leopold Stokowski, had returned for a guest appearance and, maybe to everyone's surprise, they had finished the last show with a Viennese waltz, the "General Radetsky March," which to Ella's ears sounded really more like a military parade song, with its prominent snare drum.

Dieter had been babbling to her about Johann Strauss and the Strauss family last night as he held her in the dark and tapped that march tune out with his fingertips on her back. In whispers, she had tried to argue for the superiority of Mr. John Phillip Sousa when it came to polkas, but it seemed to fall on deaf ears, as it increasingly did when this man's passions were on display and he got ahead of himself. But then, in the scantest light eeking in, bounced down to the shed from the night's low-slung clouds and the lifting of the blackout rules, he had leaned her back to look at her with that rugged smile of his, laughed at himself, and at her and cut off any debate as he kissed her.

As Ella drove their dark backroad after the disturbing night in the town hall, she knew it could not continue. Something was going to give. If not from her guilt, well then in some other even worse way.

And moments after she parked in their driveway, that something landed in her lap, or, rather, was placed in her hand. As soon as she walked in the door. In the form of a telegram that arrived this evening and that Mrs. Bunting reached to her. From the Army. They both paused for a moment, but no ... *no,* that was not how the worst news arrived. That was when two Army officers came to your door.

So she opened it. Lee had been wounded. He was in a war hospital in Italy somewhere.

It brought out everything at once and Ella's hand came up to her face as she burst into sobs, uncontrollable. Mrs. Bunting put her arm across Ella's shoulders, no doubt—Ella realized—thinking she comforted a good woman who grieved only at the news in the telegram.

Lee

Lee lay in his hospital bed clammy and hot faced. Weeks after the fight and his wounding, he knew he was not doing well and was sleeping too much. The fevers from the infected gash in his backside had come back and were worsening. What a nasty, dirty blade that Hun had stabbed him with!

"A dragon's tooth," he whispered to the nurse at his bedside, who murmured as if she understood. Only her pity was real in response, as she bid him rest quietly and she changed the cold compress on his forehead.

The sulfa drugs were not working. He knew it. And the nurses, both American and Italian, were scurrying more intently around him these past couple days, trying to clean the wound again and again to his agony, and monitoring his temperature.

"One hundred and six," he'd heard one of them whisper to the other this past hour, as they placed ice bags on him.

Now the pattern of squares in the coffered ceiling above him, in this old monastery that had been converted into a rear field hospital, swam and seemed to crisscross and re-cross—becoming the intersection of roads for military convoys, a board of checkers that moved themselves, the side of a barn and outbuildings, the windowpanes of a farmhouse.

He closed his eyes, drifting in a fretfulness that took him in to something like a dream of himself trying over and over to figure how to say goodbye to Ella.

In moments of more wakefulness, his mind knew he had not done right by her. Withheld sentiments, and rightful vows all these years. But he had never needed some damn clergyman or justice of the peace to decide his fate—nor even now to declare what they were to one another or recite his rights to stay on this earth or ascend!

Beyond his feet, on the other side of this dank hall in which he lay soaked in sweat and alternately racked with chills or burning up, was a stained-glass window, lit from the outside by the Tuscan sun. The image of an angel designed into it there ... held a wheat sheaf. The lovely figure moved and flowed, the golden grains in her arms appearing to him to bob in the breeze. She spoke something to him that he could not hear, as his eyes fluttered closed.

But then when he came round next and realized the medical team was gathered about him, it was a different kind of angel speaking to him—a nurse. A doctor was gently shaking his shoulder and talking to him too. A shipment of a new drug, "penicillin" the doc said, had at last arrived here near the front. Lee moaned as they rolled him on his side. They would give him his first dose as an injection from a needle syringe directly into his haunch, to which he relented, letting more pain take him into half-consciousness again.

33

Reese

Lifting hard, Reese grunted and threw an armful of old rusted chains up into the back of their pickup, already loaded with a broken wheelbarrow, some corroded fence wire, and a few lengths of pipe and other pieces of iron junk.

Reese closed the tailgate of the truck with a bang and clunked around to the driver's side, wearing a pair of his pop's work boots that almost sort of fit him, if he stuffed a couple socks in the front of them. It felt good to have turned twelve years old and do what he wanted.

His ma and Dieter were away, down at a meeting-visit with Farmer Tyson whose place sat just along the south property line of theirs. More talk about whether he wanted to sell another lot of his land.

"We don't need any more acres, Mother," Reese had told her, but she hadn't heeded, never did anymore. Listened to nobody, unless it was the German.

Damn this war for making everything topsy! Never caught up on farm work on account of school, never caught up on schoolwork on account of farm work—Reese was sick of it. And if he tried to remember a time before the war, it was harder and harder.

His mother had sat him down and told him about the telegrams she had received. He found that it shut his mouth about anything else and all little stuff that didn't matter these recent days, as he went around hourly thinking about his pop—injured up now and in a hospital with only strangers around him.

"I think he's going to be all right," his mother had said this morning, standing before Reese with the latest message from the Army, which she would not let him see.

Wouldn't share it with him because she didn't know for sure!

Now Reese stomped around to get in the truck as Laddie tried to jump up in with him.

"No, boy. Go on," he said, feeling bad about shooing his best buddy away but in no mood for bothers.

Reese slammed the door shut and scooched to the front of the driver's seat. Holding on to the top of the steering wheel, so he could see out good and his feet could reach the pedals easier, he started her up. He knew how. Dieter had taught him, and let him drive the truck around the farm.

He put her in reverse gear, backed careful out their driveway lane, pulled the shift lever down on the column to clunk it into first and headed toward town. Reese bumped along, bouncing in the seat, with his hands at ten o'clock and two o'clock on the steering wheel, like Dieter had showed him, and drove into Lewes.

It wasn't that hard. You just had to be careful not to push your foot in too fast or hard on the accelerator or brake, or turn the wheel too quick.

And as soon as he turned toward the main street, he saw what he was looking for on this side block. The scrap collection drive, with the Cub Scouts and Boy Scouts all around and up and down the sidewalk, helping to run it. Reese managed to steer in and stop along the curb, park her, and get out quick before he drew any attention. No one had seen who was driving.

But no sooner was he to the back of the truck, than he heard, "Well, look who it is! Farmer Reese!"

Reese cringed at the sound of Roscoe Steeves' voice. He wondered how Roscoe managed to stay a scout, with the way he annoyed everyone and the trouble he caused everywhere he went.

As Reese opened the tailgate and started dragging his stuff out to put on the heap, he heard Roscoe approaching from behind. "Y'all only stopping by? Why ain't you helping 'round here with collections, Reese Tingle?" Roscoe asked.

"Don't start, Rosc." It was Tanner's voice, as Reese tried to ignore them. "Leave it be." Several of the other boys had followed Roscoe over to see about Reese.

"Oh, that's right," Roscoe continued, "because you ain't a Scout and never did join up."

"Cut it out, Roscoe." Now Vic had come up too.

"Don't want to serve our nation," Roscoe said.

"Cain't because he didn't learn how in Cubs," said a younger boy who had turned into one of Roscoe's newest lackies.

"I might join up, maybe, if I take a mind to," Reese said like it didn't matter to him. "Got no time though."

Tanner tried to cut in again. "Sure. You can join any time, you—"

"Naw, he's too busy playing farm with the Germans to put on a uniform for America," Roscoe said.

Reese yanked off his gloves and slapped them down on the tailgate, thinking of his dad in pain and maybe in danger, and just feeling sore about everything today. He stepped closer to Roscoe's face and everybody got quiet for a second.

"Hey, your momma drive you in here just now?" Roscoe said, sudden and lowdown, one of his eyebrows going up, as he looked left and right around the truck.

"Sure, she's coming back presently," Reese said, gesturing toward the main street.

"You better go find her, then, 'cause—" Roscoe said, cocking one of his shoulders back.

"Didn't either," some of the younger boys started crowing. "I saw him!" "Driving it himself."

"Don't you boys have work to do?" a man's voice boomed next to them and they jumped. Reese spun and saw it was Mr. Gleeson, the town warden, but who was also one of the Scout guides.

"Then go on about it," he said, waving the Scouts and Cubs away and back to their tasks. "I'll help out here." And at the same time, the Troop Master over there with his silly outfit on whistled up the boys to get back to their jobs.

Reese was just as glad of it, 'cause Roscoe must be twice his weight, and his heart was pounding.

Mr. Gleeson helped him pull the rusted-out old wheelbarrow off the back of the truck and heft it up. Reese was happy to make a big loud show with this junk, to go those other boys one better, when all they were doing was loading stupid bundles of newspaper, and flattening and tying up cardboard boxes.

As they moved toward the iron-collection pile with the barrow between them, Mr. Gleeson halted and looked at Reese. "Is there any truth to what those boys were saying?" he asked.

"Sir?"

"Your momma's about here somewhere to drive, right?"

Reese let out a relieved breath. He dropped his eyes and swallowed. "She'll be by shortly," he said and kept them moving toward the junk pile.

If she could lie like she did—rotten all the time—why couldn't he?

The last thing they pulled off the truck was an old busted up ploughshare. Mr. Gleeson helped him carry it. "Them boys going on about your German help?" he asked Reese. "What about that? They transported proper back and forth to your place?"

Reese felt his neck and face color, and time seemed to stand still as they stopped with the ploughshare between them and he thought about every-thing—Dieter, Poppa Lee, and that mother of his. It was too confusing to know for sure what grown-ups had done right or wrong, or both. Too scary to know how to mess with it.

He looked up at Mr. Gleeson and simply said, "I've heared tell that prisoners, out and about in some places, might linger so's not to have to have to go back to camp."

"You 'heard tell,' huh?"

Mr. Gleeson snorted and looked at him sideways, but seemed to want to keep moving in the cold weather, and they heaved the old plough blade up atop the mess of metal with a loud crash.

Reese was relieved to thank the warden and be done. He went back to the truck and, as he did, he more felt than saw Roscoe peel off and follow him again, the Troop Master now distracted with talking to Mr. Gleeson. A gang of the boys slowly trailed after Roscoe once more when they saw they could.

"Not going to stay and help, huh?" the bonehead called as Reese whammed the pickup's tailgate closed.

"Aw, I got real war work to do. We're growing all the chickens for the Army and troops, don't you know," Reese said, as he reached up for the driver's side door.

"Hey! What are you doing?"

"Heading home, Rosc."

"Hey, you cain't drive that thing on the road!" Roscoe suddenly bellowed when he saw Reese start to step up toward the driver's seat.

"Can too. Got a farm license to drive."

"Idn't no such thing. Not till your 14."

"You watch."

"Yeah, hurry up, then," Roscoe said, seeing that it would indeed happen. "Go on and help your momma tend to her German."

Reese's hand slid slowly off the door, which still hung open. He stepped back down on the running board and then onto the street. Then he went almost nose to nose with Roscoe, who took a half-step back. He could scent this big soft kid's sour breath, smelling like meat gruel. He grabbed the ends of Roscoe's Scout scarf, pulled, then flipped the scarf and its gold clasp over the boy's shoulder

"Whoa!" Vic yelled, moving as fast as he could toward them.

"Whataya? Why I oughta …" the Roscoe said, turning sideways to Reese, and doubling up his hands.

"Yeah, but you won't," Reese said, as he turned unhurried and got up in the truck's driver's seat.

Reese started the truck and put it in gear quickly, and it lurched forward down the street. Some of the boys ran alongside him, hollering at him, and him back at them too.

"This is how she's done," he called out the window with a laugh that felt good.

He tried to speed up to get shed of them before he got to the corner, but he was only in first gear. He shifted gears in the intersection but he let the clutch out too fast again, and the pickup bucked and jumped sideways as he turned. The truck banged and scraped loudly on a street sign, as it bounced off the curb and Reese sped away down main street to hoots and howls, jeers and cheers, behind him.

Ella

"I'm growing dick!" Dieter announced to Ella.

"I beg your pardon?"

It must be a German word, she realized.

"*Thick,* you would say," he translated with a guffaw. "*Fat.*"

She patted his midsection—hard but which had indeed gained a bit of girth from the cooking she tried every blessed day to put on proper around here for everyone. It just made him more of a horse, and somehow seemed to go along with the happy-go-lucky streak about him like no man she had ever known.

But Everett was upon his last favors to her, and the town meeting had so worried him that he had conceded and was now having a POW detail assigned to Lida Crouch's farm to do some off-season work. It might quiet her for the time. Meanwhile, Ella hid Dieter in her truck's cab each morning and dropped him off at the square in town for the daily distribution of the POWs. Lida would then see him soon thereafter in the Army truck, transported proper to their place, when her own prisoners were dropped off each day.

While Dieter had waited uptown today, he had apparently slipped into the soda fountain where he knew Blacks were not allowed. Their good-countenanced friend, Mr. Rickart, who tortured over this fact and all such wrongness that he felt was mostly forced upon him, had sold Dieter a box of crullers, which their German shared with Levotas around the kerosene stove that they'd bought and installed out in the shed. An armistice had broken out between these two men, thank goodness, and so she could go back inside and tend to the farm's paperwork, leaving them to figure out what winter needs around the farm they could take care of. If only such an armistice would break out in other parts of the world!

Yesterday, another letter had arrived from Lee. Another of *several* this month ... Ella held it again.

> *I am very grateful to be alive. Lots of my fellows weren't as lucky, and I don't understand why I was.*

Every day in this short new year so far, she had not only thanked the grace of heaven that he had made it, but marveled at sentiments she saw starting to come from him.

> *The infection in my back and buttside is all but gone and the hurt is lessening. It's a miracle. Been trying to get up and walk around some. And docs say my leg is going to work better. I just have to keep at it and keep trying.*

> *Everyone in this next hospital I been moved to is very nice. And at least it's warmer down south here again, and there's food and no bullets flying in this part of Italy anyhow.*

Each note kept Ella wondering at what she read, not just at their sudden frequency, but at the sound of them, though her stomach hurt at each of his vague mentions of his injury.

On this Saturday morning, she took the letter and meant to share it with Reese if she could find him.

Her son's sullen ways, though, had only gotten worse.

School had reported to her on episodes of his combativeness. But now, she was glad to find him at the little desk in his room, surprised to see him pasting War Stamps into their booklet, which could be used to buy a war bond. She had so often asked him to help with that.

He did not acknowledge her when she walked in across the creaky floor of his bedroom.

"Hey, honey. Where did you find the money to buy more stamps?" she asked softly, surprised at how many he'd added.

"Saved a few pennies each week from my lunch money," he mumbled.

That was the boy she knew! She took a step closer and put her hand on his shoulder, but after a moment he shook it off.

"Here's another new note from your pop," she said, and laid the letter on his desk. He dropped what he was doing, and she backed away.

Downstairs again at the kitchen table, she gave up working on the farm ledgers. She pushed them away and pulled the next note she was working on to Lee back in front of her. Now that she had a better idea that her letters might actually get to him, she tried to say more of the things that one should to someone who had sacrificed so.

In three letters over the past couple weeks—heartfelt in a way that spun Ella so that it actually dizzied her a few times to stare at them—he had, perhaps for the first time clearly in these past two years, addressed his missing her and Reese and their farm and their lives.

> *Maybe you won't believe me, but I've thought every day about not being with you and Reese. I'll make that and everything else up to you when I return. This fight was something that had to be and that I had to do, and now I'm headed back to where I ought to be.*

If this was the kind of person he could return to her as, then … Yesterday, she had written him back,

> *There's no making-up you need to do for serving our country. You did us proud, Lee. And you know we been behind you all the way. Just get home here as soon as you can to be a father to my son, your son, our son.*

She tried to write only things that were true and things she was sure of.

34

Ella

Out at the crossroads leading into town, Ella slammed the door of her pickup and stormed over toward Everett. They had met at the nearest intersection to her place, where farm fields came to all four corners. He had parked his US Army car over on the grassy shoulder.

"Where is he?" she asked angrily.

Everett put up two hands. "I had to have him picked up at the end of the day yesterday."

Ella smacked him on the chest. "Why?"

"El, I can't let anyone see me even *talking* to you now," he said. "That's how bad it's got." He explained that he had picked up on chatter in town and even on the base. About a possible "arrangement" out at the Hall Farm.

"If that gets back to my direct reports and they start looking into it ... I could get cooked."

Ella slowed. "Well, then ... we can't let that happen, either," she said. "But where is he?"

Everett nodded reluctantly toward town. "At the camp here."

At the old CCC camp, on Savannah Road, not even a couple miles from here. "And he cannot roam from there," Everett said, waggling his finger at her. "What's more, he needs to be assigned elsewhere for now, for his workdays. At least for the time being, until things cool off."

Ella knew that she must look pale at this, and sunken after everything. Worn-out at this point in her years and this cursed damn war, though her 30th birthday was still months away ...

218

"I don't know what's dredged this all up again," Everett said, "because Witch Lida seems under control. I risked my neck to see that she got what she wanted. But that's the way of it now, and you best keep your peace."

Alone that night, at her kitchen table, long after Reese had gone wordlessly to bed, Ella knew what real lonesomeness felt like, all over again. A February wind pushed against the old farmhouse.

Only Levotas was here sometimes to help her run everything, especially the chicken houses. Her Black helper had come to her with a terrible story. That night of the Cab Calloway concert back in November, police officer Hale Truitt had taken his night stick to the side of a Black boy's head. Kid was no more than fourteen, according to Levotas, and Truitt had decided he was walking down the wrong street.

"Halfway knocked his ear off his head. Will probably always be that way now."

"Why didn't you tell me?" Ella asked. "And who knows about this? Was it reported?"

"What good it do to report it? That ain't going to do nothin'. And that young man still acting punch-drunk, in schoo' and everywhere from that knock in his head he took."

At this hour, Ella wished she had the energy to recapture all of her anger over this. She had a mind to go up to the town hall about it right away, but this evening there was planning needing done for the spring season. Seed and other supply orders to be written out.

She leaned forward until her forehead rested on the kitchen table and stayed there for a very long time. Bone tired from just a few days without proper help—all pride of her own ways these past years stripped out of her.

35

Reese

At school, Reese sat in the row of chairs outside the principal's office. Across from him, sat other boys who had took his side of the squabble that had broken out today. Tanner looked mad. Vic was scared. Another boy next him didn't look like he cared one way or the other, while another was still sniffling from the fight.

Roscoe and his bunch were in the principal's office first, and Reese could hear Mr. Maloney's deep voice but not see them through the dusted glass of his door. Reese's hand hurt and he still had the sensation of Roscoe's nose bending under the blow he had planted there.

Dieter had shown him. The German had put on thick gloves to catch Reese's punches when they'd practiced combinations in the back yard last year. *Jab, jab, cross.* But after Roscoe had said something about Reese's ma, it had only taken one good sock to the face of that big lug, who was in the office now still holding a handkerchief to his nose and sniveling and lying that he had been jumped.

Mr. Maloney didn't know about Reese's couple of other fights. The after-school ones. They hadn't amounted to much anyway, but this one had brought on a brawl in the hall outside the lunchroom.

People and things made Reese mad these days.

He leaned forward, his elbows on his knee, and doubled his sore left hand, admiring all that a fist like that could do, but hating the bruises forming up between his knuckles.

Ella

Ella scurried around to the side of the house to tear open an envelope from Lee. Hiding in the first well of warm, still, bright air of the season, in a spot that the sun drenched in the morning, against the clapboard siding in a spot where no one would see her, she yanked Lee's letter out and unfolded it.

> Well, Ell, here I am in jolly old England now. Yes, that's why my letters have been interrupted. They transferred me to a hospital here, in the south, near Dover, with other injured servicemen, where they specialize in exercising the wounded back "up to snuff" as they say. Only wish YOU were here to take good care of me.

Ella paused for a moment and blinked. She looked at that paragraph again. But the handwriting was Lee's and so, then, must the chipper tone ...

> I'm so grateful to be alive and to be slowly mending. So glad all over again to have you to send my letters home to. And to hear about the farm and Reese. Don't worry if he gets scrappy. That's the way that boys do at that age.

Ella flipped the letter over, and then back again, but the signature sure was Lee's. Had the nurses been telling him what to write? It was as if her correspondent was someone new.

She looked around quick, to make sure no one saw her—no one named Reese, that is, who was at the kitchen table having to do all his schoolwork there because he had been suspended this week.

Ella twisted inside herself as she folded the letter and put it back in her dress pocket. She had lost her steam for another growing season on this place, but knew that she—oh, yes, she of little faith—needed, perhaps for someone else's sake, to get back on the phone with Everett to see, damnit, what Germans she might get out to this place next week.

36

Ella

By the time spring properly arrived, Ella couldn't pick herself up anymore or even get herself out of a chair sometimes. Despite his ingenuity with such matters—and about getting to her on the sly in the past—she had not heard from Dieter.

And the letters from England had stopped. Could they only have been an illusion? Or could some young nurse be singing a different tune to Lee now?

Perhaps, then, it was as well she was alone here this month.

The amount of rousting about that she had seen from idle soldiers uptown was worrisome. Some were drunken young naval gunners who had trained nearly their entire short adult lives to do something they had never gotten to do—fire a shot at a real enemy. And if Dieter were to try to make his way here, she shuddered to think what a bunch of them might do if they found an AWOL German.

And how had it even come, these past couple of years, that she would worry about such a thing as an AWOL German? Maybe now was a chance to correct it all.

From her stoop, Ella cast a forlorn glance back to their table acres, as her pa used to call them, which needed cleared off by now, if not turned. And as for the field planting ...

The only thing springing up on schedule was her son—like an asparagus shoot, that boy. Reese was no longer one of the shorter kids in his group, and he had now felt what it was like to use his awkward, gangly new strength.

When Lee's letters had trailed off, they had taken another new tone.

I don't want to be in this place anymore. Stuck here and hobbling. But they won't give me a medical discharge to get aboard a transport and come home yet. It ought to be up to me. I feel like a POW!

How oddly the world turned, Ella thought. And why did this man remain so mysterious about his injuries?

Surely, they would not send him back to duty, even if they could. Nazi forces held just a sliver of territory between the American and Russian armies in Europe now. But what would she do if Lee Tingle were to walk right in here today, or tomorrow?

Adding to her stupor and her torpor—from a mood as low as her root cellar—she and Reese had gathered in front of their radio last week and listened to the news that their president had died. President Roosevelt was dead ...

For the first time in a long time during that radio broadcast about FDR, she had seen her son, a fretful agitator on the doorstep of adolescence—and no longer with Dieter's calming influence—hold completely still for long minutes only listening.

"He won't be able to win the war now," Reese said.

"We'll still win," Ella had said.

"Without a President?"

"We have a new President."

The coverage had gone on to describe Harry Truman reluctantly and sadly taking the oath.

Yes, her son had listened stunned, just like she had earlier this week—this time with Clarissa. In her girlfriend's living room, facing each other, hands clasped, foreheads leaned against one another. As Clarissa's baby cried in its bassinette nearby, she and her friend had wept. Now, Ella could not even speak the reason why—too horrid to repeat.

With effort on this day, Ella went out into a cool, straight-down April rain. She stepped up on an overturned bushel basket, only partly sheltered by the eaves of the shed.

She looked out over their world and over at their rickety Ford, waiting, as it always had, for her to make decisions. One last time, the dream whirled back of driving straight to Seaford or Salisbury for a new life. Leave all men behind. Take Reese with her and find a place to live, a job as a shop girl if her aunt would not employ her.

The steady rain dripped off the buds of the fruit trees in their orchard that had not been sprayed this month. Worse, sickness had come to their hen house, perhaps from the chicks they had bought from the poultry truck and from all the dampness. Already a dirty, smelly business out there that she had tired of— the chicken production—and now a portion of her flock had died. Birds with runny eyes were coughing.

Levotas' rheumatiz, as he called it, was acting up too though he had come out here long enough to help her cull the sick layers and broilers from the rest of the mass out there in that bothersome brood.

This war, this year, this dank season, had left her adrift and now locked away here.

Suddenly a breeze caught, bringing this morning's light rain into her face, snapping her around. A nightmare had come to her for the second time last night. Probably because she had read of lynchings that had continued these years, in Florida and other places south. But in her awful dream it had not been a poor Black man hanging from the rope-swing here in her yard. It had been Dieter, with Officer Hale Truitt dancing in front of a mob and laughing.

Ella concluded she could only bring wreckage around her. And so, in the increasing rain and with disappearing strength, Ella wrestled the eight-foot step ladder from their shed and set it next to that big, corded piece of hemp— the boys' rope swing, hanging down from the old cottonwood tree. Letting the rain drench her, Ella climbed as high as she could and made a loop. The ladder tottered. How easy it would be to push it out from under her by accident ... or on purpose. But instead, standing as steady as she could, and using the twist of the line as a handhold, Ella reached high and, with a knife, cut the rope and cast it to the ground, as she shivered.

Part III
If I Die Before I Wake

37

Dieter

"Eh, pardon me, doc, but might I inquire as to the route to Las Vegas?"

Dieter Schneider sat in the dark barrack that they used for kino every week—cinema, as they called it here, for prisoners in the camp at Lewes. The long frame hut was beginning to get stuffy this time of year, and before them, on the pull-down screen, played a cartoon called "Hare Meets Herr," featuring a rabbit, who was terrorizing a corpulent, lederhosen-wearing Hermann Goering in the Black Forest.

Dieter and the other Germans were unfamiliar with this character called Bugs Bunny, but they watched as the rabbit popped on a black mustache and bang of dark hair, at which point the German people, in the form of Goering, kissed the Hitler bunny's hand. Dieter rose quietly and slipped to the back. What an awful unfortunate and deadly joke his nation had turned itself into. Worse than a joke. Far worse.

As he stood for another minute and watched from the back of the hall, "Bugsenheimer Bunny" was delivered to the real cartoon Hitler, who took a terrible shock when the rabbit emerged dressed as Joseph Stalin. Seeing enough, and wondering again if he had any relatives alive still back in that land after the waves of cataclysm these past years, Dieter slipped out into the dark night.

Amidst the rows of barracks, he looked out at the starry darkness, which was just starting to come alive with the sound of summer night noises. All the critters—the chirpers and croakers and peepers. He'd had more than two years to worry about his parents who had abandoned the countryside of Schleswig-Holstein to move east to be with his father's family in Dresden, where the whispered word here was that several months ago the Americans had committed the atrocious war crime of fire-bombing the city.

Dieter watched the orange glow of cigarettes bobbing in a couple distant places about the camp. He eschewed that unhealthful practice, instead unwrapping a piece of Wrigley's Doublemint gum now and popping it in his mouth. What a burst of pleasure, he thought, as his expectation grew about what was to come tomorrow. He had been reassigned to the Hall farm as part of a three-POW rotation of group details. He would see his lover, Ella Hall, again, after more than ten weeks. Another chance, perhaps his last and best, to convince her to strike out with him. He had mapped out their flight.

Ella had spoken often of her cousin Everett at the coastline fort here, and Dieter assumed he had arranged this return. Perhaps after allowing rumors to die, about which Dieter felt helpless. He only wished he could thank the man.

But regardless of who helped, Dieter had also deemed it only a matter of destiny that he and Ella would be reunited and make their escape.

The next day, Dieter declared that all was put right now, or would be as soon as he walked into her yard. Then he saw her sitting on her back steps.

She looked thin and drawn, with dark circles under her eyes. She looked up at him slowly, almost as if not recognizing him for a moment.

He reached his hand out and she took it. He drew her to him.

"Now, we fix everything up," he said, meaning more than just this farm, which he could see had been neglected these past weeks and needed quick catch-up to the season.

And, in fact, it went well and quickly, in Dieter's estimation, with two other POWs at his bidding for ten days, though he let Levotas Clark believe that one of them was under his command.

On the few times he could get Ella alone, she would only let him hold her. Close and quiet. He could feel that she had lost weight.

Dieter pledged to himself that he would not let them be separated again. First, they would catch up on this planting season. Also for appearances, Ella told him to try to make himself seen in the POW truck, by that hen Frau Crousch, mornings and end of the day.

But a few days later, he found himself before the old bat herself, in Ella's pretty white-shell driveway on a warm, sunny afternoon that made him feel alive.

Standing a bit off from him and taking a haughty posture, the crone called, "So it's two years you've taken up residence here."

He shook his head, no. They had broken early from the fields today, the men, and had sat out back quaffing little glasses of vodka flavored with honey that one of the men had snuck along. The warmth of drink and weather flowed through him.

"We've had the finest time of our lifes here," he said to the Crousch lady. Many felt so. In a safe and prosperous land, with real, honest, tangible work and few other worries.

"Well, then … It cain't last much longer," she said, crossing her arms as she tapped her foot on the ground.

Suspecting she might be the reason he had been absented from here these past two months and more, he dubbed her the side of America he did not like—the fearful, intolerant side.

"No," he said, as the Bärenjäger they had just consumed lubricated his brain. "I will keep helping here," he declared suddenly.

She guffawed, her eyes widening. "Oh, and how do you figure on that?"

"I don't know. But I can help best here," he said, his English always improving, or at least feeling as though it did, when he'd had a couple of drinks. "I grew up on a farm before I came to America."

"Before you 'came'—?"

But the effects of the surging God-given springtime weather and his strength and health and the imbibement … It took him back in his mind to before the war, to seven years ago, he supposed. In 1938, the first girl he had ever laid with, a popular girl from down the lane in their countryside home, had been seventeen. Two years older than him, she had chased after him, till they truly found each other, the first time in a loft of hay on a spring evening—then she had come to him later that summer and showed him that she was with a child and claimed it was his. They had gotten married quietly in the back room of a church. But by the next year, he knew that life on his parents' little family farm with her and a baby that only vaguely looked like him was not to be. Not for him. With the help of a bit of money given him by his father's well-to-do family in the east, he had departed to study mechanics in Kiel, where—

"I say, oh, is that right?" the Crousch hag before him squawked again, putting on a civil tone for the first time.

Looking down at this troublesome bird, Dieter heard himself say, "A beautiful woman such as Miss Hall here, needs a man to run her farm. I know how to take care of all the needs here properly. I was a husband and father mine-self before I left home."

"Is that so?" the buzzard before Dieter said, narrowing her eyes at him. "Do tell ..."

Reese

"Hitler is dead," Reese said to Dieter.

Reese nearly barked it at him as he walked up to the back of the toolshed and put down two buckets that he used to slop their few pigs with the kitchen scraps. Dieter was sitting on the bench there, putting a new handle on a digging pitchfork.

"I know. Ist good. He will not go to Himmel."

Reese looked at him.

"*Heaven,*" the German said.

They had been given a special dispensation to have Dieter here on a Sunday to help. Reese believed that, on the sly, he would likely stay in the shed tonight.

"Last night, they say that Admiral Dönitz is in command of what is left of the Nazi regime," Dieter told Reese. "He built da U-boat fleet, you know. A madman, Reese, but klug—*clever, smart*—like all them."

"Germany has to give up now," Reese said sternly.

"Ja. We hope."

"I ain't going to school a whole week if they declare a victory," Reese said, starting to pull off his mud boots.

Dieter nodded. "But you must go to school," he said. Reese had overheard Dieter discouraging his ma from letting him off for planting season days, saying they could manage it with the other two prisoners they had coming. "You are very lucky to be in your school."

Reese stilled himself and looked at Dieter.

"I was in mine own school before all this," the German said, as he finished with the pitchfork and then explained that he had been in what sounded to Reese like some kind of technical school in some place called Keel in 1939.

"Then in 1940, I was accepted to study engineering at Universität Kiel. It was like a dream, but in 1941 I got draft to the Gottverlassene Wehrmacht!"

Reese noticed that when he started talking about something of the war that made him mad, he would slip into more German. "By 1942, they had stuck me in Kriegsmarine—*navy*—und I finished my training at the U-boat base in the Kieler Hafen."

Reese had sat down next to him on the bench. "But at least it brought me here, to this place," Dieter concluded, finishing with a gaze out across their acres and then toward their farmhouse, and mustering a half-satisfied smile after his rant.

"Will you have to leave?" Reese finally asked him very quietly, staring at his own boot laces, still unsure of what answer he wanted to hear.

"No, I won't leave. Or if I do, I will not leave for long. I will come back. I promise you."

Reese didn't know what it might all mean, or how Dieter could do that, but he said tschüß that night to Dieter and on Monday at school the news began to come in. Germany had surrendered and the next day was to be officially proclaimed VE day for the victory in Europe. President Truman had pronounced it.

"C'mon, sweetie, let's go uptown and celebrate," his mother said to him, first thing in the morning. They had not spoken to Dieter that day, nor did it seem right to go out back to him. So they jumped in the pickup and bounced toward town, laughing at their declaration that today would be a day off for both of them—from worries too.

Reese could only imagine different reactions among the POWs, but uptown, people were coursing about excitedly, gathering here and there, and Reese and his mom strolled to the cannon park, down by the canal, and listened to the sounds echoing along the coast from the cape. In their enthusiasm at the victory, the crews at Fort Miles were firing the big guns, and the booming salutes floated everywhere and through the streets here. It felt like the beginning of the end of a very long time to Reese, one that had begun when he was only a child. His mother looked out at the sky on the horizon as if watching more than the puffs of smoke from the batteries pass away.

Just a block over, in the center of town, a loudspeaker was set up and people gathered on the sidewalks and in the main street for President Truman's nine o'clock proclamation. His voice came out, a little scratchy and froggy, but strong.

This is a solemn but a glorious hour.

Reese looked around at the people listening so seriously to this wonderful news.

The flags of freedom fly over all Europe.

In the crowd, Reese stood close to his mother, who seemed to clench and knead the sleeves of her sweater.

Our rejoicing is sobered and subdued by a supreme consciousness of the terrible price we have paid to rid the world of Hitler and his evil band.

He saw a couple people holding, high above their heads, today's copies of the *Delaware Coast News* with the headline "GERMANY SURRENDERS UNCONDITIONALLY" printed in the largest letters he'd ever seen on a newspaper.

Let us not forget, my fellow Americans, the sorrow and the heartache, which today abide in the homes of so many of our neighbors—neighbors whose most priceless possession has been rendered as a sacrifice to redeem our liberty.

All at once, Reese wanted to ask his mother what this war had really meant to them—what it had cost them and what it had brought them—but it didn't seem as though either of them knew for sure now or yet, not altogether.

... to build an abiding peace, a peace rooted in justice and in law. We can build such a peace only by hard, toilsome, painstaking work.

Reese felt his mother pull him close, and he did not resist, leaning into her as the speech built.

The western world has been freed of the evil forces which for five years and longer have imprisoned the bodies and broken the lives of millions upon millions of free-born men. They have violated their churches, destroyed their homes, corrupted their children, and murdered their loved ones. Our Armies of Liberation have restored freedom to these suffering peoples, whose spirit and will the oppressors could never enslave.

Reese and his mother looked at each other, wondering at the world *they* had created out of all this and at what awful price Poppa Lee might have paid for it. Reese knew only that he had never seen his mother as happy as she was last year, when they had invented their own wartime lives, and now her face was full of anxious confusion and tears and relief, all at once.

For the triumph of spirit and of arms which we have won, and for its
promise to the peoples everywhere who join us in the love of freedom,
it is fitting that we, as a nation, give thanks to Almighty God, who has
strengthened us and given us the victory.

Reese's ears seemed to ring with those final words and he heard some crying around him. The speech was so short he wondered if he had missed some of it, as he gave up and let his mother hold him close and sniffle. Then his ears rang again in a different way as the bells of all the churches in town, including Saint Peter's just a block away, began to peal out joyously.

Around him, though, as Reese stepped back and watched, the clapping subsided and there were some hollers but mostly some handshakes and hugs, and some quiet tears.

"Why isn't everyone happier?" Reese asked his mom.

"That's why," Ella said, nodding to some on the far side of the walk among the throng calling out, "The battle is only half won!"

Of course, the Japanese had not yet been defeated…

"That's why the celebration is only halfway, honey. The war in the Pacific is still raging."

Mother Ella took him for a special early lunch at the drugstore's fountain, complete with an ice cream sundae and all the celebration chatter among the customers and the soda jerks, as kindly Mr. Rickart dashed back and forth behind the counter to feed everyone, and gave Reese a cup of extra marshmallow sauce and another of maraschino cherries to chomp on. Then all the stores closed early at noon.

"Now you must come with me," Ma Ella said.

"Where are we going?" Reese asked, then suddenly realized, as they walked toward St. Peter's.

"No."

"To the religious service of thanksgiving," she said.

But she had not made him go to Sunday school or church for a long time, so he found he could not refuse.

"We greet the grand and glorious news of Germany's surrender with a feeling of reverence." Reverend Rightmyer was already speaking when they found a seat. Reese closed his eyes and tried to drift, tired from the excitement of the last couple of hours and days. The reverend was the only man he could ever remember his mother listening to without question—in that same way the word in the newspaper headline had said, "unconditionally."

But sitting in the crowd in the wooden pews, no answers seemed to descend to him of what would come next, especially for his mother—not till they arrived home and found a telegram in the door.

His ma fumbled it open. Reese stood beside her on the front step on his tiptoes, trying to see. But she always held these and his pa's letters high when they came, so she could scan them first.

As she read with just a few quick movements of her eyes, Reese watched hints of such a tumult of emotions go across her face, as left him only guessing.

"Your father is coming home," she said.

Ella

That very same night, Ella had just turned off the lights to go upstairs—bone tired, with one weight of the world off all their shoulders and another, of her own, upon her. That question would only grow now, with—

Suddenly, her living room lit up with light sweeping across it from the outside. A car had pulled into their short lane from the road and stopped at the top of her driveway.

Ella scurried outside and saw the black-and-white—the town police car. Hale Truitt stepped out of it.

"Where is he?" Truitt asked. He sounded groggy.

"What?"

"*Where?*"

"Who?"

"Your stowaway."

"What in blazes are you talking about?"

Ella saw now that he was in his civilian clothes but had put his service belt on.

"That feckin' German that's always around here," he growled. Ella's pulse pounded, knowing that this man wasn't the only one around here who wouldn't have minded one last chance to put a bullet in a Kraut.

But just then, he staggered back a step and burped, and she could tell. He was half lit. No doubt coming from down at the DeBraak, in the same tavern where his dislike of Lee had grown over the years. Two men who were both entirely capable of arrogance.

"You're out of line, Hale. The POWs are none of your concern, as long as there's no trouble. They're managed by the Army quite well."

"Oh, there'sth trouble ol-right," he mumbled as he tried to move past her toward the back. To where she had been with Dieter this past hour and to where she knew he was sleeping satisfied and peaceful.

Ella stepped in front of Truitt. She'd had a contingency—desperate but in the back of her mind if this moment should come.

"'Trouble?'" she said. "You mean like the trouble that will come to you, if it got back how you treat the poor folk over in the Black neighborhood?"

His "huh?" came partway with a fumy belch.

"Hear you left some poor boy for good with a cock-eyed ear there last fall and a knocked noggin."

Truitt startled and then started to laugh but then stopped.

"Seems to me, that ought to be reported all the way up," Ella said, "and investigated."

Truitt harrumphed.

"I got witnesses," she said.

"Go on ahead, like I care or anybody will care." Then he tried to stick his chest out. "I know what really ought to be reported," he said, nodding back in Dieter's direction.

He tried to move past her again, but she put her index finger in the middle of his chest and halted him.

All of a sudden, he looked down at her hand, and lifted it up slowly and kissed it. She snatched it away.

"You're drunk, Hale Truitt." He took a couple unsteady steps backwards. "Now, go on."

"Just as soon as I ..." he intoned, all slurry, patting his left hip, as if he had forgotten that his gun was on his right hip.

"Listen, Hale, you and I both suffered terrible in all this, right?"

He didn't answer but retreated another couple of steps to the open door of his car. All at once, he hung over the door and dropped his head. She waited, unable to tell if he was listening or weeping or about to empty his stomach. They had all comforted him as best they knew about his brother who had been buried with honor on the hill at Bethel Cemetery here in town.

"You?" he said.

"Yes, me. I don't even know for sure that my husband is going to be able to walk when he gets back here."

Truitt murmured, "'Husband?'"

234

"How 'bout this?" Ella said, clipped and clear. "I'll give you one more chance on what I've heard about your doings, 'long as you leave us be for good."

Truitt's head, gone oddly shaggy from lack of barbering and a night of carousing, popped up angry.

She said it again. "I don't hear anything else ever happening again like that between you and Levotas' kind, and you and I are square."

"Ella Hall," he pronounced, "one a them damn crusaders, after all." But now he looked surely as if he would get sick, as he added, "I'd've never of thunk it."

With that, Truitt stayed hangdog as he got slowly back in his car.

And thusly did she sell out some poor boy whose name she didn't even know.

Through the rolled-down window, she thought she heard a "damn it" and a "Kraut *and* a nigger lover" before he drove away—leaving her to decide if she'd only keep her promise to him as long as she needed to.

38

Lee

The doors of the bus flapped open and Lee Tingle stepped out, pulling his duffle bag with him. He stood on the sidewalk of the main street in Lewes and squinted in the bright, warm sunshine.

He had taken the train only as far as Wilmington and then gotten aboard this grayliner before first light this morning.

In the dawn hours, the tidal farmlands of Delaware rolling by had reminded him strangely less of home than of the plains below Cassino. The otherwise table-flat landscape today, though, was unlike anything he had experienced for a long time since he left. In the seat of the bus, he'd twisted his garrison camp in his hands, wondering if Ella and Reese had mostly just lived on the farm or had actually kept it going as much as she said.

Yes, everything had seemed both new and familiar in that ride south down Route 9, but not so different suddenly when the bus would pass over a bridge across another salt creek or marsh that he would look down into and instead see one of the men he had trained with, sinking in a damned swamp paddy out on those Italian plains just the year before last—especially that instant coming back to him when his friend had a hole bigger than a baseball blown out of the middle of his gut, right next to Lee, as they trudged forward, the man's falling, then sinking face disappearing in the watery slop, as the whizzing sounds—

"*Tingle?*" A voice brought him out of it. "Lee Tingle?"

He looked up to see Paul Rickart.

Mr. Rickart had just stepped out of his drugstore, wiping his hands on his apron. "Yes, sir."

"Hot *damn,* boy. You're back!"

"'On a wing and a prayer.'"

"Well, look at you," Rickart said, stepping to Tingle and cuffing his shoulder gently, "and all in one piece, thank the Lord."

"Mostly."

Rickart laughed. "Well, welcome home, fella," he said, and saluted Lee. "I know you must be in a rush, but c'mon in here and have a soda on me for a minute, hey?"

Lee, all clad in Army green, tried to hide how stiffly he moved. Moments later, he found himself standing at the counter, marveling at a cold bottle of purple Nehi pop in his hand.

His stomach tightened and surged, both, at the thought of reuniting with Ella and Reese. And so, he delayed only a few more minutes with Rickart, telling him as little important about the war as he could get away with.

But outside, just then, Lee heard truck noises.

Dieter

At that moment, Dieter Schneider arrived on the main street of Lewes, outside the apothecary. For caution's sake, he'd had to return to the CCC camp these past few nights, and several trucks from that camp in Lewes still brought their POWs here to this central corner, for distribution for the day.

To his tremendous disappointment, Dieter had been reassigned this week to manage prisoners who worked at the big meat and vegetable cannery that sat just inland from here. Some of the POWs were tiring of this unpleasant work, some sloughing off, and they needed an officer with them for a while.

Dieter watched over his men in the truck, out of sight of the townsfolk as long as possible, as he waited, standing at the back of the vehicle, till the farm trucks arrived and he could disperse the prisoners assigned to field work first. As he waited, a familiar conversation broke out among his fellows, as they discussed other ways they might do right amidst the catastrophe that was this war.

In ebullient German shouts, a couple of them called to Dieter again, "We want to go fight the Japanese." He knew that they were not kidding. "We will volunteer." He had heard it in seriousness in the camp for a while now.

"They told you last year, that was not possible," Dieter said, wishing this very exchange could be heard in English by passers-by. But the high command here in America had considered this idea and roundly rejected it.

Soon, Dieter would have to convince the other contingent of this bunch in the truck to spend another hot day in that God-awful canning factory, smelling of piles of rotting vegetables and meat out behind it. And at last, he saw the farm trucks rounding into the street for the others.

Lee

In the drugstore, several customers who recognized Lee had come over to shake his hand, just as he turned and saw the commotion outside. Trucks and men.

"What the hell is that?"

"German soldiers."

"*What?*"

Lee spun a little too quickly. An impulse ran down his spine and to his hands and stopped there with this new sensation that he had no more equipment with him or gear on than the dress belt around his waist.

Rickart quickly explained about the POW camps in Delmarva, the many thousands of prisoners, and the work details.

"You got to be shittin' me," Lee said.

"Been going on for a couple years and more, Lee," Rickart said, looking at Lee as if surprised he didn't know.

Under his breath, so that only Rickart heard, Lee said, "I thought I was shed of these fuckers."

"Well, you know they been helping out at ..."

Lee looked at Rickart.

"... all about the county," he said, seeming to think of a better way to say it.

"Oh, wait till you see how easy and grand they get treated," said an old codger who had come up to clap Lee on the back, as Lee looked incredulously out at the unfolding scene on the sidewalk.

"Lee, don't worry now," Rickart said, wiping his counter real quick. "It's all been worked out. Peaceful and productive enough, I guess, till we send their asses home. You just get back now and give that family of yours a big hug."

"Peaceful? You think they know anything about that?" Lee said just loud enough that others turned and looked at him. He put his soda down on the marble counter with a bang, hefted his duffel up and left, the screen door of the fountain flapping closed behind him as he started down the sidewalk to get away from this scene. He'd have to cut just past the mess here to get around the block and over to the mechanic's shop, where he was sure he could get a lift back to the farm to surprise Ella.

Dieter

Dieter strode down the sidewalk to confirm with the guards that all the men were in their assigned transports, but, as he did, an American soldier who he didn't see until the last instant, uniformed in his off-duty dress greens, passed him, moving quickly the other way on the sidewalk. The two bumped shoulders, colliding hard enough to turn them both, just as Dieter had called out, "Mach's gut, denn!" to some of the men.

Lee

Lee spun and slowed from the collision, as he saw a "PW" painted on the shoulder of the man's shirt and recognized the bark of Deutsch that had come out of this tall clod, whose Adam's apple looked a lot like the one on the throat Lee had crushed up in the mountains with the barrel of the man's own Sturmgewehr 44 machine gun.

"Hey, *watch it!*" Lee grunted loudly to this oaf of a German who had just knocked into him. The Kraut put up his hands fast in apology as Lee, with a dark storm on his face, hesitated for a second but then made himself turn and keep on down the sidewalk, working to take the drag out of his right leg.

Ella

Ella knew the approximate date but not the exact day that Lee would arrive home. It would be just like him to shush everyone on the way in and amble up here, giving her no notice. He had sent her a message through the base at the cape, saying that it would be early this week, by the time they finished discharging him at the naval shipyard in Philadelphia.

Oh, yes, that would be his way, to come walking up the drive like he'd never left.

Ella had scarcely been able to eat for several days. But regardless of how his arrival happened, she wanted the farm looking cracker-jack, and so she'd had

Levotas and herself hustling around the yard and back lot and sheds, stowing things, mowing along the sides of the buildings, tending to animals and their pens, and generally getting things "squared away" as she always heard military fellows say.

More important, somehow Dieter and the occasional other helping prisoners had been assigned elsewhere for the next few days. Had Everett known?

As she'd toiled in the heat, she'd thought about the risky dance her dear cousin had done for her for so long. As she struggled to roll an old barrel behind the tool shed, she fought even more to know what she wanted to have happen now. She had not fixed her life in time for this! Couldn't even be sure how she wanted it fixed... And now she might make a terrible bosh of it. All because she was not a good enough person to know what was right.

Ella stopped her grunting with the barrel when she heard a vehicle approaching on the road out front. She straightened up quick and looked around the corner. But it passed by. They didn't get much traffic out here, but her head had popped up at every passing car and truck this past day or two.

She exhaled again but leaned on the barrel, feeling sick. As everything in her head and heart came together in that moment, she bent and threw up part of her meager breakfast onto the dirty ground.

Enough! There were things she could not control and so, at length, she collected herself, went up to the house, rinsed and combed out her hair, and changed her dress. It might be right for her soldier to find her unkept in work clothes, but ... Thanks to the labor, the chores in the fields and market-garden acres, and among the livestock, were caught up—as much as they ever were—this afternoon, and so, to bide her time she found herself completing the planting of the flower boxes that hung under the windows along the front of the house. She dropped in the rest of the geraniums that she had overwintered indoors, trying not to step on the places at her feet where the zinnias reseeded themselves each year and would—

Suddenly, she heard a footfall in the crushed clam shells of their driveway, and she spun to see a green-clad man with a big duffle bag up on his shoulder. *Lee.*

She threw down her trowel and gloves. "Lee!"

He was not walking very fast, but he tossed his bag and stepped to her.

"Hi there, Ella," he said, with a wan smile.

Had she forgotten how dark-complected he could look with that hair and with tanned skin? Had he somehow become more so after two years in Italy— and more handsome?

They embraced. Or had she forgotten how solid he was? So squarely built.

But how close or how long to embrace? Neither seemed to know.

"You're beautiful as ever," he said warmly, as Laddie spun circles in front of him and whined and pawed his legs, and Lee cupped his other hand lovingly behind Ella's head.

"I'm just so glad it's all over for you, Lee," she said. "And that you've come through." She held him back and looked him up and down. "Thank you for what you've done over there and for returning to us."

"I'm glad too," he said.

She was having just as much trouble as she knew she would to find words that were honest and right. It pained her nearly to tears. And how strange to see him in a uniform and so manicured.

"How did you get here?"

"Got dropped," he said, nodding his head back north towards the nearest crossroads, "but I wanted to walk this last piece."

"Of course," she said, as he took his first moment to pull his eyes from her and to look up and around at the farm. She knew how much newness he would see. Fixed-up and painted outbuildings, new equipment here and there, and, most of all the two long poultry houses.

Later, Ella couldn't quite remember what they had said clumsily and awkwardly to each other, except that Lee had kept looking all about and admiring the place.

"Well, I'll be," he kept saying.

"Farming has changed these last few years, Lee," Ella said, feeling odd. "Farm production has more than doubled in this country, during the war," she added like a silly girl trying to figure out what to say in a class presentation or on a first date. "We worked our fannies off."

"Was that alfalfa I saw in the upper fields?"

"Part of the new crop rotation."

Lee lifted his cap and scratched his barbered head.

"I don't understand how you managed it," he said.

"I found help," she said. Then, "Here," with some hesitation she took his hand, "let me show you," and led him back into the farmyards.

241

Reese

Reese woke on a warm summer morning, later than usual, and a sound came to him. A sound he had once known. His mother and father talking downstairs! Then he remembered, he was waking again today to a house where his pop was home. And that he'd been in his dad's embrace these last couple days.

He listened, unable to make out the words. But the voices came to him as though from the past, when he had still been a kid, not "a bean sprout of twelve," as his mother now called him. It seemed much longer than two and a half years ago that things had been normal, twice that really since this never-ending war, or fear of it, had taken over.

Reese rose and walked quietly in his bare feet toward the hall. He wanted to run downstairs and hug his pop again, but his folks were having a talk.

Reese had arrived home the day before yesterday from an outing on the bay with his chums to find this father home. Poppa Lee looked different and the same. When they embraced, his dad felt and even smelled like dad. But different too. Spicey. He'd never known him to use an aftershave.

And he moved different too, like sore still.

"You okay, Pop?" Reese had asked, holding his dad's hand as they'd stood out in the backyard, looking each other up and down big-eyed.

"Sure. Got nicked in the backside is all," he said, rubbing his haunch. "It'll be okay."

They'd had a quiet dinner that first night, just the three of them. Reese wanted to ask his pa everything, amidst his mother's glances to slow down.

Still, he had gotten Pop Lee talking about days at sea and beaches in Italy and "hard awful work of pushing the enemy back" and mountains in Italy and nice British people and gardens around a hospital in England.

But his father tired too. And his ma had insisted they let him rest.

This morning, upon his father's third day home, Reese stood quietly at the top of the steps, glad to hear his folks catching up more and more. Wanting it to move past everything else. Hoping to hear his ma in that chattering way when she felt good and his pop's voice booming out confident.

But he heard his ma saying, "The war has changed us all."

"But it's over," his pop said.

He could not hear his mother say anything to that.

"What news of Clarissa and Rand?" his pop asked. His ma had always dubbed them Reese's honorary aunt and uncle.

"What's wrong?" his father asked.

"Well, they had a baby," she said.

"Hell yeah," his pop said in surprise and celebration. "If that's so, then why—"

He heard his ma scooch her chair back, though, and say, "Oh, there'll be time for all that."

Reese knew why she didn't want to tell. So he dressed quick to go down to his pa but then paused again at the top of the steps when he heard his pop saying, "I'll take a look at your ledgers a little bit later."

"You're welcome to, but there's no need. You can trust—" It sounded as though his mother was about to say, "You can trust me," but she stopped and said, "You can trust that I've kept the books properly and that they're nicely in order and in the black, thank you."

There was silence below and Reese sat down at the top of steps—even knowing he ought to be past earwigging like this. When next he heard his father's voice, it was further away, as if in their living room, and as if looking back across their land.

"That middle twenty acres ought to be in something by now."

Reese could clearly make out what his father said about the big strip of land that separated their upper and lower fields.

"No, that's to be fallow these months," his mother called from the kitchen. Reese never remembered her speaking to his father this way. "We're resting that soil while we restore it with the chicken litter first, for late-season planting."

"'We?'"

Reese felt his hand tighten on the stair rail.

"Me and everyone who's helped me," his ma said.

He heard his father ask something he couldn't make out.

After the next silence, his mother's voice came from the living room as well. Reese stepped down and leaned over the rail.

"Lee Tingle, you left me here on this farm, and I've managed to keep it."

"Yes, you sure have. But I didn't leave you. I was called."

"You answered a calling."

His mother's voice was more muffled now, softer and more quavery, and Reese strained to hear.

"Listen, Lee, I'm sure you did many brave things that you'll share with us in time, and we are proud of you—and thanking the Lord that you made it safe and are back. But you've come back to *my* farm now."

"Always was, El..."

"Because you wanted it that way, and so it's become."

He couldn't hear his pop say anything to that.

"Now let's see what you want it to be," his ma added.

It fretted Reese all that night and he woke to a fear that Dieter might be assigned back to them by today. He'd never in his life seen his pop sleep in, well past dawn—and for some reason on their sofa since he'd got back—but Reese went down and roused him while his ma rested for once. Reese made boiled grits for him and his pa and, as they ate, asked nothing other than what chow was like in the Army and out on the battlefield. Then he convinced his pop to hike down to the canal with him.

His father looked confused for a moment by the notion but then whispered, "I'm glad for the excuse, and doctors said I'm supposed to walk as much as I can."

He was none too fast, but he kept up. His pop's right leg kind of yanked up and around a little when he walked. Reese covered his sadness at it and tried to take no notice.

Reese led him down and showed him the old skiff that they'd always kept stashed by the canal—the one Reese had used during his dad's absence. Reese had covered her with tarps so she wouldn't weather, and plugged some leaks with resin and shellac. He'd painted her and put her up on blocks so she would not sit on the ground. It was the first time he had seen his pop smile all the way and let out a laugh since he had been home.

Reese had enough tackle and dried bait hidden under the boat that they could decide right then and there to go for a float and a fish.

"This is real fine, son," his father said, once they were bobbing in the warm sun on a slack high tide in the canal. "Why did you call her the Davis?"

Reese felt himself stiffen. He had painted "*USS Davis*" in white letters on the front of the bow on either side. He'd clean forgotten.

"After the *Davis,* Pop. You know, the American destroyer," Reese said quietly, trying to turn attention back to their fishing lines.

"Why that one?"

Caught, he had to say it now.

"Because it went down this spring from a U-boat torpedo." Just two months ago with all hundred men aboard lost.

His pop looked at him, then nodded in agreement. Then stopped—

"The *Davis?*" His father lowered his fishing pole. "Wudn't that the one Rand Ellis was assigned to?"

Reese leaned forward, unable to meet his pop's eyes. But when this man looked at him and asked him a question, he could only ever answer truthful. It was what scared him the most about having his pop back.

But this one, at least, he would answer for his ma, nodding yes.

"And your Aunt Clarissa with their new baby ...?" His father's mouth hung open. "Rand Ellis, lost at sea ...?"

Wind out of the west had taken their drift too far into the tidal grass.

"He knew about the child?"

"Yes, sir. Uncle Rand got the news some weeks before he went down with the ship," Reese answered, trying not to go blubbery like his ma and like he had when he'd first heard the news and known his father was shipping home at the same time.

Ma Ella should be doing this telling! Just like she ought on other things too.

Reese put his pole down and took hold of the oars to get them back in the middle of the canal.

"But they found that sub *and killed it,* Pop," he said, quick and hopeful, looking up into his father's eyes. "From the air and from the other destroyers," he added quickly.

But his father looked pale.

"You all right, Pa?"

"Sure, bud."

But the war had followed his father home and even out here, and dwelled with them again now.

"That was out there, though, while the battle was still going," Reese said, nodding toward the cape and the Atlantic, as he pulled his oars back in and put a piece of dried clam on the hook at the bottom of his father's rig. They had all heard of rogue U-boats still out there that had refused to surrender, but ... Rumors mostly.

"Yep, I don't think there's any subs back here in this canal, bub," his pop said, looking like he fought his way out of a daze, and trying hard for a grin.

Reese nodded seriously, then less so, as they let the shifting tide start to take them south again along the inland waterway.

"Atta boy," his father said. He gave Reese a quick rub on his shoulders, but then a far-away expression came back on his face again.

Lee

"Who is that man back there?" Lee asked Ella.

Lee stood at the back door of their farmhouse, looking out toward the edge of their fields, past a picnic table that someone had built in their back yard during the years he was away. Lee had sat right there with Ella just yesterday, as she had leaned forward on her elbows, her face hidden in her hair. Lee had placed his hands on her arms to try to comfort her, after she had told him fully of Clarissa's mourning.

"She will never be the same again," she had lamented, and then oddly added, "like lots of us. And poor Rand, probably killed in his bunk as he slept. I spent as many days with her as I could, this spring when the news came."

Lee had learned that—my God—the *Davis* has been the last US naval vessel lost in the Battle of the Atlantic.

This morning, though, his woman seemed to have regained herself. Lee only wished he could say the same, in these mixed-up-feeling days since his return, as he gazed far across to some sturdy-looking fellow who was working in the distance out on their land.

Try as he might, Lee had not yet been able to rise early, as had he once done. And he and Ella had kept separate beds. He knew it best for now.

As he had dressed this morning, though, he'd thought he'd heard a truck stop by briefly.

"He's just one of the helpers who has been assigned to us from time to time," Ella answered curtly.

"You've become one good boss-woman and overseer," Lee said cheerfully, looking at Ella for a chuckle.

Perhaps she would laugh with him again, in time, Lee thought, as he tightened the strap on his farming dungarees for the first time, still curious though.

"He's a hand who's learned the jobs around here," Ella said. She seemed to at least try for an airy tone. "Let him be. He knows what to do."

Ella then insisted, right away, that Lee come down to the basement with her and help with a shelf that had collapsed this past winter and a door that was off its hinges.

"Be along, presently," Lee called to her, as soon as she went to the cellar. But as she began busying herself down there, he went quietly out back, and toward the fields. He had took a mind to thank this laborer out there and any others who'd lent a hand, whoever they were.

Dieter

Out on a dirty rise on the mid-fields, where the corner gate led into the animal pasturing, Dieter repaired some wiring that one of the heifers had pushed down. He muddled over how odd his Ella had acted these past few days, neither coming to meet or greet him. He wondered again at what he had blabbed to Lida Crousch. He wanted a chance to correct himself and make clear to her that he'd had no contact—in fact, from 1939 through 1941—with the young woman who he had been forced to marry. He knew only from his family that she had stopped insisting that the child was his and then had fatigued of farming life in their village and had fled to the city. He was not even sure of her whereabouts by the time the German navy had swept him up.

Dieter worried that Crousch had said something false or misconstrued to Ella, with whom he'd wrongly shared little about his previous life. That was his fault but he would correct it by—

Dieter raised his head suddenly. A man was approaching him. A man he did not know. Dressed in overalls and work clothes. The man was solidly built, with dark hair and eyes. He raised his hand as he approached and then walked up.

"I want to thank you, sir, for whatever-all it is you've done here," he said.

Dieter straightened the rest of the way and nodded. Something told him to stay mum, even as in the same instant he could not help himself from saying, "You are welcome, of course."

Lee

Lee had extended his hand, but now dropped it slowly, hearing that deep almost-lispy cut at English that he knew too well, from prisoners they had taken, but now from this strapping blond-haired, blue-eyed man before him.

How could—? A German accent? Then he spotted the "PW," painted on the shoulder of his shirt. Was this the same lug of a POW that he had run into on the sidewalk uptown?

"Lee Tingle," Lee finished, not being able to stop himself, growing almost inaudible even as he said it.

Dieter

Dieter had all of a sudden guessed as much, with a jolt running through him. He had seen pictures up at the farmhouse.

"Okay, yes. I did not know you have returned to here," Dieter heard himself babble.

Lee

That same clipped guttural voicing that Lee had heard through smoky wood lines and hedgerows, behind walls and moving and retreating along village blocks and past rocky crevasses, and in lines of captives, some overly pleased to have been caught and not killed, and finally, in the end, below a rocky mountain-top lip over which a German mountain patrol had come and then tried to kill his platoon, and—

Lee took a step back.

Dieter

Dieter, his pulse racing, realized that his hand had slipped around instinctively, protectively, close to the hammer that he knew hung on his belt—horrified at the very thought of it.

Lee

Lee's nostrils flared. But, with all his will, he turned without another word and stalked back to the farmhouse.

39

Ella

"You didn't inform me properly," Ella heard Lee say again as he faced her from the hallway and she stood in the kitchen. "Didn't alert me that you had German prisoners working on this farm."

Lee loomed there. Squared-off and solid like an athlete, his hands shoved in his pockets and his feet spread wide.

"Okay, Lee, you're right. But please don't talk to me like I'm one of your enlisted men," she asked him, not wanting to feel like some recalcitrant soldier of his at this moment.

She placed her hands on the back of one of the chairs. In fact, the chair that Dieter had often sat in.

"All right, then, but you didn't trust me enough to tell me about them," he said, motioning out back to the farm.

"No," Ella agreed. "I didn't—or hadn't yet. I didn't believe you'd take it right … especially now, so fast. I don't know. I'm sorry."

"And I have to find it out on my own recon?"

Ella stared at him for a second. "You see, this is what I mean," she said. "And I'm sorry if I don't know all the right ways to bring you back into this place, Lee, but you don't seem all the way back. And so that's why, and you'll have to forgive me my weaknesses if you are to become part of us again."

As they spoke, more than a week had gone since that first and only encounter between the two men out back, and Lee had not acknowledged Dieter's presence any further until today.

He had sulked around on a slow simmer, a low boil that—

"I want them out of here," Lee said, in a low tone. "All Germans."

"No. Who will work this place then?"

Everett had informed her that many of the German POWs would not go home until next year—or at least that a good portion of them would be retained until the end of this current farming season.

Lee stepped fully into the kitchen, scowling.

"Levotas is getting older and more cantankerous by the day," Ella went on. "Unless I'm supposed to pay full wage to farm hands."

"Ella, I am *back,*" he said, starting to raise his voice.

"Mmm-hmm. How much? And in what way? And are you back in body too?"

"I'm okay."

"Why haven't you picked up anything heavy with your right arm?"

Her one-time and maybe-yet common-law husband stilled at the question. She had seen it from the moment he had carried his duffle bag up their driveway, and since.

"Shoulder was damaged in the fight too," he said, dropping his eyes, rolling his shoulder and flexing his arm and his fist.

He had mentioned "the fight" a couple of times but had not told them anything else about it. She knew only from the letter she had received from the Army that a stab wound suffered in combat with the enemy accounted for his limp.

"Tell me," she said.

"Something cracked and something tore when I hit the ground. It's okay now," he said, extending his arm straight out.

"I'm so sorry for that too," she said, as she went to him.

She reached up and inspected and worked his shoulder gently with both hands.

His face was close to hers and she crinkled her nose when he breathed on her. "That won't help you either," she said. The smell of alcohol.

She had tried to give him warm, friendly patience. Now it was time for something else.

"Okay, you say you're back"

"*Yes.*"

"I need more than 'back.' Are you back to you and back *better,* like I started to see in your letters?"

"Sure."

"Prove it to us all."

She saw his face cloud again. "Well, you'll just have to see, won't ya?" he said.

250

But it happened again two days later, with him railing at her.

"In the meantime, I ain't working with them," Lee said, waving toward their acres. Somewhere along the rear of the farm, Dieter and another prisoner were clearing brush today. "Damned cockamamie arrangement ..."

Lee took a sudden step and smacked his hand on the table. "You know our 5th Army lost twenty thousand men beating those bastards back up the peninsula. Many more times that in wounded too."

Ella held a breath. She had not heard an exact figure. All those just from the 5th ... Horrible.

"You're going to have to decide," he grumbled as he ambled off, but it sounded more like a threat than a question.

At the end of the day, Ella was out at the top of their lane, in the driveway for the POW pick-up. She wanted to watch over this and at least see Dieter for a moment.

"Is it okay?" Dieter said to her quietly as he walked by. "You okay?"

She nodded.

"We will talk," she reassured him.

"No, I want to see you. We can—"

"And don't come back!" someone hollered, making Ella jump. She looked over to see Lee ambling towards them, moving like some saddle-sore cowboy, as he barked at the Germans at the back of the truck.

"Had enough of you sausage-eaters. Git!" he said, gesturing with those big hands and forearms of his. In one, he held a can of beer. She'd suspected that he had a case of beer around here somewhere, and only wondered at how he had gotten it. Black market from the base was the only way, since the metal scarcity had stopped canned beer for the public years ago.

He shook the can as he strode toward them. "Here!" He punched a hole in it with a can opener. "Some of the piss water y'all lap up like momma's milk." And just that fast he tossed the can toward the prisoners, rolling it underhand in at their feet, like laying a grenade under them and their vehicle.

The beer sprayed over the men's feet as Ella reached the space between Lee and the Germans, to slow him.

"Get in," she shouted over her shoulder to the three Germans who stood at the back of the truck, staring.

She put a hand on each of Lee's shoulders and succeeded in stopping him. Then she turned him partway back around.

Ella made a quick glance back and saw that Dieter and his big boots had come to a dead stop at the tailgate of the truck—not removing himself until he saw that this collision between Ella and Lee didn't get worse.

Lee saw it too. "What are *you* looking at?" he called out, but the Army-corporal driver moved Dieter quickly into the truck, and Ella kept Lee where he was until they drove out.

Dieter

The black-and-white film showed more images of concentration camp prisoners. Scantily clad in the cold. Thin, drawn, emaciated. Malnourished, hair shaved, and looking sick.

To the clatter of the projector, Dieter and his fellow prisoners watched in the hot, darkened commons hall of the POW camp. It was the eyes, of those people … The eyes of the death-camp prisoners in these film reels that Dieter could not stop seeing. That followed him afterwards.

He could not endure any more such faces. Deep, dark, sunken. Glazed over in the damnation they had experienced, and now in forever shock and eternal alteration.

Then came the bodies, in piles of rag clothes or naked. Dumped in ditches. And, of course the bones, stacks of bones.

"Please, no more Knochenfilme," Dieter's men had pleaded with him. The "films of *bones*" as they called them, which all prisoners in all the camps were forced to watch.

But Dieter could do nothing, and would not have stopped these showings anyway. And it was compulsory this evening again, to see the newest reel of the atrocities.

The very next day, Dieter stood out in the prison yard before a huge bonfire with hundreds of his fellow POWs, and he hurled his German uniform into the flames. Most of the other men in the camp did the same with theirs, while others simply looked confused and a few still denied that it could be possible—the extent of what they had seen in the pictures.

But for the bulk of the men, the burning of the uniforms they had been captured in was the least and, unfortunately, the most they could do at the moment to try to express their shock and anger at the crimes their nation had committed—and for which they would always share guilt.

Dieter stared into the flames, wondering what more they would discover had happened in their homeland in the years since they had left. He had embarked from Kiel aboard the U-858 in December of 1941. Theirs had been agonizingly long, *months*-long, voyages with too much killing. And the few times they had returned—beating all the odds among U-boats by returning at all, let alone repeatedly—they had berthed in Hamburg, only briefly, making it even harder to get word to family. Nothing at all to be known of the girl who had once called him husband, and father of her child, or tried to.

Dieter watched his lieutenant-commander's jacket smoking and turning from gray to black. On that day when he and the helpers at Ella's farm had been drinking the honey vodka, he knew he had made a terrible mistake by saying anything to Frau Crousch about that young woman and child that he had thought of at home and long discounted. He had tried to find a way back to Ella's neighbor lady so that he could explain or retract, tried asking for a day's assignment back to her farm—to head her off.

If he could only know Ella's heart now, with her before-man back on the farm. It scared him to go there now and—

Dieter had to step back as the breeze shifted and the inferno before him reached its peak in the hot, dry, dusty summer air, and the incinerating stench came into his face. Was there any chance that his family had not died in the Dresden firestorm precipitated by the allies?

"Did you know about the concentration camps?" Ella had asked him quickly last week, as he'd readied to mount the truck again at the end of another day.

"I think for most of us the answer is yes," he said very somberly, but then explained that they knew of relocation camps and in some cases knew that these were work camps. They had been given to understand that they were camps for resistors too but they did not know these to be such places of suffering or death. "That is our fault. It seems most those bad things happened in the east, and we knew little of that front."

But in the sadness with which Ella looked back at him, he knew the horrible inadequacy of his answer.

Lee

With heavy shirt and gloves on, Lee walked into the barnyard. He saw Ella standing next to the two gas cans he had filled—the long-nozzled ones they used to set burns out in the fields.

"The bottom acres," Lee said. "Gonna burn that corn scrub off."

He was bound for what he had discovered to be the new southmost section of their land. Ella had been offered an early-producing sweet-corn seed variety by the extension office and had her "helpers" put it in by April. It wasn't a lot of acres but apparently she'd gotten good money for being the first farm around here to get table corn to the markets this month. The stalks and husks and all left over after the harvester went through needed clearing this summer, so they could get winter wheat in.

"That there is still too green to burn," Ella said.

Lee stopped. "Well, don't you just know everything now? Maybe you don't need me around here anymore."

"Lee ..."

As they stood facing each other in silence, the far western horizon drew Lee's eyes off. At length, he said, "You know most of my regiment is getting retrained and sent across to fight the Japs."

He thought he saw a shiver go through her. From the news, they all knew that the Japanese were dug in and unrelenting in places like Iwo Jima and Okinawa.

"I want to go too," he said.

"Lee, stop it."

But inside him was something he could not turn off.

"I want to fight the Nips."

He watched Ella purse her lips hard in complete disquiet, and he thought of their encounter with her cousin Everett yesterday up town. The man had made himself damn scarce since Lee's return, not even dropping by to welcome him home, and had acted even more awkward than normal when they'd run into him. Conversation had gone to the war, of course. Everett had mentioned the military hearsay—that it could cost another million American lives to take the Japanese home islands and mainland, if they were to try.

Lee stepped past Ella and picked up the burn cans to go.

"You need some help tending that," Ella called after him about the fire he would now set.

"I can manage."

Some hours later, Lee returned to the farmyard at a slow walk with his empty cans. He allowed now that the woman had been right. The fields had only half burned. But that hadn't kept the fire from jumping a couple times to the next-door field and copse of wood, and he'd barely been able to beat it out on his own.

A shit morning's work, he thought, as he reached the barnyard, dirty, hot, and tired—his throat dry, in need of a drink, a real drink—but then stopped.

There, behind the storage shed, he spotted his wife. Working next to the big damn German. Her, with her clipboard in her hand. Him moving sacks of seed and calling off to her, as she took stock of their supply.

But what stood him still was not that this job was done between the two of them, or that they were working together, or even the easy, practiced way in which they did—no, it was her *manner* with the man.

Lee moved around to the corner of the barn so he could hear.

The German was chatting conversationally with Ella. "We have collected almost one thousand dollars from the men's pays and saved it from this past year—then sent it to the American Red Kreuz—the Red *Cross*."

"That's wonderful, Dieter," Ella said and reached up and patted his back.

Not a minute later they had turned to something else and he heard her laugh with the man.

In the smell of smoke still drifting from their new south acres, Lee felt his own fire ripple through him, hotter than anything else he had felt this morning. For some cursed reason—as he tasted still the fine ash and the residue all over him from the crap job he'd just done—his mind leapt back to the memory of a flame-thrower unit that he had witnessed a squad of the German mountaineers use against an American dugout in the hills, a way up north of Cassino. Too far down across a canyon for his regiment to get there in time to help. But not too far away for them to hear the screaming sounds of the men trapped inside, a sound that transported his mind to the moaning that burn victims had made next him in the first field hospital he had arrived in—groans of pain all night long.

Then, as Lee came back to the here-and-now, he saw his wife give the German a quick rub on the back of his neck. It was not so much that Ella had touched the German, or how she had touched him. Or even how long it had been since she had touched Lee like that. Instead, it was in her voice—not the words but the way she burbled and bubbled with him. It was her *way* with him, as she smiled in a kind of smile that had been withheld from him so far.

And with that, Lee knew again the animal engine in him. And that it was ready to take over. Knew he wasn't quite right yet. And that he would only partly remember what he did in the next minute if he did not turn away.

Reese

Reese manned his produce stand at the crossroads, unmoving in the heat, as he tapped his fingers. If people would just drive by easy, they would see he had sweet corn. Silver-queen white. A few bushel that they had kept in the spring house, still from that first crop. Tomatoes, big and early because they'd started them up in April in the cold frames. String beans coming now, several peck to sell.

Upon his wooden crate, he moved further under the shade of the plyboard top that he and Poppa Lee had put over the stand. Last week, that pop had helped him fix and paint up this little structure for the season.

It was good to get away on another summer day. From that place that was so betwixt and between. Wasn't right around there, amongst them. Felt like he couldn't be with his people anymore ... What with all that went unsaid and that still lingered. And he searched daily for how to help it run its course ...

Then yesterday, he'd seen his ma sneak a smooch to Dieter's cheek before he loaded on the truck to go back to the camp—and that was it. It brought back all he had known over this past year and two, and he would endure it no longer.

But as he repositioned his "FARM FRESH" sign against the front of his stand, he told himself that all that grown-up wrongness was not why he had cleared out again today. No, he needed to raise up some money if he was to buy that canoe that had caught his fancy. One of the new Grummans that had just started coming out that he had seen at the marine store over at the boatyard. Made out of aluminum! Why, he could practically carry it himself. With that boat, he'd paddle up to Milford and beyond and down to Rehoboth and further to Indian River if he could time the tides right and—

Reese stopped daydreaming as a car coming down the road slowed up. The road and the car were dusty, putting up a trail behind. A Hudson ... The widow

Crouch's old boat! Well, at least she might buy from him. She stopped right in front, got out, and walked over.

"My, ain't you early with all this," she declared looking down her nose at his offerings. "Guess it's easy when y'all have so much help around the place," she said, raising an eyebrow at him. "Still, huh?"

He knew who she meant.

"Yes, ma'am."

Before him, he had a nasty critter. He thanked goodness that he had long since graduated out of her class at Sunday school. But, just the same, the woman could be used like a megaphone to the world if you wanted or didn't want to spread some whisperings.

"And now with that brave father of yours home. Must have been quite a shock for him, when he saw who was helping around your place."

Reese's jaw tightened. He ought to've known this might come.

"Guess he doesn't need to know," she said, feigning a whisper, "that one of them didn't spend much time at the camp last year." She did not meet his eye but used her thumbnail to peel back a husk and inspect the corn. "Lived with y'all mostly, hey?"

Reese felt a pit in his gut. But here was maybe a way. And, anyhow, she already knew. "I suppose," he said.

"Family style?"

All motion went out of Reese. One of those pauses came again when time stopped—like he could reach out and touch it and pluck it in its stillness. In a flash, he relived everything he had known, good and bad, with those three adults back on his farm. But his mother needed help 'cause she was stuck and he knew what the widow was good for too. "I guess," he answered.

She tossed the corn down with no interest now.

"But what of it, Mrs. Crouch?" he said abruptly, suddenly trying to reel it back in, almost quick as he had said it.

"Well now, don't get fresh, young man." But then she went back to a tone as if browsing again. "Let's be civil."

She disregarded the green beans completely.

"Well, I reckon your poppa won't have to worry about it much longer," she said, as she pointed to a couple of the larger tomatoes that she would take. "Now that they'll be shipping that lot home."

His friend Dieter … who had been his pal too. But who was in the way of everything now!

"Truth be known, I'll bet that big one will be in a hurry to skedaddle back," she went on, as she poked for coinage in her little needlepoint pouch that looked so tight and lightly used he expected to see moths flying out of. "What with that wife and child of his waiting for him back home on his farm. Longing for him I'm sure back in that black Fatherland of theirs. Damned as it is now!"

Reese suddenly fumbled the change he was counting out for her. Wife and child? Dieter had a family in Germany? And a farm yet?

But he made himself stare stony at the widow, who narrowed her eyes at him too. "On account of he told me himself," she said with a nod.

Then she half-heartedly wished him luck with his selling and was off with herself and her brown paper bag of two tomatoes. He wanted to tell her not to come back and to holler out, "You're fired as my customer!" but his tongue stuck to his mouth.

"You go on ahead and let it be known, if you want," she said back over her shoulder as she walked away.

Ella

Out at the road in front of their place, Lee greeted the Army driver and got in the long green car with the white star on the side. He closed the car door with a bang, as Ella peeked out from behind the lace curtains she had put in their front windows, and the car roared off with a puff of smokey exhaust.

"I'll take the day to myself," Lee had said.

As soon as he was out of sight and the Army vehicle disappeared around the corner at the crossroads, Ella jumped in their pickup, and minutes later, pulled into a parking spot at Saint Peter's.

She never needed an excuse to seek out Reverend Rightmyer, but with tired arms she lifted a box of canned foods out of the bed of the truck anyway.

When she set down her box of big blue Mason jars, sealed and labelled, with a thud on the table in the rectory, she said, "For your Red Cross larder."

Nelson Rightmyer nodded appreciation.

"But Ella, the War in the Atlantic is won, you know."

"Of course," she said, pushing straggled hair behind her ear as she gazed at the packed and suspended vegetables and meats and fruits that she and Dieter had farmed and put by. "Then for the church pantry."

"Surely," he said as he took the box, but stood there in his work clothes looking at her.

"Can we walk?" she asked.

They strolled the path from the rectory up toward the church, through the old cemetery. Nelson asked after everyone's whereabouts today. They had relented at last and let Reese join up the Boy Scouts real fast so he could go to the scout camp this week with his new chums Tanner and Vic, over at the Chesapeake upon the North East River.

And what about her farm help? Nelson worked hard to make that come out like a casual question. Dieter and another prisoner were working in the market fields today, probably picking forty bushel at least of zucchini for the fast truck to Philadelphia.

She felt his relief when she quickly added that Lee was away too. He had caught that lift to the Armed Services office in Dover to finish some of his veteran's paperwork. He had planned no more than that, she was certain, from the way he had dressed and the few things he carried—no walking across the hall to the re-enlistment office today and no slipping out to the bar, she made him promise.

"Other days, though, I dare not leave the farm, Nelson," she said, stopping in her tracks and letting it come through in her voice. "Not any time they are both there."

"Of course." She needed explain no further.

She grabbed the arm of his shirt, stopped him, and blurted out. "How much longer can I do this?" Finding chores at opposite ends of her place for them. Each day, directing Dieter accordingly ...

The option of ending Dieter's service with them was so obvious that her rector didn't even speak it. He kept his lips tight and shook his head.

She stepped closer, even as she could not bear the sound of her own voice. Imploring.

"Nelson, is it possible to love two people at the same time?"

He swallowed hard and dropped his eyes, then fumbled in the pocket of his dungarees.

Or was it possible then to all of a sudden discover that you don't love either of them?

Reverend pulled out a pair of gloves and handed them to her and, as if in an invitation to wait for his answer, said, "Come help me," and nodded her over toward the cemetery.

Sometime later, Ella's gloved hands were yanking at the grass and weeds around one of the ancient tombstones. She was on all fours in the hot summer sun, as Nelson worked alongside her at the next grave marker over, likewise clearing out the growth that was too close to these randomly spaced, cockeyed, and historic old monuments for the lawnmower to get to.

They had said little more as they worked upon the graves of those who had come before them in this place, in the parish of this seafaring church, including some who had been born in the 1600s. Pilots of the bay, river, and ocean. Patriots of the war for Independence, veterans of the war of 1812, even a governor and senator, all interred here.

"Oww." Ella pulled her hand back as it brushed against something rough—an old piece of iron sticking out of the ground beside one of the stones. "What's this?"

Nelson gestured to the marker. "Henry McCracken, a long-time ship's captain." The date of death said 1868. "He requested that his anchor be buried with him. That's one of its flukes sticking out."

Ella straightened up on her knees in the warm grass, and rocked back on her haunches, thankful for a cooling breeze that puffed in from the direction of the bay and the ocean, and she thought about her kith and kin, and Lee's, tied to this place for generations. Then about the anchor with which her father had decorated their front walk.

"You didn't answer my question," she said all at once to the rector.

He was working a pair of clippers around a marker, and now he stopped. "Lord forgive me for saying it this way, but—while I wish the best for these men of yours—what I care about is *you*, Ella, and your well-being." He looked up east and to the wisps of white clouds undulating through the blue summer sky. "And how you…I mean to say, think about the last time we were together."

It had been the last survivor incident that Nelson helped with, just a few months earlier. He had rung her up and asked her if she could get over to the Coast Guard station as fast as possible.

When she got there, he was already dispatching the sailors that had arrived at the pier in Lewes after their freighter had been sunk by one of the last of the prowling U-boats. Yes, indeed her pastor had been there that day, going from one man to the next, evaluating each, one at a time, according to what care or housing he might need, and overseeing the ambulance services.

They looked steadily at each other now, recalling the hell they had seen one more time on the faces of these men.

"Have you been able to push that all away ..." Nelson said, shaking his head and seeming to struggle for the right words. "Much less ... believe that you could leave that and everything behind, in the way you might be thinking of?"

During that hour at the life-saving station, he'd had her distributing blank Western Union message forms so that the sailors could notify family members that they had survived the sinking.

She had to fill the silence now with something. "How many survivors do think you helped?" she asked. During this war.

"Hundreds," he said. "More than any other town on this Atlantic coast, I'll warrant that. Buried too many, too."

That day, some of the survivors' hands had trembled too much to fill anything out, so she had done it for them, taking the information from them and carefully scribing it.

Some of the sailors from that day remained here still at Beebe Hospital.

"I don't want life to be even *harder* for you," Nelson went on. He was speaking to her now as nothing other than her friend. And as ever, he would never say anything directly about Lee, for or against.

"Thank you," Ella said as she rose suddenly. "I think I need to go home."

Some days later, on a stinky hot morning, Ella crossed the farmyard in back of her place, feeling like she stormed across the yard.

Lee was off on an errand and then he would go seek some company at the VFW. Reese was to return from Scout camp tomorrow.

When she had rounded past here, behind their farmyard, just ten days ago, she had heard Reese's voice. Then Lee's, the two of them laughing together, over on the far side of the poultry house, the operation of which Lee had appropriated. They followed each other about, Reese showing his pop the many things he'd learned about helping out here, so that the two of them ended up—

Her thoughts flipped as she spotted Dieter up toward the farthest end of their market garden. He was raking off the zuke vines while he minded the picker they had here today, a migrant working through their beans just the next lot over.

She strode to the German. He straightened up seeing her coming so quickly toward him.

"You *lied* to me," she said and took a tearful swing at his head, which he mostly ducked.

Reese had only been able to share it with her in the form of a letter that he had mailed to her from his summer camp.

"You have a wife and children back in your country," she said, her voice cracking.

"No," Dieter said, holding up his hands. "No, they weren't and I don't even know them anymore."

Some day she would have to forgive the boy for telling her what he had discovered, and then sharing it with her only in a letter. It was to be expected, though, with what he knew.

"Haven't seen them for a long time before this war starts," Dieter was babbling quickly.

Yes, everything was about his father now, with her son. Lee Tingle got all the credit, not just for permitting him to go to scout camp but for winning the war that Dieter was a symbol of.

"That child? He's not mine, I don't think."

"You 'don't *think?*'"

Yes, a wounded Lee had arrived into their lives and Ella had returned a kind of invisible knife into his back with Dieter's lingering presence and all her weakness.

"They not still alive, I don't think."

The migrant picker was staring at them, but she doubted he spoke English.

"You 'don't *think?*'" Ella hollered at Dieter again and gave him a shove, before she gave him her back and strode away.

Lee

On an early morning, Lee worked next to Ella's cousin Everett out by the Fort Miles gate, where surplus Army supplies had been set out for the taking. Lee was sure that the farm could use some of these lockers and hoses and great spools of wire and such, and Everett had invited him to be the first to pick from it.

But now Lee suspected it was an excuse for Lieutenant Everett Hall to corner him—something he didn't need.

"Leave him be, Lee. Like I said. I'm telling you," Everett spoke, as the two of them hefted up an empty 50-gallon barrel into the back of the farm's pickup.

But Lee had left the Army at the same rank as Everett, and so, with a grin, he said, "I don't think a lieutenant can order a lieutenant about."

He spoke it trying to lighten the mood and get the man off it! But Everett would not let go.

"That's my advice to you," Ella's cousin said. "Leave it be. They're friends. Just ride it out."

It rubbed Lee wrong and he said, "All the same, why don't you tell me when you going to get these devils out of here?"

"It's not up to me, Lee."

Lee wondered if this was the truth.

But Everett kept on. "It's up to your— To Ella and her needs," he said. "For her, *her* farm, and to how long these laborers are kept here stateside by the government."

"Her 'needs?' It might be up to more than that," Lee growled, feeling the last few years well up inside him again. "You ought see how I have to skirt around to stay away from those buggers, and what I want to do when I hear him sprechen that dirty-douche Deutsch talk on our place."

"*Lee,*" Everett shouted, as he hurled a bundle of oak stakes into the truck bed. "If you stay hot-headed about this, that could be the end of it. And the end of the return you wanted for yourself." He tried to take a hold of Lee's elbow. "You're not where you need to be yet, my friend. You need to be all the way back with us, and there's a ways to go."

Lee knew that Everett had seen it in other men returning from the war.

"You don't have to tell me."

"You're not all the way with us still."

"No, I'm not," Lee said, yanking his arm away.

"Why, you can't even meet my eyes or other people's half the time."

Lee let out a pshaw, and a doubtful "Please," and turned from him.

"You're home now, Lee. You're not soldiering anymore."

Lee let them quiet as he motioned for Everett to help him heft up a bale of wire fencing.

"The work those prisoners did was a Godsend, and a blessing to your ... to that place you're on—and to plenty of other folk," Everett said. "To the war effort, for that matter! It was damn hard to manage it, but we pulled it off. And they cooperated dutifully."

Lee harrumphed. One of his cronies last night at the tavern had made a comment about that one big oaf of a German having served as the "man of the farm" while Lee was away. Lee had left prompt out the rear of the bar to keep himself from thrashing the drunk varmint to an inch of his life. But it confirmed to him that the Kraut goon had been on their place for much more of his deployment than Lee had realized.

"You want to be with a fine woman, right?" Everett was asking, his voice rising again.

"Sure."

"In fact, the most quality one I know? Not perfect but closest I've ever seen?"

"Of course."

"You always have wanted to. Just didn't know how, so you all but twiddled it away."

"I know that. I know it now too."

Everett was leaning in, not letting off. "Then, darn it, Lee Tingle, don't mess with things there for the moment. Whatever farm set-up is still in place, it's just the way you found it when you got back, that's all. And here's the one thing you can do, just let it be and let it go ... Let it *run its course*. And everything will come out all right for you and El, one way or the other."

"'Or the other?'" Lee barked, then shouldered Everett away from the back of the truck and slammed the tailgate shut.

"That's if you're a wise man," Everett said, standing his ground.

But as Lee got in and drove away, with no thank-you to Everett, he felt a dark turn in himself.

"Mind my words!" Ella's cousin hollered after him, as Lee wondered why the man seemed so involved in all this.

But now, he headed straight back, all the way along wondering if this world he had returned to was just upside down. Full of Nazi lovers or was he just going crazy?

He needed to do some good in this hour, though, with what was turning inside him, as he drove back through and then out of town to get back to their farm.

Still did, as he approached the Crouch farm, and then got an idea—with all this booty in the back of the truck. Widow's place could use some of this loot too. He was sure.

Lida Crouch came running out when she saw him stopping by to her.

"Why I'll be," she called out minutes later and clapped her hands, as she watched Lee roll three big bales of fencing that would be good for chickens out of the back of the truck.

"Sure is nice to have menfolk back," Lida said. "I hope your Ella appreciates."

"You'd think," Lee grumbled, as he toted the bales over to the side of her drive.

"Well, she's been a ... *resourceful* one, I suppose is the word, and as I guess you know," Lida continued.

Lee slowed up and looked at her.

"I trust you guessed by now, dear, and heard and don't doubt it—and damn the luck that it comes to me to say it, if I even need to, that she took—" Here Lida stopped for an instant and had to clear a frog in her throat. "—full advantage of what was available to her while you were gone."

Lee's eyes were upon her like a rifle shot. He studied her hard, but she held his eyes and let the most mournful and woebegone look stay on her face. "Oh, honey." She nodded yes, to be sure he took her awful meaning. And let her chin quiver. In case he had any doubt.

Looking only straight ahead, then, he moved back toward his truck, noticing that he was opening and closing his right hand over and over, as he got in saying nothing more, and drove off toward the Hall farm, pointing himself with intent.

Dieter

Dieter kicked a coffee can so hard it flew half the length of the soccer field in the POW camp near Milford that he had been transferred back to, suddenly last evening, for some reason that he did not understand. The instruction had come from up high somewhere, he was sure. He wondered if Ella's cousin was somehow behind it again.

What a terrible turn, he thought, when he could have been helping Ella on this busy summer day and planning with her for a quick slip-away.

How fast could he get another audience with her to explain more! The last he had heard anything about that girl back in his homeland that Ella was so upset about—the last he had known anything of her or her boy—was when his U-858 had been berthed briefly in Hamburg, early in 1942, and he had been able to pick up a post from one of their family friends in Plön that said she and the child had moved east to Lübeck, the medieval-looking village—that beautiful, red-brick Hanseatic League town, near the Baltic. Ella must understand that this young woman who had claimed him had been lost to him, by intent of them both for years before he last departed Germany.

Dieter began glancing this way and that, at the many easy ways available to escape this camp.

40

Reese

On another hot-as-blazes afternoon, the electrical fan whirred in the corner of the living room, but Reese could only feel it blowing more warm air on him. His mother fanned herself with a *McCall's* magazine.

Reese had told her that they ought to go up town to get a cool drink at the drugstore. But he'd said it without much gusto. Neither of them wanted to move right now in the heat. Last week had brought news of the atomic bombs dropped by America on Hiroshima and Nagasaki. Single bombs big enough to level a city. No one knew what to think or what it all meant, and it made a person feel more scared than proud.

But it had unleashed rumors that the war might be done soon, and everyone had got kind of quiet and fretful-like. Even more so his ma, especially, he noticed, on any day when she didn't know exactly where pop or Dieter were.

The news droned on their radio, turned down low because it was bringing them nothing new other than awful estimates of how many might have died in those bombings. Then just barely cutting through the sticky room, he heard his mother. "What say we go on up to the auditorium and take in one of the 'talkies,' as your gramps used to say." She tried to laugh.

Heck, yes! Not an hour later, he found himself and her sitting in the darkened coolness of that movie hall, waiting for *The Three Caballeros* to start. It was a film by Mr. Walter Disney and his animation studio, and the other boys said you had to see it for the way it mixed together a regular movie with cartoons figures such that—

Suddenly, the lights came back up and Reese turned quickly to Ella with a groan. Was there a problem with the movie reel, or had the projector blown a bulb?

"May we have your attention, please." A loud voice came over the PA. His ma got a look on her face like there might be a fire in the house.

"The announcement has come through: the Japanese have surrendered. The war is over." Reese and Ella looked at each other with eyes as big as they would ever go. "I repeat, Japan has surrendered. The World War is over."

They let out a shout, along with everyone else in the place, and Reese let his ma grab him in a quick clench, through which he hugged her back. "C'mon, you!" she cried and jumped up, grabbing him by the wrist, so their popcorn flew across the floor as they rushed out.

On the sidewalk, in the early evening light, the din came from everywhere. The air raid signals and fire sirens were sounding out. Not in the short bursts that would have had Reese scurrying a couple of years ago but in long happy wails. And the church bells were going full tilt.

Reese and his mom let the joy come into their hearts and on their faces, as people poured out into the street. It seemed to Reese that all the nervousness of the past few days exploded now in an uproar that continued to grow. He didn't even mind his mother pulling him by the hand as they walked toward the center of town.

Soon, the fire trucks rolled by, making all the noise they could, so Reese had to press his hands over his ears. People poured out of their houses, hollering, some banging on pots and pans, and shaking hands and hugging and kissing their neighbors.

As Reese and his ma approached the main street of town, they met throngs of happy, screaming, crying people. Customers had rushed out of the diner, forgetting about their food. In minutes, parades of cars where driving through the streets, honking and with their people hanging out and waving.

"They had just enough gas left in their cars, and they won't have to worry about it now!" Reese yelled to his mom, finding he made giddy gabber as he added to the victory whoops. But his ma had somehow grown quieter over these minutes, more somber even as they went deeper into the celebration. Reese supposed she was thinking about all that had passed and how things had changed.

"C'mon, Ma," he said, and led her down the block and in the direction of the canal at the front of the town. People were all milling and rushing and running and dancing and talking loud as they approached the intersection below the bridge.

All of a sudden, Reese recognized a figure coming toward them, over the bridge.

Pop. "Look it!" he said to his mom, pointing to his Poppa Lee approaching right down the middle of the street.

His father had on a white T-shirt and his work jeans. His hitchy step made for a worse limp in boot heels on the hard-top road as he made his way toward them.

"He's a hero, Mom."

"Oh, is that so?"

"I saw it."

His mother looked at him.

"In the *letter* from the Army. You didn't see it? Came yesterday. Pop opened it and left it on the table by the front door, so I saw." She frowned like she didn't know. "He's getting awards!"

"'Awards?' *Medals,* you mean? Well, a Purple Heart, I suppose, sure," his mom said, her words slowing.

"Yes, and a silver one."

His mother blinked with her mouth open as she looked at him.

"A Silver Star?"

"Yes!" It was all in the letter. "A Silver Star, and he's supposed to report to the base up in Dover to receive it and ..."

But it seemed his mother had stopped listening to him, her eyes filled up. She looked up at Pop Lee as he walked to them. And the tears dropped.

He didn't know what to do, other than thinking it served her right. Anyone knew she should have behaved and be nicer to him. If she could have been so sweet with the German all this time, she could manage with his father now.

Reese watched as his mother reached both her hands out for his father to take. For a long second, and then an even longer one, his father did not take those hands. At last he did, slowly but with no squeeze. They held each other that way for some seconds. If only his pa would smile as much as Reese had learned from Dieter that men could.

Ella

Ella released the big strong hands holding hers and ... let Dieter engulf her in a hug. They were at the back side of the farm, behind the farthest outbuilding, where no one would see them.

She had thought twice about having ambushed him and not having given him a chance to explain about his past. And now, her big German would not relax his embrace on her, and she did not squirm, having tried hard to take him at his word about the woman and the boy back in his homeland. Because what if she never knew and never saw him again by tomorrow or the next day and still never knew? For today, she was asking him an even more urgent question. "Why?" with her head against his shoulder. "Why do you have to go?"

He had just revealed, haltingly, that he was to be scheduled among the first of the POWs to ship back to his country.

Ella trembled at the speed with which it was all happening.

"I don't know why," he said.

She pushed back, leaning away with both her forearms against his chest. "You're first because you have a wife and child—that's the reason, isn't it?"

"I *don't* have a wife und child, but—" He hesitated. "That was something I told them when we arrived here, first time, only because—"

Ella put a hand to his mouth, for him to keep his voice low. She was not sure of Lee or Reese's whereabouts this hour.

"—because everyone was asked," he said, gently lowering her hand, "and ... I thought it might help me in some ways to just say ja."

Ella fell against him again, every time wondering if it might be the last.

"These have been da happiest two years of mine life."

He stopped gazing out across their fields and pressed his lips against the top of her head.

"We can never have it back again," Ella said, barely audible. Not here. And never like it was.

"We can!" he said, gently taking hold of her shoulders and leaning her back, so that she would look up at him. "You said yourself that you had another dream than being on this farm."

"Whisper," she breathed, putting a finger to his lips, which he gently brushed away.

"I have saved almost five hundred dollars from my work here. We can use it to start new."

She tried for the thousandth time to fully envision such a wild gambit. How could he believe this could work? And how could she fully trust anything he dreamt up or said? With the way he had kept his past life from her?

"You want to know again why, I said nothing about that girl and her boy back home?" He dipped his head down so he could fasten her eyes. "Is also because I love you, mein Ella, und I would not let any wrong story come between that."

Dieter was leaning back against the shed now, with both arms wrapped around her, while Ella tried to keep her ears perked up, to be sure they remained alone. There she stayed for some time. Taking Reese with them, perhaps they would find some big town or city in the West, as Dieter had spoken longingly about, where he could pretend to be an American and they would slowly—

Her eyes blinked open at the sound of Dieter's voice, singing. *Singing.* Softly again. To himself, to her. A song she had heard him start crooning half-jokingly last fall, and then more seriously after the two of them had heard Kate Smith sing it in her radio broadcast. "Don't Fence Me In," was all over the airwaves again, now that Bing Crosby and the Andrews Sisters had recorded it too.

And so she found herself in long moments now as her German lover sang about riding through wide open land and skies, with a lament about never wanting to be fenced in again.

Dieter had fatigued so awfully badly at being sent from the farm here back to the POW camp this year. Now he continued to croon sadly, in English lyrics about a dream of wandering to the mountains.

How sweetly silly and melancholy to hear her big German singing a cowboy song with his heavy accent. She wasn't sure he even understood all the words about wanting free of hobbles, but he certainly put feeling into the lines about cresting a ridge to watch the moon rise over the West.

Lee

The next day, Lee came around the side of their big equipment shed pushing a wheelbarrow that one of their hands had left out by the field. He suspected the big, dumb German had done it.

For Lee at last, this all needed to end now. And with the heat on this blaring mid-August day ... He was in no mind for an inch of it. How had he been able to hold himself off over what he now believed might have happened in his absence? And with Reese having revealed yesterday that this one was a goddamned U-boat officer ...

Lee stopped suddenly. Voices came out of the side window of the shed that he was standing right next to. He leaned against the window frame and could just see inside. There, Ella was next to the work bench, wearing only her a loose, clingy summer dress. Now she re-tied her hair behind her head, looking a beautiful mess on this dirty summer workday.

"But how can you say that you *know* they are dead?" she asked the German. Schneider was his name, who he suddenly saw was across from her, hanging tools up on the rack. "We both pray they are not."

"Of course, but the town to which they moved, Lübeck, was der first to be bombed from the air," Schneider said, turning to her. "The German regime, you know, was not only ones to commit crimes of war. Lübeck was first to be flattened by the RAF, then, later, closer to my home, Kiel."

"I'm sorry."

"But I tell you, by then, I hardly knew of her."

Lee set his wheelbarrow the rest of the way down silently, and straightened. He could not believe the familiarity with which the two inside the shed spoke, and the German's sneaky command of English.

"But that is all by, and we hope all sides put it behind und only pray for survivors. Put in der past, like this, listen to this, my El. I am one of the ones who hast completed mine democracy classes at the prisoner camp."

Lee felt dizzy. The Kraut was speaking like this to his wife and the mother of his son—or at least the woman who had asked him over and over again all those years to stand up and, in the eyes of God and everyone, to *become* his wife by vows.

"You see, mein Liebchen, this means good chance I will not be sent to Frankreich or England for work for another year before my … repatriates …"

He couldn't hear all the way, but the Hun seemed to search and fumble for the word "repatriation."

"… to Germany."

"Please …" Lee heard Ella's voice breaking, as she tried to cut in.

"I will be free. We will be free," the man said, as Lee's chest rose and he felt his forearms tighten.

But he stuck still for a moment longer as the German described his classes on the atrocities of the Third Reich and how they had included teaching about the Jewish people. Gazing across with a big grin to Ella, he said, "I know all about Georg Gershwin und Franz Kafka und Albert Einstein now," and he chuckled.

"Oh, Dieter …"

There was some kind of desperation in her voice. Lee heard a scurry and feared what he might see next between them, but then, through the window, he perceived a form slip by. He took three quick steps and peeked around the corner and saw Ella exit the shed silently, while the German was blabbing on, his head in his work. Ella hurrying away, her arms wrapped around herself, clutching at herself, upset.

In a moment, she was out of sight. And, just that fast, Lee was in the doorway of the shed.

Thinking the footsteps were still Ella's, and with his back to the door as he shelved some cans of nails, the big German kept on with, "I like Benny Goodman!" And he har-harred.

Lee wondered if this big asshole had been drinking, as the prisoner spun around, saying, "I am a democrat now, so—" and then froze.

"No, you're not. You're a bullshitter," Lee said.

"Herr Tingle."

"No. Mr. Tingle to you, for the two more minutes it's going to take for me to kick your ass out of here for good."

Lee rushed him. The German dropped the can in his hand only in time to brace himself. Lee crashed into him, sending the German against the side of the shed.

Lee pulled up and stood above him. Then he was atop the man cocking his fist back before the Kraut would catch his breath.

But suddenly, the enemy tied up his arms, leaving them grappling long enough for his adversary to roll and rock once until, using all of his weight and strength, he managed to thrust Lee back, as tools fell off the wall he was against.

"Stop!" the German bellowed.

This one was bigger and gamer than Lee had even thought. But Lee was faster and, as the German tried to regain his feet, Lee put him down with a kick to his ankle, then landed with one knee on the German's chest, as the man just had time to scream, "Halt! It's wrong you—" before Lee's hands closed around his throat.

The German tried to gain control of Lee's wrists but Lee could now bear down with all his weight, as he watched this enemy gasp and try to draw air.

In this passing instant of fate, Lee wondered if the man in his grip now understood that this was exactly what he and his ilk deserved and a fitting way for it all to end. "Had it coming," Lee growled, for the wrong that the damn Kriegsmarine had done to thousands of victims, and then for presuming to insert himself on Lee's farm and lay claim to its queen.

"Brought this on yourself," Lee said through bared teeth and spittle. He intended it as the last words the German would hear and hoped that, indeed, it was the German's final sentiments as well as the man began to dim ...

With the German in a death grip, Lee could hear the rest of the battle around him too. The others fighting. The boom of artillery, the crack and rattle of fire-arms. Men hollering, some wailing, others fighting by hand.

Until something cut through that yelling. A voice. His own? Telling him how awful it was. Must stop. No more. Something broke inside him that he could no longer bear.

"No more fighting and killing ..." he mumbled, over the German's purple, choking face. Lee felt his hands loosen for a moment. But the hollering was not his fellows and their enemies, or even himself. It was a shriller, younger voice that cracked.

"Fight! Help, Mama! Stop!"

His son's voice. Sounding like it was coming across the barnyard.

That second that Lee had leaned back and straightened was just instant enough for the man beneath him to pull one leg up, plant his boot hard in Lee's midsection, and send Lee back against the worktable behind him.

Through the doorway, he saw his son racing toward the entrance of the shed, whimpering.

Lee began to rise quickly then collapsed again wanting it all to just end. But the beast in him coiled for a last time and moved him back to the balls of his feet, as both men prepared to charge each other once more.

That swiftly, though, Ella came through the door behind Reese, shouting, "*No,* it's my fault. Stop!"

Reese reached Lee just in time to land his hands on the the Lee's shoulders, the boy throwing all of himself into it, and pushing him back onto his rear. "No! No."

Ella turned hard and met Schneider, putting her weight against him, just as he was rising.

"It's all on me. *Please stop,*" she said, pressing him back down.

Ella

In that moment, having thrown herself and her son between the two combatants to stop them, Ella looked left and right, trying to discern if she could any longer see a difference, good or bad, between these men, or in her feelings for them.

She had ahold of Dieter's shirt. "That's it. It's over," she said, holding him in place.

All became still in the shed, save for four people gasping, and the youngest crying.

41

Ella

Ella waited for her cousin Everett, for what felt like it might be a last time to meet him in that low, long, bunk-shaped building that held the servicemen's lounge at Fort Miles. The warm Indian-summer day was bright outside.

Everett—a man who always looked like he had just come from a barber—seemed a bit crumpled and mussed today. As they greeted, Ella moved toward one of the sitting-room arrangements. Everett reached out and took her elbow, and gently stopped her.

A door at the end of the lounge opened and several staff officers exited and passed by them, tossing a couple of uncomfortable looks at them. The tag on the door said, "Colonel Robert E. Phillips, commanding officer of the Harbor Defenses of the Delaware."

"Let's walk," Everett said quietly.

They took a pathway out toward the ocean.

"Everything okay?" Ella asked.

"Sure. The war has just worn people down."

Nothing truer could be said, she thought.

They strolled up the rise, toward the overlook at the top of the big gun battery that was hidden here within the dune.

Ella had confided to Everett about the fight on the farm. And of course, he had immediately reassigned their POW elsewhere. She had not seen Dieter since.

"You making out all right?" Everett asked, sounding tired himself as they reached the top of the path, on a sandy, scrubby knoll atop the great gun emplacement.

"We're okay."

On an impulse, Ella stepped up atop the picnic table here at the overlook for a better view of the miles up and down the shoreline. "If only this war had never come," she said. "To the millions lost and hurt. And to us ..."

"Of course."

"How can so much time pass in just a few years?" Ella said, "You'll find it odd, Ev, but I sometimes pine for before, when it was just Reese and Lee and me, and I never knew anything could be different."

She saw in his eyes that Everett understood.

"But you've set the stage to make it better. Remember, El, that was a time *under* Lee. You've said so yourself. And now it will be different."

"It's why I yearn, too, for the way it was last year and the year before, when I at least imagined things could be very different or even perfect."

Her cousin struggled with what to say. And again, it was her fault.

"It was a dream," she added.

With that, they stood in silence and surveyed the vast vista before them. The ocean sparkled in the September sun and they could see as far south along the coast as Rehoboth and clearly make out Cape May northeasterly from here across the wide mouth of the Delaware Bay. Guarding that, beneath their feet, were the tremendous guns that had ended up never firing a shot at an enemy during this war.

"I have something new, though, now," Ella said, perking up, brightening as she looked down into her dear cuz's amethyst eyes. "These past weeks, I can see it. A promise." She reached down and put a hand on Everett's shoulder. "Mostly unspoken, but real. A man back on the farm who is yielding to me now, often, who ... *defers* to me already, as it makes sense. A partnership starting, I think, with someone who knows what he left behind and almost lost."

"Does he understand ... *everything*?" Everett asked hesitantly, keeping his face noncommittal.

"No, but enough. And no matter what else he thinks, we've spoken many times these past weeks, and I've convinced him that Dieter helped save our farm, and so our lives there, and that that's all he needs to know."

In one of those moments, she had found Lee leaning against the big old cottonwood tree back in their farmyard, beneath a rope that she guessed he must think had broken off. She had cupped his head in her hands and said, "He became part of our farm for a time."

All the fight had gone out of Lee by then, but he asked, "What else was he here?"

"He was part of us because he was considerate and companionable to us all. That's all that matters."

Hearing that they were hashing this out, Everett seemed to relax some. He stepped up on the bench of the picnic table so they were closer, and so they could put their arms around one another, eyes casting out again into the endless view of air and water.

"You've got a son who's a teenager now."

"Just."

"But he's thankful to have his home ... restored."

Everett turned his face toward her.

"Changed," Ella continued, "and Reese sees his father at least a little better, and for what he wants him to be."

Far down below them, as far as they could see left and right, the endless sea roiled gently into the sandy shoreline. Down there on the beach, a surf caster with a great long pole hurled his line out. Over there a fishing boat. In the distance, a freighter safely approached the bay with nothing to fear. And no one patrolling this coast now but the seagulls.

"You must be happy to be done," Ella finally said, stepping down onto the seat, so she was next to him. She knew that Everett was very close to the end of his service term.

"Well, it's here already," he said. "Decided on this week."

Ella was confused. Here was what he had been holding back! "What?"

"Listen, so you know—and like we knew it might, word got back to base command about the, your, *our* ... arrangement at your farm."

Ella swallowed hard.

"There was an investigation into the allocation of the POW labor from the fort over the past couple of years. It came on a complaint."

"Oh, God, Ev. Don't say it. I'm so sorry. It didn't—?"

"Yeah, my discharge. It was put through as 'Other than Honorable' because of the matter of the prisoners, and it just wasn't worth fighting."

Ella bent over involuntarily and moaned.

"It's okay. You weren't the only farm I did some special favors for, but they talked to ... folks. Your neighbors ... We got a little too loosey-goosey with things and how we let the prisoners dwell here and there." He laughed bitterly. "But, hey, we knew that might happen, right?"

Ella would have trouble remembering the next few minutes, other than stepping into the beach plum bushes next to the path and doubling over, sick at what her cousin had just shared—and then him stopping her from storming back to the quarters to tell some other version of the story to Colonel Phillips.

For Ella, at last, it only made the end-point more absolute and the need for it—especially so long as Dieter dwelled dangerously yet on this peninsula. Put all further life-indulgences behind her as memories—and not leave it up to events anymore, as she so badly had.

Dieter

Dieter put on a dark suit coat and pulled a fedora down over his eyes in the darkness. Then he pushed the fence wire back in a place he knew it was cut, and he slid out into the night from Camp Saulsbury.

Out on the main route south, he stood on the shoulder of the road with his thumb out, as a trucker pulled over.

Ella

Not an hour later, Ella was lying in her bed, sore, and staring at the ceiling with the sensation that a bear snored next to her.

But as she tried to close her eyes and recover and think of a more apt comparison—letting Lee Tingle back into her bed maybe more like allowing a jackhammer powered by a volcano under her sheets and atop her and between her legs—she wondered if she heard a sound.

With a blank feeling on her face, Ella had been trying to let the explosion and energy and strength of this man, with all its sin and shortcoming, pleasure and pain, authenticity and renewal, settle out and calm within her and the bedroom. Before she permitted him in here and in *her*, she had told him that if she ever witnessed or learned of anything again in their lives like she had come upon in the shed with him and Dieter, all would be over.

He had not argued, but had warned, "Just so for you."

With the loss for words that afflicted the two of them then, both were simply asking for each other's help and consigning to a new try.

But even with that, tonight, in this hour, felt like maybe too soon. Too fast. Until they knew better or for certain what they were to each other.

Ella turned in the sheets, only wishing more air would flow through the house this evening, when she heard something again, this time a tap sound on the screen of their bedroom window. A large bug had collided with it?

Then another "bap" and another right after. She could not believe it, if it could be. In one noiseless glide of the slightest movement, she was on her bare feet and to the window, where below, an all too familiar figure, in the diffused moonlight, waved at her.

Down and out in her nightgown, like a flowing white shadow, she took hold of Dieter and they went across the lawn and behind a copse of trees near the front of their property.

Reese

Reese Tingle's eyes fluttered open. Something had woken him. He whipped his covers off, slid his feet into his slippers, and walked silently into the hallway. He turned up the steps, to his third-floor attic-space lookout. To the dormer window that had been his spotting tower all through the war.

Ella

Under the dim-to-dark shelter of a locust tree, beneath a low-set sky that glowed now from the return of lights to the world beyond, and crouching behind a row of winterberry bushes, Ella and Dieter held onto each other.

"My God, Dieter," Ella whispered, shaking him for having taken this risk.

Just that evening, she had come out of town, past the USO club in Lewes. Now she squeezed Dieter's arms at the thought of what some of these GIs might do if they stumbled out into the night and found a disguised German hiking towards a back road.

Dieter

Seeing Ella's fear, Dieter patted the side of her face but inwardly despaired, knowing he would always only be what he was here now to these people.

Reese

Reese Tingle enjoyed the openness of his viewpoint, as he leaned on his elbows on the windowsill. The breeze from the sea and bay and tidal marshes travelled to him and across his face.

Dieter

Over on the other side of the grass of the front yard and the Hall's clam-shell driveway, Dieter felt the woman he had loved reach up and move her fingertips across a place on his neck where he still had a bruise from the hold that Lee Tingle had taken upon his life.

Dieter gently drew her hand away.

"I understand," her German whispered. "Why he did and what he has gone through."

Reese

At his perch that he imagined was his crow's nest atop this farmhouse that was the sailing vessel of their lives, Reese could make out only one light moving across the waterworld far out before them. Because the air was so humid this evening, he could spot the running lights of only one tanker or a transport ship perhaps. Squinting out at that yellow twinkle, his breathing went to short breaths when he thought that Dieter would be sailing away forever soon on one of those ships.

But he would not permit that man to return here ever to trigger another nightmare like the one he and his mother had broken up in the tool shed last month.

Just then, he saw headlights coming toward them, and guessed who it was. Officer Truitt on his nightly patrol around the outskirts of town.

Ella

Across the yard, behind the bushes, Ella went onto one knee and pulled her once-lover down in a crouch with her. She suspected who they saw approaching.

The patrol car coasted by but, as its lights raked their front, it did not slow or pop its brights as always in the past but continued on—a bit slower, but still on—where the road curved past their house.

Reese

Reese wondered if there had been something odd in the periphery of his vision but the headlights had slid past too quickly. When the police car rounded past them and on into the night, he leaned further out the window and listened and looked and squinted into the darkness down toward the bottom of the lane. Was that movement within the shadows of that clump of trees out at the far corner of their property near the road? Probably just the breeze blowing the tree boughs in the light that bounced down from the clouds tonight.

42

Ella

In an early evening sun, already taking on that slant of autumn, Ella stood at the bottom of her driveway. Behind her, at the top of the drive, she knew that Lee waited, looking on. But in front of her now stood Dieter.

The Army had permitted a last drop-off of some of the prisoners who were going home. One more brief visit to say farewell, in some cases with families that they had become close to. And to gather any things. What might they have left behind these months or years? And pick up gifts or exchange mementos with their employers. Dieter's satchel lay next to his feet. In it, his work clothes and a bag of the cookies that Ella had baked. He would also find a flask of elderberry wine that she had tucked in there.

The truck to pick Dieter up would be back around very soon.

They spoke so that only they could hear.

"I will come back," he said.

"No."

"You come to Europe. We will marry und return here."

"Here comes your truck."

Moments passed, and Ella glanced back to where Reese had come and stood next to his father. Darn if Laddie the collie didn't come sit right next to them too, like some damn painting—the three of them posed there. And all the while, the sound of the truck grew louder until it stopped just near them and idled.

Ella opened her mouth but then, just in the next instant, turned her head and saw the two men's eyes meet. In that connection, she believed she witnessed a just-discernable nod between them.

Understanding? Acceptance? Sadness? Regret? Resentment? Murder? Peace? All of it!

Without turning all the way back, Ella reached out and shook Dieter's hand. Then, feeling a whole part of her dying, she pivoted slowly and made her way back up the driveway toward Lee and Reese. It seemed like miles to get back to them. But the windows to the house and the living room on this side were open. And for some stupid reason, the words of Douglas MacArthur, which they had sat in there and listened to loudly just a few weeks ago, seemed to drift out the windows to her again. Aboard the battleship Missouri, as the Japanese and American officials signed the surrender documents, the general had announced, "Let us pray that peace be restored to the world and that God will preserve it always. *These proceedings are closed.*"

As she stopped next to Lee, turned toward the road again, and put her arm around Reese, they all looked back at Dieter. Suddenly, Reese moved out from under her hand and strode down the drive toward the German.

Ella reached for him but then stopped, as she and Lee watched him approach Dieter.

"He was a nice and good man," Ella said.

She looked up to see what response this might draw from Lee and was stunned to see the droop-eyed-sad-but-resigned look by which he took her at her word.

"So am I," he said, his eyes hot, but not with anger. Ella had never seen him cry before, in all the time she had known him, which seemed now like her whole life, and she looked away.

Lee had, of course, found the small bed that Dieter had used in their tool shed, perhaps assuming it had been set up there for one of their transient workers. And so it *had* been ...

And there, Lee had set up camp. "I will sleep out here until you are sure where you want me."

She had not argued.

And in this moment she could just make out what her son said to Dieter.

"Goodbye."

"We had fun," Dieter said.

"I'm sorry."

"No 'sorry.'"

"... and that you have to go, and all ..."

284

But it seemed Reese's lips clamped and quivered.

Ella believed she might never have seen the kind of strength from a man that she witnessed now from the one at the bottom of her driveway.

"Tschüß, then, my buddy. You be good to them."

"Just 'Tschüß?'" she thought she heard her son say.

Ella knew it only meant "Bye."

"Not auf wiedersehen?" Reese said. He knew that word too—"*until we see each other again.*"

But Dieter just winked to the boy and swung onto the truck.

Postlude

Ella

Leaves, yellow and orange, swirled down in the fall sunlight, as Ella peered out at the church gardens and held Lee's hand.

Before them, Reverend Rightmyer flipped through his service primer. Suddenly, he excused himself to go get a proper copy of the marriage vows.

They could hear him fussing partway to himself, rummaging at the back of the room, behind the altar. "You'd think I knew them in my sleep by now." So many new marriages with men returning from the war!

Lee took the moment to draw Ella in closer.

"You're crying," he said tenderly.

"A little."

She had said nearly the same thing to Nelson Rightmyer just a few days ago, sitting alone with him here in the front pew of this church.

"Your dilemma is over," Nelson had said to her. "Your world improved and decided. Be happy, please."

She had tried for years to bring Lee to this decision and this moment, before the war had come. And now?

"Nothing to be gained by dwelling on what might have been," her friend the rector had said distractedly three days ago, placing his hands atop hers.

Today, Nelson was scurrying about, preparing for a big, fancy wedding for another woman that Ella knew from high school—another who had only just now chosen her beau and her future.

On their way driving here today, Ella and Lee had seen the For Sale sign out on front of Lida Crouch's farm. Whoever might have once helped her keep the place—her nephews or sons—had not wanted to return to it, or perhaps to her.

"Well, there's that anyway," Ella had said, not sure if Lee understood.

Peering through the open windows of the church to her right, Ella could just spot a lovely new housewares shop that had opened up across the block on the main street of their little town. It was not unlike the one in which she had been offered a partnership in Seaford those years ago.

But she willed her attention back to today and these nuptials that they had decided would be just for the two of them. They had wanted Clarissa and Everett to stand with them, but Clarissa had at last confided to Ella that her baby was not Rand Ellis' child. Ella had done some quick math in her head and on a calendar and realized, of course, the child could not quite be his. In fact, Clarissa admitted, she wasn't sure whose child it was. My, what a time-out-of-time and out of character she must have had in the shipyard during her assignment there! Yes, her friend's own doings had made her an even safer confidante for Ella. And Clarissa had declared she could never feel right standing in a church again. Meanwhile, Everett had left the county for a journey of discovery, west across the country.

Reese? Well, he had always considered the two of them to be married. So, no need to drag him to something that ... seemed so overdue.

Now Lee's thick, calloused hand came up and wiped a tear from her cheek, his other arm holding her around the waist, as Nelson arrived back before them again straightening out his tunic. At length, Ella slid her arm around Lee and pulled him in too. Pulled him as close as she could.

Through the window next to her Ella could also see over into the fellowship hall of the rectory, just a few feet across the garden and the old cemetery of the church. The dropping sun was clearly lighting up the kitchen and pantry. All at once, on the shelves at one of the hall's windows there, she could just spy a row of tall, blue Mason jars with light cutting through them, and she recognized them at once as the ones she had brought here this past summer. She could just make out that a jar of preserved orange butternut squash sat next to one holding large pickles, with labels on the side, on which she knew the handwriting was Dieter's.

Afterword

The sinkings off of America's East Coast during World War II and the presence and role of POWs in the US during the war are part of the history of that time that is little known by most. For accuracy and descriptions—including names and dates of vessel losses, presence of German prisoners on the Delmarva Peninsula, and many other details of the war-time venue depicted here—I am particularly indebted to Michael Morgan for his brief volume *World War II and the Delaware Coast* (The History Press, 2016, www.historypress.net)

For me and my family of native Delawareans, Lewes has been a part of our lives for generations. It is a town with a rare mix of both the earthy and the salty.

All praise to the soldiers, farmers, and ordinary citizens who did their duty in America in the great conflagration of the 1940s.

Acknowledgements

I want to thank my wife, son, and daughter—Linda, Beau, and Bailey—for their patience and understanding lo' these decades, as I pursued my writing "habit." And for their encouragement. Additional thanks to Beau for helping to formulate the idea for *Ella's War* when he was a youngster fascinated with Lewes, farming, World War II, U-boats, German POWs, and the like, and for insisting I write this.

Special thanks, too, to the Rebel Writers of Bucks County (www.rebel-writers.org), my longtime novelist critique group. That crucible of honest feedback—and support and camaraderie—has helped me to hone my craft and keep after it. Particular thanks for their input on this novel project go to my Rebel writing pals Chris Bauer, Dave Jarrett, Melissa Sullivan, and Martha Holland, and to the late John Wirebach.

My gratitude as well to my sister and brother, Kimberly and Greg Allen, for beta reading my projects and for their undying cheerleading of my efforts—and to my parents for their faith in me, and my grandparents for their stories of Lewes, Delaware. Gratefulness, too, to the team at Vine Leaves Press for their vision.

Additional forever appreciation goes to my lifelong writing compadre Ron Suskind and his unswerving confidence in my chops, as well to those hallowed halls of the University of Virginia's English Department, which helped put a dream in me.

Vine Leaves Press

Enjoyed this book?
Go to *vineleavespress.com* to find more.
Subscribe to our newsletter: